Figments

For permissions contact: cm@cm-brown.com

Cover Artwork by Castiel Flores

Cover Layout by Erica Lynn Evans

Edited by Lily Ingersoll

ISBN: 978-1-963266-08-5

Visit the author on the Internet

http://www.therunespring.com

At first, people didn't really notice. It happened first in the wild places. That was where the largest groups of Figments appeared. The Fairy Kingdoms in the forests of Ireland cemented Figments in recorded history. While the situation did not improve, until London, everyone could just ignore the odd happenings. People had been claiming to see monsters in the woods since the beginning of time.

London made it impossible to ignore the truth, and it remains empty to this day, taken over from top to bottom by a Cheshire Cat colony. They seem content to stay within the borders of the city as no one has seen a Cheshire Cat elsewhere, but no one who goes into London comes out again.

Every generation had its historical events – the sort of moments that everyone remembered where they were when they occurred. Those memories have faded. No one remembers them anymore, not since the Emergence. The Emergence was the single most overwhelming event to happen in the history of the world to that point. What we know now is that belief is a natural metaphysical force. A force that builds up over time until the laws of reality can no longer contain it. When that energy finally burst its confines and started leaking into reality, it was in the form of Figments – creatures that had been imagined by people over all the years of our existence.

Not every creature we ever came up with gets a membership card to reality, mind you, and we still don't know the exact criteria that lets something manifest in our world. Still, we know that many creatures from books and myths now wander our world, and not all of them are friendly.

The years following the Emergence were surprisingly less chaotic than they should have been. Humans quickly learned what sorts of Figments were dangerous to them and which ones were not. Except for a select few areas like London, there just wasn't much need for the kind of panic something like this should cause. Any place with a high quotient of religious zealotry seemed to draw the more monstrous Figments like moths to a flame. Nearly every country on Earth now has a few small areas that are blasted-out wastelands that represent the most concentrated kinds of hatred, but the panic from those was short-lived.

Once everyone in those areas was gone and the Figments had taken over, you couldn't go back into them. However, the things that lived there didn't come out, either. It took more than a few years for things to really start going off the rails. It wasn't until children started to manifest their own personal Figments that things really went sideways. Why, you might ask? Because with those manifestations came Auras: supernatural abilities that were unique to those with Figments. With the help of their Figments, these people could do miraculous things, but no one ever saw it that way.

Most people just called us Demons.

"Teresa, it's time for school!" her mother shouted up the stairs. Trick rolled over in her bed. Her mother was the only one that ever called her Teresa anymore. Trick froze when she felt a small lump of something soft under the covers beside her. She looked across the room at her dresser. The stuffed puppy that she hadn't slept with since she was six was still there, next to the mirror, as it always was. So, what was in the bed next to her? She would have noticed if their cat, Tassels, was in the bed. She always got overheated when the big butterscotch tomcat slept beside her. Besides, the enormous tomcat was a lot bigger than the cantaloupe-sized lump under her covers.

Trick pulled back the covers to reveal a ball of blue and purple fur. Recognition set in instantly. She scrambled back away, and almost fell off of her bed. She slid to the floor and peeked over the side of the bed just enough so she could watch the tiny blue ball of fur.

"BelleBelle?" Trick whispered.

She had imagined this creature when she was five years old and obsessed with Figments. Her name was Anabelle, and in five-year-old Trick's little world, she could turn Trick into any Figment that she wanted. She had played monsters with her friends, and Anabelle had let her believe she was one. But Anabelle was definitely not real. Their home had been largely safe from Figments. They didn't go camping ever since someone saw a dragon coming out of Raquette Lake.

Other than that, her life had been pretty normal. When her parents had found her playing pretend with her friends, though, they had been very upset. They had worried about this very thing happening. "No no no no no! This is so bad," Trick whispered. She closed her eyes and tried to imagine that this wasn't happening. She squeezed them shut as hard as she could and imagined that her imaginary friend Anabelle was not laying in the bed. She knew that once she had a Figment it would never go away. She might not ever grow up. Some kids who had gotten Figments stopped getting older altogether. She didn't want to be stuck as a kid forever, though she couldn't say why.

Trick opened one eye first and let out a low groan when the bundle of blue and purple fur remained in place on her bed without any sign of disappearing. She reached out tentatively and prodded the ball of blue fur. A soft trilling noise came from the bundle of fur, and it uncurled. Its body was small, roundish like a rabbit. Its odd paws were a little overlarge for the size of the creature. All four of them were a strange combination of a cat's paw and a human hand. Its head was shaped like a leopard, but in miniature, and there was something not quite right about it. It had large, rounded ears with fur ruffs all the way around them. Its eyes were a little too large, like a puppy that wasn't quite full grown yet, and purple like the clouded spots in its fur all the way through, except for a large blue pupil in the middle that matched the rest of its fur.

Anabelle got to her paws and stretched like a cat. Two long tails unfurled from around her paws. They were more than twice the length of the creature's body and seemed to float as if weightless. They were thin and covered in short, dense blue fur with wide purple stripes along their length. They each had a puff ball of purple fur at the end, and each one had a bow tied just below the puff ball. The bows each had a golden bead at the center in the shape of a tiny cartoon kitten face. Trick remembered that the bows would change at random. She wondered if they would still do that.

"Mmmhmm?" Anabelle trilled as she looked up at Trick. Then, her eyes darted around a little wild. She floated up off of Trick's bed and spun slowly in a circle, looking all around Trick's bedroom. "How did I get here?" Trick just groaned again and slumped to the ground between her bed and the wall. Her life was over.

Anabelle floated down towards Trick. The color of her large eyes swirled like a pool of water, bleeding from purple to a dark grey that approached black. The light blue pupil was more clearly visible in the middle of the dark grey. "Trick, what's the matter?" she asked, her voice a light churr that seemed to tickle the inside of Trick's ears.

"You're the matter. You're not supposed to be here. I'm gonna to get in big trouble because you're not supposed to be here!"

There were worse stories than kids who never got any older. There were stories about kids that went missing after getting their own Figment. People hated kids who got their own Figments. They were treated like freaks, and even Trick had avoided the boy in her school who had come to school one day with what looked like a stuffed green tiger with orange stripes riding on his shoulder. It turned out that his Figment gave him the power to teleport short distances with a thought. He had been the boy who had stopped getting older. He was a year older than her, but he would never look any older than twelve as far as anyone could tell.

Anabelle's ears drooped, and her eyes swirled again, changing to an extremely pale blue. "M'sorry, Trick. I didn't mean to come," Anabelle apologized. Tears welled in her eyes. "I don't think I can go away now, but I can try if you don't want me."

Trick felt awful, but she remembered what people had said about Dylan, the boy with the stuffed tiger Figment. They had called him a Demon. Trick didn't want people to think she was a Demon. Anabelle started to become transparent and fade away, like the image from a projector that had been shut off. Trick hadn't thought that it was possible. She held up a hand to try to stop Anabelle, but it was too late. She vanished.

Trick shouldn't feel like this about her imaginary friend. Anabelle had never been real. So why did what she had just done hurt her heart so much? If it was bad to have a Figment, shouldn't she feel good that she had gotten rid of Anabelle before anyone had seen her?

"BelleBelle," Trick intoned sadly, tears welling up in her eyes.

She sniffed them back. If she cried now, her mother would know something was wrong. She didn't want to talk about what had happened. If she didn't get to keep Anabelle, she certainly didn't want anyone to know that she had come in the first place. She watched the spot where Anabelle had first appeared until her mother called her again.

"Teresa?! You're gonna be late for school. Come get some breakfast!" her mother called up the stairs.

"Ok, Mom! I'm coming!" She kept her tears out of her voice.

Trick pulled out her favorite purple overalls and a pink t-shirt with a swarm of cartoon butterflies on the chest. She donned them in a hurry and took the time to French braid her long red hair into a single long tail. She selected a purple bow from a bowl full on her dresser to match her overalls and tied off her braid with it, placing the perfect little purple bow at the end of her braid. She looked back at her bed one last time before she grabbed her purple backpack from a hook by her door. She swung it over her shoulder and opened the door before trotting down the stairs and plopping it down by the front door on her way to the kitchen. Her mother was at the stove cooking eggs and bacon. There was a plate on the table for her already, containing a single egg, two pieces of toast, and three pieces of bacon.

"Hurry up and eat. You're gonna miss your bus and neither your father nor I have the time to take you to school this morning. Sorry, sweetie."

"S'ok, Mom. If I miss the bus, I can walk."

Trick stacked the egg and bacon between both slices of toast. She squirted some ketchup onto the sandwich, and started eating it as she headed for the door.

"Don't get ketchup on your shirt!" her mother called after her.

Trick took a bite out of the sandwich and put it on the table by the door next to her parents' bowl of keys while she shrugged into her backpack. Shooting out the door, she made it out to the sidewalk just as the bus driver opened the doors to the bus. She entered the bus and paused at the top of the stairs. There, sitting in the first seat with two seats between him and the rest of the kids, was Dylan.

Dylan had close-cropped brown hair that almost matched the color of his skin. He wore a dark green t-shirt, black jeans and black Adidas sneakers with blue trim. Sitting on his shoulder was his Figment. It was as she remembered it – a stuffed tiger with green fur and orange stripes. Its bright blue embroidered eyes were somehow filled with intelligence and mischief. It grinned at her, showing two little plush fangs. It waved its paw at her as she stopped to stare at them. She almost sat down next to Dylan to ask him what it was like to have a Figment. She couldn't, though.

"Find a seat, kid. We haven't got all day," the bus driver, Gus said.

Trick ran past Dylan and towards the back of the bus. She took the second to last seat, next to her best friend. Edmund was a little taller than her and had his black hair in dozens of tight braids that ran from the front of his head to the back, where they hung to about shoulder length. His coffee-colored skin made for a rich compliment to his dark hair. He was dressed in a blue t-shirt and black cargo shorts that he stubbornly wore even though it was starting to get colder. He had small, round, wire-rimmed glasses. He was reading a book, but she couldn't see the title.

"Hey, Trick. How'd it go with your parents?" He looked up from his book and saw the look on her face. He slid over in the seat so that she would have room to sit down beside him.

"I totally forgot to ask them with everything happening this morning! I'll text my Dad at lunch and ask him. Don't let me forget." Edmund frowned.

"Trick! We are going this weekend!"

Trick slid into the seat as the bus pulled away from the curb. She swallowed and thought about telling him what had distracted her from asking her parents this morning about going on the camping trip with Eddy's family. She didn't think they would let her go. They were paranoid about running into some monster out in the woods, but Eddy's family had their own private cabin in the woods. They always went on one last weekend trip after school started to finish closing up the camp for the winter. Now she wasn't sure she should go at all. What if Anabelle came back? She said she wasn't sure that she could leave now that she had come.

"What's the matter, Trick? Your face has that scrunched-up thinking look." Eddy closed up his folder and slid it into his backpack.

"I want to tell you, Eddy, but if I do, you can't tell anyone about it. Not anyone, not ever. You promise?" Trick asked. He looked at her for a long moment. She held up her fist with the pinky finger out. "Pinky swear, Eddy." He nodded and hooked his pinky around hers. She pulled off her backpack and held it in her lap.

"I got a Figment this morning, Eddy, but I told her I didn't want her, and she disappeared."

Eddy's mouth dropped open, and he leaned closer to her. "No, freaking, way! Why would you do that? Figments give you magic powers!"

She waved her hands at him frantically even though he kept his voice down to a whisper. "Eddddddy, keep it down," she hissed.

He rolled his eyes at her. "I'm whispering. How much more down do you want?" Eddy said sardonically.

"Eddy! This is serious. Look at what happened to Dylan when he got his Figment. Everyone makes fun of him, and they treat him…" She trailed off and just shivered.

"Trick, those kids are just jealous. He can *teleport!*" Eddy put excited emphasis on the word. "I'm jealous! It is the coolest thing ever!" Eddy gushed.

"You can't tell anyone. You pinky swore!" Trick chided.

"I won't tell anyone. Besides, if she's gone, what does it matter?"

"Because you know what they told us, Eddy. Once you have a Figment, there's no getting rid of it. I think she's going to come back."

"Well what are you going to do about it if she does?"

Trick just stared into the distance and shook her head. She had no idea whatsoever.

Chapter Two
"Our Figments"

The bell buzzed, and everyone started shuffling their books into their backpacks. It was Trick's lunch period, and Eddy's, too. They were in different classes most of the morning because Eddy needed to take Spanish, but Trick was already bilingual. Everyone in her family spoke both English and German except her Dad. His German was passable at best. He had never been good at it, but her mom kept trying to teach him how to speak it. He could understand it, but still couldn't speak it well. Her mother made them speak it all day on days off from school so that they never got out of practice.

Trick slung her backpack over her shoulder and trotted out into the hall with the sea of other kids, then took a left, pausing at her locker to grab her lunch box. She then headed for the cafeteria and sat down at the corner table where she and Eddy always sat. He came in a few minutes later, but had to go through the lunch line before coming over to the table and sitting down. He looked around for a long minute to make sure that no one was going to sit down next to him.

"So, did she come back?" Eddy asked excitedly. Trick shook her head. She felt both relieved and guilty.

"I haven't seen her, but I don't think a Figment can just go away, Eddy. What am I gonna to do?" Trick asked dejectedly.

"What do you mean what are you gonna to do?" Eddy rolled his eyes and picked up his turkey sandwich, biting into it. "You're gonna get magic powers!" he added after swallowing.

"Yeah, like Dylan. So everyone can hate me," Trick grumbled. She prodded at her sandwich but didn't feel very hungry.

"I wouldn't hate you. I don't hate Dylan. We just don't have any of the same interests. He's into sports, and I'm a nature nerd," Eddy said matter-of-factly.

"Did you hear about that kid from Texas who got the Figment that lets him heal people who are hurt or sick?

They're saying the government came and took him from his family." Trick finally picked up her sandwich and took a bite.

"The internet says that's just a rumor."

"What if it isn't?" Trick took another bite from her sandwich. She noticed that her mother had left a sticky note with a smiley face drawn on it in the lid of her lunchbox. "And that isn't the only bad thing that has happened to kids with Figments. I don't think I want to be a little kid forever," Trick groused.

She took another bite, and then slowly chewed the sandwich. She put the rest of it back in her lunchbox. Her stomach was churning, and she thought if she ate anymore, she might throw up.

"I don't think that'll happen to you. Dylan is the first kid anyone has ever heard of that stopped getting older," Eddy reassured her. She wanted to believe him, because even though she had only known for hours that she had Anabelle, she still felt awful for sending her away.

"Eddy, Dylan is at least the tenth kid who stopped getting older. Don't try to make me feel better that way. I'm not stupid." Trick rebuked.

Eddy shook his head and looked hurt. He took out his phone and tapped the screen a few times. He pulled up the Farfetched website. It was like Wikipedia for Figments – a huge internet encyclopedia with everything the human race knew about Figments in it. They had a list of every known kid who had gotten a Figment, what their powers were, and anything odd about them since they got their Figment.

Dylan had actually made his own entry on the page hoping that it would make it so that people were not afraid of him. It hadn't worked very well, though some people had started paying him to take them with him on short teleport jumps to different places. He could only jump as far as he could see, but there didn't seem to be any limit on how many times he could do it. Given a half hour, or so, he could literally jump across the country. He could take anyone with him as long as they were holding his hand or holding his Figment, Tigs.

Apparently, Dylan had quickly discovered that if he took certain routes, he could jump thirty or forty miles at once. Sometimes, he could go a lot further, according to what he had put on Farfetched. Eddy did a search on Farfetched and showed Trick the screen. Dylan Hicks was the only person on the list of people who had stopped aging.

"Ok, fine, but it could happen. What if she gives me the same magic power I imagined she could when I was a kid, and I end up stuck as some big monster Figment? What then, Eddy?" Trick grumbled. She looked up at the clock and decided she didn't want to be hungry the rest of the day, and began to force herself to eat.

Eddy just shrugged. "There are dozens of kids with shape-shifting Figments. They have all been able to change back to human, except that one kid from Alaska who turned into a talking polar bear… but Farfetched says he can change back, he just doesn't. Apparently, he likes being a bear better." Eddy shrugged again. He was more optimistic about the situation than she was.

"If you think this is so great, then why aren't you sitting around dreaming up a Figment as hard as you can?" Trick asked sarcastically.

"What makes you think I haven't been?" he asked sourly.

Trick stared at him in open amazement, "but why would you want people to treat you like Dylan?"

"Have you ever asked Dylan what it is like to have a Figment of your own?" Eddy asked in a harsh whisper. Trick just shook her head. She had been having that very same thought earlier. "Maybe you should." Eddy snapped a little angrily.

"Eddy, you know I like Dylan. I don't think of him like that. I just thought that after they said he couldn't play any sports with his Figment around, and he had to quit all the sports teams, he wouldn't like his Figment very much."

Trick looked over to where Dylan was sitting alone in the corner of the lunchroom. She was careful not to stare for too long before she got her eyes back on what remained of her sandwich. She forced herself to finish it.

"You should go talk to him. I did, after all the jocks told him that he couldn't play sports with Tigs around. I wanted to invite him to come camping with my family, but I stupidly asked him if he would like it better if Tigs hadn't come." Eddy shook his head.

Dylan got up and walked towards the door. He dumped what was left on his tray in the trash and left it on top of the bin before heading out through the double doors that lead out to the fields behind the school. He went out there sometimes during lunch to play with a hacky sack. Trick finished her sandwich, zipped her lunchbox closed, and got up.

"See you in social studies class?" Eddy asked.

"Sure hope so," Trick replied.

She slung her backpack on her shoulder and headed for the double doors. She followed Dylan outside where he was a little ways away from the door, skillfully juggling the hacky sack with his feet. She walked towards him. He saw her out of the corner of his eye, but he didn't say anything. He just kept juggling the hacky sack. Tigs somehow maintained a perfect perch on his shoulder no matter how Dylan moved. Maybe all Figments could float like Anabelle had been able to that morning? She leaned up against the wall of the school and waited for him to finish. When he finally kicked the hacky sack high into the air and held his hand out until the little round footbag fell into it, Trick was actually staring. He was amazing with that thing.

"Wow, that's awesome," Trick said.

"Thanks. It's the only thing I get to do anymore. Why are you out here with me? Aren't you worried everyone will make fun of you for talkin' to me?" Dylan observed.

Tigs waved to her from Dylan's shoulder with its little plush paw.

"I'm sorry people make fun of you, but I wouldn't," Trick said. Dylan just shrugged.

"People are stupid, but I've had Tigs for a year now. I'm over it. If people want to think that I'm a monster because of Tigs, let 'em."

"Does he talk?"

The little tiger's face sort of morphed in a cartoon scowl.

"Tigs is a she." Dylan smirked.

"Oh, I'm sorry!" Trick faltered.

"It's alright. It's pretty impossible to tell. She's just fooling with you. She does it to anyone who is interested in us. It's our own little joke," Dylan explained, "No, she can't talk. I can hear her in my head, though. She likes you." Tigs grinned, her little plush fangs showing. "What did you come out here for? You've never followed me out here before." Trick took a deep breath.

"You, and her. What's it like? I mean you care about her a lot. You gave up..." Trick trailed off when Dylan frowned at her.

"Look. Your name's Teresa, right?" Dylan asked.

"Everyone calls me Trick."

"Trick. Tigs is the best thing that ever happened to me. If you think sports or some bunch of idiots is worth anything compared to Tigs, you're crazy. She's my best friend, and I'd trade anything for her. That's what it's like," Dylan glowered.

"I didn't mean it like that. I told you I wouldn't ever make fun of you." Trick reassured.

"Then why would you ask me something like that?" Dylan rebuked, and then his face lit with recognition. "Oh, you didn't," he whispered.

"When I was six, I had an imaginary friend, and when I woke up this morning, she was in my bed. But I thought of all the terrible things that people did to you, and I sent her away," Trick explained.

Dylan tilted his head as if he were listening to something that Trick couldn't hear. Then his face became really worried, and a little angry.

"Call her back right now. You don't know what you did," He shook his fist under her nose. "Call her back. If you don't, she'll die, and you might, too," Dylan growled.

"What?" Trick yelped.

"You idiot! Figments are part of us. If she's your Figment, she's a piece of what makes you, you. The only way you can kill a Figment is to send them away and not believe in them when they first show up. But she's part of you. If she disappears for real, you could too," Dylan cautioned.

"How do you know that?" Trick blurted worriedly.

"Because Tigs told me. Call her. Even if people make fun of you, it's worth it. She'll always be your friend, for the rest of your life, even if it's forever." Dylan lifted Tigs off his shoulder and hugged her. Trick looked around worriedly.

"No one's going to see. Not everyone will be able to see her right away. It took like a month for people to be able to see Tigs," Dylan reassured.

"So how do I…?"

"Just call her name. If she isn't gone, she'll show up right away."

"How does she know all this?" Trick asked. Dylan just shrugged.

"She's a Figment…?" Dylan said a little skeptically, as if to say a wizard did it. Trick made a little moaning sound.

"My life is so over," Trick grumbled. Dylan just grinned at her.

"BelleBelle?" Trick asked in a whisper. Nothing happened, and Dylan started to look worried again. "Anabelle, please come out?"

"You said you didn't want me," a small voice seemed to float in from thin air.

"I'm sorry. I was scared."

Finally, Anabelle faded into view from wherever it was that she was hiding. She appeared at first all in blue, without her purple spots and stripes. Those were the last thing to fade into view. The bows on her tail had changed. Instead of the tiny kitten faces they sported this morning, the bows had frightened looking little skulls in a dull grey metal at their center. Anabelle's eyes were a sad, stormy grey color. She flew into Trick's chest, and Trick hugged her.

"Please don't send me away again." Anabelle's whispered voice was frightened.

"I won't. I promise." Trick vowed. Dylan put Tigs back up on his shoulder and picked up his backpack. He slung it over the opposite shoulder.

"Almost time for class again, and I gotta change for gym class. People will make fun of you once they can see her, but I'll still be your friend if you want," Dylan offered.

"I think I'd like that." Trick let Anabelle go, and she floated around Trick as she picked up her things. Dylan reached out and scratched Anabelle on the head as he passed.

"I thought you said no one else could see her?"

"Other people with Figments can always see," Dylan explained. "Since we're the only two around here, and I'm not going to tell anyone, she's invisible. You should figure out what your powers are. You might need them," Dylan added over his shoulder as he headed for the doors leading back into school.

"Why?"

"I had to dodge a few fights before my old friends left me alone. My powers helped. If yours can't help, you tell me, and I will," Dylan called back. He went inside, and left Trick standing with Anabelle floating next to her.

"Can our powers help us?" Trick asked.

"I can turn us into almost any other Figment, and you'll get all of their powers." Trick's mouth fell open. She blinked, and then asked.

"Any other Figment? You can make us into a dragon? Or a unicorn?" Trick gasped.

"Um… not a dragon or a unicorn. They're too magical. Too many people believing in them for me to make us one of them on just our magic, but we can do lots of things. You used to like werewolves and Cheshire Cats," Anabelle suggested. Cheshire Cats had gained a lot scarier of a reputation after they chased everyone out of London.

"What do you mean by us?" Trick asked.

"Well, yeah! Do you know how to fly or work a tail or walk on all fours?" Anabelle wiggled her four odd paws. Trick shook her head. "Well, I do. That's part of my magic. When you become a Figment, I live inside of your head, and help you understand how to work the powers and the body so that you don't have to. It would take you a long time to learn how to do all the things Figments do if you didn't have me.

You still have to practice some, but I can help a lot." Trick looked around.

"Can we do it right now? How long does it take?" Trick asked.

"It only takes a second, but it's gonna be kinda boring if you don't have a mirror to see, and won't Eddy want to see too?" Anabelle cautioned.

"How do you know about Eddy?" Trick asked. Anabelle rolled her large eyes.

"I came from your imagination silly. I know lots of things that you know. At least the stuff that isn't boring," Anabelle explained.

"How long until everyone can see you, instead of just me?" Trick asked. Anabelle made a little shrugging motion with her front paws.

"Probably until someone who doesn't know how to keep a secret sees us use our magic. I know some things about how we work, but none of us knows everything. I bet it took a long time for someone to see Tigs and Dylan use their teleporting."

"People call them Auras. Magic powers that kids get when they have a Figment," Trick said. Anabelle rolled her eyes again.

"Whatever. Until someone starts making noise about us having an Aura, I'll probably stay invisible."

The doors opened, and Eddy poked his head outside, and looked around. He spotted Trick and came over. "So, what did he say?"

"You already asked him," Trick smirked. Eddy looked a little sheepish.

"It was about two days after I made the stupid mistake of asking him if he would rather she hadn't come," Eddy admitted.

"You really do want a Figment of your own," Trick said in amazement.

"Yes!" Eddy gushed, "Trick, until your parents yelled at you, that was all we ever talked about. Then we started reading things with magic powers in them. Now kids like us are really getting Auras from their Figments. You had a chance to have your own!" Trick pushed some of her hair out of her face and hooked it behind her ear.

"I still do," Trick admitted, and Eddy's face lit up with excitement. He looked around.

"Is she here, why can't I see her?"

"She's hovering around your head. She doesn't think you'll be able to see her until you see us use our Aura."

"Well, what are you waiting for?" Eddy prodded. The bell started to ring inside the building, and they both looked up, startled.

"We're gonna be late. Will anyone else see her?" Eddy asked.

"Just Dylan, but we don't have any classes together."

"After school. You gotta show me!"

"I'll show you if you help me figure out what I'm going to tell my parents. This is what they were so worried about."

"Deal. As long as I get to see your Aura first!"

They both had to run to make it to social studies class. Anabelle perched weightlessly on her shoulder as she ran.

"Why are we running?" Anabelle asked.

She may know things about Figments, and magic, but she had no idea what was going on in the human world. Trick guessed those were the boring bits Anabelle had mentioned.

"We're gonna be late for class. We'll get in trouble if we don't make it," Trick whispered urgently.

"I don't know what a class is," Anabelle said. Trick almost laughed.

"You'll learn. I'll teach you everything you need to know." Trick added as they raced down the hallway. "Just don't talk while we're in class. I can't talk back or everyone'll think I'm crazy."

"Ok. Can I move around? No one can see me."

"Sure, just don't do anything to silly or you'll have me laughing."

"No promises."

Trick and Eddy both slowed down as they made it to the door. They walked through it just as the bell was ringing the second time. Both she and Eddy couldn't stand social studies.

They sat at the back of the class and flipped open their books when prompted by the teacher. When she turned to write on the board, Eddy made goofy stabbing motions at her back with his pencil. Mrs. Ekard didn't like them very much just because they didn't like social studies. It wasn't that they didn't try hard at the class, but neither of them could ever get all the facts straight. She scowled over their tests whenever they took one.

Apparently, that was one of the things that Anabelle knew, because she floated towards the front of the room. Trick was unable to say anything without disrupting class, so she had to try to hide her amusement when Anabelle started to move her mouth in sync with everything the teacher said. She rolled over onto her back and started doing it upside down. She floated near the Teacher the entire time, but she was very careful not to touch her.

Trick wondered if people would feel it if Anabelle touched them. She suspected they would, and that would be the end of her being hidden. Trick sat there shaking with barely contained laughter as Anabelle continued to make faces and mimic the teacher. It was the longest thirty minutes of her life, shaking both in laughter and fear that the teacher would notice her shaking. She didn't retain a single thing from that class.

When the bell rang, Anabelle zipped back over to Trick, who had managed to not laugh for an entire five seconds after the bell before she burst into gasping giggles. Mrs. Ekard glared at her, but since class was over there wasn't really anything she could do about it. Trick could not stop laughing, and Eddy just sat there with a confused grin on his face.

"What is so funny?" Eddy prompted.

"BelleBelle was mocking the teacher the entire class!"

"Oh, no wonder you were the only one almost dying of laughter. Why do you call her BelleBelle? Didn't you say you named her Anabelle?"

Trick just shrugged. "I don't know. It just sounded better to me a few years ago?"

They began the walk home, and Trick shivered, wishing she had worn warmer pants. Her overalls were usually warm enough this time of the year, but it was a lot colder than normal. She wrapped her arms around herself. Her thin fleece jacket wasn't warm enough for today.

"We could just turn into something with warm fur?" Anabelle suggested.

"Not out here! Everyone would see!" Trick rebuked quickly. Anabelle just made her odd paw shrugging motion and floated off towards the houses on the side of the street.

"It's gonna get really weird with you talking to her if I can't hear her." Eddy laughed a little.

"Tigs and Anabelle both think that if you see us use our Aura, you'll be able to see her."

As they got closer to her house, Eddy got back on track. "Don't forget we have to ask your parents about going to camp."

Trick had completely forgotten about it in all the fuss with BelleBelle. They ran up the front stairs to Trick's house. She opened the door, and she could tell that the house was empty. Her mother hadn't made it home from work yet. That was normal. Her older brother wouldn't be home for hours. He had an after-school job. She closed the door, and they both put their boots on the shoe trays by the door. Eddy dropped his backpack. Trick ran up the stairs and down the hallway to her room. She hung her pack on the hook by the door, and Anabelle floated to the middle of her room.

"It had more pink before," Anabelle said, looking around at the posters on the purple walls.

"Dad repainted it last year for me. Pink was mom and dad's idea. I like purple the best," Trick explained.

"I know. I just remember all the pink, or at least you remember all the pink and I do too."

"BelleBelle, is it gonna hurt when we use our Aura?" Trick asked. She couldn't imagine how she could transform into a Figment without it having some effect on her. Anabelle spun around in the air and got a quizzical look. Her tails actually formed a question mark in the air, which made Trick laugh.

"What? No it won't hurt. You won't feel anything when we change."

"And we get all the magic of whatever we turn into?" She was just now realizing what that meant. She was going to have a lot of dangerous powers. Anabelle seemed to be able to read her mind.

"Don't worry. I know how to use all their powers. I won't let us do anything bad with them." Anabelle reassured.

"Alright, alright. Is it hard for you to do it? I want to show Eddy, but we have to change back before my family gets home."

Anabelle shook her head. "Nope, it's what you made me to do, but if we do something big it might take longer to change back."

"Can we do Figments that other kids have? Like Tigs?" Trick asked. Anabelle shook her head right away.

"Nope. Tigs only has Dylan's belief to make her magic from. The only reason we can do magic from other Figments is that when we turn into a Figment we share all the belief that made them."

"I don't get it." Trick looked to Anabelle quizzically.

"I'm not sure you're ever going to, but Eddy's waiting for us. If you want to show him our magic, pick something small. Like a little fairy, or a Cheshire Cat, or maybe a Gryphon. Having wings is fun."

"Maybe Eddy will have some suggestions," Trick said and went back out to the living room. Eddy had turned on the television and was waiting for her.

"Ok, I think I'm ready," Trick said, her voice a little uncertain.

"This is gonna be awesome. What are you going to turn into?" Eddy asked eagerly.

"I don't know. Any ideas?" Trick asked, and Anabelle looked at Eddy with interest.

"Oh, do something spooky. Like a Black Dog!" Eddy suggested.

"We can only do Figments, not animals."

"I think he means a Barghest. It's a Figment from Ireland," Anabelle explained as Eddy opened his mouth to answer her. Trick held up a hand while she listened to Anabelle.

"Do you know every Figment in the world?" Trick asked. Anabelle nodded, then shook her head.

"Not really. I learn about them when people mention them. I know all the ones that you knew, but when someone mentions a new Figment I learn about them. As soon as Eddy said the Black Dog I knew what it was," she explained.

"You gotta hurry up and change. Not being able to hear or see her is getting weird."

"Can we do it?" Trick asked.

"Sure, but the house will get all messy."

"Huh?"

"Barghests give off a black dust. They leave smudgy black footprints all over the place. Plus, they're super scary. It's part of their magic. Eddy would get really scared if we turned into that," Anabelle explained.

"BelleBelle says that a Black Dog wouldn't be a good idea."

"Why not?"

"Because its magic scares people, and because it'll make a mess in the house." Eddy gave her a quizzical look, and she continued. "We're running out of time. Let's do a werewolf."

"What kind of werewolf? There are a few," Anabelle asked

"Oh, do one of the big dire wolf looking ones that the Park Rangers in Alaska have been working with!" Eddy suggested.

Everyone knew about them. The deal the National Park Services had made with the werewolves was all over the news and the internet.

"How does it work? Aren't they sort of human?" Trick asked.

"No they aren't. Some Werewolves can look mostly human, but never completely human. I can go right to their werewolf shape for this, though," Anabelle said.

"Ok, will I fit in here?" Their house was not small, but it was not enormous either. She remembered reading on the internet that they were pretty big.

Eddy piped up, "No way. They're huge, like as big as a polar bear. Let's go out on the deck. No one can see us over the fence back there."

He jumped up from the couch and raced out to grab his shoes. He hopped on one foot as he pulled on his boot. Trick didn't bother with her shoes. She would have paws in a second or two. She went out through the sliding glass doors in the kitchen, and down the stairs to the low deck. Her dad had built it a few years back, and he carefully scraped and painted it every couple of years to make sure it didn't wear out. Eddy sat down in one of the lawn chairs to watch, and Trick looked nervous.

"All right, I'm ready, BelleBelle." Trick squeezed her eyes shut and made little fists of her hands like she was preparing to get a shot from the doctor. Anabelle chirped with laughter.

"You should open your eyes. This is going to be fun." Anabelle laughed.

Trick opened her, though she didn't unball her fists. Anabelle suddenly flew at her in a blur. Trick held up her hands defensively, but Anabelle flew right through them as if she were a ghost. She had gone completely transparent, and was glowing brightly like a blue and purple star. She hit Trick's chest and vanished in an explosion of blue light that blinded Trick for a moment. She blinked the flash from her watery eyes, and she realized that she was standing on all fours, and she was huge. Way, way bigger than Eddy, and she felt odd. She lifted her right front paw for a moment.

[Wait a second. This is our first time, and I need to see how you work inside.] Anabelle's voice whispered inside of Trick's head.

She put her right front paw down and looked over towards the sliding glass doors, where they showed her reflection. She was an absolutely enormous white wolf. They had not been lying about the size. She was almost as big as her dad's car. She felt so super strong. She touched her doggy tongue to her huge pointed fangs, and then noticed Eddy was looking at her in gape-mouthed wonder.

"Holy shit," he whispered. She laid her ears back at him. Her mother hated it when people cursed. "I could ride you like a pony," Eddy laughed. Trick lifted her lips away from massive fangs as long as his hand as if to say she would love to see him try. "Whoa! Keep those things to yourself, girl!" He got off his chair carefully, as if he was afraid he would startle her.

[*Can we talk when we're like this?*] Trick thought the question and hoped that Anabelle would hear her.

[*Ummmmm, werewolves aren't really made for talking,*] Anabelle replied. [*Ok, you should be able to walk now. Can you feel our tail?*] Trick thought about it for a moment, and she could feel her gently swaying tail. She made it wag faster when Eddy approached her slowly.

[*I can feel it! I have a tail!*] She squealed in delight.

"Can I..." Eddy held up his hand in a wordless gesture.

She sniffed his hand, and the smell was almost like it was talking to her. **This is Eddy,** it said. She realized she could smell hundreds of other things that she couldn't identify. Things that were trying to speak to her through her nose.

[*Hold on, I can help with the smells,*] Anabelle said inside of her head.

Eddy reached out and touched the side of her enormous muzzle. He carefully ran his fingers through the fur there. Trick realized how ecstatic Eddy was from his smell. She could smell how he felt. This was amazing! She leaned into Eddy's tiny fingers on her muzzle, and he scratched her face like he did with his dog. It felt really nice. Then she smelled something new. It said to her, **there is a cat in the corner of the yard.**

She had to go investigate that smell! The deck creaked when she jumped off onto the lawn. She put her nose to the ground and charged towards the back corner of the fence.

[*Careful, you're going to squish that poor cat and wreck the fence.*] Anabelle warned inside of her head.

Eddy was running to catch up with her, when she shoved her nose through the shrubs at the back corner of the property. A tiny black and white ball of fur was cowering away from her. It hissed and spit as she pushed her nose closer. She snuffled at the cat. It was their second cat, Socks. Trick didn't want to scare their cat, so she backed out of the bush. Eddy watched her for a second.

"That was a little scary, Trick. You're so huge and strong," Eddy noted. She turned her head to him and nodded. "Your eyes look really cool, two different colors like that. Did you do that on purpose?" Eddy asked, and Trick tilted her head questioningly.

[We should change back. We used up a lot of our magic to do this. If we don't change back we'll be stuck this way for a while,] Anabelle warned.

[Is it always going to be like this?] Trick asked.

[Nah, just the first time or two while I learn how to work with you.] Anabelle responded, before another flash of blinding blue light, and they were Trick and Anabelle again. Eddy took one look at her, and then whipped around, facing away from her.

"Uh Trick, you're missing some things," Eddy quavered embarrassedly. Trick looked down and turned bright red. She was stark naked. She tried desperately to cover herself with her hands, but it was a futile effort.

"Anabelle!" Trick squealed.

"Oh, ummm, hold on a second. They'll fade back in," Anabelle said, a truly mortified look on her feline face. "I'm so sorry, Trick!" she squeaked.

Trick stood perfectly still, shivering in the cold autumn air, completely unsure of what she should do. Then, less than a minute later, her clothing faded back into view as if it had been there all along, and they just couldn't see it. Trick let out a sigh of relief.

"Okay, Eddy. Is that going to happen every time we change back?!" Trick growled at Anabelle.

"No. I promise I'll bring them back right away from now on. Remember, I'm new at this too," she apologized. Eddy turned back around when he heard her voice.

"Wow," he whispered, "She's amazing."

"Thank you," Anabelle said.

"I didn't think you would be able to talk, like Tigs can't."

"Tigs can't talk because Dylan's magic is different than ours. She had to inhabit the body of something real to manifest here, so she took over the body of Dylan's little sister's stuffed tiger. They actually thought that she was his little sister's Figment until Dylan started hearing her inside of his head," Anabelle explained.

"How do you know?" Trick asked.

"We talked while you and Dylan were talking. She told me," Anabelle said.

"Trick, do you realize what this means?" Eddy asked.

"That kids at school are going to try and make me give them werewolf rides?" Trick laughed.

"No, doofus. It means you can have almost any magic powers you want!" Eddy exclaimed. "Anabelle is the coolest Figment in the world. You guys are gonna be famous!"

"No no no nope! You are not putting me on Farfetched. My parents are going to freak out about this already. Nope! I don't want to be famous."

"What are your parents going to freak out about?" Trick cringed as her mother's voice came from the house.

"She wants to go camping with us this weekend, Mrs. Strand," Eddy covered for her without missing a beat. Her mother did not look convinced.

"I really would rather she not go out into the woods Eddy," her mother said.

"We aren't going to be camping out in the woods. We're going to our private camp," Eddy explained. Trick's mother looked skeptically at them both.

"If I say yes, and that's only after I talk to your parents, Eddy, I still want to know what you two were talking about when I got here," Her mother said knowingly. Trick looked bewildered, and her mother rolled her eyes. "A trip to Eddy's camp isn't going to make you famous, Teresa."

"It's not like you can keep it a secret forever, Trick." Eddy sighed.

"Do we have to show her our Aura too? Because I'm pretty sure if I turn into a werewolf, she's gonna freak," Trick whispered.

"Not anymore. You can just touch me, and I can make her see," Anabelle responded. Her mother's face was getting more, and more worried by the minute. Trick held out her hand, and Anabelle landed on her hand.

"Mom, this is Anabelle. My Figment."

Chapter Three
"Unexpected Effects"

Trick's mother stared at Anabelle for a few long moments before her eyes rolled up into her head and she collapsed to the deck with a loud thud. Trick rushed over to her, Anabelle floating worriedly beside. She crouched over her mother, but had no idea what to do.

"I think she's alright," Eddy said.

Trick took a pillow off of a deck chair and slid it beneath her mother's head. About thirty seconds later, her mother spoke in German.

"Baby, you need to make it go away."

"I can't, Mama. I promised I wouldn't, and it could be bad for me if I did," Trick said.

"Oh, Teresa, this will not end well," her mother said before finally sitting up. She saw Eddy and sighed. She switched back to English, "Eddy, can you make it home on your own? I need to talk to Teresa."

Eddy nodded and stood up. "I'll be fine, Mrs. Strand." He went into the house, and a minute later, she heard the front door close behind him.

"Teresa, you don't know what's going to happen when people find out you have a Figment."

"If we don't tell anyone, and I'm careful about not letting people see me use my Aura, no one will be able to see Anabelle," Trick reassured. Her mother looked a little relieved at that news.

"Teresa, when I was a little girl, there was a girl at my school that got her own Figment. When everyone found out, they did not treat her well. She ran away, and we never saw her again. They say she went into London and never came out. She was a good girl, and she saved someone's life with her Aura, which was why everyone knew. They should have been grateful, but they weren't. I don't want anything to happen to you, Teresa." Her mother put her hand on the side of Trick's face. She looked at Anabelle. "You will protect my daughter?"

"I'll do my best," Anabelle promised.

Finally, her mother heaved a huge sigh. "Are you going to show your father and brother?" her mother asked as if there were some choice in the matter.

"I don't think it would be a good idea to try to keep her hidden from them. If I do, they could tell someone without knowing they aren't supposed to," Trick said. Her mother smiled at her.

"I think that's smart, but maybe tell them what's going to happen before you show them… and have them sit down first," her mother advised. She rubbed the back of her head for emphasis and grimaced. That was when they both heard the door open.

Trick's brother wouldn't be home for a couple of hours yet, so it must have been her dad. She and her mother went inside to greet him. Her mother kissed him on the cheek and took the grocery bag he was carrying, then went into the kitchen and started to fix dinner. Trick was left standing in the breezeway with her father, who was now slipping off his shoes. He looked at her and he raised a brow at the look on her face.

"What's going on, Trickster?" he asked. He had been the one to give her the nickname.

"I've got something to tell you, Dad, but Mom says you should probably sit down before I do."

He shot her a confused look, then laughed a little and tousled her hair as he moved into the living room. He sat down in his comfy recliner. "Alright, lay it on me."

"Dad, when I woke up this morning, I had a Figment." He paused, and his eyes went a little wide for moment, and they darted around the room. Then he burst into laughter.

"Oh, that's a good joke! You got me, Trick!"

She held out her hand to one side of her head, palm up as if to draw the eye of a crowd to something she was presenting. Anabelle faded into view, floating just above Trick's hand, and her father's mouth fell open.

"My god, you weren't kidding."

"Not this time, Daddy."

"She's beautiful," her father said.

That was not the reaction she had been expecting from her father. Her mother had, after all, been upset when she had first seen Anabelle only an hour earlier. "You're not mad?" she asked sheepishly.

"What? Why would I be mad?"

"Because I *am* upset, and worried," her mother called out on the way back from the kitchen. She came in from the hallway with a dish towel in her hands.

"Trick, were you trying to make Anabelle come to you?" her father asked.

"That isn't the point," her mother said as Trick responded.

"No, I wasn't trying…" she looked at her mother to see if she was going to say anything else. When she didn't, Trick went on, "but I'm glad she came."

Her father paused for a long moment looking between the two of them. "Trick, can you give Mommy and Daddy a minute to talk?"

Trick sighed, "I won't try to make her go away now that she's here."

Her Father nodded, "We won't ask you to."

"Mom already did," Trick grumbled, and then left through the kitchen onto the back deck. Anabelle had remained silent throughout the entire conversation.

"I'm sorry, Trick. I didn't want to make problems for you." Her ears and whiskers drooped.

"BelleBelle, how do Figments get made?" Trick held out her hands, and Anabelle alighted in her arms.

"I don't know. The first thing I remember is when you woke me up. I don't know how I got here. I knew some things, but only stuff you knew and how to use our Aura. Tigs doesn't know either. I asked her that, too. According to her, she has asked a lot of other Figments, and even the oldest ones she could find don't know. She even had Dylan take her to Ireland on a weekend to talk to Fairies. They don't know either. They told her if she really wanted to know, she would need to find The White God, whatever that's supposed to mean."

Trick had no idea either. "I wonder what they're talkin' about," Trick mumbled as she leaned against the deck railing and looked out over the back yard.

"You could hear them if we changed into a werewolf again," Anabelle suggested.

Trick shrugged. "They're fighting. Mom usually wins, but I don't think she will this time. He gets a look on his face when he's ready to dig in his heels."

Anabelle's expression turned worried. Trick wasn't sure how she knew it was a worried look. Anabelle's semi-feline face didn't have the same sort of facial expressions that a human did.

"BelleBelle, I promised you that I wouldn't send you away again, and I won't. I don't care what they say. But my Dad is an artist, and he has always been a lot less strict than Mom. He thinks Figments and magic are amazing. I think that's how you got here."

Trick sighed. She knew her mother was right. Having Anabelle was not always going to be fun, and she was almost certainly going to be light on friends after this. Now that her Mother had been so upset, she felt like it was going to be a lot harder than she thought. She hoped that at least her father would support her.

The doors slid open behind her, interrupting her thoughts. Her Father joined her on the deck, and she could see her mother at the stove in the kitchen past him. She did not look terribly happy, but the worried expression was gone. Her father had a guarded grin on his face, and she could tell that he had won the argument just like she thought he would. He frowned when he saw the look on her face.

"Hey kiddo, don't worry about your Mom. She'll adjust. She's just worried that people won't understand. I think that she probably thinks you won't understand why people are treating you differently, but I also think that maybe you already thought of that."

"I know that people are going to make fun of me, just like Dylan when he first got Tigs," Trick admitted.

Her father nodded, "People are afraid of things they don't understand, Trick, and fear makes people do stupid things. So, you're right. They are going to make fun of you. When they do, Trick, you know you can talk to me about it, and your Mom will help you too. Just give her time to understand why Anabelle is so special to you. I don't think she ever had an imaginary friend, but I did, and I know how special they can be. Do you know what your Aura can do yet?"

"Sure. Our Aura lets us change into other Figments," she said.

Her father raised an eyebrow, "You can shapeshift?"

"Sort of? I can't turn into just anything. Just other Figments, and just ones that there are a lot of. We get all the magic powers that the Figment has."

Her Father's eyes went a little wide as he processed that. "Could you turn into a dragon?" he asked excitedly.

"No, but we did a werewolf earlier. Anabelle says dragons are too big. We don't have enough whatever it is that makes up Figments to do something as big as a dragon," Trick explained.

"A werewolf? You mean like the big ones the park rangers are working with?"

Trick smiled, thinking it funny that it was almost the exact same thing that Eddy had said. "Yep. A huge white one just like that."

"Oh, that's the coolest!" Her Father could be like a big kid sometimes. It was one of the things she loved the most about him. He kept his inner child on the outside. "Can you show me?"

"Umm, I don't know. We just changed for Eddy. I think we need a little time before we do it again?" Trick said uncertainly. She looked at Anabelle.

"If we do it right now, it'll make us tired. We need some time to recover," Anabelle explained.

Her father leaned back away from them for a moment, looking a little startled. "You talk!"

"Why does everyone think that I shouldn't talk?"

Her father shook his head. "Because... you know what... you're right. You're a Figment, not a cat. But you look sort of like a cat, so that's probably why," He reasoned.

Anabelle shrugged, "Makes sense I guess."

"Dinner!" her mother called from the kitchen.

"We'll be right in, dear!" her father called back.

"Trick, your mom isn't wrong that you're going to have some problems because of this, but I think that you'll get through them just fine. I'll help, and so will your mother."

Trick put her arms around his waist and hugged him. "Thanks, Dad."

"That's what Dads are for, kiddo."

They both went inside, and her mother seemed to be in a better mood. Dinner went uneventfully, and Trick was doing her homework with Anabelle floating over her shoulder when she noticed something odd. She could feel the tail she had in her werewolf shape, as if she still had it. Slowly, frightened of what she was about to see, Trick stood up. She walked toward the mirror hanging on the back of the door. She turned around, and noticed there was a bulge in the seat of her overalls.

"Anabelle..." Trick said. Anabelle had taken up residence on top of her bookcase and was napping. Her eyes slid open. "Yes?"

"Please tell me that when I take off my overalls I'm not going to find a tail."

"Well, of course you have a tail. It's left over from using our Aura." Trick took down the top of her overalls, and a large wolf's tail covered in white fur spilled out. It fell almost to her ankles and curled at the tip.

"Anabelle, this is super bad. How long is this going to last?" Trick asked a little hysterically.

"Until we change into something else or change into the werewolf shape and back again. Whenever we use a shape for the first time, there'll be some left over magic. What's the problem? It looks like a fine tail."

"I can't have a tail! I can't wear any of my clothes like this! If I have a tail at school tomorrow, everyone is going to know I have a Figment," Trick fretted.

Anabelle seemed genuinely confused as to why this was a problem.

"You can just wear a dress for now and we can do a quick change in the morning to get rid of it." Anabelle rolled over onto her back and looked at Trick upside-down.

Trick shucked out of her overalls and tossed them into the laundry basket by the door. She went to her closet and started sliding things from one side to the other on their hangers until she reached her dresses. She picked out a one-piece green one with long sleeves and a knee-length skirt. A large, round patch with a stylized tree of life in the middle was stitched into the chest of the bodice. Trick took a pair of matching green leggings out of her dresser and pulled them on. Thankfully, the waistband of the leggings was stretchy enough that it flexed around the base of her tail so they stayed up just fine.

"Can we do this on purpose? You know, only transform parts?" Trick asked.

"I think so, if we practice, but I'm tired right now," Anabelle complained. She stretched her paws over her head and yawned hugely, her tongue curling in a feline way.

"Me too, but I have to finish my homework first. I'm not going to wake up with other werewolf parts, am I?" Trick looked at her chair, and then at her tail. She turned the chair sideways so her tail could hang off the edge. Her math homework didn't take her much longer, and she felt her tail wagging of its own accord when she finally closed her math book. She groaned at the feeling, and glared daggers at Anabelle.

"Do you have any idea how weird this is?" Trick said, pointing behind her with her thumb.

Anabelle's eyes opened to slits. She lifted her own tails and waved them both at Trick for emphasis.

"You had a tail when we were the werewolf earlier," Anabelle mumbled sleepily.

"That was different. I'm not a werewolf anymore. I'm not supposed to have a tail!" Trick growled in consternation.

"You do know that this isn't gonna get less weird, right?" Anabelle said, her voice a little more awake than it had been.

Trick sighed and fidgeted with her dress. She pulled it down over her tail, and her tail lifted it back up again.

"You're sure we're gonna to be able to get rid of this tomorrow? I can't go to school like this," Trick complained.

"If you let me sleep, we'll be able to. We'll be able to do a lot of transformations after tonight."

"Why after tonight?"

Anabelle rolled back over and grumbled, "You're not going to let me sleep, are you?"

"I have a bazillion questions, BelleBelle. You're going to have to answer a few."

Anabelle stretched and sighed, "Because I'm your Figment, but when you sent me away, you disrupted our bond a little. It'll take a day or so for our bond to settle again. Once it does, we'll be able to do a lot of transformations in a day."

"A day or so? Or so? How long is or so? The part about the tail needing to be gone before school tomorrow?" Trick blurted out, a touch hysterically.

"Calm down," Anabelle said, "It's not the end of the world, and if you let me sleep, it'll get done a lot faster. I can adjust our bond in my dreams."

"How does that even make any sense?"

Anabelle rolled her eyes.

"There are things I can do in dreams. I can see our bond, and our magic. And I can protect you from bad dreams, too."

"How do you know all this?" Trick grumbled in annoyance.

"How many times are you going to ask me that? I don't know! There's lots of stuff in my head. I don't know where it came from. It's just there!" Anabelle shouted uncomfortably.

Trick sighed, "Sorry, BelleBelle."

Anabelle sighed in response. "I'm not going to have all the answers to your questions, Trick. I don't even know what I'm supposed to be here for besides being your Figment."

There was a knock on the door frame, and they both looked up to see Trick's father standing in the doorway.

"No one knows that, anyways," he said. "Sorry. I heard you shouting, and I just wanted to make sure everything is all..." He trailed off as he seemed to realize she had changed her clothes. Then he saw her tail sticking out from beneath the hem of her dress. He raised an eyebrow. "Trickster, you know you have a tail?"

"I hadn't noticed, Dad," she snarked.

"Should I be worried?"

"Maybe? I don't know, Dad."

"No, it's just a side effect of using a new shape for the first time. When we can change again tomorrow, it'll go away," Anabelle said peevishly from her place atop the dresser.

Her father didn't look terribly convinced. "Alright, just be careful your mother doesn't see you. You know I'm almost as interested in Figments as you are, but she's worried something terrible is going to happen now that you have one. Besides, none of us really know how Figments work, so she's also probably worried that what you can do is dangerous," her father explained.

Anabelle lifted her head and looked at him.

"It isn't dangerous at all. Our magic is safe for us to use." She sounded almost offended.

Her father held up his hands in mute entreaty.

"I know, but she doesn't. Kids have only been getting Figments since we were kids. That's pretty new, and no one really knows how what you can do with your Aura works, so we don't really know if it is safe. I believe you, Anabelle, but I want to believe, and I have read all the accounts of how far kids' Figments have gone to protect them. But Trick's mom hasn't. She's worried you're going to hurt her daughter somehow. Do you understand?"

Anabelle nodded her head. "But I promised her I would protect Trick."

"I know you did, but you're going to have to give her a little time. Go on and brush your teeth, Trick. I'll keep your mom distracted so she doesn't see your..." He thought for a moment. "side effect." He finished with a smirk.

"Can we watch a movie before we go to sleep?" Trick asked. Her father looked pointedly at the clock.

"Promise I get to see you use your Aura tomorrow, and I'll keep your mom occupied so she doesn't see the light under your door and bust you, kiddo," her father said conspiratorially. She hugged him, and then ran for the bathroom. He looked to Anabelle, and his eyes got hard.

"I love my daughter more than life itself, so please be truthful with me. Is what you can do going to hurt my daughter?" he asked seriously.

Anabelle got her feet under her and sat up. "Using our Aura will not hurt her at all. There may be a few side effects, but none that will hurt her physically," Anabelle affirmed.

"What about emotionally?"

Anabelle tilted her head, "I can't stop other people from treating her badly, but I'll do my best to make sure she feels good about herself."

"You seem different, now that she isn't here."

"Sounding more adult isn't difficult for me, but I'm her Figment," Anabelle explained.

"Alright. Thanks for telling me the truth. You can call me Dad too," he confided with a little grin.

Trick dashed back into the room. She had swapped her green dress for a long nightshirt with a unicorn on the front. She hung her dress on a hook by the door so it'd be ready for tomorrow.

"One movie, night owl, then straight to sleep," her father reminded.

"Sure, Dad." Trick hugged him again. "Thanks for helping, Dad."

"Anytime, kiddo. Good Night Teresa," he said and then closed the door behind him.

Trick turned on her TV and was asleep before the opening credits rolled on the movie.

Trick woke up to the feeling of something tiny shaking her shoulder.

"Trick!" Anabelle drew out the word desperately.

"Mmmwha?" Trick mumbled as she woke up to not only the sound of Anabelle, but the sound of her alarm clock going off. She reached over to the small table beside her bed and dismissed the alarm before flopping back on the bed. "I was having a good dream, BelleBelle. What's the matter?" Trick shielded her eyes from the daylight streaming in through the crack in her closed curtains.

"You broke it!" Anabelle exclaimed, her voice distraught.

"What are you talking about?" Trick closed her hands into fists and rubbed the sleep from her eyes.

"Trick, when you sent me away yesterday, you cracked our bond. I can't get our magic lined back up the way it should be. I tried as hard as I could, but it wouldn't go back to the way it should be." Anabelle quavered hopelessly. "I fixed the crack, but the bond is all muzzy and crinkled when I look at it in my dreams."

"Wait, does that mean..." Trick trailed off and raked the blankets off her body. She knew what she would find when she did, though. Peaking from the hem of her rumpled night shirt was the tip of a fluffy white tail. When she thought about it, the tip of the tail twitched. She groaned, "It's not going to go away even if we change, is it?"

"No, it's worse than that!" Anabelle moaned. "It will wear off after a while, but until it does, if we change into new things, you'll get more parts that aren't yours."

"BelleBelle, how long is a while?"

"I don't know, Trick. The magic is all wrong. It's not how it is supposed to be, and I don't know what to do to fix it. I tried everything that I know how to do to smooth it out. Every time I get it just right, it kinks up again." She put her head down on the bedspread dejectedly and put her paws over her nose. "I tried, Trick," she mumbled dismally. Tears leaked down the sides of her muzzle, and Trick sighed. She hadn't even known Anabelle could cry. She put her hand on Anabelle's head.

"It's ok, Anabelle. It's ok. It was going to get out someday. Even if we got all through school without someone seeing us change, it was going to happen someday," Trick comforted. She looked down at the tip of the tail sticking out of the bottom of her night shirt.

"Maybe I can wear a long dress, and just make sure it doesn't stick out of the bottom?" she wondered aloud. She sighed after a minute and shook her head. "Nah, that won't ever work. I can't sit on the silly thing." Trick swung her legs out of bed and slid to the floor. Anabelle looked up.

"How come you're not mad?" Anabelle asked awkwardly.

Trick just shrugged. "It's not going to get better if I get mad, is it?"

Anabelle shook her head. "I guess not."

"Will it get better on its own, or are we stuck this way forever?"

"The bond or the tail?"

"The bond."

"I think we're stuck this way. I'm supposed to be able to smooth out problems with our bond, but the magic got busted. All I can tell for sure is that it will only happen when we use a new shape, and that it will wear off, but I don't know how long it will take."

Trick sighed and took the green dress down off the hook by the door. There was a knock on the door.

"I'm awake, Mom," Trick called out.

"It's Dad."

"Hey, I meant to ask you. Did Bobby ever come home last night?" Trick popped the door open and took the green dress back to her bed.

"Oh, I forgot to tell you. No, he went straight from work to stay with a friend of his. They're moving into the dormitories at college this week. He won't be back until tomorrow afternoon earliest."

Trick's older brother, Robert, had been born seven years before her. Their parents both had been in their early twenties, and after the hard times they had, they decided that they wanted to wait until they were better established financially before they had another child. That was why her brother was almost twice her age. He had been her best friend when she was really little, until she met Eddy. She still told him everything. She was hoping to tell him all about Anabelle before he left for college.

"Will he be back before he goes off to college?" Trick asked.

"Yeah. Semester doesn't start for another week. They're just getting everything moved into the dorms this weekend," her father explained.

"Him and Jack?" Trick asked. Bobby and Jack had been inseparable since they were kids. Trick liked Jack. Unlike a lot of Bobby's other friends, he had never complained when Bobby said they had to take Trick with them on some adventure or other.

"Who else is Bobby gonna put in his dorm room at college? He'll never get anything done without Jack," her father explained.

Her father liked Jack too. Bobby never was short on smarts, quite the opposite. Bobby was too smart. If he didn't have Jack to keep him on task, he would get bored and never finish his homework. They helped each other. When Jack couldn't figure out something, Bobby would help. When Bobby started slacking off, Jack would help. Her father said they were like a matched set of book ends. The books wouldn't stand up without both of them.

"Mom's already gone to work, so I'll make you breakfast. You want to show me your Aura?" he asked a little excitedly. Her father loved the idea of magic, and always had, even before Figments showed up in the world. He was an artist, and had his own small advertising firm that came up with logos and creative marketing art, but his real passion was drawing comic books. He even had a couple of very successful comics under a penname.

"Okay, but I can only show you the werewolf for now. BelleBelle told me this morning that when I sent her away yesterday, it did something to our magic. Now when we change into new Figments, I'm going to end up with parts of me like the tail for a while after we change back."

Her father looked to where Anabelle was on the bed.

"I thought you said it wouldn't hurt her?" he demanded a little angrily.

Anabelle looked down. "It won't hurt either of us, but when Trick sent me away, it did something to our bond that I can't fix yet. When we change back, the magic doesn't all flow out the way it should. Some of it stays trapped in her body, and it leaks out slow, so after we change back, as the magic leaks out, something will change again on its own. I can't do anything that will hurt her."

Her father looked puzzled for a moment. "What do you mean?"

Anabelle looked at Trick, and then sighed. "I'm <u>her</u> Figment," Anabelle said the same way she had the day before, putting the emphasis on her, like that explained everything. Her father looked confused for a minute, but then his eyes went a little wide.

"You mean it literally. You're like a slave," her father speculated.

Anabelle shrugged a little. "That is not a nice way to say it, but yes. The magic of our bond means that she can control me if she wants to. I can't ever do anything she doesn't want me to. There's a little wiggle room for me, but not much."

Trick turned to her, "Did I do that?"

Anabelle shook her head.

"No, that's the way it is for all Figments that belong to one person. It is alright, Trick. I'm happy with it being this way. I'm your Figment, and you're my companion. I wouldn't want to be without you no matter what."

"I'm sorry I doubted you. I didn't mean to drag that out of you," her father said.

"You had to know, and eventually, she would have learned enough about our magic to know," Anabelle admitted, but her voice said she wasn't happy to have revealed it.

She wasn't happy Trick's father was forcing her to have this grown-up talk in front of Trick. It could put a strain on her relationship with Trick. It would be better if Trick didn't know that. Not because it would have let Anabelle get away with anything, it wouldn't have. She could hear Trick's thoughts. There was never any question about whether or not she knew if Trick really wanted her not to do something. But Trick would always wonder if she was responsible for everything Anabelle did.

For the most part, Anabelle would never do anything that Trick didn't want, anyway. Their interests were singular because of their bond, but there were times when Anabelle would go the extra mile in the protection of her Companion, where she might do something that she was sure was the right thing to do even if Trick wasn't. It was part of that wiggle room she had talked about. She could also do some things that Trick wouldn't strictly want her to do so long as they didn't do any harm, like what she had done making fun of the teacher.

"Why didn't you want to tell me?" Trick asked.

"Because whatever put all of this into my head tells me that it would be better if you didn't know yet. I would have told you all of this as you learned more about our bond." It would be a few years before Trick would understand, and Anabelle would tell her then, but her father seemed to get it.

"Trick, Anabelle doesn't want you to think that the things she does are your fault, and if you know that she can't do anything that you don't want her to, then she' s worried you will think everything she does is your fault." Her father explained it well, and Anabelle felt some respect for him, because she would have had no idea how to tell Trick in a way she would understand. Trick looked worriedly at Anabelle.

"But isn't it? If she can't do anything without me letting her?"

"It's complicated, Trick. Until you understand more about how our bond works, you just have to trust me. You won't know enough for a long time to know how to actually give me a command to make me do something against my will, and by then, I hope that you won't want to. But unless you do force me do something, everything I do is my decision," Anabelle explained. Trick sat down on the bed and put the dress down beside her.

"You didn't need to know all of this now, Trick. It's too soon. I wanted us to learn all these things together."

Anabelle eyed her father in annoyance. She understood why the man had needed to know, he wanted to make sure his daughter was safe. But she wished that he had trusted her when she told him the first time that she wouldn't hurt his daughter.

"I screwed things up," her father sighed. "I'm just afraid for Trick."

"Yes, you did, but it's too late now," Anabelle said. "No point in being angry over something I can't change."

"We're going to be late for school if we don't get going," Trick interjected. She started to take things out of her dresser.

"Why don't you take a sick day and stay home with me today, kiddo? I'll call into school and let them know you are out sick. I think growing a tail constitutes a good reason for a sick day." He closed the door so she could get dressed.

She took off her night shirt and hung it up next to the door. She pulled on her green leggings, and then pulled the green tree of life dress over her head. She got it settled and went out to the kitchen, where her father was just putting down his cell phone. Trick climbed up onto one of the stools next to the island that sat between the kitchen and the dining room.

"I should have gone, Dad. They're just going to know tomorrow," Trick said as Anabelle landed in her lap.

"Maybe by tomorrow, you'll be able to fix whatever is broken, or maybe it'll wear off," her father suggested optimistically. Trick rolled her eyes.

"I can try, but I need to be able to sleep," Anabelle said.

"Let's get something to eat first. You do eat?" Trick's father asked.

"I don't know, honestly. There's nothing in my memory about eating."

"It is so strange that you know so much but your memory is so short," her father said. He started taking pans out of the drawers next to the stove, setting them on the stovetop, and then went to the refrigerator.

"I think it might be the way all Figments like me are made. We need to know things to help the people we're bonded to," Anabelle pondered.

"Well, maybe someone out there thinks that you shouldn't have to spend a lifetime learning everything you need to know?" He suggested as he retrieved some eggs and bacon from the refrigerator, placing them next to the stove. Trick exchanged a look with Anabelle, who just shrugged a little.

"Well, if I'm going to stay home from school, I might as well have Eddy bring my homework so I'm not behind," Trick said. She took her cell phone out of a little pocket on the front of her dress and texted Eddy to ask him to do so.

"Sounds like a good plan, Trickster," her father replied.

A few minutes later, Eddy texted back, asking if she was ok. She told him that she was, but that she was having a little trouble with her Aura. He replied, letting her know that he would bring her homework over, and she could tell him all about it then. Meanwhile, her father was flipping pancakes, and Anabelle was floating around his head. She was flitting between the pans, sniffing things.

"Mmmm, this one smells good," Anabelle said, floating over the pan of sizzling bacon. Her father chuckled.

"Never fails. Everyone loves bacon." He picked up a piece that was cooling on a plate and held it up to Anabelle. She took it carefully in her strange paws. She sniffed it again, and hesitantly took a bite of it.

"It's good!" She exclaimed after some thoughtful chewing.

"I just wish I knew if it was good for you," her father said.

"It sure tastes good," Anabelle said enthusiastically.

She gobbled down the first piece, and hovered closer to the plate. Her father chuckled, and then held up a second piece of bacon. Anabelle snatched it greedily and hovered back towards Trick, nibbling at the bacon. She finished it in short order. Her father came over to the island with two plates loaded down with eggs and bacon. He set the smaller of the two in front of Trick. Trick took another piece of bacon and held it out to Anabelle. She rolled over lazily onto her back, and then reached out with her front paws to take it. It seemed that she did not have much room in her stomach for food, because she nibbled at it much more slowly than the first two. Trick dug into her food with abandon like she always did. Her father grinned.

"So, if you can't get rid of the tail by tomorrow you're just going to tell everyone about Anabelle?"

"I don't know what else to do. We can't keep it a secret forever," Trick spluttered around a mouthful of eggs.

"Don't talk with your mouth full," her father reminded. Trick rolled her eyes and swallowed her food. Her father continued, "Why can't you? No one can see Anabelle unless you let them, and you don't have to use your Aura where anyone can see. If you just make sure no one sees you change, there's no way for them to tell you from any other Figment, right?"

"I guess, but if I show up at school with a tail or something, people are going to know." Trick took another bite and chewed. Anabelle alighted on the tabletop on her back. She looked at them both upside-down.

"Well sure, but if you can hide it until it goes away on its own, no one's ever gonna know," her dad said. Trick lifted her tail and waved it at him.

"How do I hide this?" Trick asked skeptically.

"Well it won't be easy, but I can try to help you. You can wear ankle-length dresses to hide the tail for now if it isn't gone by tomorrow."

Trick finished the last of her bacon, and her father took the plate to the dishwasher.

"Want to show me your Aura now?"

Trick grinned and Anabelle perked up, floating from the table and flipping over. Trick remembered how big the werewolf shape had been.

"I won't fit in here. Let's go out in the back yard," Trick said and went out through the sliding doors. Her father followed her.

"When we change back this time, the clothing has to come first," Trick whispered.

"I said it was an accident," Anabelle groused.

"What was an accident?" her father probed. Trick blushed bright red. She tried to think of a lie, but her father's stern expression pulled the truth out of her.

"When we changed back earlier, it took a minute for my clothes to come back," Trick said embarrassedly. Her father started to laugh, but then cut off and gave her a hard look.

"Oh god, Eddy saw you naked, didn't he? I'm sorry I laughed."

"It's ok, Daddy. Eddy turned around real fast. I think he might have turned as red as me."

"It was an accident. It was the first time we ever changed," Anabelle fumed.

"It's ok. I'm sure Eddy was the perfect gentleman. Come on, show me already! The suspense is killing me!"

"Ok, here goes," Trick said.

She looked at Anabelle. Anabelle landed in Trick's hands, and Trick hugged her to her chest. Then, there was the flash of blue light, and suddenly she was on four paws again, but it felt different this time. Everything seemed more like she knew what she was doing. Right away, she could control her tail, and her sense of smell seemed even more like someone was whispering in her ear. Her hearing, too, jumped out. She could hear her father's heartbeat if she paid close enough attention.

"Whoa! That's the most amazing thing I have ever seen!"

Trick padded across the deck, boards creaking under her weight, and sat down in front of her father, who now seemed very small by comparison. He held out his hand, and she sniffed it. **This is dad**, the scent said, and then, **That is oil, fat,**

and meat of some kind. His hands smelled like bacon, and she licked his fingers before she could stop herself. Her tongue was more than large enough to engulf most of his hand. Her sense of smell was almost overwhelming.

[I can help you process all the smells, but it would be better if you learned how yourself. Lots of Figments have better senses than humans, so we'll be doing it a lot. The more you learn how to do it yourself, the more I can pay attention to other things,] Anabelle said inside of her head.

[Is that why it seems like the smells are words? Are you doing that?]

[No, that's just how your brain interprets it. I'm just translating what things are, but if I stop, it will still come to you as words, but they'll make less sense.]

"Eww, Trick!" her father said with a laugh. "God, look at those teeth." Trick peeled her lips back from her fangs so he could see them better. "Geez! Don't bite anyone with those things!"

When she tried to laugh, a chuffing sound came out of her throat. She shook her head, and then turned towards the bushes again. The smell coming from there said, **This is the cat, but it isn't here now.** That modifier at the end hadn't been there before.

[How long can we stay like this?] Trick asked.

[For as long as we want, now. You could stay in this form permanently, if you wanted to. The first time we changed, I had to use a lot of magic energy, but now that we have done it before, changing takes almost none, and once the change is done, the magic you need comes from the same source where the werewolves get it instead of from inside of you.] Anabelle's explanation was vague, and Trick didn't fully understand, but before she could ask any more questions, Anabelle continued on. *[You're going to have to trust me for now, Trick. There's a lot that you have to learn before I can really help you understand how our magic works.]*

[Ok.] Trick turned her attention back to her father. He had been talking, and she hadn't been listening because of her internal dialogue with Anabelle. She tilted her head at him, but he didn't seem to get it. She was about to change back

when her father got up and started to walk around her with
interest.

"God, you're enormous. Good thing we don't have to feed
a werewolf. We'd be bankrupt in a week!" He reached out
and touched her side. She stood still while he ran his fingers
through her fur. "It's softer than I thought it would be. This is
so cool." The enthusiasm was clear in his voice. "I wonder
how fast you can run, and if you have super strength like
them."

[We do. We have all the powers that the northern tribes have,]
Anabelle filled in.

[Let's change back so we can talk to him.]

Anabelle gave a mental nod, then the flash of blue light
returned. Trick immediately patted herself down before the
light even started to fade. Her dress was there just fine. Her
tail was also there, and she made an unhappy noise.

"I told you the clothes would come back right this time,"
Anabelle huffed.

"I was hoping the tail would go away," Trick fumed.

"Told you it wouldn't."

"What's it feel like?" her father interjected.

"Well, we haven't done much yet. I feel really strong, I can
hear things that are really far away, and the smells talk to me."

"The smells… talk to you?" her father asked skeptically.

"Yep. When I smell something, I sort of hear a description
of what I'm smelling in my head."

"You're like a little super hero," he laughed.

"Yeah, if super heroes got Figment body parts," Trick
sassed, waving her tail at him.

"Some heroes have problems with their powers at first.
You'll figure it out. Tell you what, if you want to try out your
powers a little more, I can drive you out to the woods today. I
know some places that you can run around and no one will see
you."

"I'm not a super hero, Dad," she complained, "but I would
like go out where I can play as a werewolf. I feel like I could
run so fast. Anabelle says we get all of their powers." Her
father nodded.

"Go grab a jacket, and I'll pack us a lunch. Mom'll be home late tonight, and your brother won't be back until tomorrow. We should have plenty of time to drive up North. I know just the place."

Her father had grown up much further north than where they lived now. He liked being closer to work, but he still remembered all the places he had visited when he was a kid. She grabbed her green fleece jacket and turned to find Anabelle staring at her very intently.

"What?"

"Not sure," Anabelle said. She shrugged a bit and floated lazily around the room, slowly rolling over and over again. Trick gave her an exasperated look.

"You're kinda weird, ya know."

"I'm *your* imaginary friend."

"Not very imaginary anymore," Trick shot back.

She picked up her smaller hiking pack. It had some things in it that her father always made her take when they went hiking or camping. He had taught her how to use all of them. It contained a good pocket knife, some waterproof matches, and three small cans of Sterno to help her light a fire if she needed to, some granola bars, a big bottle of water, and some small hand warmers. She shrugged into her jacket, and then pulled the backpack on. She slipped on a pair of comfortable green round-toed shoes, and then had a thought.

"How much stuff can we carry when we change?" she asked Anabelle. She knew her clothes would change with her and come back after she changed back, but what about the rest?

"Not a lot. Clothing will change with us. The backpack is probably too much to for our magic to handle. We can try it. If it is too much, it will just drop on the ground when we're done changing."

"How do you fly?" Trick asked as she opened the door.

"I'unno, I just do." Anabelle floated out the door behind Trick. Trick noticed that the bows on Anabelle's tails were now made of a shiny silver cloth with gold beads in the shape of little wolf heads.

"Do you pick the bows on your tails?"

"Nope, you do. You can change them if you really think about it," Anabelle explained. When Trick got back to the kitchen, her father was making sandwiches. He had two thermoses that were probably filled with soup.

"Toss me your water bottle," her father said. She took off the pack and slid the stainless-steel vacuum bottle out of it. She tossed the bottle to him, and he caught it in one hand before filling it with water and ice. He handed it back to her, and she slid it into her pack.

"I'm worried about Mom. She was really mad about Anabelle," Trick mused. She had always had a good relationship with both her parents, and it looked like this was going to come between her and her mother.

"She wasn't mad. She was just worried about you. I told you, kiddo, your Mom'll be fine. You just need to give her time to adjust." Trick stared at the bows on Anabelle's gently waving tails. She thought about them changing from the silvery cloth to green to match her dress, and the gold changing to purple plastic because purple was her favorite color. After a long minute, the silver color bled into green, and then the wolf heads popped from gold to purple.

"Neat!" Trick said. Anabelle swished her tails around where she could see them.

"Good. That's your first lesson in how our magic works. You can communicate with me just by thinking about it if you want. It isn't the same as when we're sharing a body, but I can feel what you want me to do," Anabelle explained. Her father came out of the kitchen with his hiking pack on his shoulder.

"Ready?" He asked.

"Yep! Let's go!"

Chapter Five
"Run"

It took about an hour and a half to reach the place her father had in mind. Black Creek was fairly remote and while people fished along it all the time, there was a lot of woodland. They parked at a bend in the creek, surrounded by the deep woods of the Adirondacks. Even if they did run into someone else, as long as no one saw her change, there was no danger of anyone finding out who she was. If someone saw her in her werewolf shape, they would probably just run away.

Trick and Anabelle got out of the car and shifted into the werewolf shape. Like Anabelle had said, the pack fell off to the ground when they changed. Her father picked up her pack and set it back in the car and locked it.

"Pretty sure that you would survive better in that body than I could with all my gear," he said. Trick dropped her jaw in a doggy grin. Her father took his fly fishing rod out of the back of the car.

"Go on. I assume you can find your way back to me from my scent. I doubt there is anything around here strong enough to hurt you like that. If you have all of their magic, I doubt anything could really hurt you. I'll do some fishing," her father said.

[Can we?] Trick asked in her head.

[Yep,] Anabelle replied.

Trick gave a nod, which felt distinctly odd in the werewolf body. She turned to the woods and yelped in glee before racing into the trees in a blur of speed. At first, she stumbled over roots and hidden limbs in the undergrowth.

[Running on four paws is weird,] Trick thought.

[It's because I'm still learning how to work with you. You'll get better every minute. Just keep running.]

Trick did. She pushed a little harder, and the trees turned into blurs in the corners of her vision as she darted between them. She raced along the creek, turning toward the water when she reached a bend. The creek was at least fifty feet across, and she was about to find out how far she could jump.

[Trick, we'll go way too far!] Anabelle squeaked, but it was already too late.

Trick shot towards the edge of the creek, and the muscles in her hind quarters bunched up. She exploded into the air, clearing the creek easily before smashing into the trees with a startled yip, branches slapping her in the face. Trick lost control of her body for a moment.

Anabelle took over and righted them as they tumbled through the tree limbs. Somehow, she managed to flip them over, and they landed on all four paws, skidding through sharp stones. Trick felt them slicing through the pads of her paws, and she yowled in pain. Her reaction blocked Anabelle's control for a moment, sending them tumbling over a fallen log, rolling ass over tea kettle until they fetched up hard against the trunk of a tree. Trick laid there dazed for a long moment. She struggled to get up reflexively.

[No, don't get up yet. Your paws are regenerating, and you broke some of the small bones there, too.] Anabelle cautioned.

Trick groaned, *[It hurts.]*

[It'll get better in a few seconds. Just stay still.]

A few minutes later the pain in her paws faded, just like Anabelle said it would.

[Sorry, BelleBelle. That was my fault.]

[You're going to make mistakes, Trick. You don't ever have to apologize to me. Just make sure you don't ever do that off a cliff or something.]

[BelleBelle, what happens if we get hurt, and then change back while we are hurt?] Trick asked concernedly.

[The hurts stay. Lots of Figments have self-healing powers, so it will usually be better to wait to change back.]

Trick rolled herself over onto four paws again and panted for a minute.

[Ewww, I'm drooling all over the place!]

[Yes, and you should keep your tongue stuck out like that, or you'll get it in your fur. Werewolves, just like real wolves, can't sweat.]

[Oh, ewww, gross! I sweat through my tongue?]

[Sort of.] Anabelle's voice rang with laughter inside Trick's head.

It was then that Trick suddenly realized her nose was trying to get a message through to her. **This is something that does not belong here,** it said. She didn't know how her nose knew that it was out of place, but it certainly did.

[Do you know what that smell is?] Trick asked.

[It's another Figment. You're smelling magic. It has a unique scent,] Anabelle replied. [It's something small. Probably just a nymph, or some sort of forest spirit. Don't worry. They can't tell we aren't just another werewolf.]

[Are you sure?]

[No. There may be some Figments who could tell, but I don't know about them yet. Big powerful things like Dragons, maybe they can tell, but it is definitely not a dragon.]

[Can we go see what it is? Do you think it is safe?] Trick asked skeptically. She felt Anabelle's reply as a sort of mental shrug.

[Whatever it is will probably run away if you chase it. Nymphs and Dryads are really fast in the woods.]

Trick turned towards the smell. She darted into the trees, kicking up gravel and dirt as her claws dug into the ground. She was a little more cautious with her speed this time. She arrowed through the trees towards the smell, and whatever it was, she caught it by surprise because it didn't try to run until it was too late.

Trick burst through the underbrush and nearly landed on top of a small creature that looked sort of like a raccoon. Unlike a raccoon, it was wearing clothing, a long green jacket that reached almost to the ground and a hat. The golden-buttoned jacket was stenciled with leaves all over. The hat was a tiny, round affair, brimless, with a golden bell-like ball atop, though it didn't make any noise when the creature startled back away from her. She could see the creature's puffy, ringed tail and little muzzle. Its face was covered with dark grey fur, aside from a white mask around its eyes.

[Trick, kill it!] Anabelle said frantically.

[What? Why?]

[Because it's a pooka! It will use its magic to confuse us, and we could be lost out here for a long, long time! It would go after our family too! Either kill it, or we have to run!]

Trick stood for a frozen, crystalline moment, trying to decide what to do. The thing didn't look like it was going to attack them. It looked terrified of her. Its whiskers twitched, and its eyes were very wide. Anabelle realized that the message wasn't getting through.

[Trick, that thing is not afraid of you! It looks that way on purpose! Run, run, run!] Anabelle's voice rang inside of her head, snapping Trick out of indecision.

Trick bolted away as fast as she could. She turned around faster than she thought was possible and darted into the woods. Branches snapped off as she bulled frantically through the trees away from it. She had never been so afraid in her life. She ran full-tilt down a hill, and then when she came to a narrow corridor that was filled with deadfall trees, she bunched her muscles and leapt thirty feet into the air. She cleared the deadfall trees with ease, but branches raked at her as she blurred through them. She made it back to the creek, and this time when she leapt over the creek, she made it without nearly killing herself. She had made it <u>miles</u> through the woods while she was running, and it looked as if her father had walked quite a ways while he was fishing.

[Is it chasing us?] she gasped inside of her head to Anabelle.

[Slow down, and breathe deeply through your nose.]

Trick slowed to a trot just long enough to take a deep breath through her nose. A number of scents came to her. The sheer number confused her until she felt Anabelle sorting through them to help her. **This is a pine tree. This is the smell of running water. This is magic.** This last scent concerned her the most, but after a moment, she got the sense from Anabelle that the smell of the magic was far off. She slowed down a little more and took another deep breath. **These are oak trees. These are maple trees. That is Dad.** Trick slowed to a stop and looked around. She realized they were close to the car. Her father's scent here was a little faint, but it was easy to follow.

[What's a pooka?]

[It's a type of fairy. It can change its shape, and they're known for cursing people so that they can't find their way out of the woods forever, among other things.]

Trick put her nose to the ground and started to trail her father's scent. She needed to get to him, and get them out of there right away. If that thing was still wandering around the woods, it was still dangerous to them. It could still find them. She began to pick up speed as her worry filled her mind. The wind shifted, and started blowing at her back. She lost her father's scent in that wind.

[No!] She slowed down and started casting about with her nose near the ground, trying to pick up his scent. It led into the water, and stopped there.

[No need to panic. He went in the water here. Just follow the creek and you'll find him,] Anabelle advised.

Trick turned and ran down the creek in the direction that her father had been going. He had gone a long way, because it took her five minutes and several bends in the creek to find him. He was standing in the water, wearing hip waders. He was whipping his fly fishing rod in a complicated pattern to get all the fishing line into the air for a cast. She slowed to a halt on the bank of the creek and sat down. She didn't particularly want to change back because she wanted to get out of the woods quickly. She thought that her father could ride on her back to get back to the car faster.

[That won't work,] Anabelle advised.

[Why not?]

[Because there's nothing for him to hold on to. We're not a horse, and even if we changed into something like a horse, it's not as easy to ride a horse as you think it is, but it would still be better if we didn't change back. Werewolves have some resistance to magic, and we can defend ourselves if we have to.]

[I don't know anything about defending myself, BelleBelle.]

[But I do, and I can control our body if you give me permission.]

Her father looked up from what he was doing after casting his line. He saw her sitting there and grinned. He waved at her, and began reeling in his line.

"Done already?"

[We can change back and forth a whole bunch now. Change back so we can talk to him.]

They changed back in a flash of blue light, and Trick checked her clothing. Then, her father saw the expression on her face. He hurried out of the water.

"What's the matter, Trick?"

"We saw a dangerous Figment out in the woods. Anabelle thinks we should go."

Her father's expression shifted to one of annoyance.

"Great, now I can't even fish the creek anymore. Your mother will have a fit."

"Well, if you don't tell her, and you give us a little time, we'll be able to change into something that can protect us from magic," Anabelle suggested.

"We can?" Trick asked skeptically.

"There are a few Figments that can protect against all magic," Anabelle explained. "Some fairies are particularly good at it. Also, elementals can ground out any magic thrown at them."

It was odd when Anabelle recited these facts. She sounded completely different, and her eyes lost focus. It was as if she was reading it all from a book that only she could see.

"Alright, we can go," her father said. He fiddled with the basket on his belt, and she could see some fish tails sticking out of the basket.

"I'm gonna change back to the wolf just in case," Trick said. Her father looked around a little nervously. She made the change back, and surprisingly, she realized that changing didn't make her feel like it did the first time. She actually felt quite good.

[Yeah. It will take a lot more changes now for us to get tired. I told you it would.]

[I know. I just haven't gotten used to any of this yet.]

Her father couldn't run through the woods like she could, but he made his way back to the car at a rapid pace. They circled around him, sniffing the air to make sure that no one else came close to them. There were a few normal animals. **This is a deer. This is a squirrel. A few days ago, a cougar passed this way.**

[How do real werewolves put up with this all the time? I can barely hear myself think with all these smells.]

[You'd have to ask one of them.]

They had gotten about halfway back to the car when she smelled something. **This is something that does not belong here, but not the same something.** Trick froze, and started turning in a circle until she was facing the direction the smell was coming from.

"We mean it no harm," a melodious voice floated from the bushes. It was not loud, but it was smooth. "It is a long way from home. We have never seen one of its kind around here before."

Trick saw a flash of golden eyes in the bushes for a moment, but then they blinked and did not return. She bared her teeth and growled.

"It is rude. Perhaps it is afraid of us?" the voice said.

Trick turned, following the sound of its voice. She knew she couldn't wait for this thing. Her father was getting too far away.

"We mean it no harm," the voice repeated, as if it could sense that she was about to leave, and it did not want her to go.

She couldn't talk, and she couldn't change back, because if she did, she would be defenseless against whatever this thing was.

[Do you know what it is?] Trick asked Anabelle mentally.

[I have to see it, or hear the name of the creature to know what it is.]

"Maybe if it could see us, it would not be afraid?" the voice mused.

[Tilt your head, drop one ear, and lift the other,] Anabelle advised. Trick took a long moment to figure out how to control her ears, and then did what Anabelle suggested.

"It has a question, or perhaps an answer. We will show it."

A sleek, black form emerged from the bushes. It was much smaller than Trick's werewolf shape. It had large golden eyes, and a grinning mouth full of sharp-looking teeth. It floated a couple of feet off the ground. Once it was clear of the bushes, she could see that it was striped with dark grey from the tip of its tail to its neck. It had a stripe over its eyes too.

[It's a Cheshire Cat,] Anabelle said.

[But no one has ever seen one outside of London.]

[You can't see a Cheshire Cat if it doesn't want you to. They can be anywhere at any time they want. They can't hurt people physically, though. They can make people pretty crazy if they want to for some reason, but they can't physically hurt people. It's part of their magic.]

[Can't hurt people?]

[Their magic stops working if they hurt someone.]

[And what does their magic do?]

"It is not startled. It recognizes one of us. It seems to be elsewhere though. I know it understands us. It can change back to speak to us."

[It expects us to change back to the semi-human shape that Werewolves have,] Trick mused continuing the mental dialogue with Anabelle.

[We might be fine. You do have a tail. Werewolves in their human shape always have some wolf features.]

[It will see you, though.]

[I don't have to leave your body for a while if we change back.]

Trick wasn't sure why she felt like she should talk to this Figment. Cheshire Cats chased everyone out of London. They said that some people had been driven entirely insane by Cheshire Cats. Its golden eyes watched her carefully.

"It wonders about the stories it has heard of us. It wonders if we will attempt to drive it mad."

Trick had Anabelle change them back. She made sure to curl her tail up so that it was obvious.

"I've heard a lot of bad things," Trick said tentatively.

It watched her with curious eyes. "It is not a werewolf." The Cheshire Cat floated higher into the air, and its body faded away, leaving behind only its eyes and mouth floating in the air.

"I am a werewolf," Trick attempted.

"Lies fall from its lips. It does not change like a werewolf," the cat replied. Its eyes and mouth floated around her in the air. They started to roll, and its body appeared in a swirl of black smoke as it turned upside-down.

"I am a werewolf," Trick repeated.

"It smells like a werewolf. It has a tail like a werewolf would. But it does not change like a werewolf. Perhaps it is a different kind of werewolf. Perhaps it is not like those in the Alaskan tribes. But it helps the human stay safe from the pooka."

Trick turned to leave, and the Cat spoke again quickly.

"It need not fear the pooka any longer. We have shooed it along its way." Trick paused and looked back. "Truly we do not think it will come near with us here, and there are no other Figments nearby. It can stay." The cat floated closer examining her with its golden eyes.

"What are you doing out here?" Trick asked. She turned back to the little clearing.

"We are looking for those Spelled by The White God. We thought that it might be one of the Spelled," the Cat explained. Trick just shook her head. The White God again. 'Who was The White God?' she thought, but she didn't say anything. She just shook her head.

"But if you are not one of the Spelled, merely a werewolf, then we must look elsewhere," the Cat continued.

[He's talking about us, I think. The Spelled. People who get their own Figments,] Anabelle mused.

[Should we tell him?]

[Why would we?]

"It seems to be elsewhere again. It tilts its head like it is listening to something we cannot hear," the Cat said a little testily.

"I don't know if I should be talking to you. I'm thinking," Trick stalled.

[Well, Tigs said something about someone called the White God didn't she?] Trick thought at Anabelle.

"It seems like it is making a much bigger decision than simply deciding to converse. We think it is lying again."

Trick rolled her eyes.

[I don't know what to do,] Anabelle admitted.

[I don't know either. Maybe dad will know what to do.]

[If we want to talk to it again, we have to tell it what we are. It won't be here when we come back if we don't.]

[Come out,] Trick said.

Anabelle emerged in a smaller flash of light.

"You were right. I'm not a werewolf. I can be one. I can be any Figment that I want," Trick admitted.

"It is one of the Spelled, and it fooled even our senses. It is talented, and it is rude. But, perhaps it will do better than the last dozen," the Cat mused as it floated around her.

"I don't know if I should talk to you anymore," Trick said. The Cat's eyes roved over her as if searching for something.

"It is very young. The others were not so young as it," The Cat said after a moment.

"I have a name. I'm Trick, and this is Anabelle."

The Cat said nothing for a long moment.

"It should be careful-careful. It does not know that to give its name is a dangerous thing. We understand. It is young, it should seek advice from its elders. We will be nearby when it wishes to speak to us again." The Cat faded away in a puff of black smoke before Trick could protest.

"What the heck was that all about?" Trick wondered aloud.

"Who knows? I'll remember it all to tell Dad, though."

They changed back into the werewolf shape and dashed into the woods. It did not take them long to catch up to their father. They were still about a mile away from the car when they caught up. Despite what the Cat had said, Trick still thought it would be a good idea to go home. She stepped out from the underbrush and trotted next to her father.

"You were gone for a bit. Are you ok?" her father asked. Trick gave a soft, affirmative growl. It took them about half an hour to get back to the car. When she changed back, her father looked at her oddly. "What took you so long to catch up back there?"

"I ran into something out in the woods. A Cheshire Cat. It told me some things that I'm not sure about," Trick said. They got into the car, and Anabelle recited all the details of their encounter with the Cheshire Cat. Her father didn't say anything for a long time, and they were almost halfway home when he finally spoke.

"I don't get it either, Trick. You're just a kid. What could they want you to do?" If he didn't know, she had no chance of figuring it out.

Chapter Six
"Luck"

When Trick woke up the next morning, there was a knot in her stomach. She tried to feel her tail, but she couldn't, so she assumed it had fallen asleep. When she finally looked around for Anabelle, she noticed that her Figment was nowhere to be seen.

"BelleBelle?" The lid to the laundry hamper flipped open, and Anabelle floated out. She looked exhausted. Her ears were drooping, and her fur was sticking out in different directions. "What happened to you?" Anabelle spun over slowly so she was upside-down.

"I didn't get any real sleep last night at all. I was working in our dreams all night trying to fix our magic," Anabelle said dejectedly.

"Oh, god. I still have a tail, huh?"

"No. I fixed it a little. The left-over magic from each first change will take a couple of days to get out of your body now, so if we want to be able to use more than our werewolf form, we will at least know how long it is going to take for the magic to wear off." Anabelle yawned wide, her tongue curling.

"That's great, Anabelle!"

"It's the best we are ever going to get, Trick. I don't know how to do it any better."

"It's alright, BelleBelle. This is my fault. At least we can go back to school today."

"Teresa! Time to get up." Her mother's voice called from the door.

"Already up, Mom," Trick shouted back and swung her legs out of bed.

Her mother opened the door to her room, entered, and sat on the bed next to Trick.

"I'm sorry about the other day. I shouldn't have asked you to do that. I just don't want you to go through what I saw my friend go through when I was little. She was one of the first kids in the world to get a Figment," her mother said.

"I know, Mom."

"Your Dad thinks that we should keep you home from school until you have a better handle on your magic."

"Uh-uh. I wanna go back to school. And we've got it figured out. Anabelle fixed it."

"Well, you can stay out for a few more days if you like. We can cover for you." Her mother smiled.

"Nah, then I'll just have all that homework to do. I'm okay, Mom. I can go back to school today."

"Well, your father said you had a problem."

Trick looked up. "Oh, I didn't think he was gonna tell you."

Her mother laughed, "He lay down in bed last night and said…" Her mother began a passable imitation of her father's voice. "Our daughter has grown a tail, and has no idea when it is going to go away."

Trick laughed. "Yeah, that's what Anabelle fixed, but if we change into more Figments, we'll have other things that we have to wait for them to wear off. It will take a couple of days for each," Trick continued. Her mother looked a little worried. "It won't hurt me. It just takes a little time to wear off," Trick tried to reassured her. Her mother did not look enthusiastic about the prospect. "Don't worry, Mom. I will be careful to keep it a secret for as long as I can," Trick said.

Anabelle seemed to have fallen asleep floating lazily in a circle near the ceiling of her room. Her mother looked up when a soft snore escaped the Figment.

"Is she alright?"

"Yes, she was just awake all night trying to fix our magic. She's really tired."

"That's why you don't have a tail today?"

"Mhmm."

Her mother looked up thoughtfully at Anabelle. "Well, you better get ready for school. I'll give you a ride in, if you like." Her mother put her arms around Trick and hugged her tight. "I love you."

"I love you too, Mom."

Her mom got up from her bed. "I'll go make you some breakfast."

Trick had showered the night before, so she tossed her night shirt in the hamper. She put her hair up in pigtails with two purple scrunchies, and then went to her closet. She decided that from now on, just in case she ended up with another tail, that dresses would be best. She kind of wished that she had more long dresses because if she did end up with a tail again, somehow, it would cover it better, but most of her dresses were knee-length.

She took a pair of purple leggings out of her dresser along with a short-sleeve wool dress in blue. To them, she added a pair of blue Mary Jane flats. The round-toed shoes were her favorites since she couldn't find any in purple. She got dressed, and looked up to where Anabelle floated near the ceiling.

"Are you going to be alright?" Trick asked. Anabelle opened one eye and looked down at her.

"I'll be fine once I get some real sleep."

"Do you want to stay here and sleep?"

Anabelle shook her head. "I can't. I have to be with you. I'll sleep inside of you today, at least until you need me, or I feel better."

Annabelle floated closer to Trick. Trick held out her hands, and Anabelle landed in her arms. There was a flash of blue light that made Trick blink. Anabelle was gone.

"This is so weird," Trick said aloud.

[I know. You'll understand one day when you have a better grasp on magic. I'm your living magic, so I'm a part of you. That's why I can do this.]

Trick walked to her desk and sat down, opening her laptop computer. She checked her e-mail, and found a few from Eddy wanting to know what happened yesterday. She replied, letting him know that she would tell him everything in school today.

[What do you mean by that? How do you know I'll understand?] Trick thought at Anabelle. She got the distinct impression of a shrug in reply.

[I don't know. I just know that I'm supposed to say that, and that it is true.]

[Go to sleep. I won't bug you unless I need you,] Trick thought at Anabelle.

[I am asleep,] Anabelle replied.

Trick sighed, and went back to what she was doing on the computer. She opened the Farfetched website and searched The White God. She had a feeling that the Cheshire Cat in the woods had told her something that no one else knew: that the kids who were getting Figments all these years weren't getting them at random. Someone or something was giving them magic powers. There wasn't very much on the website, but there was a little blurb that said a few people who had spoken to Figments had heard them mention The White God. She realized after she closed her laptop that if she really wanted to know how she had gotten Anabelle, she was going to have to keep looking for The White God.

She grabbed her backpack, and started stuffing her homework inside. Eddy had dropped off everything while she and her father had been out yesterday, and even though the social studies was not her best subject, she had finished it all. At least she wouldn't have to listen to a lecture from Mrs. Ekard. She could smell bacon cooking in the kitchen, and she went that way. Her mother had made her a sandwich on an English muffin.

"Hurry up and eat, Teresa. We're already running late." Her mother turned around, munching on a piece of bacon. "Oh, I like the blue one, but I thought you didn't like dresses so much anymore?"

Trick shrugged. "I don't mind them. I just thought pants were easier, but if I'm going to grow a tail or something the next time I change, a dress might be better."

"Very practical," her mother laughed. She smoothed down her own grey business skirt. "My daughter, the shapeshifter," her mother groaned. "What happened to the worst thing I had to worry about happening was you liking some boy?"

Trick rolled her eyes, "Boys are boring."

Her mother laughed a little more. "Don't let Eddy hear you say that." She picked up her keys and purse off the counter.

"Well, Eddy isn't just some boy, he's my friend," Trick said, and her mother's laughter once again filled the air.

"Let's go. I let the school know you're going to be a little late while you were getting dressed."

The drive into school was uneventful, and when she finally made it to shop class, she was only about ten minutes late. Eddy was sitting in their normal spot, not far from the back door of the class room that lead out to the wood shop.

"Mr. Kitnam is going to have some words for you after class. You know how he gets when people are late," Eddy whispered when she sat down next to him.

The balding man at the front of the classroom was hanging up a huge piece of paper on the chalk board with instructions all over it. The fringe of hair he had left had gone silver, and he wore a tan button up work shirt over a pair of black slacks. Every year, Mr. Kitnam had everyone do a single class project. Everyone got a part of it, and each student's part made up half of their grade for the year. The projects got a little harder every year. This would be their second year in his class. Trick liked Mr. Kitnam. He was one of the only teachers that called her Trick and not Teresa. But he really hated it when people were late to class, even her. He had scowled a little when she came in the room.

"We've gotta talk after class. Something happened yesterday, and I don't know what to do about it," Trick said.

She took out her notebook and pencil and started taking notes as Mr. Kitnam explained to them how the project was going to be divided up for this year. Over the course of the year, he would teach them everything they needed to know to get the project done, and then at the end of the year, he would help everyone to put it all together. The bell rang, and everyone shuffled their books into their backpacks.

"So what happened?" Eddy asked as soon as they got out into the hall.

"Not here, Eddy. I don't want anyone to hear."

"Don't want anyone to hear what?" a voice asked from behind them. Trick turned around, and found Dylan and Tigs behind them.

"Oh, good. I was going to come find you next," Trick said.

"Why?" Dylan asked.

"Because Anabelle said that Tigs knows something that might help us."

"We have study hall this period. What about you, Dylan?" Eddy asked.

"I can skip class if you think it's important."

"I don't know how important it is, but it might have something to do with how we got our Figments," Trick said. Dylan's interest sharpened.

"Alright. Ms. Tintle won't mind if I skip Math. I'm her best student. I'll just tell her I wasn't feeling well and get my homework after class," Dylan said.

The study hall was an open period, so no one would really notice if they all disappeared for a bit. They went downstairs and headed outside. It was only second period, so there was no lunch going on, which left the field out back empty.

"So, spill. What happened to you yesterday?" Dylan asked.

"After I did my first transformation, about an hour after I changed back, I grew a tail. I did something to our magic when I sent Anabelle away, but that's not the important part. My dad took me out to the woods so I could run around as a werewolf, and see what it was like. When we were out there, we ran into a Cheshire Cat," Trick explained. She told them everything that had happened to her in the woods.

"Other Figments have told Tigs that if we could find The White God, we could get answers about how to use our magic and how Tigs got here. You think that whoever this White God is, the Cheshire Cats know where to find him?" Dylan asked.

"Maybe. I don't know. But Anabelle and I would both like to know how she got here. I think Tigs wants to know, too." Trick said. The little stuffed tiger riding on Dylan's shoulder gave an exaggerated nod.

"Yeah, she does," Dylan said, "but all the Cheshire Cats are on the other side of the world. I mean, we jumped across the ocean one weekend to see the fairies, but it was not a fun trip."

"Why?" Eddy asked.

"We have to teleport up to the top of a mountain, and then teleport nonstop across the ocean from there. I have to do it fast so that we don't fall too far, or we'll be going too fast when we get there, and we'll kill ourselves when we hit the ground. It takes about forty jumps to get all the way there, and by the time I do, I'm exhausted. It took us all weekend to get enough energy back to jump back here, and I spent a bunch of my money doing it," Dylan said.

[We can help with that. We can turn into something big enough to carry them that can fly,] Anabelle chimed in inside of Trick's head.

"What if we could turn into something that can fly that could carry you?" Trick relayed the idea for Anabelle.

Dylan looked thoughtful. He exchanged a long look with Tigs. "That would probably help, as long as it isn't too big."

"I don't know how big it would have to be. Anabelle just suggested it, but I don't think she knows what sort of Figment we could turn into that could carry us all."

"Did you figure out your magic?" Dylan asked.

"A little. I know how to change, but there are side effects if I do. And Anabelle can learn about new Figments just by someone saying their name around her."

Dylan looked around. "Where is she, anyway?"

"She's inside of me. She can sort of turn herself into a part of me?" Trick said uncertainly.

"I've heard of that. Some of the other shapeshifter kids on Farfetched say that's how they change, too," Eddy said.

"So what could fly that could carry all of us?" Dylan asked.

"What about a gryphon? They're supposed to be pretty big, big enough that they are having problems with them eating whole cows in India," Eddy suggested.

"How do you know all this?" Dylan asked skeptically.

"I read about it on the internet," Eddy said.

"He's a little obsessed with Figments," Trick said, earning her a scowl from Eddy.

"Why shouldn't I be? Figments are magic! It couldn't possibly be cooler." Eddy growled at them defensively.

"No, Eddy its fine. I'm just not used to people thinking my powers are cool," Dylan placated.

"I don't get why everyone is so afraid of you."

Dylan sighed, "Then you aren't thinking very hard, Eddy. I can go anywhere I can see. Nothing can stop me. I don't age. What's it going to be like in five or ten years when I have learned everything there is to know about my power? What about a hundred years from now? They're afraid of what I can do," Dylan said a little testily.

"Sorry. Didn't think about it like that, but it's still not fair. You don't do that."

Dylan just shrugged. "It's alright. I just get worked up because I've only had Tigs for a year, and no one else has ever actually liked what we can do. Even the people who've paid me for quick trips are terrified."

"How much do you charge people?" asked Trick.

"A lot. My parents put it all in a college fund for me, but I keep a little bit in cash for myself. We spent most of it the last time we went to see the Fairies, though. We had to take camping gear, and I had to tell my parents that I was staying over at a friend's house for the weekend. It only takes about a minute to actually do the jumps to get over there. Do you even know where you want to go?"

"No idea," Trick said. *[Can we even turn into a gryphon?]* She asked Anabelle inside her head.

[Sure,] came the sleepy reply.

[Is it big enough to carry everyone at once?]

[Yep, but riding a gryphon would be harder than they think. There's nothing to hold on to. We would need a way to keep them on our back.]

"Anabelle says that riding a gryphon would be hard because there's nothing to hold onto. We would need a way for you to hold on."

"We can work something out," Eddy said confidently.

"But you said the Cheshire Cat told you that it would be around if you needed to talk to it again," Dylan pointed out.

"So we should try to talk to it after school," Eddy decided.

"Alright. We can go to the park after school and try to talk to him?" She had no idea if the cat even had a gender. "I think if we go to my house and call a Cheshire Cat there, my Mom will have a meltdown," Trick said.

"Then the park is probably our best bet. After school, we'll go," Dylan said.

"Why do I feel like this is a bad idea?" Trick groaned.

"Because we'll probably all end up crazy. It is a Cheshire Cat, after all," Eddy said.

"No, I don't think that. I just feel like we have no idea what we're getting into," Trick said.

"Well, I guess it is lucky we have two of the most magical kids on earth then. You guys can do anything," Eddy said. Trick scowled at him. "What?!" Eddy yelped.

"I can't change into other things without ending up with who knows what animal parts for days. Some luck we have," Trick complained.

"Well we'll just have to do all our adventuring on the weekend then." Eddy suggested. Trick rolled her eyes.

"We better get to class," Dylan reminded, before poking Trick in the chest, "and you should think about just telling everyone about your Figment. It'll make your life easier."

"How?"

"You'll see after a while of trying to hide everything that it's just easier if everyone knows." Dylan said as he walked through the doors back into the school.

The rest of the day went by at a snail's pace. Both she and Eddy had nothing but boring classes on Thursday. Trick spent the entire day appearing as if she were daydreaming. Mrs. Ekard noticed during social studies and yelled at her. Trick apologized to Mrs. Ekard, making an excuse about not feeling well, and managed to avoid detention.

[*Should we be trying to figure this out?*] Trick thought to Anabelle.

[*People have been trying to figure out where Figments come from for a long time. Maybe if we find out, we can fix our magic so the side effects aren't so inconvenient,*] came the reply.

[*I just don't want to get into trouble.*]

Trick was worried that she might get involved in something that could get her hurt, or worse, get Eddy and Dylan hurt. She worried that the stories on the internet were true; that someone might come and take her away from her parents if they found out she had powers.

"Trick?" Eddy's voice finally broke into her thoughts. Trick looked around and realized their algebra class was mostly empty. Everyone but she, Eddy, and the Teacher had left.

"Yeah, Eddy. Sorry, I was just thinking unhappy thoughts." Trick shoved her books into her book bag, and then slung it over her shoulder. She left the room, and he jogged to catch up with her after picking up his own backpack.

"Are you alright, Trick?" Eddy asked, concern in his voice.

"No. I don't think it's a good idea to try to figure this out on our own, Eddy. It could be dangerous. We could get into big trouble." Trick fidgeted with the skirt of her blue dress.

"There's no one to teach you about how to use your powers Trick. Even Dylan has questions that no one will help him with. This might be the only chance that either of you have to learn. At least, we should go talk to the Cat. It might know something that will help?" Eddy suggested. Trick sighed. Eddy wasn't going to let this go.

"Alright, fine. We'll go talk to the stupid cat."

They stopped at their lockers and dropped off the books they didn't need for the long weekend. Luckily, they had an extra day off thanks to some roof repairs nobody had realized were needed until after school started. Trick took only her social studies book. She had done all the homework for her other classes during her two study halls and lunch. Eddy had helped her get through the math. She understood it, but without his help, it would have been much harder to get it all right.

"Hey, you guys ready? If this crazy thing attacks us, grab ahold of me and I'll get us away," Dylan advised. He didn't have a backpack, and was wearing a heavy leather jacket. He had come out of a side hallway, and there was someone trailing behind him.

"Who's this?" Trick asked suspiciously. Dylan turned around and frowned.

"That's my little sister, Tamara. Is everything alright, Mara?"

Tamara was around seven years old. She wore a pink dress with long sleeves and a Hello Kitty print on the front. She carried a matching pink backpack in her right hand. Her appearance was a surprise to Dylan as she was going to the elementary school up the street. Clearly it wasn't the first time she had found Dylan at the high school, though.

"Tracy said you would take me home," mumbled Mara shyly.

"Liar. You're just hoping to go home the fun way," Dylan smirked. Through his grin, Trick could see clearly how much he liked his little sister. Mara twisted the toe of her pink sneaker on the floor tiles by way of a reply. "I'll take you home, but you can't tell Mom or Dad. Deal?" Dylan said. Mara hooted in glee and ran across the hall. "I'll meet you guys at the park in a few minutes," Dylan said to the others.

"Alright," Trick said.

Dylan took Mara's hand and glanced around quickly to be sure that there was no one else in the hallway. Tigs waved to them from Dylan's shoulder, and then a flash of light consumed their view. Trick shielded her eyes, and when the light died down, Dylan and Mara were gone.

"That was the coolest thing I have ever seen." Eddy whispered. "Well except for you changing into a werewolf." Eddy finished.

"You really are such a nerd," Trick snarked as she slung her backpack over her shoulder.

Eddy just grinned at her, "Guilty as charged."

They left the school and headed down Main Street. All the houses here were old, and some of them showed the weight of their years. They cut between what used to be the old video store and a church, to a long-used short cut: a hole in the fence that had been there as long as they had been coming to the park. The basketball hoops there were missing their nets, and no one bothered to replace them. It was surprisingly empty. Usually, there were a few kids here after school, but it was getting colder.

The pair headed for the woods on the other side of the park. There, they found a steep hill, and just past the wood line was a trail that lead up the hill. It was all private property, but no one ever came around to kick them out, so all the kids used it. There were about a dozen small clearings in the woods where kids hung out in small groups. The pair checked them all, not wanting an audience for talking with the Cheshire Cat, but no one was there. They sat down on two logs across from each other. Sometimes, kids built fires here, in the largest of the clearings. Trick and Eddy didn't have to wait long. After a few minutes, they heard a pop, and Dylan and Tigs appeared behind Eddy. He looked around warily then came to sit on one of the empty logs.

"Is it here?" Dylan asked.

"I haven't called for it yet," Trick replied.

A moment later, Anabelle emerged from Trick's chest. She was transparent like a ghost for a few seconds as she floated to the log beside Trick. She alighted there, and then became completely solid.

"Hi Dylan, Hi Tigs, Hey Eddy. Sorry I was asleep all day. It took a lot of energy to fix our magic last night."

Anabelle rubbed her eyes with her forepaws and made a soft trilling noise. She yawned hugely, and then rolled over onto her back with her paws up in the air. She let her tongue loll out of her muzzle, and everyone laughed.

"How are we gonna to do this?" Dylan asked.

"Perhaps we can assist them with this conundrum."

Everyone jumped startled by the voice that came from what seemed like all around them. They all looked around, and when they looked back, the black and grey striped Cheshire Cat was in the circle between them. They all leaned back away from the creature, and Dylan jumped back, flipping backwards over the log he was sitting on. There was a flash of white light, and he appeared standing, about ten feet away. Tigs was sitting on his head, somehow looking dazed.

"Holy crap, you scared the hell out of me!" Dylan yelped. The cat grinned its Cheshire grin at him, full of sharp teeth.

"Manifestly true. We apologize. It is our nature. We cannot be anything but what we are," the Cat said. Dylan came back to sit down on his log.

"It wished to speak with us?" the Cat inquired.

"We have questions," Trick replied.

"We have answers, but we advise them to hurry. The pooka overheard our talk, and it has told others. They know that we have taken an interest in it," cautioned the cat. Everyone exchanged looks.

"What are you talking about?" Dylan asked.

"We are concerned that now that they know it could make the decision, they will come for it," the cat explained.

"Who?" Trick asked with a hint of a quiver in her voice.

"Figments. Many of them do not wish to return to the place between. Its fearful world has sent us back many times. They hope that if they get to one of the Spelled, they can force it to decide," the Cat explained.

"Decide what?" Eddy probed.

"It is not our place to tell it this thing. We cannot taint its decision. It must discover its own path to the White God."

"Well, what good are you?" Trick huffed. The cat's huge eyes narrowed.

"It is rude again. If it is to be so rude, we do not have to entertain its questions," the Cat hissed. It began to fade away. Dylan shot her an annoyed look.

"I was not rude to you. Please stay. I have questions too," Dylan implored. The cat's eyes turned to him.

"It is young as well, but we sense it would not be equal to the task of deciding. What is its question?" The Cat's grin spread ear to ear. It was creepy.

"What can you tell us?"

"It asks a very smart question. We can tell it that if it seeks answers to why it was Spelled, it can find them. It should seek them among the Diné. Their Figments are among the eldest. It can discover what it wishes to know among them."

"You don't actually know, do you?" Dylan challenged. The cat went completely transparent, leaving behind only its eyes and Cheshire grin.

"We are but guards. We cannot let it pass until it has walked the correct path. Only when it has solved the riddle of how it got its Figment will it find its way to the White God," the Cat's ambulatory mouth divulged, and then its eyes and mouth faded away.

"What's it talking about? The Diné?" Dylan asked. Eddy took out his phone and started tapping the screen.

"It's a Native American word," Eddy explained as he scrolled. "It's mostly used by the Navajo and the Apache. According to this, it means The People. Dylan, how long would it take you to get us to Arizona?"

"I've never gone to Arizona. Probably about twenty minutes, once I know how to get there. How far away is it?"

Eddy tapped away at his phone for a minute.

"About two thousand miles."

"Is it higher up or lower?"

Eddy gave him a quizzical look.

"One of the first things I learned when I ran away last year is that when you go a long way, how far up or down it is matters. If it's higher, I can't just go straight in a direction. If I did that, I might teleport inside of a rock. I almost teleported into a mountain the first time. Tigs saved us both," Dylan explained.

Eddy swiped through his phone.

"It's higher up than here," Eddy advised.

"Then we need to get higher up. What about your idea of turning into something big enough to carry us all?" Dylan asked, looking toward Trick.

"Lots of flying things aren't really made for people to ride on them," Anabelle spoke up. "A gryphon is big enough to carry both of you, but there's nothing for you to hold on to. And flying is a pretty bumpy ride. And we would have to practice, too. I can help Trick fly right, but it won't be very smooth until she does it for herself a little."

"How does teleporting that far work? I thought you have to be able to see where you're going," Eddy wondered. Dylan wiggled his hand in the air.

"It depends on how many times I've been to a place before. There are a few places I can teleport to from anywhere. Like my bedroom in my house. I can jump back there no matter where I am."

"How many places do you have like that?" Eddy asked. Dylan just shrugged.

"I haven't ever counted. Tigs says there are nine. They're mostly here in the States. If I don't go to them a lot, I lose them, so I tend to port to them once a week. But none of them are close to Arizona. Why Arizona?"

Eddy let his phone down so everyone could see the screen. There was a map that showed the Navajo Reservation.

"According to this, the Navajo used the word Diné the most, so it's probably a good idea to start with them."

"Well, if Trick isn't going to be able to fly us, we are going to have to practice a little. When I'm going a really long way, the best way to do it is for me to teleport up high, usually a few thousand feet into the sky, and then teleport in the direction I'm going. If I have to take people with me that way, you have to really hold onto me or Tigs, or else we'll lose you when we teleport. We'll fall a little, but we have to make each port so fast that if I lose one of you, I won't be able to find you again," Dylan explained. All of them suddenly looked uneasy.

"That sounds like it would not be fun," Eddy said after a moment.

"Falling a few thousand feet? Pretty sure it would be fun until the sudden stop," Dylan shot back a sardonically.

"Maybe we should get our parents to help," Trick suggested. Dylan shook his head.

"My parents wouldn't help us with this. They're too afraid of us," Dylan said dejectedly.

"My dad will help us. He thinks that magic and Figments are amazing," Trick said.

"I don't think it's a good idea. I don't even think we should take Eddy. He doesn't have any powers of his own. He can't protect himself. No offense, Eddy. You're smarter than both of us put together," Dylan said. Eddy shook his head.

"None taken. I'm coming anyway. There's no way I'm missing this. If anything tries to eat me, I'll duck behind you, Trick," Eddy smirked.

"It's not a joke, Eddy," Dylan rebuked.

"Who's joking?" Eddy pointed at Trick. "She can turn into a werewolf the size of a car."

"You were serious about that?" Dylan marveled.

Trick nodded. She looked around warily, then held her hand out to Anabelle. Anabelle put a paw on her fingertips, and the flash of light came. The transformation felt different this time. It didn't take any effort at all to get used to her tail, or to being on all fours. It just felt natural now.

"Holy crap!" Dylan yelped louder than when the Cheshire Cat had appeared, though he didn't disappear this time. "You're freaking huge!" Trick dropped her mouth open in a doggy grin. "Look at those freaking teeth!" Trick changed back, and Anabelle yawned on the log next to her.

"We gotta try new things soon. The Werewolf is getting boring," Anabelle said.

"Yeah, because I need a tail, or wings, or feathers left over," Trick shot back.

"We have to practice sometime," Anabelle replied. Trick sighed, and looked at Eddy.

"Will your parents keep it a secret if I look a little… odd this weekend?" Trick couldn't think of a better place than Eddy's cabin to spend a few days looking a little weird. There wouldn't be anyone around to see her except him and his parents. Eddy looked uncertain.

"I have no clue. They've never been upset about my "unhealthy fascination" with Figments." He made air quotes with his fingers around unhealthy fascination.

"Who told you that?" Dylan asked. Eddy just shrugged.

"It doesn't matter. I don't believe there's anything unhealthy about it. Maybe you're right, Dylan. Maybe people have good reasons to be scared of you guys, but who are they going to come to for help when people start doing bad things with their Auras?"

"Everyone's going to be sorry when they need your help." Dylan tilted his head, and then exchanged a look with Tigs.

"I never thought of it that way, but you're right," responded Trick. Trick took a deep breath and stood up.

"We should get going. I have some time, and I don't know about you, Dylan, but your mom is going to be wondering where you are, Eddy," Trick suggested. Eddy nodded, and stood up, dusting off the seat of his pants.

"My parents won't come looking for me, but they'll want to know what I'm up to. I'll see how hard it is to get to the Navajo Reservation this weekend while you guys are gone. I might be able to get to know the place well enough to teleport there in one jump if we're lucky."

"Good Luck," Eddy said. Dylan and Tigs vanished in a flash of white light.

"Eddy, before you head home, what do you think would be good things for us to try turning into? You know a ton about Figments. Which ones have the best magic powers?" Trick asked.

"I'll e-mail you a list of good ones. I'd start with a Cheshire Cat. No one can even touch them or hurt them. They can fly, and they can become invisible. A lot of people even think they can walk through walls." Eddy said. Trick narrowed her eyes.

"You're just hoping I end up looking like an anime cat girl!" Trick accused. Eddy spluttered, and Trick started to laugh. His face scrunched up, and he grinned.

"Nope, that was all your idea. You're the one that put on the frilly dress and cat ears for Halloween last year," he sassed. Trick blushed. The cat girl *had* been her idea.

"Jerk!" Trick shot back. Eddy began to laugh. He picked up his backpack and put it on.

"Oh, don't be so sore. It's not very often I get one over on you. Besides, you make a cute cat girl." Trick rolled her eyes then she sighed.

"Don't tell your parents yet. I'll ask my Dad what he thinks I should do."

"Sure." Eddy nodded and headed down the trail. Trick looked around again, and shrugged.

"Wanna try out a Cheshire Cat?" Trick asked Anabelle. Anabelle brightened immediately.

"Yes!" Anabelle effused.

"Can I pick what gets left over?" Trick wondered. Anabelle floated up from the log and flipped upside down.

"Maybe. I can try, but you have to tell me what you're hoping for."

"Something we can cover up? I can wear a hat to cover animal ears. A long dress to cover a tail." Trick slowed to a stop.

"What's the matter, Trick?"

"I'm thinking Dylan is right."

"About what?"

"That it's going to be extremely hard to keep our powers hidden from people."

"I don't mind trying."

"I know, BelleBelle. It would just be a lot easier if people knew." Trick sighed.

"In some ways, it would. In others, it wouldn't." Anabelle floated lazily around Trick's head.

"What do you mean by that?" Trick asked.

"Sure, we could change whenever we wanted, but it isn't going to feel good when people make fun of you because you have a tail, cat ears, or a lot more than that, if we do a lot of changes at once." Trick's expression changed as a worry crossed her mind.

"Anabelle, if we do too many new changes in a row, could we hurt ourselves?"

"No. What can happen is we won't be able to change back to your normal shape. We would still be able to switch between Figments we had already done." Trick's face fell, and she pulled her hand back from Anabelle. Anabelle went on quickly. "Not permanently, Trick, but for a few days, while the magic gets out of our body. And remember, it's only when our body hasn't experienced that particular magic yet. If we stick with things we have already been before, it won't happen." Trick reached out again, and Anabelle floated closer. Trick grinned.

"Come on, BelleBelle, this is going to be fun." Anabelle perked up and flashed Trick a feline grin. She flew into Trick's arms, and the flash of light came.

Chapter Eight
"On Our Own"

Dylan popped into existence in his bedroom. He sighed in regret. He had friends, and he was lying to them. It didn't feel good. He hadn't spoken to his parents in over a month. His mother and father had not been terribly interested in what he did. Having a boy had not fit into their plans. Once they had Tracy, and then Tamara, he didn't really matter to them anymore.

He had hated his younger sister Tracy at first. According to his parents, she could do no wrong. But eventually, he realized that Tracy liked him regardless of how his parents treated him. His parents were the ones who didn't care because he wasn't a girl. He wasn't sure why it mattered, but to them, it did. That was why he had played every sport he could.

Anything that kept him away from home was something that he pursued with vigor. Tigs had been a blessing to him, because she had made his parents even less likely to want to be around him. Tigs had also made it so that he could take care of himself, even at his age. He was the black sheep of the family, but it didn't really bother him anymore. His parents had gotten a real surprise with Tamara. They couldn't fit her into their tidy little box either.

Tamara loved him, and spent more time with him than she ever did with her older sister. Tamara loved his magic. She thought it was the coolest thing in the universe, and no matter what they did, they couldn't get Tamara interested in anything else more than her awesome big bro who could do real magic. But he didn't think he could explain to Trick or Eddy about what his life at home was like. They wouldn't understand why his parents acted like they did. He certainly didn't get it.

[Humans are weird.] Tigs said into his mind.

[Thanks *so* much.] Dylan replied with amusement.

[You're not human anymore, Dylan.]

[What?] Dylan's surprise filled his mental voice.

[You're not really human anymore. Magic changes you. Humans cannot use magic.]

[I don't feel any different. Are you ever going to stop keeping secrets from me?] Dylan asked as he started going through his closet.

[I'm not trying to,] Tigs replied dejectedly.

Dylan emptied his books onto his little desk, and packed some clothes. He had been taking some small jobs transporting things cross-country without telling his parents. When someone had approached his parents and offered a substantial amount of money for Dylan to teleport him cross-country, they had taken it. They had split it three ways, saying that it would be a college fund for him and his sisters. He doubted he would ever see any of it. He felt a little jealous of his new friends. Their parents actually cared about them, and Trick at least didn't seem to have any of the kinds of grown-up thoughts that Dylan was forced to have.

[Your new friends are real friends, Dylan,] Tigs encouraged.

Dylan continued to stuff clothes into his backpack. He went to his closet, and dug through it silently. He took down the small lock box that he had bought and hidden there, and opened it. Inside were bundles of cash. He peeled a few hundred dollar bills off of one of the bundles, and stuffed them into his backpack.

[How do you know?] asked Dylan. Tigs made a little shrugging motion he could see in the corner of his eye.

[I just do.]

Dylan closed the lock box and stowed it hidden in the back of his closet.

[You should tell them everything. They would help if they could,] Tigs added

[Ok.] Dylan sighed.

[They are already helping more than anyone else has.]

[I said ok. We'll talk to them soon.]

Tigs gave a little nod, *[Arizona?]*

[Yeah, we have to see how hard it is to get there. See how much stuff is in the way.]

Tigs nodded in agreement. Dylan picked up his backpack and looked at Tigs on the bed. She was getting up to a standing position.

[Must you strap me to that bag? This stupid body doesn't move very well as it is,] Tigs complained. Dylan shrugged.

[You could just stay inside the pack, but you end up all scrunched up and you complain about that just as much.] Tigs watched him for a minute then he heard her mental sigh. *[I'm sorry, Tigs. I'm going to look like I'm twelve for the rest of my life. It's odd enough without you riding on my shoulder in places where they don't know me.]*

[Yeah but you are twelve right now.]

Dylan shrugged. *[Not the point.]*

Tigs rolled her eyes, which was always interesting to watch as they were embroidered. Somehow, Tigs inhabiting the plush toy had animated parts of it with a semblance of life.

[I'll go inside the bag this time. I hate being buckled to the back of it like that. I can't get myself free with these paws.] Tigs held up her plush tiger paws. They were soft and rounded, with no digits beyond a sort of thumb, like a mitten.

[I'll see if I can find a new way to clip you in that you can get out of it on your own as soon as we get back.]

Dylan took his clothes back out of the bag and started folding them properly so they would take up less room in the pack. When he was done, he held the pack open, and Tigs climbed inside. He snagged his leather aviator jacket and slipped it on. The warm lining helped him get through the cold spots he had to teleport to. He slung the pack over his shoulder, and then put his arm through the other side.

[You ok in there?]

[Yeah, more room this time.]

[Good.]

Dylan turned around, and something moving in his back yard caught his eye through the bedroom window. He watched in growing horror as three black shapes slid over the fence. They were small, maybe four feet tall, and in the dying light of evening, he could see that they were definitely not human. They wore black form-fitting clothing, and their stocky, squarish bodies made their lack of humanity clear.

Dylan watched as they approached the back of the house. As they did, they started to fade away. His eyes widened as they reached out with their hands. They seemed to pick up the long shadows around the yard like swaths of fabric. They swathed themselves in the shadow and disappeared from view.

[*What are those things?*] Dylan asked.

[*No idea, but they're here for you. We should confront them, or they'll come in looking for you. They might hurt our sisters. If they know that we're gone, they'll follow.*]

"Tigs, that means we can never come home," said Dylan, completely forgetting to use their telepathic link.

[*I don't know what it means, Dylan. Maybe they'll give up if keep jumping around for a while? We should ask Trick. Maybe she can turn into something scary to get rid of them.*]

Dylan could just barely make out the group of Goblins prowling across his back yard. They were nearly invisible, but if he focused, he could see the movement. He called up his power, and appeared on his back porch. The flash of white light from his magic seemed to do something to whatever the goblins had done to hide themselves. Suddenly, he could see them easily, though their shapes looked muddled somehow.

"You're here for me, but I'm not staying, so leave my family out of whatever this is," Dylan challenged.

He didn't even know if they understood English, but they immediately drew out glittering daggers. Dylan yelped, and his power kicked in on reflex. He was standing at the summit of Mount Marcy in the Adirondacks.

[*Tigs, are they going to leave? Do we have to go back?*]

[*I don't know.*]

[*We have to go back. What's the closest direct jump to home without going home?*]

[*The Ghost Trail.*] It was the spot in the woods where they had met with the Cheshire Cat with Trick and Eddy earlier that day.

[*That's a lot closer to Trick's house than ours.*]

[*We should go for help. She can help Dylan,*] Tigs pleaded with him. Dylan shook his head.

[No, we can do this on our own. Let's go. We can teleport those little things far away. What's the farthest spot we can go to?]

Tigs thought for a long moment. It was odd, but Dylan could tell the difference between her thinking at him and her thinking to herself.

[That spot above the volcano,] Tigs advised. Dylan shook his head.

[We can't drop them from there. They will fall into the volcano from there.]

[The next place is that spot in Alaska where you like to watch the killer whales.]

[That works. Let's do it.]

[If we do that, and they get stuck there, we can't ever go back there. You'll have to find a new whale watching spot,] Tigs said with some amusement.

They appeared at the spot in the woods everyone called the Ghost Trail. From there, it took a few seconds to make the eight teleports to his back yard. The flash of white light faded, and Dylan looked around, but there were no fuzzy see through shapes like there had been before. He ported to his bedroom. He opened his bedroom door slowly, and crept into the hallway. He made it to the stairs, and looked through the gap. His sisters were sitting on the couch with their father watching TV. He slunk a little further down the stairs so he could see into the kitchen. His mother was in there, stacking dishes. He sighed in relief and crept back up the stairs. He closed the door to his room silently, and then ported back to the Ghost Trail.

[What are we doing back here?] Tigs asked.

[We have to warn Trick. I don't think they'll go after Eddy, he doesn't have a Figment. But they might go after Trick.]

He felt Tigs' mental assent. They made two jumps from the Ghost Trail, and ended up on Trick's front step. Dylan knocked on the door rapidly. He heard footsteps inside, and a woman opened the door.

"Hello. Wait, you're Dylan Marsh," Trick's mother gestured to Tigs. Dylan nodded.

"This is Tigs. I need to talk to Trick," Dylan blurted
frantically. Trick's mother seemed to pick up on his stress
right away.

"What's the matter?" she asked. Dylan hesitated. She
didn't have any powers.

"A lot," Dylan said. "Can I come in Mrs…" He trailed off.
He didn't know Trick's last name.

"Strand," Trick's Mother finished for him. "Trick is up in
her room, but what is the matter?"

"Just something that happened at school," Dylan replied.
Trick's mother looked at him suspiciously as if she knew that
he was lying, but she didn't want to say it for some reason.
Still, she stepped out of the way and gestured to the stairs.

"Second door on the right up the stairs is her room. Trick,
your friend is here!" Trick's mom shouted.

Dylan didn't wait. He teleported to the top of the stairs.
The door to Trick's room opened just as he teleported down
the hallway to the room. He felt the odd sensation of having
teleported into the same space where someone was already
standing. Trick let out a grunt, and tumbled back into her
room. Anabelle swooped out of the way and spun into the
corner of the room, floating in the air.

"Oh god I'm so sorry!" Dylan exclaimed.

"What happened?" Trick grumbled.

"I think it's a safety mechanism for my magic. If I try to
teleport into the same place where something already is,
things get displaced. If it's something that is lighter than me, it
gets moved out of the way. If it's heavier than me, I get
moved out of the way." Trick opened her mouth, but Dylan
spoke over her. "No time for that. Figments came to my
house looking for me. We have to go right now." Dylan came
into the room and stood, looking out the window.

"Go?"

"Trick, your parents don't have any powers, and you can't
use your powers right yet. We have to go someplace safe."

"For how long?"

"Until we can find out how to make them leave us alone."

"But that could take forever, and how are we going to find out without help from our parents?" Dylan just shook his head. He hadn't figured out anything. He just knew they had to run for now. "What are we going to tell everyone?" asked Trick. Dylan stood by her window, looking out into the back yard. Fuzzy shapes were coming over the fence.

"We don't have time for that. We don't have time for anything. They are here!" Trick got up from the floor where she had landed.

"Dylan, who is here?"

"I don't know what they are."

Anabelle moved next to him, peering out the window. Her huge, round eyes were luminous, like someone was shining headlights into a deer's eyes.

"Goblins. Those are goblins." Anabelle whispered.

"Augh! We could turn into one of those... things," Trick said, having received a mental picture from Anabelle. Anabelle nodded. "Let's not, ever," finished Trick.

Dylan looked over at her and noticed that she was wearing a purple boonie hat, with pigtails hanging down either side of her head.

"What is that hat?" Dylan asked.

Trick grabbed the brim and pulled it down. She groaned, and then pulled the hat off. When she did a large pair of mottled blue and grey cat ears popped up through her hair. Dylan's eyes went wide. Everyone recognized patterns like that. There were hundreds of pictures of Cheshire Cats on the internet. Surprisingly, none of them looked like quite like the one from the movie. They all had unique patterns in their fur, and so did Trick. She had looked over the neon blue looking whorls and spirals in her fur when she became the cat. She really liked her pattern, but she sort of wished the rest of her fur was some other color than the ugly dark grey that backed her neon blue patterns.

"You turned into a Cheshire Cat?" blurted Dylan. Trick nodded, twisting the hat in her hands. "You look so cool!" He reached up towards her ears, but then he pulled his hand back when she glared at him. "Sorry!" Dylan said hurriedly, and then looked back out the window.

The fuzzy shapes had dropped whatever camouflage they had been using. Black, squarish shapes sat balanced on the edge of the fence. Why would they stop like that? Tigs popped her head out of the backpack next to Dylan's.

[Why aren't they trying to get in?] she asked inside of his head.

[I don't know. Maybe they don't want to try and fight Trick and us at the same time?] Tigs swiveled her head around to look at Trick and Anabelle.

[They're tons more powerful than we are. All that Aura.] The thought was not really meant for Dylan to hear. Sometimes, though, she caught him off-guard by not breaking their telepathic link while she was thinking private thoughts.

[You think so?]

[Yes. Can't you see the Aura around her? It's a little scary.]

[I don't see anything.]

[Well those things can probably feel it. What if she turned into something really big and powerful? There are lots of Figments that can't be killed, ones strong enough to twist those things like a pretzel.]

"You really like the ears?" Trick asked nervously. Dylan rolled his eyes.

"Trick, there are things outside that want to kidnap us," Dylan chided, trying to get her to focus. "We have to go. Can you pack a bag?"

"I have to ask my parents," Trick replied. Dylan wiped his hand over his face.

"Trick, pack your things. Our parents don't have Auras. They'll just get hurt. We are on our own," Dylan said with finality.

Trick frantically wracked her brain for ways to solve this problem as she stuffed clothes into her backpack. Anabelle hovered nearby, concern on her tiny feline face. If she just left, her parents would be looking for her. She put her cell phone into her backpack.

"I'll be right back," Dylan said. He had been thinking that if they were going to be gone for a long time, it might be better to bring all of his savings with him. Before Trick could say anything, he disappeared in a flash of white light.

"Trick, we can't leave without telling Mom and Dad." Anabelle reminded.

"I know, BelleBelle, but what if Dylan is right?" Trick felt tears well in her eyes as she thought of Figments attacking her parents.

"We could kill them," Anabelle half-suggested grimly. Trick gulped noisily and shook her head.

"Can't we just scare them away?"

"I think more of them will just come back."

"Are there any Figments you know of that could make them go away?"

Anabelle looked at her dubiously for a long moment, and then a villainous grin spread around her muzzle.

"I know what we can do!" Anabelle trilled gleefully. "We can be one of Coyote." Trick stared at her blankly. Anabelle sighed. "Just do what I say, and prepare to have cat ears and a coyote's tail when we're done."

Trick made a dissatisfied groan, and then held out her arms. Anabelle flew into her arms, and the blue flash of light surrounded them. When Trick blinked away the spots floating in her vision from the flash, she realized she was standing on all fours. It wasn't like being a werewolf, though. She was smaller, probably about the same size as the Cheshire Cat body she had been in earlier.

[*What are we?*] Trick thought to Anabelle.

[*An avatar of Coyote. He is a Native American god with lots of neat powers. One of them is that he can make little parts of himself go off on their own. There are hundreds of the Figment versions of him running around. We have lots of new powers, and while we are in this form, we can't die.*]

[*How does this help?*]

[*Well, Coyote can walk through shadows, has the luck of the draw, can look like anyone or anything he wants, and is probably the best trickster in the history of the world.*]

[*I don't know what that all means.*]

[*It means that we are going to make this a lot harder than it is worth to those Goblins until they go away.*]

Then, Trick felt an odd sensation. It was like she had spun herself wildly in a circle and was uncontrollably dizzy. She couldn't focus for a second, then all of the sudden, everything snapped into focus.

[*What was…*] Trick trailed off as she realized that she knew a number of new things.

She knew that in this form, she could step into a shadow and step out of any other shadow within her line of sight. She knew that she could not die, but that wasn't the same as being invincible. As an Avatar of Coyote, she could be harmed, she could even be killed, but if she died in this form, she would come back to life within a few days. Coyote could never actually die, and neither could any of his manifestations. She could look like anyone or anything that she could imagine. Though unlike her power, she would not actually become the creatures, only make illusions of them. She could sense that she was part of something much, much larger. Part of the god Coyote. Suddenly, she could feel his eyes on her.

[*What is this, what is this?*] a new voice came into her head. [*To take on even a small bit of my magic, and become me. To steal my very self from me the thief of thieves.*] A cackling laugh filled with genuine mirth filled her head. [*A trickster to boot, how appropriate you are, little thing. I like you already. Be clever with my powers, child.*] Then the feeling of eyes on her fled.

[*That was terrifying,*] Anabelle's quavering voice came back into Trick's mind.

[*At least he liked us?*] replied Trick in a similarly quaking mental voice.

[*I didn't think he was actually real. I thought his avatars were just normal Figments.*]

[*What did you do just before he started talking?*]

[*Something I should have been able to do the whole time. I can give you my instincts about the powers of Figments we become. It doesn't teach you everything I know about a particular Figment. It just lets you use their power right away without having to learn absolutely everything.*]

[*When we are safe again, we really need to talk about everything we can do with our Aura.*]

Trick looked outside, and saw the goblins were moving down into her yard. The sun was going down, and there were plenty of shadows now. Trick looked at them eyes narrowed with mischief. She stepped through a shadow in the corner of her room like it was a doorway. She came out through the shadow cast by the fence over the shrubs in her back yard. She dropped her jaw open in a doggy grin as she watched goblins creep forward.

[*Be careful, Trick. Coyote has no fear, but if you get hurt, it will really hurt.*] Anabelle warned, but it seemed like Trick could barely hear her. She received a distracted affirmative from Trick's mind.

Trick slipped out from between the bushes in perfect silence. Only with Coyote's luck was it possible that not even a scrape of sound was heard. As soon as Trick was clear of the bushes, she imagined herself in the shape of one of the goblins. The illusion came together perfectly. She padded across the ground, and as she went past the goblins, Trick rammed her shoulder into the one on the right. It made the goblin stumble into the one to the right of it. She kept right on walking, giving the goblins just enough time to see her. Then, she walked into the shadow of the picnic table nearby.

The goblin she had shoved had stumbled into the one to the right of it. Trick walked out of the shadow beneath the bushes again. She watched as the goblin she had bumped turned and shoved the one to its left. It pointed at its companion, and shouted in a language that Trick didn't

understand. Its companion looked confused, and said
something back in a tone of annoyance that Trick understood
perfectly.

[*We should try to lead them away.*] Anabelle suggested. Trick
eyed the goblins.

[*I want to rile them up so that when they chase us, they don't
stop.*]

Laughter accompanied Trick's thoughts. It was a bit
infectious, and Anabelle laughed a little, too, as the goblins
fought. They were winding down when inspiration struck
Trick. She understood that Coyote's power of having the luck
of the draw on his side meant that if things were going to go
wrong, they wouldn't go wrong for her. It wasn't foolproof,
and other Avatars of Coyote understood that you had to
already be working a situation to your advantage, or it would
fail at the worst possible moment. Trick gained the same
understanding through Anabelle's knowledge.

Trick darted out of the shrubs. She shot across the back
yard at a speed that easily matched the top speed of her
werewolf shape. She leapt and crashed paws-first into the
back of one of the goblins. She rode the creature to the
ground, and stood there on his back. She let her jaw fall open
into a doggy grin, and the other goblins stared at her,
incredulity on their mottled green and black faces. She
lowered her front half into a playful posture and let out a little
yip.

The goblin she had bumped earlier yelled something in
that foreign tongue, and snatched at the long dagger on his
belt. Just at that moment, the dagger inexplicably stuck in its
sheath. The goblin yanked himself off balance, trying to free
his dagger. Trick yipped again, and then darted off towards
the fence. She couldn't see the shadows on the other side of
the fence, but the ones in her bedroom were within her line of
sight. She jumped through the shadow of the fence and
landed in her bedroom. Then, she jumped onto her bed so she
could see out of the window, instinctively knowing that if she
could see the shadow in the forest outside, she could get to it.

Standing on her bed gave her a good view of the forest, and
she jumped across the room, going through the shadow her

dresser was casting. She landed outside of the fence in the woods. She let out a taunting series of yips, and Anabelle laughed gleefully inside of her head. She saw the fence shaking as the goblins threw themselves onto it from the other side.

[They know that you're the one they are after, Trick.] Anabelle said.

[How do you know?]

[I can understand them. They think that if they catch you, they can use you to catch Dylan.]

[We'll see how they feel about that after we have a little more fun with them.]

Trick waited until they clambered over the fence, and then dropped to the ground. They looked around, and Trick let out a mocking yip to draw their attention. The one struggling goblin finally yanked his long dagger free. He pointed it at Trick, and yelled something in his native language. Trick bolted into the trees with the mocking laughter of Coyote trailing behind her.

The woods behind her house were not enormous, but she ran to the little clearing in the middle of it. There were tree stumps everywhere in the little clearing, a familiar place where she and Eddy had camped several times. She stopped in the middle of the clearing and jumped up on top of one of the stumps. This would be perfect. There were shadows everywhere that would let her scramble through them without any danger of being hurt. She didn't think she could hurt them herself, but if they managed to hurt each other, she couldn't do anything about that.

The goblins ran into the clearing a minute later and slowed to a stop, looking for her. They spread out in a loose line, making their way to the middle of the clearing. There was a small, loose group of trees in the middle of the clearing, and they assumed that Trick was hiding there. She ran out of the shadow of a stump behind them. She shouldered her way through the middle of the small figures, and then jumped into the trees. She caught a tree branch in her teeth and spun in the air, yanking it back. The first goblin who ran in after her took the branch in the face when she let it go. It smashed him back out of the little group of trees, and he tumbled into his friends, who had gathered behind him.

Trick ran into a shadow of a tree, and out of another behind the goblins. They were arguing angrily with the one who had tumbled into them. They all had their daggers out, and Trick noticed the way one of them was holding his dagger. She ran up behind them and bumped her head into the hand holding the dagger. It shot forward, jabbing into the buttocks of the one in front of him. Trick darted away before they could see her, disappearing into the shadows, chased by the shout of the goblin that had been prodded. When she came out of the shadows, the goblins were squabbling loudly, waving their daggers at each other. Trick had to squash the urge to let out yips of laughter.

She could feel the luck with her, and ran between the legs of all of the goblins, making certain they saw her. She darted into the large copse, and they chased her inside. They stumbled through the low pine limbs, pausing to look around as they got inside. Trick could see them moving through the trees as the pine boughs moved before them.

The collection of trees was odd. It was a ring of pine trees, with a larger collection of trees inside that weren't like any of the other ones in the woods near Trick's house. They were an explosion of limbs right from the ground up. With so many of the trees around, the limbs were like a maze of living wood. Trick and Eddy had spent endless hours climbing through the trees. It was their favorite place to be. Trick scrambled through the limbs more quickly on four paws than she had ever been able to before. The goblins came after her, and once they were well into the morass of limbs, Trick climbed into the limbs above them.

She watched them from above. A plan began to form, and then she jumped through a shadow from the treetops. She stepped out onto a branch that was at head height for one of the goblins. It immediately saw her, and drew back its dagger. It swung in a blur, but Trick was already moving. She stepped through the shadows, and out at ground level. She heard the sound of metal on wood. It was followed by a sharp snapping sound, and she turned just in time to see the limb she had been standing on spinning away from the tree. It smashed into the face of one of the other goblins.

Trick couldn't help herself. She let out a cackling yip. The goblins all looked up into the trees, but they couldn't catch sight of her tan pelt against the bark of the trees. They started yelling at each other in earnest now. Clearly, only the one who had swung at her had seen her, and the others thought he had done something stupid.

[Oh, My. Those are not nice words,] Anabelle giggled.

Trick waited for the one that was clearly in charge to shout the others down. Then, she walked through the shadow of the tree trunk, emerging between the one in charge and one coming around the tree trunk to see what all the commotion was about. The goblin let out a high-pitched shriek of anger and lunged at her. She kept walking right through the shadow of the goblin in front of her. She appeared back in the trees just in time for the attacking goblin to smash into the legs of the leader.

She realized that as it got darker, it was going to get harder and harder to walk through the shadows. Something about the difference between light and shadow made Coyote's magic work. If it was dark, there would be much less shadow to walk through. Luckily for her, the errant attack caused a brawl to break out between all four goblins.

She couldn't help but let out a noise that she didn't think any normal coyote would ever be capable of. It was an eerie, cackling laughter that unlike her earlier yips, echoed off the trees. It brought the brawling goblins up short. They froze mid-punch, and their heads whipped about, searching for the source of the laughter. Her sensitive coyote ears picked up whispers between the goblins.

[They are afraid. They are whispering about curses,] Anabelle said with a little bit of laughter in her voice. *[Can you do that again?]*

[I don't know what I did that time.]

Trick walked through the shrinking shadows, and appeared just on the edge of the copse of trees. She turned back, and tried to remember how she had gotten the laugh out of her throat. She realized suddenly that she didn't need to frighten the goblins any further. They had run from the copse and were sprinting across the clearing, away from her house. It didn't take them long to disappear into the woods without a trace.

Trick trotted back to the fence and realized that she had no way to get back over it. She couldn't see the shadows on the other side. She had climbed over her fence dozens of times. She looked around, but nobody could possibly see her from where she was. She and Anabelle split apart in a flash of blue light. She made a face, feeling the tingling sensation of what she now knew was magic leaking out of her body in two places instead of just one. She didn't need to look to know that the tail was there.

Instead, she ran to the big rock at the corner of the fence. She clambered up onto the large boulder. From there, she could jump just high enough to catch the top of the fence. Her feet scrabbled against the wood of the fence, but she finally pulled herself over the top. She rolled off the top of the fence as she had done hundreds of times, landing softly in the big round shrub at its base. Anabelle floated beside her.

"I um, I made your tail match your ears at least?" Anabelle said tentatively.

Trick rolled out of the bushes, and then turned her whole body to look behind her. A long tail, half as long as she was tall, covered in mottled blue and grey fur, floated sedately behind her. It came out through a hole in her dress.

"You fixed my dress?"

"Yeah," came Anabelle's soft reply. Trick began to laugh.

"BelleBelle, it's fine! It's actually kinda cool, like Dylan said. Come on, we have to get back inside. He'll be back soon," Trick said.

Anabelle floated closer, and they changed. Emerging from the flash of light, they had become a large mottled blue and grey Cheshire Cat. The stripes that made up the whorls in her fur got wider in some places, making her pattern look not only swirled but mottled. It turned out that lots of people were right. Cheshire Cats could indeed walk through walls.

She used that power now, and squeezed through *someplace else* that let her go through the walls of her house. She didn't become visible again until she was back in her room. Dylan still wasn't there. She floated just above the bed, spinning lazily so that her paws were up in the air.

Being in the form of the Cheshire Cat gave her an odd way of looking at things. Nothing looked quite right unless she was upside-down. Their thoughts were nothing like a human's thoughts. She wasn't sure how she'd describe the thoughts running through her head. It was like a jumble of disordered ideas was tumbling around the inside of her head. Every one of the ideas made her grin manically, as if every thought a Cheshire Cat ever had was wildly amusing to the cat. There was a flash of white light in her room, and Dylan appeared next to the window again. She floated closer to Dylan while he looked out of the window searching for the goblins.

"The goblins are gone," Trick said in a slow, melodious version of her voice from behind him. When he turned around, Trick was floating less than a foot away from him. The huge, pointed teeth of her Cheshire grin were at eye-level with him.

"What the crap?" Dylan squeaked.

He jumped back away from her. He tripped over her laundry basket and flipped backwards. He ended up slumped against the back wall of her closet. Tigs had fallen from his shoulder and was pushing herself up to her plush feet from beneath the mound of dirty clothes that had flown out of Trick's laundry basket.

"It's just me," Trick continued, but she couldn't stop grinning even as Dylan shivered. "You really are pretty jumpy."

"That is outrageously creepy." Trick flipped herself over right side up again.

"They have a lot of neat powers, but they can't actually hurt anyone."

"Unless you count scaring someone to death," Dylan observed. Trick continued to roll, hovering in midair until she was upside-down again.

"Do you still think we have to leave?" Trick wondered in the odd, slow, melodic tone of her Cheshire Cat voice.

"Why wouldn't we?"

"Because I scared the goblins almost to death. Maybe they'll tell everyone else to leave us alone."

"I don't know, Trick."

"Are you two alright up there?" Trick's mother shouted up the stairs.

"We're fine, Mrs. Strand!" Dylan shouted in reply.

"Teresa?" her mother shouted. Trick rolled her enormous eyes. A quick blue flash of light later, Trick was sitting on the bed with Anabelle in her lap.

"We're fine, Mom!" She lowered her voice back to normal levels. "I can't go, Dylan. I have to talk to my parents. They'll know what to do." Dylan looked uncertain. He noticed the long, mottled blue and grey tail swishing behind Trick on the bed.

"Whoa. You're getting more Cheshire Cat parts. Are you all right?" Trick nodded.

"Yeah. They'll go away after a couple of days. Well, unless we want to keep them." Trick paused for a moment, and then looked towards Anabelle.

"Yes, we can do partial transformations, but they don't give us any of the magic powers," Anabelle confirmed. Trick got up and went out into the hallway, leaving Dylan and Tigs standing in her room.

[Told you she would help,] Tigs said into his head.

[I still think we should get away from here.]

[Away isn't going to help us, Dylan. We don't know what we are doing,] Tigs said, and then pointed out the door. *[Maybe they can help.]*

Chapter Ten
"Help"

Trick descended the stairs. Her mother and father were watching something on television when she came around the couch.

"Hey, sweetie. What did your friend need?" her mother asked. Trick sat down on the hassock between the couch and the television.

"He came to tell me that Figments were trying to come and get me," Trick replied. Dylan had come down the stairs, and she saw him now standing in the hallway.

"What?" her father interjected. He looked around warily.

"I chased them away, Daddy, but Dylan thinks they'll be back. We saw the Cheshire Cat again," Trick informed. She recounted their talk with the Cheshire Cat to her parents. When she was done, her parents just stared at her.

"That's a lot of thinking," Dylan added. Her father recovered first.

"You can't just run off to the other side of the country," he said. Dylan just rolled his eyes as if to say I told you so.

"But if we don't get help, there'll be more Figments. Trick scared away these ones. What if something too big to scare away comes?" Dylan urged. Trick's parents exchanged a look.

"You're just kids, Dylan. We can't let you go off on your own. What do your parents have to say about this?" Trick's mother said.

"My parents don't care about what I do," Dylan divulged. He entered the room and stood next to Trick. Trick's Father just stared at him.

"What do you mean?"

Dylan just shrugged, "They won't even notice I'm not around for days."

Trick's Father rubbed his temples. "We can deal with that later. Trick can't go. We'll call the police. They can protect us."

"You know that won't help," Dylan sighed, "but I can't make anyone do anything. Trick, I'll tell you what I find out in

Arizona." He vanished in a flash of white light. Trick glared at her parents.

"He's my friend, and those things would have hurt us if he didn't come to tell us," Trick admonished.

"Teresa, we can't let you go someplace you might get hurt," her mother rejoined.

"I could have gotten hurt right here tonight! You could have gotten hurt!" Trick shouted.

"Trick, we're your parents. It's our job to protect you," her father added.

"You can't. Those goblins tonight had swords and magic. They could've killed you." Tears rolled down her cheeks. "Because of us."

"This is exactly what I was afraid of," Trick's mother said. "People get Figments, and terrible things happen to them."

Anabelle's ears folded back. Trick felt her face twist up in anger. She stood up, and her hands balled into tiny fists.

"Anabelle saved you both tonight." Trick sniffled back her tears. "You don't get to blame her for this!" She stormed out of the living room. Her mother stood up.

"Don't, Hannah. She is right," her father added. She turned on him.

"Robert, she is a child!" She didn't quite shout, but she wasn't far from it.

"She is a child that now has amazing magical powers. I know this is not what we were prepared for, but we can't exactly keep her here anymore if she doesn't want to stay."

"So what are you suggesting?"

"I'm suggesting that if we want to have any sort of relationship with our daughter, we are going to have to be a little more flexible about how much we try to restrict her from doing things she feels are right. I don't want to just let her run off either, but can you think of some way to stop her now? You haven't seen her yet, Hannah. She can become a werewolf too big to fit in the living room. And those ears and that tail sure look like they belong to a Cheshire Cat. If I understand her Aura right, she can turn into any Figment she wants." He could tell that his wife didn't understand what he was saying. "Hannah, it means she can have literally any magic powers she wants."

"But she's just a kid. She doesn't know anything about being out in the world, Robert."

"That's what I'm trying to say. Either we can try to teach her as much as we can and give her a safe place to come home to, or she isn't going to come home at all. With her powers, we would never find her." Hannah ground her teeth.

"We can't, Robert. She could get hurt. She could die. How would we even know?" She left the room and went up the stairs. She peeked around the edge of Trick's door. The room was completely empty.

"Teresa?" She checked the closet, but Trick was gone. "Robert!" A moment later, Trick's father came through the door. "She's gone!" She clutched at this neck and sobbed.

Trick stood outside, having taken Coyote's shape again. She had no idea how to catch up with Dylan, but she had some clothes in a backpack along with a cell phone. It was just small enough for her to carry in her mouth. She couldn't stay at home. They knew where she lived. She couldn't keep her parents safe. She had to get help, and the only help was two thousand miles away in Arizona.

She ran through the woods, and headed for the Ghost Trail. It was near dark, but her coyote eyes made it almost as bright as daylight. She ran along trails that she had followed a hundred times to get to the Ghost Trail. She stopped when she got to the place where they had met with the Cat. She dropped her backpack, and changed back to her human shape. Anabelle floated nearby, and Trick noticed that her fur was giving off a soft glow like a black light. She floated closer to Trick as she rummaged through her backpack and pulled out her cell phone.

"Who are you going to call?" Anabelle asked.

"I'm going to try Dylan first."

She scrolled through her contact list and found Dylan, making the call and putting him on speaker. She sat down on one of the logs and Anabelle floated down to alight on Trick's lap. Trick ran her fingers through Anabelle's fur, and instantly felt better. The phone rang for almost a minute. Finally, the line picked up.

"Hey there, this is Dylan. You know what to do."

"Dylan, this is Trick. Please call me back the second you get this. You're going to need my help. I'm at the Ghost Trail."

She thumbed the end call button, then noticed Eddy's name on her contact list. She wanted to call him badly, but if she got him involved, he could get hurt just as easily as her parents could. She was about to put her phone back when it rang. Dad was calling. She dragged her finger across the screen, sending the call to voicemail. She slid the phone into her backpack, and looked down at Anabelle. Her fur was still giving off a soft purple glow.

"Do you always glow like that? I haven't noticed you glowing like this in our bedroom."

"I don't know. I'm a little scared. I know you're right. If we stayed, Mom and Dad would get hurt trying to protect us, but what are we going to do, Trick?" Anabelle's eyes swirled and changed color to a pale yellow, glowing dimly in the light.

"I don't know either, BelleBelle."

"You'll get help," sounded a voice from the ring of trees. Trick spun around, but already knew who was standing there.

"Hey, Eddy," Trick grumbled.

"Hey, Trick. Your Dad called me. He said your phone was off, and asked if I knew where you were. I told him I might. Why didn't you call me, Trick?"

"You didn't see the goblins, Eddy. They had swords, and they could be almost invisible with their magic. I have magic. I can be Figments that can't get hurt."

"But you can't run away, Trick."

"I'm not running away, Eddy. I don't wanna be all alone. I wanna go home. But those things would kill Mom and Dad. They want me for something, and if I don't find out what, I can't stay home without people getting hurt."

"But we're just kids, Trick. You tell me all the time that I'm the smartest person you know. Still, I'm just a kid, and I know there are a lot of things that are easy for them that I can't do."

"It doesn't matter, Eddy. I have to try."

Eddy sighed, "It's like talking to a wall. Alright, Trick, but there's no way you are going without me." He reached behind a tree and pulled out two backpacks much larger than Trick's. They had sleeping bags rolled up on top of them.

"No, Eddy. You can't come with me."

"If you don't take me with you, I'll tell your parents everything you're going to do. You're not going without me. My parents are going to ground me for life so this better be worth it."

Trick burst out into a little sobbing laugh.

"You know we can make Eddy into a Figment?" Anabelle suggested. Trick's laughing cut off, and she and Eddy both stared at Anabelle, speechless.

"What?" Eddy said after a moment.

"How?" Trick asked at the same time.

Anabelle looked back and forth between them. After a moment, she settled on Trick's question.

"We can gift our power to someone for the span of a single transformation. It's dangerous because Eddy wouldn't be able to change back on his own. If something happens to us, he'll be stuck that way," explained Anabelle.

"Can we do it for anyone?" Trick asked. Anabelle shook her head.

"Nun uh. Only people like Eddy."

"What do you mean?" Eddy asked. He brought the backpacks closer to the logs, and rummaged through his. He took out a small, battery-powered lantern. He opened it and light filled the little clearing.

"You're compatible with our magic. I can't explain how it works, but it would only work for you."

"But I could get stuck that way? Forever?"

Anabelle nodded.

"If something happened to us, you wouldn't be able to change back, but if you want to come, we can make you into a

Cheshire Cat. That way, you can go incorporeal, and you can fly, and…" Eddy cut Anabelle off.

"Ok, I get it. I don't have magic powers. If things get dangerous, feel free to zap me."

As much as Eddy had wanted magic powers since he could remember, he didn't want to be fuzzy and cat-shaped for the rest of his life. Especially since as far as anyone knew, Cheshire Cats lived forever. He could deal with being grounded for the rest of his natural life, but he thought that if he went home floating and furry, his parents would probably die of shock.

"Why didn't you tell us before?" Trick asked Anabelle. Anabelle made an exasperated noise.

"I didn't know before. Trick, I promise I'm not keeping anything from you." Anabelle whined pitifully. "I don't know why I don't know one moment, and then I do the next moment!" Her high-pitched trill was miserable.

"Okay! It's okay, Anabelle," replied Trick soothingly, "I believe you."

"So what are we doing next?" Eddy said.

"Well, I'm waiting for Dylan to call me back. I don't want to leave my phone on for too long."

"Probably a good idea." Eddy took his phone out of his pocket and turned it off as well.

"If Dylan doesn't come back, I guess we'll have to fly to Arizona."

"Fly? How?"

"As a gryphon like you suggested." Eddy's surprise was clear on his face.

"Don't you have enough… extra parts?" Eddy gestured to her ears and tail. Trick shrugged. She put her purple boonie hat on, covering her ears.

"They'll go away in a couple of days." Trick said tiredly. She fussed with the skirt of her blue dress. "How long should we wait?" Trick dug through her bag and took out her phone. She turned it back on. As soon as her background image appeared on the screen, the phone started to ring. Dylan's number appeared shortly after, and she answered the call.

"Trick, what happened?" Dylan asked before she could even say hello.

"I left home, and so did Eddy. We need to help each other. If everyone is chasing us all over the place, our parents will be safe."

"Are you still at the Ghost Trail?"

"Yeah, we were just getting ready to leave."

There was a flash of white light that made the forest as bright as the middle of the day for a long moment. When it faded, Dylan was tucking his phone back into the pocket of his leather jacket. Trick put her phone back into her little purple backpack.

"I was halfway to Arizona," Dylan said.

"Sorry, Dylan. My parents didn't want to let me go, but you're right. More Figments are gonna to come lookin' for us."

"Alright, but we have to go."

Tigs poked her head out of Dylan's backpack. He reached up and helped her out. Trick noticed that Dylan was carrying a backpack like the ones that Eddy brought now. She was no stranger to camping gear. Her parents used to take her camping a lot. She picked up the pack that Eddy had brought for her. She opened it, and stuffed her smaller one inside. She shrugged herself into the backpack.

"Both of you have to hold onto Tigs. No matter what happens, do not let go of her. Please don't throw up on her. She absolutely hates going through the laundry."

Trick burst out into giggles, "Sorry. I won't." Eddy took a grip around one of Tigs' tiny plush paws, and Trick took the other one.

"This is going to take a whole bunch of jumps. We'll get there in about three minutes. Just hold on," Dylan cautioned. Then, the wind was rushing by.

They were somewhere in the sky, thousands of feet above the ground. Trick looked down, and saw the lights of their home town twinkling below. Then, they started to fall. She clutched to Tigs' tiny plush paw for dear life. Then, they were floating through the air somewhere else. It was impossible to tell where. Just as they started to fall, there was another jarring movement, and she was looking down to see an enormous city below. Then more dark land below. It went on like that for a full minute before she noticed that it was starting to get lighter out.

She could see flat, beautiful grasslands below, dotted with tiny houses spaced enormous distances from one another. Then, it was suddenly much brighter, and the air was a lot warmer. She felt Anabelle clinging to her shirt, and she looked down to see a huge river far below. She tried to ask Anabelle what was the matter, but her words vanished into the void between teleports. It all went by so fast that it was impossible for any of them to keep track of where they were. Trick's fingers started to hurt from her white knuckled grip on Tigs' plush paw. She felt Anabelle slip inside of her head.

[That's better. Tigs says we are almost there. She says when we get there, if you want to turn into something that can fly to get down to the ground, it'll probably be easier than landing with Dylan,] Anabelle relayed.

[Will Eddy be alright?]

[Yeah. Tigs just says it is a little bumpy when they go such a long way. Nothing life-threatening.]

They appeared over a huge stretch of desert. The air was baking hot, and Trick could tell that they were much lower than they had been before.

"Where are we?" Trick yelled.

"Over the Navajo Reservation. A place called Red Valley for now," Dylan yelled back, "If you want to let go and fly down on your own, it'll be a smoother ride."

"OK!"

Trick noticed that the whole time they had been talking, they really hadn't fallen very much further down. Trick let go of Tigs and thought about the Cheshire Cat form. The transformation was instantaneous, and she began to float in midair without really trying to. Then, she rolled over upside-down for a moment to make everything look normal. She tilted her body so she was facing the ground, and started to pick up speed. She realized that floating in space like that was the natural state. To actually go up or down, she had to exert mental effort to make her body heavier. Otherwise, she would just float wherever she stopped concentrating.

She saw Dylan, Tigs, and Eddy appear just a little ways further down. Then they vanished, and appeared a lot further down. When she finally caught up with them, they were laying on the ground. Eddy was clutching Tigs for dear life, and she was wiggling her arms and legs trying to get away from him.

"Eddy, you can open your eyes," Trick said as she floated above him. Eddy's eyes popped open. Then, he groaned.

"It's not that bad. We weren't going that fast when we landed," Dylan grumbled.

"Hey-ya that was *some* landing, youngins!" called a man's voice with a deep, mellifluous accent. Dylan whipped around, and Trick floated past him. For some reason, she felt like she knew this man.

"You're him," Trick said. The young man had a sheet of black hair that fell nearly to his waist, and she had no idea what he was wearing. It was light tan fabric, covered in tiny colored beads in various places. He grinned manically at her.

"Nah. I'm just a little piece of him. Like what you did, little sister. A Figment, as you call us. But our mutual friend warned me that you might be comin', and you might even need to be pointed in the right direction?"

Trick changed back to her human form, and Anabelle floated down to rest on her shoulder.

"We are trying to find out more about how we got our Figments, Mister," Trick said.

"Shoot, little sister, don't call me Mister. Just looking at you reminds me how old I am." His grin was infectious, and it made Trick smile too. "Now, that's a big question you got there, little sister, and Old Coyote hisself can get you all pointed in the right direction." He turned on his heel, and started to walk away. "But you're goin'ta have to do something for me if you all want me to take ya to him."

"Wait a second!" Dylan said. The man's form melted away, and in his place stood a coyote about twice the size of any coyote that ever lived. It winked at him, and turned to walk away down the path.

"What the heck is going on?!" Dylan yelled at the canine.

"I think he wants us to follow him." Trick picked up her pack and put it on. She ran off down the path after the coyote. Dylan and Eddy exchanged a look.

"I should have just let her turn me into a frog or whatever," Eddy grumbled.

He put his backpack on, and headed down the trail. Dylan looked at Tigs. She just held up her plush paws in a gesture that Dylan recognized as her form of a shrug. He took off his bomber jacket and tied the sleeves around his waist. It was a lot hotter on the ground here than it was in the sky. He shouldered his pack and picked up Tigs. He situated her on his shoulder, and took off to catch up with the others.

The coyote lead them into the desert for almost an hour before they came to a large cave. The canine disappeared into the cave, and they all hesitated at the mouth. It was almost pitch black within.

"How do we know this guy is trying to help us?" Eddy asked suspiciously.

"When I scared off the goblins, I was a Figment like him. I can feel him somehow. He won't lie to us," replied Trick.

"Okay, but if anything bad starts to happen, I want you to grab onto Tigs or me, and I'll take us someplace far away," Dylan said.

Trick and Eddy nodded. They all went into the cave. A moment later, Eddy took out the battery-powered lantern. He opened it and light filled the sandstone cave. It was beautiful, if a bit scary. Orange and white striated stalactites hung down from the ceiling, and matching stalagmites grew up from the floor. Matching each other, they could have been the teeth of some giant monster. Trick liked them, though. The orange and white made her think of the trees in Dr. Seuss books. The cave roof got a little lower as the path took a sharp bend. From around the corner, they could see the flickering light of a fire. It made shadows dance through the rock formations, hinting at creatures that were not really there.

Trick lead the way through the romping shadows, and turned the corner to find the coyote sitting next to a small fire inside of a circle of stones. There were a number of lawn chairs and large rocks pulled up around the fire. The coyote was sitting atop one of the rocks, and it waited patiently for them to find seats around the fire. It was slowly starting to get dark again, and despite how hot it had been outside, Trick could feel a chill coming on. She scooted her lawn chair closer to the fire and pulled her backpack closer. Anabelle alighted in her lap and seemed to fall asleep immediately.

Once they were all situated, the coyote became a man again. Trick couldn't tell how old he was. He seemed young.

He didn't have gray hair, and he didn't move like an old man, but his face was lined,   and when he grinned, lines crinkled at the corners of his eyes.

"What's your name?" Trick asked.

"They call me Shadow Runner this time around. Just Runner to my friends," the man said.

"Are we your friends?" Eddy asked skeptically.

"Well, that depends on how you define friends, little brother. I would say I like you youngins enough to have you call me Runner. Now hush. I have a story to tell you, and when I'm done, I'll send you off to take care of what you're here to do."

The man raised his hands, and the shadows around the cave ceased to move. Trick gasped in amazement as the shadows gathered on the smooth cave ceiling. They appeared to be a circle of people looking down at all of them.

"Long ago, in the time before this time, The People were plentiful in this land. It was a time of bounty, and the wisest of The People wielded the power of great magic through their totem spirits."

The shadows swirled. They reformed to show silhouettes of full corn fields, with shadows of people walking between the rows. The shadow of a dog trotted across the cave roof to meet up with a man at the edge of the fields.

"Then, a great medicine man of The People saw a vision which warned him that a time was coming when the magic of The People would flee this world, and not return for long ages of men. A time when men from across the world would come, and if all of those among The People did not use the time they had to cast a great magic to protect The People from these men, their way of life would be destroyed."

The shadows changed to show the silhouette of a massive bonfire. Around the fire danced hundreds of silhouettes of men. A breeze blew through the cave, and on the wind the faint sounds of chanting filled the cave.

"But men's hearts can be dark places, and some of those old medicine men did not wish to give up their powers. Not even to protect their own people."

The shadows above swirled again, and a circle floated across the ceiling of the cave that Trick somehow knew represented the moon. Below it, silhouettes of men beckoned to animals. A wolf, a bear, a big cat of some kind, and many others that Trick did not immediately recognize. As soon as the animals drew close enough, spears of darkness leapt from the men and stabbed into the animals.

"In their fear and greed, they consumed their totem spirits, and took on their shapes." The men transformed into the animals that they had stabbed their spears into. "So through their evil, they took on the lives of their totems. They gained endless life and great magic power, but to keep this power, they must kill and kill, taking the skins of their victims to sustain their power." The shadows burst apart, and returned to just flickering shapes on the walls of the cave.

"Though some have been slain in the ages since their betrayal caused the near extermination of The People. Not all could be found. Without their aid, the protections faded before the white men came, and they still roam the land to this day." Shadow Runner finished the story, and the affable expression returned to his face.

"What does this have to do with us?" Eddy asked.

"If you all wish for the help of Old Coyote hisself, you're gonna to need to do a service for The People, little brother. Not far from here, there is a village of The People, and there abouts, some mighty strange things been happenin'. Follow the road to the village and find out what is hiding in that place. Put a stop to it if you can," Shadow Runner explained.

"But why us? We're just kids," Dylan said.

"Just kids can't sling magic about like y'all can. Trust in your powers, little brother. Besides, y'all have your Figments to back you up. They won't let y'all get hurt. Go on now, youngins." Shadow Runner's shape then melted away into the huge coyote. He walked into one of the flickering shadows, and vanished completely.

"This sounds like a bad idea," Eddy said after a long minute.

"But what else can we do?" Trick asked.

"Nothing if we want to find out where our Figments came from," said Dylan, "and he's right. We have lots of our own magic."

"Maybe there are other places we could go to get help? There are more Native American reservations we could try," Eddy suggested.

[We're meant to be here. I can feel it,] Tigs said into Dylan's head. *[Anabelle and I will keep you safe.]* Dylan shook his head at Eddy.

"Tigs thinks we are supposed to do this."

"I think so too. We have to help if we can," agreed Anabelle.

"But what if it is one of these things? It kills people to take their skins!" Eddy's voice crept into mild hysteria.

"Eddy! We'll be alright. If anything happens, Dylan can get us out of there in a second," Trick reassured.

She was very nervous herself, but she didn't want Eddy to get freaked out. If they ever wanted to go home, they had to do this. They decided it would be best to leave their things in the cave. They all brought their cell phones just in case they got split up.

"Somehow, I feel like we aren't going to fit in around here," Dylan said, remembering the bronze skin and odd clothing Shadow Runner had been wearing.

"I can go have a look around without anyone seeing me," Trick offered. She handed her phone to Eddy, and then took on the coyote shape.

"Man, I cannot get over how cool that is!" Dylan said. Tigs gave him a look, and Dylan grinned back. "No, I wouldn't trade you for that power. Teleporting is pretty amazing too."

Trick trotted off towards a cactus, and disappeared into its shadow. She came out of the shadow of a building in the town. Trick trotted toward the back of the building on Anabelle's advice, and quickly saw that their clothing wouldn't be terribly out of place after all. The girls had dresses a lot like hers, though they were made of a lighter fabric. Some wore blue jeans and t-shirts. Except for the fact that everyone was bronze-skinned, they would just be another three kids. Trick could just stay in the form of the coyote, and people would likely just mistake her for a dog.

[*Do you see anything odd, BelleBelle?*] Trick asked.

[*You can't see it yet, but there's something wrong with everyone. There's something wrong with their Auras.*]

[*I didn't think that regular people had Auras?*]

Anabelle made an exasperated sound inside of her head. [*Of course they do. Normal people can't make magic with their Auras. Their Auras are trapped inside of their bodies. Ours can go outside. But with a little practice, you can see normal people's auras. These people don't have much Aura left. I can barely see them.*]

[*Is it hurting them?*]

[*Yes, badly. There are some that are going to die soon.*] Anabelle's voice was concerned.

[*Can we help them?*]

[*Not without changing to a new Figment.*]

[*We can be something that can help them?*] Trick asked in wonder.

[*There are more Native American Figments like Coyote, though there aren't as many of those as Coyote has, we can take the shape of a manifestation of the Great Bear. The Avatars of Bear are magical healers. We can make them better that way.*] Trick sat and watched from the shadows for a long while. The people moved slowly, and seemed aimless.

[*How many Figments do you know about?*] Trick asked.

[*A few hundred that I actually know about. I also know exactly how many types of Figments there are in the world, but I don't know about all of them until I hear their names.*]

[*That makes no sense,*] Trick grumbled.

[*How do you think I feel with all these gaps inside of my head?*] whimpered Anabelle.

[*Oh it's alright, BelleBelle. I just wish I could help.*]

[*You can. Get Eddy to talk about more Figments.*]

[*Alright, we can do that. Eddy loves talking about Figments.*]

Trick turned around and trotted back to the spot where she could see the cactus. She walked into the shadow of the building and emerged from the cactus' shadow. She then trotted back to where the boys were waiting for her and changed back to her human form, Anabelle floating along beside her.

"They don't dress a lot different than us. I think Runner was just showing off for us," Trick advised.

"Did you see anything else?" Eddy asked.

Trick shook her head.

"Anabelle did, though. She thinks there is something wrong with the people here."

"Is it a good idea for us to go down there then?" Dylan worried. They had walked a little further forward so that they could see the town from the top of the hill. It was not a big place. It was a group of maybe ten or fifteen buildings surrounded by fifty or sixty houses and trailers. The buildings all had a faded look, like they had been painted with washed-out water colors.

"I don't know. I could make Eddy into another coyote, and we could look around better without anyone really knowing," Trick suggested. Eddy looked a little taken aback. Dylan looked shocked.

"How the heck can you do that?" Dylan asked.

"Eddy has been Trick's best friend since they were really little. His Aura is aligned with Trick's. She can give her magic to him. But Trick, if you do that, we won't be able to change into anything new for a little while," Anabelle reminded.

"I'm gonna look a little more weird after this," Trick said.

Eddy just shrugged. Dylan pointed at Tigs and rolled his eyes. Trick had hidden her tail by keeping it wrapped around her hips beneath her dress, and her ears had been hidden beneath the purple boonie hat she was wearing.

"I don't think I'm gonna be able to hide whatever happens next. This will be our third new change."

"Into what?" Dylan asked.

Anabelle landed on Trick's shoulder, and the now-familiar flash of blue light surrounded her. When it faded away, a huge Kodiak bear was standing where Trick had been. Unlike the coyote that was indistinguishable from the real animal, the bear had odd white markings, like a stripe painted across its eyes. Three bands of color circled its right forefoot, purple, blue, and green. Tied into the fur behind one ear were two large feathers, one black, one white. Trick shifted from one set of feet to the other, trying to get used to the huge body. It was even bigger than her werewolf form. She understood the most basic parts of the magic of the bear.

"That's the coolest thing I've ever seen," Eddy said. He came tentatively closer, and reached up to touch the feathers in Trick's fur. He did so gently.

"I wonder what all the colors are for," Eddy wondered aloud. Trick couldn't answer him, but she knew. It was part of the little bit of knowledge that she had gotten from Anabelle in the change.

[What can we change this time? Is there anything we can hide?] Trick asked, preparing to change back so she could change Eddy and herself.

[Not really. If we send it to your hands or feet you'll end up with paws, and you can't wear your boots with paws.]

[Alright, fine, just do whatever is easiest.]

[Your nose and a little of your face is probably easiest.]

Trick took a few trundling steps back from Eddy, and then made the transformation back to her human form. Her magic came a little easier each time. Now, she barely had to think about changing and it happened.

"Uh, Trick, there's something on your face," Eddy said. Trick lashed her tail once, and then rolled her eyes.

"It'll all go away in a couple of days. I told you I would look a little weirder." She could feel how different her nose was. She could twitch it back and forth. "What does it look like?"

"Cute, like your mom painted a really good cat nose on you for Halloween," Eddy said. "Uh, that's not going to happen to me, is it?" he asked with some concern.

"Nope. When we gift you our magic, it will all come back when we take it away," Anabelle reassured.

"So what am I supposed to do?" Dylan asked. Trick just shrugged.

"You can wait here if you want, or you can go into town, and see what you can find out. We won't be far away."

"Alright. I can at least go to the little store there and get us some drinks and stuff."

"Ready, Eddy?" Trick asked.

"Not even close," he said.

Trick laughed, and then put her hand on his shoulder. Eddy stood stock still as the flash of blue light faded. He looked at Trick, and tilted his head. His vision was all weird. It was like he was watching an old black and white movie, but there were subtle hints of blue and yellow laced throughout the picture. He stumbled to one side, but then suddenly felt like he had been living in this body for a long time. He steadied himself on his four paws.

Shadows now had odd, dimly-glowing outlines around them, as if they were objectives in a video game. He tried to look back at his own body, but he could only see his rear end and a waving tail. He noticed he was not the same color as Trick. His body was darker colored, but his vision didn't allow him to distinguish the different colors. He could only tell that his tail looked almost black, while Trick's tail and fur looked closer to grey.

[Are you alright, Eddy?] Anabelle's voice sounded in his head.

[This is so weird.]

[Just give yourself a minute to get used to it. I've put what you need to use that body in your head. Your brain will pick it all up in a minute.]

[How come I can hear you?]

[As long as you're part of our magic, I can talk to you mind to mind. When you feel okay, follow us into town. Trick and I are just going to walk around and listen at houses to see what we can hear. You can hear a lot better now, so if you get close enough to a house, you can hear what's going on inside.]

Eddy saw Trick turn and trot off toward the cactus she had gone to earlier. This time, he saw what happened. She used the shadow there like it was a doorway. She walked right through it, and came out of the shadow at the house down in town. Eddy took one step, and then another. Within a few steps, he had the hang of it. It was odd how bright everything looked. It had been edging slowly closer to full dark for about a half an hour, but now it looked like daylight again, even if everything was in black and white.

"Good Luck," Dylan said, and Eddy nodded to him.

He opened his mouth to try to say something on instinct, but only a yip of sound came out. Eddy paused for a second, and then realized what had happened. He shook his head before turning to the shadow of the cactus. He noticed that the outline of the shadow was dimmer now. He somehow understood that it meant the shadow was fading. With everything becoming darker and no sources of light, the cactus' shadow was growing indistinguishable from the darkness around it. Once that happened, it would no longer function as a doorway for him.

Once he got closer to it, he looked down at the town, wondering if that would happen with the shadows of the buildings. The town had street lights, and front porch lights, however. Plenty of sharply defined shadows down there. He looked at the one Trick had used. He stopped on the edge of the cactus shadow. He decided to pick a different shadow, one from a trailer on the opposite side of the street. When he looked at it, the outline brightened from a dim white to a bright blue. He walked through the shadow of the cactus.

The sensation of passing through it was odd, like he was going into a tunnel beneath a mountain. He got the feeling that the whole mountain was pressing down on him and that if anything went wrong, it would fall down and crush him. He shivered when he came out of the shadow of the trailer. He felt his ears flatten in reaction to the sensation.

[This is so weird.]

[What?] Anabelle asked.

[The way my face reacts to the way I feel. Why do I know that I should flatten my ears when I feel something unsettling?]

[Oh, it's part of what I put in your head. Animals have a lot more ways of communicating than just verbal. You humans talk too much. Animals don't need to talk to tell each other how they are feeling.]

Eddy's ears perked up when he heard someone talking in the trailer. Surprisingly, he could hear them almost as well as if he had been inside, but they weren't talking about anything

of interest. Eddy moved on to the next house. He had
wended his way between several trailers and houses by the
time he heard something that drew his attention. The voice
was male, and had the same accent as Shadow Runner had.

"… since she came to town, everyone has been stumbling
about in a daze. I don't care if I have to drive to a hospital in
Albuquerque, I'm not taking Aiya to her." He continued in a
language that Eddy didn't understand.

[Anabelle?] Eddy asked.

*[Hold on, Eddy. We are watching over Dylan. He's in the little
grocery store, and it wasn't going well at first. They wanted to know
what he was doing on the reservation. But he showed them his Aura,
and said he was just visiting for the night. He said he didn't know he
was on the reservation.]*

Eddy left the shadow of the house he had been listening at.
He saw the little grocery store at the end of the lane. Eddy
looked around and saw the fuzzy shadow cast from a
telephone pole. It was just wide enough for him to squeeze his
coyote body through. He went through the shadow and came
out beside of the store. He instinctively lifted his nose and
sniffed around. He paused as he heard words inside of his
head that he realized a moment later were his brain translating
smells. It said **this is Trick**. The smell lead around the corner
to the back of the store.

He found Trick with her ear pressed against the wall of the
store. He joined her, lifting one of his ears and letting the
other one fall. He discovered that folding one of his ears down
blocked sound almost as well as sticking a finger into it.
Convenient when you didn't have fingers.

"… have you seen any other kids like me?" Dylan asked.

"Not around these parts. Though there is a girl we have
heard about on the other side of the Res that has her own
magic powers," a deep male voice replied. It had a slight
Native American accent.

"I heard on the internet that some Native American
shamans have gotten Figments. I've just been traveling
around trying to see if anyone knows more about them."

"Not anyone that I've heard of, kid, but you're welcome to
go ask old Doc Whitefeather. She's a real doctor, and may be

able to tell you more. Shaman is not our word, young man, so I wouldn't use it around her, were I you. Her house is a couple miles out to the west of town. I wouldn't go tonight, though, if you don't know your way around. Even a couple miles out of town you can get lost in the desert pretty easily, and there are rattlers out there as well."

"Rattlers?"

"Rattlesnakes. Very poisonous."

"Maybe I'll come back tomorrow then. Thanks, mister."

"Hey kid, don't let the police catch you sleeping in that cave. You'll be in big trouble."

"Thanks again."

When Dylan exited the store, he exchanged a glance with Tigs. Trick moved closer to the street, and let out a little yip at him. When he saw her, he hurried into the alleyway between the tiny grocery store and the building next to it. He followed her behind the building. She changed back to her human form, and Anabelle floated just above her left shoulder.

"I'm not going to change you back just yet, Eddy, just in case."

Eddy bobbed his head, and moved a little closer to them. He looked back at his body for a moment, and then carefully lifted his tail out of the way. He sat down as slowly as he possibly could, like he wasn't quite sure how his body worked.

"You'll be fine. We will change you back as soon as we are all safe."

"The guy in the store said that it might be dangerous to try and walk around out here at night," Dylan related.

"We heard everything through the wall," Trick advised.

Eddy let out a little yip, and they both looked down at him. Anabelle floated down closer to Eddy.

"What's he saying, BelleBelle?" Trick asked.

Anabelle flicked one of her tails at Trick in a little shooing motion to quiet her. A few tense seconds passed before Anabelle started to speak.

"He says he heard two people arguing about taking someone to a hospital. He didn't hear the whole conversation but he says that someone didn't want to take someone to her. He thinks it might be the doctor that the person in the store was talking about."

"Wouldn't they want to take someone to the closest doctor?" Dylan asked.

"Maybe there is something wrong with the doctor here?" Trick asked. Dylan just shrugged.

"Eddy says that the person said they would drive to Albuquerque instead. How far away is that?" Anabelle asked.

Dylan took out his phone, but there wasn't very good cell reception where they were. He put his phone away, and then looked at Tigs.

"She says it is a long way."

Trick understood then that Dylan and Tigs had the same problem that she and Anabelle did. She understood that somehow Tigs and Anabelle were learning new things they could do all the time. It was just like going to school for Trick. She learned new things in class, and they learned new things by using their powers, but there were no teachers. Somehow, just their magic was just teaching them things.

"So where are we going to stay tonight?" Trick asked worriedly. She had never been away from home without adults around.

"I've got a good place. I don't think we want to come back here until the sun is going down," said Dylan. "I'll meet you back at the cave."

"Alright."

Trick held out her hand to Anabelle, and after a quick flash of light, she became the coyote again. She led Eddy around to the other side of the store. She pointed with her nose to one of the telephone poles at the far end of the street. The light on it was casting a shadow. Eddy bobbed his head once, and Trick walked into the shadow of the building. She waited at the edge of town for Eddy to come through the shadow. Finally, after a long moment, his nose poked out of the shadow, and then the rest of him followed.

[Is there any way I can talk to him?] Trick asked. She got a mental negative from Anabelle.

[I don't know how I would do that.]

[Well, just tell him I'm gonna run as fast as I can, and he should follow me.]

Trick took off running down the road. It was so much fun to run on four paws. She couldn't believe how slow she was in her human form. The walk that had taken them so long zipped past on coyote paws. It was only a few minutes before they were trotting into the mouth of the cave, tongues lolling out of their mouths. They came around the bend in the cave, and found Dylan had laid out the things he had bought at the small grocery store.

"I hope you guys are ok with turkey sandwiches and water," Dylan said as they padded fully into the circle of light provided by his lantern. Trick split from Anabelle and changed back to her human shape.

"How do we change him back?" Trick gestured towards Eddy.

"We need a few minutes to change him back," Anabelle said. Eddy whimpered a little. "Don't worry. We won't leave you stuck that way, Eddy. We just have to wait for our magic to build back up from our change. Trick, eat something. It'll make things go faster," Anabelle advised.

Dylan held out half a turkey sub wrapped in wax paper and a small bag of sour cream and onion potato chips. Trick's favorite kind. She unwrapped the sandwich and started to eat it. It was real turkey, not the deli stuff, and it was really good. It didn't take her long to go through the sandwich. She was about to tear into the bag of chips, when Anabelle floated down from where she had been circling above them.

"That's good enough. We can change him back now."

Trick reached down to where Eddy had laid down at her side. She put her hand on his head, and the usual flash of blue filled the cave. The light subsided, and for a moment, Trick thought that Eddy was going to be naked like she had been the first time. However, as his body faded back into view, his clothing snapped into reality with a small, audible pop of sound. Dylan gave Eddy a sandwich and a bag of chips too. He tried to talk between bites, but was only partially successful.

"I can't believe," he paused for a bite, "how cool that was. I can," Another bite. "Run so fast," then a drink of water, "like that."

"Eddy. Eat first, talk later," Trick chided with a little laugh. Dylan took out another half of turkey sub from the plastic grocery bag, and held it out for Trick.

"Thanks, Dylan."

"It was weird, the two people talking sounded really scared. They weren't yelling, they were almost whispering like they didn't want anyone to hear it." Eddy popped the last of his sandwich into his mouth.

"You think that is what he wanted us to find?"

"Probably, but what can we do about it?" Trick asked.

"We'll have to figure that out tomorrow. I've been here long enough to be able to teleport directly back to this cave," Dylan said.

"Can you take us someplace where we can use our cell phones? I want to text my parents so they at least know we are alright," Trick asked. Dylan thought for a minute.

"Yeah. One of the permanent teleports is just above San Francisco. Good cell reception there."

Everyone picked up their backpacks. Dylan took Tigs down off his shoulder, and then held her out to Trick with both hands. Trick took her carefully.

"How do you stay put on his shoulder like that?" Trick asked the stuffed tiger.

"She says their magic does it," Anabelle imparted.

Eddy took one of Tigs' paws.

"This isn't going involve us falling until we are dead from it, right?" Eddy grinned. Dylan rolled his eyes.

"No, chicken. We are going the easy way this time. San Francisco first. I'm taking us to a place overlooking the Golden Gate Bridge called Vista Point. I like to go there at night," Dylan said.

Then they were standing in a small area with an old looking park bench. There was red clay covering the ground, and to the right were a long line of empty parking spaces. Trick looked up, and then clutched Tigs to her chest. The

Golden Gate Bridge stretched out across the bay, lit by hundreds of street lights. The glow reflected off of the water of the bay, and the view was breathtaking.

"Is this why you come here?" Trick asked in wonder.

"Nah, I just like the bench." Dylan sat down on the park bench. Eddy, and Trick both laughed .

"Hurry up so we can get some sleep. I want to sleep in my own bed sometime this century without Figments trying to crawl through the walls of my house," Dylan grumbled. Trick and Eddy both took out their cell phones and turned them on.

Chapter Twelve
"Hidden"

Trick rolled over and yawned far wider than any human being ever could. The place Dylan had taken them to set up their little campout was a nice flat area, high on the side of a mountain on the Hawaiian Island of Oahu. Trick had quickly discovered that even with a comfortable sleeping bag, sleeping on the ground stinks. It was weird to her because she had slept on the ground plenty of times with her parents. She didn't remember it being as uncomfortable as it was when she had tried to sleep last night.

Anabelle had suggested she try getting some sleep as one of their other shapes – the Cheshire Cat. Trick wasn't sure if she would ever sleep in a bed again. She had floated bonelessly, with her paws stretched over her head all night, a few inches off the ground. It was the most comfortable sleep she'd ever had in her entire life.

"Okay, that tongue curl with all those teeth is really creepy looking." Dylan's voice was sleepy.

"If you slept as good as I did last night, you'd never sleep anywhere but floating off the ground again. I certainly don't think I will."

"Still creepy."

Trick's Cheshire grin spread from ear to ear, provoking a shiver from Dylan. She rolled over in the air.

"Admit it. I'm adorable," Trick smirked, wiggling her ears at him.

"If by adorable you mean-high octane nightmare fuel."

"I think she's cute," Eddy mumbled, half-asleep, before pulling the turned-down front of his sleeping bag over his head, "but a lot more adorable when sleeping." He rolled over onto his side with his back to them.

Dylan waved Trick away from their little camp. She floated along behind him, and they walked a few dozen yards away from where Eddy was sleeping .

"We can let him sleep. It's not going to get dark in Arizona for a few hours," Dylan suggested.

"How do you know?"

Dylan held up his cell phone.

"I didn't know anything about time zones until a few months ago when Tigs and I started jumping all over the place. I teleported back to San Francisco earlier while you guys were still asleep to look some stuff up on my phone. You drool when you sleep upside-down, by the way."

Dylan laughed at Trick's enormous frown.

"I wanted to ask you. People usually react pretty badly to kids with Figments. How do you get around all that?" Trick asked.

"I don't, not all the time. Before you started listening in at the store, the guy behind the counter said the Navajo have a lot different view of kids with Figments. Usually, I have to do a lot of fast talking to get people to trust me at all, or keep Tigs hidden." Tigs nodded her head in agreement. Dylan held up his phone, which showed a screen full of text.

"So what did you find out?" Trick asked with a very feline purr.

"The story that Shadow Runner told us yesterday? If what he told us about is what is hiding in that village, there is no way we can stop it."

"Why would you say that?"

"Because that story he told us is about something they call a Skinwalker."

Trick felt a mental shiver from Anabelle.

[Trick, can we please change back so I can talk?]

[Sure.] The flash of light came and went. Trick took a seat on a log, and Dylan sat down on the stump of a tree.

"Skinwalkers are from the last era. They were like you, but when the decision happened, they didn't want to lose their magic, so they killed their Figments to keep their power. They," she paused, "devoured their Figments." Anabelle sounded like she was going to be sick.

"I have so many questions I don't know which one to ask first." Dylan said. "I'll start with how do you know that?"

"Because they're learning through their magic somehow. Anabelle learns things about Figments, and I'm willing to bet that Tigs learns things about teleporting. The more you do it the more they learn," Trick said.

"Really?" Dylan's voice was skeptical.

"I honestly don't know. I'm just guessing."

"Considering that Tigs just told me yesterday that she can now tell how far away we are from a place just by hearing the name of the place I think it's a pretty good guess. She hasn't been able to do that ever before."

"So why can't we stop it?"

"Because they can't die. They are like the combination of a human and their Figment. They get all the powers of both," Anabelle explained.

"I don't get it. I don't have any powers without you."

Anabelle took a deep breath and let out a long sigh.

"Yet. You don't have any powers without me *yet*. We'll always be much better when we're together, but eventually, you'll be able to do a lot of things on your own."

"BelleBelle, I'm never ever sending you away again. Not ever."

"What do you mean yet?" Dylan asked.

"Tigs and I work with the magic you already have. It's like if you shout as loud as you can, but then both Trick and you shout at the same time, the sound is louder because there are two of you. That's what having a Figment does, only better. We make your magic a lot, lot stronger, but the more you use magic, the easier it gets. So eventually, after using your magic for a long time, your body gets used to it you'll be able to use your magic without our help."

Dylan nodded, and then scratched Tigs on the head.

"Don't worry. I'm yours forever, Tigs."

"What does that do to us?" Trick asked.

"Over time, most of the people who have Figments will cease to age because of the magic energy that you work with regularly. Sometimes there are other side effects," Anabelle explained.

"Other side effects?" Trick asked.

Anabelle sighed, "I can't predict it for everyone, but eventually you in particular would have likely resembled the

Figment of your choosing a little bit. Pointy ears, different nose, maybe a tail but I don't think so."

[*The reason you stopped aging right away is because Teleporting gives off a lot of energy, and so much energy going through your body all at once stopped you from getting any older. Sorry,*] Tigs apologized inside of Dylan's head.

"Oh, Tigs, don't apologize. Eventually I'll get a driver's license to make people believe how old I am." Dylan chuckled.

"So I'm gonna look like this permanently some day?" Trick asked, alarmed.

"No, no, silly. I told you before this will fade away. We can decide, as your body takes on more magic and we get older, how you want to look. It will be little things. You'll see," Anabelle assured her.

"What about the other things you said? What is the last era, and the decision?" Dylan had been listening carefully. Anabelle thought about it.

"I don't know," Anabelle said. "That's everything I got when you started talking about the Skinwalkers."

Dylan groaned in frustration.

"So what are we going to do?" Trick asked.

"We can beat the Skinwalker," Anabelle said, her voice not nearly as confident as her words.

"What? If they can't die, how can we beat them?" Trick asked.

"The Great Bear's healing magic can separate the Figment from the human if we can get close enough to touch them."

"How many Figments come from there?" Dylan asked. He had seen Trick become a magical coyote and a magical bear. "Do all animals have magical powers?"

"I don't think so, but I don't know. All I know about is the Figments that come from Coyote, Bear, and Owl. They all have different powers. But I know there are lots more that come from the last era," Anabelle explained. Dylan frowned.

"The last era again," Dylan grumbled.

Anabelle made an odd motion with her shoulders that took a moment to recognize as shrug. "I'm sorry."

Dylan sighed, "It's not your fault. Are you two hungry? Do you eat, Anabelle?"

She bobbed her head. "I can, but as long as Trick eats, I don't get hungry. But I like bacon."

"That's odd. Tigs said the same thing when she first came," Dylan observed.

"Food?" Trick asked.

"Oh yeah, there is a diner nearby to one of my permanent teleports that's open all the time. We can order food, and I can go there to pick it up."

They headed back to their little camp. Eddy had been sleeping the entire time. Trick shook him awake.

"Hey Eddy, we are getting breakfast. You hungry?"

He stretched his arms out of his sleeping bag. "Mmm, food sounds good. But where are we going to get it?"

"I'll go for it. It's from a diner. I like the food there. It's still breakfast time there, but if I don't go soon, it'll be lunch time," Dylan explained.

"How are we going to pay for it? I don't have a lot of money." Eddy reached for his backpack. Dylan shook his head.

"Don't worry about it. I've got plenty of money. What do you want?"

Eddy retrieved a notebook from his bag and wrote down his order. He handed it to Trick, who added her own, including an extra order of bacon for Anabelle.

"Back soon," Dylan said as he picked up Tigs where she had been sitting by the remains of last night's fire. They vanished in the usual flash of white light.

"Um, if he doesn't come back, how are we going to get down from here?" Eddy asked.

"As Cheshire Cats." Trick held out her hand for Anabelle, and she came closer. The transformation back to the Cheshire Cat took less than a second. Trick rolled over onto her back, floating a couple of feet off the ground.

"Did I miss anything? I was tired," Eddy asked.

"Dylan thinks he knows what we are supposed to stop back in Arizona. He thinks it's a Skinwalker." Trick's blue and grey-striped ears twitched as they caught a noise off in the trees down the hill – footsteps. "Eddy, someone is coming up the mountain."

"I don't think anyone can get to us here without some mountain climbing gear."

The area was only about fifty feet square, jutting out from the mountain. No trees grew on the flat patch, which was surrounded by trees growing from the mountainside, the tops of which were over twenty feet above the edge of the outcrop. They were definitely shielded from view. Trick hoped that would be enough, but she could hear someone milling around at the bottom of the outcrop over a hundred feet below. She floated towards the edge of the outcropping.

"Trick!" Eddy hissed.

"I can go see who it is, Eddy. They won't ever see me."

Cheshire Cats couldn't teleport like Dylan, but they could move over short distances instantly. She peaked over the edge, but couldn't actually see anyone through the canopy of the trees. Still, her ears told her where the person was. She slid out of reality, and appeared at the bottom of the outcropping. Trick concentrated on the idea that her body wasn't really there, letting it fade away until only her eyes were visible. The magic responded to her thought immediately.

[This is what you meant about me getting better with magic huh?] Trick asked.

[Magic is basically about learning how to concentrate in such a way that it knows you are thinking at it. That is a huge oversimplification, but it is the basic idea.]

They floated towards the sound of footsteps. Trick peaked through the undergrowth, and saw a figure clad in green slacks and a grey shirt peering up the escarpment, looking toward the camp. Trick thought it was a woman, because a long black braid hung down from beneath their tan hat, almost to her waist.

"Hello!" The person's voice was not outrageously high, but it was definitely that of a woman. Trick floated away, concentrating on her body becoming solid again. She slipped out of reality, reappearing back at the top of the escarpment.

She floated to the camp where Eddy was shoveling dirt over the fire. He had heard the woman shouting.

"I think it's a park ranger. They probably saw the smoke from our fire."

Trick didn't know a lot about being out in the forest, but Eddy did. He was a Boy Scout, and his family loved to camp. His face fell.

"They won't go away until they can get up here and check on it. They'll be worried about it getting bigger."

"Maybe I can scare her away?" Trick hissed to Eddy

"We could get in big trouble," came Eddy's whispered reply.

A flash of light signaled Dylan's return. He was about to say something when he noticed the look on Eddy's face and Trick's flattened ears.

"What is it?"

"There is a park ranger down at the bottom of the outcropping." Trick's melodious voice made the sentence feel longer than it was.

"Oh is that all? It's probably Lani. It's fine she knows me. Be right back."

Dylan vanished, and about thirty seconds later, he returned with the park ranger. She was not as tall as she had looked on the slope, though she was taller than everyone else there, and Trick thought she was quite pretty. Her face was a little different than the people she was used to seeing. She had a wide nose, tilted almond-shaped eyes, and bronze-colored skin that was a little darker than the people on the Navajo reservation where they were yesterday. The ranger opened her mouth, but then her eyes landed on Trick. There was a clear hiccup in her ability to speak, but finally she smiled shakily.

"Aloha, kids," the ranger quivered.

Trick realized that she was scaring the woman, but didn't want to change back to her human shape.

"Don't worry. I'm normally human. I won't hurt you."

Trick tried to smile reassuringly, but her toothy grin made the woman shiver. Trick flattened her ears on instinct. She didn't want to risk this woman somehow telling people about who she was, so she didn't want to change back to her human shape. Still, she didn't want to scare her.

[*We are thousands of miles away from home, and she seems nice. And you don't really look like yourself right now,*] prompted Anabelle

[*I hope you're right.*]

Trick shifted back to her mostly-human form, though Anabelle didn't leave her body.

"Sorry. I didn't mean to scare you."

"Wow. That's some Aura. You can turn into Figments?"

"Yep, any one that I want."

"Amazing."

Dylan piped up, "Lani, this is my friend Trick, and that is my friend Eddy."

"Guys, this is Kehaulani Kekoa. Did I say it right?"

Lani nodded. "Mahalo, Dylan. It's good to see you again. I figured it was you up here. Didn't know you were bringing friends now. You can all call me Lani. I'm just checking on the fire. I can't really stop you coming up here, and I don't really want to. Just be careful to clean up, and not leave anything behind."

"Sure thing, Lani. No one will ever know we were here. Promise." Clearly, Dylan thought highly of this woman.

"I'm glad to see you have some friends, Dylan. Come back any time you like. Could you save me the walk down the mountain?"

"Sure." He held Tigs out to her, and Lani took her gingerly.

"Hey, Tigs."

Tigs waved a little plush paw at her, and then they disappeared. Dylan returned a few minutes later.

"What was that all about?" Eddy asked.

"Lani caught me up here the third or fourth time I came here. She knew someone had been coming up here because she saw the smoke from my fires, but she ended up camping out here for almost a week waiting for me. She was pretty ticked at first, because she was worried I would start a big fire out here. I helped her get back down the mountain, and helped her with her job a little. She's my friend now. She's one of the only people who doesn't seem to be scared of Tigs and I. Well before you guys."

Dylan's phone beeped in his pocket. "Shoot! Late for the food. Be right back!" Dylan and Tigs vanished.

They were only gone for about five minutes before returning with a plastic bag filled with takeout containers. They sat down on the logs around the doused fire pit and started eating. Dylan and Trick told Eddy about what they had been discussing while he was sleeping. Eddy started to take out his phone to look up things about Skinwalkers, but Dylan told him that there just wasn't much on the internet about them.

"So, how do you even know you can do anything about one?" Eddy asked Trick.

Trick just shrugged, chewing on a mouthful of pancake, and pointed at Anabelle with a piece of bacon. Anabelle snatched it up, and then floated through the air on her back like an otter, munching on the bacon.

"She said that the magic the Bear can do can let us beat the Skinwalker. We just have to touch it," Trick said after swallowing her bite.

"Can you make me another Bear Figment? If there are two of us, it'll probably be easier to tackle this thing."

Anabelle floated towards the middle and shook her head. "Not for a few days. Not right now."

"Why not?"

"Because…" Anabelle trailed off. "You're not going to understand this even if I explain it. We just can't."

Eddy's expression turned dumbfounded. "Did you just call me stupid?" Eddy started grinning, but kept his head down so Annabelle couldn't see.

"Oh no, Eddy. I just mean that…" Anabelle trailed off as she floated closer to Eddy. She finally floated close enough to see his grin. "Jerk!" She whipped around, and whacked him with a soft tuft of fur on one of her tails.

"Hey!" he laughed and batted at her. She dipped under his swinging hands, and trilled a little laugh.

"What are we going to do?" Dylan interjected. He bit into his breakfast sandwich.

"We don't even know if it is what we think it is. How do we find out?" Trick asked.

"That's easy. Tigs and I can see it," Anabelle said. "The hard part is that a Skinwalker will be able to see us too, and they are really dangerous. They can make you sick just by pointing at you."

"Awesome." Dylan's voice dripped with sarcasm. He finished his sandwich and looked at his phone. "Well, we better figure it out, because it's going to be getting dark in Arizona soon."

Dylan started packing up his things, and Eddy shoveled the rest of his omelet into his mouth. Trick finished her pancakes, leaving the last of the bacon for Anabelle. She packed up her sleeping bag, and looked at her cell phone. There was almost no reception up there.

"We should check our messages before we go back to the reservation to talk to that doctor," Trick advised. Dylan nodded in agreement.

Once they all had their backpacks on, Trick picked up Tigs from the edge of a stump, where she had been swinging her plush legs over the edge. She and Eddy each took one of Tigs' plush paws. They all appeared at the spot overlooking the Golden Gate Bridge. Trick and Eddy took out their phones. The messages from Trick's parents were pretty frantic. They demanded she tell them where she had gone, and that she come home right then. Eddy's were much worse.

"I'm literally grounded for the rest of my life. Thanks so much, Trick," he grumbled.

Trick grinned at him. "I don't seem to remember anyone holding a gun to your head."

Eddy stuck his tongue out at her. Both sent messages back, but Trick noticed Dylan hadn't even checked his phone.

"Aren't your parents going to be looking for you?"

Dylan just shook his head, and then scowled at Tigs for a long moment. Trick suspected they were having a mental conversation.

[They are. I can't hear it but I can tell when they are talking,] Anabelle confirmed. Trick didn't respond, and just watched Dylan.

"Fine! I'll tell them!" Dylan yelled at Tigs after a long moment. Her plush ears folded back, and her expression turned deeply sad.

"My parents don't care about me! You two don't have a freaking clue because I don't tell anyone, but they only care about my sisters. They think I'm worthless, especially since I got Tigs! I'm on my own. I don't have parents anymore. They'll kick me out the second I'm old enough."

Trick's eyes went a little wide at Dylan's outburst.

"Dylan, I didn't know. I'm sorry."

"Well now you know." Dylan sighed. "Can we shut up about it?"

"Sure."

Trick wanted to help, but she had no idea what to do, turning her attention instead to her parents' messages. She replied that she couldn't come home, but she was fine, and that she would keep sending messages when she could.

"Yeah, that's fine." Eddy agreed. Dylan seemed to deflate with relief. He put a hand on Tigs' head.

"Sorry, Tigs. Sorry. You know how this makes me feel." Tigs didn't look convinced, but she patted him on the cheek with one of her tiny paws.

"We can talk about this more later. We should get going," Trick said. Dylan nodded.

In a flash, they were back in the cave where they had spoken with Shadow Runner the day before. The sun was going down outside, but it was still extremely hot. Trick shifted, becoming a Cheshire Cat once more. She floated up into the sky, as Dylan teleported Eddy toward town, stopping at the hill where they'd stopped the night before in order to try and see the doctor's house.

The clerk in the store had said it was a few miles outside of town, and Dylan said if she got up high enough, she could find the place pretty easily. The desert was beautiful from this high up. The buildings looked like doll houses, and the people looked like ants. Slow-moving ants, thanks to their lethargy. After a moment, she found the road heading out of town towards the doctor's office. She floated back down, rolling over and over before she came to hover beside Dylan and Eddy.

"It's that way." Trick pointed with a forepaw.

Dylan put one hand on Eddy's shoulder, and Trick picked up Tigs off of Dylan's. They all vanished, appearing on a hill over a mile away, before disappearing again to appear atop a dune even further down the road. That was when they finally got into sight of the doctor's office.

There were actually two buildings – a squat, square one that was clearly the office, and a second, a quarter mile behind the first, that looked like it might be the doctor's house. A short road connected the two. The house was a small, cozy affair, built from bright orange adobe. Flowering cacti traced both sides of the path made by a stone walkway leading from the driveway to the front door.

Trick groaned, "It's still so hot."

"You think all that fur you have is helping?"

Trick rolled her huge feline eyes, and then her body disappeared out of existence, leaving behind only her toothy grin and her huge feline eyes.

"Just because I can't see your body doesn't mean…" Eddy trailed off when found his hand passed right through the space where her body had been.

"Yeah, it's not really there," Trick grinned. "I'm going to take a quick look and see if the doctor is the one we are looking for."

Bodiless, she floated towards the office. Dylan teleported himself and Eddy toward a rock formation about a mile away. They could still see the building, but the rock formation kept them out of the sun. Trick moved to the window and peeked through. She found her vision as a Cheshire Cat more like her normal vision than that of the bear or coyote forms she'd taken earlier, or she did at first, at least.

When she looked at the three people sitting in the small waiting room, her vision changed. The colors faded until everything looked like a weathered painting. Around each person shone a cloud of brightly colored light. Each was a little bit different, and the light stopped about two inches away from their skin. One woman's glowed purple with motes of white, lines of dark red shooting through it. She sat with her head bowed, and it looked like she had been crying. She was holding a blue towel tied tightly around her left hand. She wore a yellow sundress that once had been the color of the sun, but now looked more like a faded buttercup. Lurid dark red light pulsed around that hand.

[*Her hand is hurt. That's why she looks like that. The purple and red show fear and pain,*] Anabelle explained.

The next one was a man wearing a black t-shirt and worn out jeans. He had dark brown cowboy boots on, and a belt festooned with beads, the buckle in the shape of a wolf's head. A short, bright red feather hung from his neck on a strip of leather. His cloud shone purple like the woman's, though it was much lighter. A swirling red cloud hovered over his stomach.

The third person was the worst. Most of their cloud was an angry red, outlined with deep purple that had been pushed to the edge.

[*They're super sick. It's something that's in their whole body for all that red in their Aura,*] Anabelle explained.

[*Is there anything we can do to help them?*]

[*Sure, but we would have to be the Bear.*]

[*Maybe later. I don't think Shadow Runner sent us here for that.*]

Trick floated around the back of the building, where she found two more windows. Through the first, she could see a vacant exam room, containing a padded exam table topped with fresh paper. Trick was about to move on when the door opened. She floated to the side of the window. It was unlikely that they would see her eyes, colored as closely to the sky as they were.

She moved to the top of the window, spinning upside-down so that only the tops of her eyes would be visible if someone happened to look. It was the woman that Anabelle had said was super sick. She realized that she hadn't noticed how the woman was dressed. She was dressed in a very expensive suit jacket and matching business skirt. She had the same bronze-colored skin as everyone else, and was wearing a beautiful gold necklace, hung with feathers. Trick thought it was very odd that someone dressed like that would have such an odd necklace.

The other woman in the room was older. She was not elderly, but not young either. She had the same bronze skin, and wore her long black hair in two braids tied off with small, beaded decorations at the bases and ends. A lab coat hid the rest of her clothes except a pair of sensible round-toed black shoes.

None of that was what caught Trick's attention, however. The cloud of lights floating about the woman was almost blindingly bright. A rainbow of blues, whites, and the brightest viridian greens pulsated around the woman. It practically filled the entire room.

[She's definitely not human. She's a Figment,] Anabelle said with authority.

[Is she a Skinwalker?] Trick asked, frightened.

[Nuh uh. Not her. She's something else.]

Trick heard doors closing somewhere else in the building and moved to investigate. Moving around the edge of the building, she spied someone walking out to the small parking lot. This person had almost no cloud of lights around them. Only a thin line of sickly lurid green remained.

[That's very bad. That's what everyone else in the town looks like.]

Hearing someone talking, Trick floated back to the window. When she came back to the window, Anabelle immediately gasped inside of her head. There was someone else in the room now. The Figment woman was gone, and in her place was a young man wearing dark green nurse's scrubs. He held a clipboard, and was flipping through pages. The thing that truly drew Trick's eye was the shifting black cloud of smoke that surrounded the young man. Around his neck was a necklace holding a gemstone glowing with a pulsing bright blue, white, and green light. It looked like the same cloud of lights that surrounded the old doctor woman. The man's eyes were glowing a deep blood red, and they were staring directly at her.

[*That's a Skinwalker!*] Anabelle shouted inside of their head.

Trick immediately slipped out of reality. She appeared at the limit of their ability to translocate, a few hundred yards away. Immediately, she disappeared again, running away as fast as she could concentrate on the magic. She finally appeared in the shadow of the rock where Dylan and Eddy were waiting, panting harshly.

"Dylan! We have to go far away!" Trick shouted. She switched back to her human form and picked up her pack. She grabbed onto one of Dylan's arms with surprising strength. Eddy was already holding Tigs, and they all vanished in the flash of teleportation.

Trick gasped on the ground, having run to the edge of the escarpment and thrown up over the side the moment they had appeared on the outcropping in Hawaii.

"It's eating people."

That was what she had understood the second it had looked into her eyes. It looked at her like food. It wasn't eating them in the real sense. It was worse than that. It was eating their magic.

"It's eating their souls," Trick lamented, nausea in her voice.

"Trick, what did it look like?" Dylan asked.

Trick flopped backwards to sit on the ground, then suddenly yelped and jumped up, yanking her tail out from beneath her. Eddy stifled a laugh, earning him a glare from Trick. She took a long few minutes to catch her breath before telling them what she had seen. By the time she was done, all three of them seemed dumbfounded.

"What about the old woman? If she is a Figment, maybe she can help us?" Eddy suggested.

"I don't think she even knows what he is," Trick said.

"Maybe we should find her and tell her," Dylan suggested.

"But we don't even know who or what <u>she</u> is," Trick complained.

"We can find out for sure pretty easily," Anabelle announced while floating closer to Trick, flipping over onto her back much as Trick while wearing the body of a Cheshire Cat. "If we can get close enough to touch her, I can tell what kind of Figment she is."

"Why would a Figment be acting like a human doctor?" Eddy wondered.

"How should I know?" Trick asked.

"No, he's right. It's weird," Dylan said.

"Not all wild Figments are bad, Dylan. Some of them are really super helpful," Anabelle shot back.

"Sorry," Dylan said.

"But you're not wrong. Her Aura was really, really strong," Anabelle said. "Figments as strong as her usually don't care much for humans."

"So how does that help us?" Eddy asked.

"I have no idea."

"So we still need to get close enough to touch her. How are we going to do that?" Trick asked.

"Coyote. We should be able to use the shadows to get close enough without her seeing us," suggested Anabelle.

Dylan exchanged a look with Tigs. "I feel like you're doing everything."

"The fact that we couldn't have gotten across the country without you?" Trick asked.

Dylan sighed, "Alright, are you ready to go back, then? You were really scared."

"You didn't see that thing." Trick swallowed and looked at Anabelle. Anabelle gave her an encouraging toothy smile. It was weird how she could use human expression despite that she was clearly feline. It worked, and Trick got to her feet. "Ok, let's go."

They decided that everyone should leave their gear behind except for Dylan, who had all the money. When they finally got back to the building, the sun was near the horizon, darkness beginning to set in. There were still lights on in the building. Trick had taken the shape of the coyote, and she had changed Eddy to match.

Anabelle had assured her that it didn't matter if she or Eddy was the one who got close enough to touch the old woman. She would still be able to tell what the woman was. Dylan had stayed back, but not very far away, so they could run to him and get away if they needed to. They had been circling the building for an hour when the lights inside finally went out. Moments later, it came out of the building. Trick was glad she couldn't see the awful aura coming off of that thing while wearing the form of the coyote.

The Skinwalker paused to look around slowly. Trick shrunk back behind the landscaping she was hiding behind, and the monstrous thing shrugged off its paranoia. It went to a newish red SUV, got in, and drove away. Trick sniffed at the air, and the acrid smell of the creature filled her nose. **This is a vile evil creature,** the smell said to her, which was the most descriptive a smell had ever been for her so far.

She wiggled her way back out of the landscaping when the doctor didn't emerge from the building. She started to sniff around, and wended her way back through the landscaping, towards the back of the building. As soon as she rounded the corner of the building, she spotted the woman, who was leaning up against it, watching her carefully.

"Come to make mischief, little sister?" the woman smirked. Her smile made Trick feel warm inside, like when her grandmother baked her cookies. The woman tilted her head a little and then squinted her eyes.

"Oh ho!" The woman began to laugh. She slapped her knee, and tears began to leak from her eyes. "Oh, child, you are something, aren't you? I bet you were quite a shock to that old dog. Come, child, I won't hurt you," the doctor said. Trick slinked cautiously closer, feeling like she could trust this woman, for some reason.

"I assume you have a reason for seeking me out? You obviously know that I'm not human."

Trick bobbed her head. She sniffed the air, but the smell of the Skinwalker was fading, so she felt a little more secure.

"Worried about eavesdroppers? Well come on, then, my home is not far."

The woman pushed herself away from the building and walked toward the small house behind it. Anabelle told Eddy where they were going, and he slipped out of the building's shadow. He had been quietly following the Skinwalker out of town.

[He doesn't live here. He drove out of town,] Eddy reported as he came up next to her. The woman looked over her shoulder and smiled at Eddy, too. Dylan appeared a moment later, with Tigs on his shoulder.

"I didn't think that there were any more of the Spelled among the Diné," the woman said, opening the door and letting everyone inside. Trick slid back into her human form, letting Anabelle out into the world beside her, and the doctor's mouth let out a soft 'o' of surprise.

"Well aren't you just cute as a button." She looked at them all expectantly.

"I'm Teresa, but my friends call me Trick. This is Dylan, and that's Eddy." Trick gestured to Dylan, and then to Eddy, still in the body of the coyote.

"Is he one of my brothers, then?" the doctor asked.

"No, he's my best friend. I can change him just like me."

Anabelle chimed in, "But right now our magic isn't strong enough to change him back right away." The doctor nodded.

"My name is Doctor Nascha Whitefeather. So you are two of the Spelled then. What are you doing way out here?"

Trick looked at Anabelle. *[What kind of Figment is she?]*_She asked mentally.

[She's an avatar of the Bear. Like the Bear we can become.]

"We're here because we're trying to find out how we got our Figments. One of the Coyotes told us that if we found out what was happening here, he would help us find out how we got our Figments." Trick went on to tell Nascha why it was so important to them. Nascha looked up at the ceiling, and mumbled some words in a language that she didn't understand. She would have to ask Anabelle later if she knew what Nascha had said.

"And you found me," Nascha said with a motherly grin. She waved her hand to invite them to sit in the living room as she moved to the kitchen.

Her little house was neat and clean. The living room had beautiful woven throw rugs on the hardwood floors, and was neatly decorated with feathered adornments. It was a large, open space that connected to the entrance with a step down. They took their shoes off, and left them on a shoe tray before stepping down. Trick patted some of the dust off of her light blue sundress. Interestingly, the pieces of furniture in the living area around the large modern flat panel television were older looking affairs – two recliners and a small couch, all in rust orange fabric that matched the carpets. They were extremely comfortable, though, and Trick swung her legs against the recliner while Anabelle lay in her lap.

"I think what he meant for us to find was the Skinwalker that is working as your nurse," Trick said.

There was a loud sound of breaking glass. Trick jumped up, and almost switched forms to the werewolf.

"Do not say that word. Child, you do not know what you are doing. Call it the creature or monster. Do not say its name. They gain power for everyone who fears them." Nascha's voice was low and dangerous.

"I'm sorry. I didn't know," Trick said.

Nascha took a deep breath. "How could one of the Eaters get so close to me?" Nascha whispered.

Anabelle floated up having been displaced from Trick's lap and stared at her for a long minute. Eventually, Nascha took a deep breath and held her hands out to either side as if to say 'What?'

"It has your magic, or magic from another one of the Bear," Anabelle said, still staring at Nascha.

Nascha's eyes went very wide, and she opened her mouth. Anabelle's eyes narrowed, and the woman's mouth snapped shut before she could say anything. Anabelle nodded, and Nascha took another deep breath it seemed she used them to calm herself often.

"Well, I certainly passed nothing to the creature, but it could have defeated another of us to take the magic from them."

"It keeps it in a crystal around its neck, but I think it only affects you because it's the same as your magic." Anabelle floated back to Trick, and landed on her lap again.

Nascha lowered her eyes to the ground. They darted back and forth frantically, and she turned listlessly back to the kitchen. She slowly cleaned up the broken cup, and then started to make tea again. A few minutes later, she brought a tray with four cups on it. It had a small pile of cookies in the middle.

"Children, you don't know what I owe you for this. One of those things could find no place better than my clinic to fill its greed. It is bold, for my folk are some of the only ones who can destroy one of the Eaters of Souls. Bold, and stupid," Nascha said angrily.

Trick reached out and took a big handful of the cookies, then offered one to Eddy, who had settled down next to her feet. He took it carefully, as if he wasn't sure how to eat the thing. A moment later, he had snapped the cookie in half, licking the pieces up from the rug.

"You okay, Eddy? It's gonna take a little while before I build up enough magic to change you back." He lifted his head and bobbed it once.

"You know one of the powers of we avatars is to change back to our human forms. If your power works the way I think that it does, he should be able to change back on his own. Though, if he is not one of the Diné, he may look a little different than he normally does. I've never seen another of the Children who was not one of the Diné," Nascha advised.

"I'm still learning, and so is Anabelle."

"Our transformation magic doesn't all transfer to him that way. He can't change shapes without our help, even if the Figment he is wearing at the time can," Anabelle informed.

"So you learn by mention?" Nascha asked

"I'm not sure what that means."

"It is a power that some of our kind have when it comes to certain narrow areas of expertise. Mention something about their area of expertise that they don't know, and they learn it automatically. Your area of expertise is apparently Figments. What the Diné once called totem spirits, and a hundred other names that everyone has forgotten by now. I can't tell you how you got your Figments. I was never a member of a Spelled pairing, so I don't know how they were made. But if anyone would know how it is done it is the old dog himself," Nascha explained.

Trick looked down to Eddy, "I can change you back now if you want."

Eddy looked up at her. Then looked around at everyone. He bobbed his head once. Trick reached down and touched two fingers to the top of his head. There was a flash of light, and then Eddy stood there, wearing a pair of shorts and a green t-shirt.

"It's nice to meet you, ma'am," Eddy said, and then took a seat at the opposite end of the couch from her.

"And you, Eddy."

"I'm surprised you aren't worried that we are out here on our own," Dylan said.

"I'm not human, Dylan, and I recognize the power you three hold. Even the strongest Figments would not lightly approach you to attempt to do harm. Not if they have any wits."

"Someone should have told those goblins that," Anabelle grumbled. Nascha looked at Anabelle, but did not ask for any explanation.

"Regardless, your duty is discharged here, children. Now that I'm aware, I can take care of the creature with little trouble. He may have found a way to cleverly hide beneath my eyes, but his magics are no match for that of the Great Bear," Nascha explained.

Trick looked up and shook her head. "I don't think so. We haven't stopped that thing yet," Trick insisted.

Nascha shook her head. "I recognize your power, child, but creatures such as that thing are very dangerous when cornered. No child, if the wily old dog doesn't acknowledge that you have done your service to the Diné, return to me, and I will speak to the Great Bear on your behalf."

Nascha finished her tea, and she reached to the table to put her cup down. The cup got over the tray, but tumbled out of her fingers. Her eyes went wide, and then suddenly, she was transforming. Her transformation was not like Trick's. Her body began to grow, and Eddy scrambled away from her as her clothing faded away. Beneath the clothing was a thick coating of brown fur. She fell forward onto all fours, and her hands and feet reformed into paws.

In less than thirty seconds, Nascha had become a massive bear, similar to the form that Trick had taken, though the colors of the rings in her fur and across her face were very different. She also had far more feathers – dozens hung on a

string around her huge neck. Her eyes had gone blank, and
the whites were shot through with broken blood vessels.
Then, that faded away, and her eyes were the eyes of a Bear.
She turned slowly towards the front door of her house. She
clambered over the couch, cutting huge holes in the fabric with
her claws. Her muscles twitched with every movement, as if
she were fighting against the motion. Still, she tipped over the
couch, and trundled towards the door.

"What is going on?" Trick whispered.

"Something is attacking her with magic. She can't control
herself. I think it's the monster," Anabelle whispered.

Trick got up, but she had no idea what to do.

"What do we do?" Eddy asked.

Dylan grabbed his backpack, and looked like he was about
to vanish. Eddy was looking at Trick, and at first, she looked
terrified, like she was about to run away, too. Then, Anabelle
landed lightly on her shoulder and situated herself there.
Trick paused, and obviously Anabelle was saying something
to her in her mind. Her face smoothed over, and her hands
fisted until her tiny knuckles turned white.

"I want to go home. And this thing is in our way. So we
are going to stop it," Trick growled angrily. "You guys can go
if you want. You don't have to stay. I'll do it."

"Nuh uh. I'm not leaving you alone," Eddy said. "Make
me the coyote again. There's lots of shadows out there. I can
distract it."

Trick held out her hand for him, and he grabbed it. The
blue flash of light faded, leaving behind the large coyote
version of Eddy.

"Be careful, Eddy. Don't stand still where it can see you,"
Anabelle warned.

Eddy bobbed his head and then looked around the room.
Not having a good view of any of the shadows outside, Eddy
went to the back door of the house and looked back at Trick.
She found the door locked, and opened it as quietly as she
could to let Eddy out.

"What am I supposed to do?" Dylan asked.

"I hope nothing," Anabelle said. "I didn't tell Eddy but if something bad happens to him, he can come back from it. It'll hurt a lot, though, so I want him to be careful. But we can't protect you the same way. You have to be our escape if this goes really wrong. If Trick and I can't get our paws on that monster, we'll switch to our Cheshire Cat form and slip away. If that happens, you have to get to Eddy and teleport him away. We'll meet at the cave, and then you can take us really far away."

"Who put you in charge?" Dylan was frightened, but she could see he wanted to help.

"If you have a better idea, let's hear it." Anabelle's voice was a growling trill of anger. Dylan made a frustrated grunt.

"Fine." Dylan put his backpack fully on and then looked out the back window. He vanished in a flash of white light.

Trick looked out the front window. It looked like the Skinwalker had been walking away down the path with Nascha a few steps behind him. It had stopped when Eddy had come out onto the path growling at it. It seemed not to know what to think of him. It lifted a hand, but as soon as it did, Eddy dashed off through a shadow. Trick could tell that he appeared not too far away, but definitely out of sight.

"We should use the Cheshire Cat form to get above him, and then turn into the Bear and drop on top of him," Anabelle suggested. Trick nodded.

"I have taken the totem spirit of the Bear, and I can do the same to you, dog! I'm more powerful than any of you!" The Skinwalker shouted. "Stupid cackling dog."

It started to walk towards the doctor's office again. Nascha followed him like a pet dog. Trick took the shape of the Cheshire Cat. She waited for a long moment, and Eddy popped back out of another shadow. He darted behind the Skinwalker and bit at the back of its leg. He kept right on going into the shadow of one of the manicured cacti on the other side of the walk. The Skinwalker screamed in fury and spun around. Trick slipped out of reality, and appeared in the air, hovering above the Skinwalker.

[Let's go, BelleBelle.]

In an instant, she took the shape of the enormous Bear. She landed on top of the Skinwalker, crushing it to the ground. Anabelle had told her that her healing magic could separate the human from the Figment it had consumed. She concentrated on the magic flowing into her huge body, and the bands of color all over her body shimmered with light as the magic passed through her. She could feel the Skinwalker struggling beneath her massive bulk, but there was no way it was going to get free before she completed her work. Then something huge smashed into Trick.

For a moment, she lost track of where she was, and Anabelle took over their body. She rolled over and over, trying to shove away the massive bulk of Nascha. Nascha, for her part, was attempting to sink her claws into Trick's side. Amazingly, Anabelle fought her like she had done it thousands of times. She kept rolling their body until Nascha was thrown off. Trick roared in anger, but that was as much control as she had. She was learning quickly from everything Anabelle was doing, but she didn't try to interfere with Anabelle's control.

It was like riding a rollercoaster as it flung her body about. It was an odd experience, being a passenger in her own body. She and Anabelle faced off with Nascha. Nascha roared, and charged at her in a massive wave of fur and muscle. Anabelle shuffled their body just a little to one side to throw off Nascha's aim. She waited for the last moment when Nascha reared up to slash at her with her claws. Then, Anabelle launched their body forward, smashing their shoulder into Nascha's chest. There was a resounding cracking sound as they smashed into her. Nascha tumbled backwards, and Anabelle didn't hesitate for a second. She plowed through Nascha, shoving her aside, and shot towards the Skinwalker who was just then attempting to rise.

[*Get the magic ready! I can't do it. It only comes for you.*] Anabelle shouted inside of their head.

Trick noticed why the Skinwalker hadn't been able to get up. It had bite marks all over its body. Eddy had been harassing it. It had a vicious wound in the back of one leg, and a serious gash across the back of its neck. Even as she raced towards the Skinwalker, she saw Eddy sprinting out of the shadow of the round flowering cacti on one side of the path. He skidded to a halt when he saw her barreling towards the Skinwalker. He yelped, and spun around, darting back towards the shadow.

Before he could get back to the shadow the Skinwalker lifted its hand. It roared a word that Trick did not understand, and a livid red glow surrounded its hand like a neon sign. Eddy made the most terrible whining noise she had ever heard in her life, but then he tumbled through the shadow he had been headed towards and he was gone. Trick didn't stop. Anabelle shouted inside of their head, but Trick blocked it out. She concentrated on the healing magic, and the markings began to glow again. The Skinwalker flipped itself onto its back, and glared at her with putrid red eyes. It raised that same hand to her, but it was far too late.

Anabelle reared up, and came down on top of the creature with both front paws. Trick could feel the magic much better this time. She concentrated on forcing it out through their massive paws and into the Skinwalker. The markings painted into her fur brightened intensely, to a level that was just barely short of blinding. Dirt and sand flew everywhere when their paws smashed into the Skinwalker's chest, directly on the crystal it wore there.

There was a shriek of indescribable sound that sent Trick and Anabelle deaf from being so close to it. Still, Anabelle pushed their paws down as hard as she could, even as their paws were burned by the light of the power coursing through the crystal. The crystal burst with a crash of sound, and then Trick could hear nothing more. Sight left them as well, the explosion of blue and green light that shot away from the Skinwalker's destroyed trinket blinding them.

She tumbled to a stop twenty feet away, her massive body crushing a huge bed of beautiful pink flowers. When Trick was finally able to blink the light from her blinded eyes, Anabelle was shouting inside of her head.

[*Oh please wake up Trick. Please. Eddy is really hurt. That thing cursed him. I can't do it without you.*] The voice inside of Trick's head sounded as if it were sobbing

[*Ahhh! BelleBelle, it hurts!*] Trick tried to move her bear body, but she was still a little disoriented.

[*Our paws are burned, and we are laying on bed of cactuses. I'll get us up, we have to heal Eddy.*]

A moment later, Trick felt Anabelle controlling their body, helping them to stand up. Then, the Skinwalker emerged from the cloud of sand like a wraith from the shadows. Its burning red eyes fixed on her, and it lifted its hand to point at her.

"Die," it said.

But nothing happened. The cloud of dust receded away from the creature. There was a circle of blasted-out flesh on his chest where the crystal had exploded. That was not what had stopped him, however.

Nascha stood next to him, her hand like a band of iron around his wrist. She had changed back to her human form, and she was beautiful. She was clothed in a flowing robe of blue and white fabric that shimmered with internal light. It was belted with glowing green roots, and from the belt hung feathers made of light in a spectrum of color that ran from white to blue to green and back again in a coruscating wave of light. Her eyes were like two burning viridian stars. The necklace around her neck, which had also been decorated with feathers, was like a collar of white light hanging loosely around her neck. She smiled at Trick and nodded to her in thanks. She twisted her body and shoved the Skinwalker back.

"That is quite enough," she said, and then started to chant. It was quiet at first, a slow, stirring sound that made all of Trick's fur stand up on end. Trick moved closer to Nascha. Nascha rested a hand in the thick ruff of fur around Trick's neck. Trick immediately felt better. The burns on her paws vanished, and all of the little hurts she had taken in the fight faded away.

[*Eddy!*] Anabelle yelled inside of her head.

Nascha looked down, and dazzled them both again with her quiet smile.

[Do not worry. I have turned the creature's magic back upon it. Your friend is unharmed,] Nascha's strong voice sounded inside of their mind. She continued her steady chant. *[Go to them. Dylan took him, and they are waiting for you behind the house. I must dance with this thing to see it cleansed. You have done well, little sister. Wait inside, as I would have words with you.]* She released her grip on Trick's thick fur.

Trick ran for the back of the house. She changed mid-step from the form of the Great Bear to her human shape. She ran as fast as she could, and when she skidded around the corner of the house, she found Dylan and Tigs sitting on the ground. Eddy, still in the shape of the Coyote, was lying there with his head on Dylan's leg. All three of them were covered head to toe in dirt and dust. Eddy's ears perked up, and he opened his eyes to look at her.

Somehow, Trick could tell he looked tired, but he wasn't hurt. She had to check anyway. She ran to them, dropping to her knees when she got to them. She started running her hands through Eddy's fur to make sure that he wasn't hurt anywhere.

"Oh god, Eddy, are you alright? That thing did something to you." The words tumbled out of her falling over themselves she said them so quickly.

"He says he is fine, Trick, but would like to be changed back," Anabelle relayed.

"Oh yeah," Trick said. The change only took a moment, and then Eddy was sitting there. Apparently, the shapeshifting didn't get rid of the dirt, because he was still covered head to toe. If anything, the red dust stood out even more against his dark skin.

"That was terrifying. I was so scared I thought I was gonna puke. Can we not do that again?"

Trick just shrugged. She had no idea what they were going to be doing over the next few days. She looked down at the ground. She felt terrible for making Eddy do that.

"We can take you home if you want, Eddy," Trick offered.

"What? Trick, don't be stupid. You're my best friend, and I'm gonna help you so we can all go home." Then he hugged her, and she felt immensely better.

"I may have actually puked," Dylan muttered into the silence that followed. Trick burst out laughing. She couldn't help it. Dylan grinned at her wanly, "At least I felt better afterwards?"

Trick couldn't stop laughing. Then, all the sound was blasted away from them. At that moment, Nascha's chant became something so much bigger than a sound. For a few minutes, all they could hear was her voice, but it wasn't only her voice. It was like they were in a huge sports stadium and everyone was cheering at once. The volume of a thousand voices chanting a beautiful harmonized beat filled the air. It drowned out every other sound.

All three of them got up and ran for the front of the house. When they rounded the corner, they were nearly blinded by the dazzling lights of the magic that Nascha had called. A column of dim white light had surrounded both Nascha and the Skinwalker. Standing next to Nascha was a gargantuan Bear. Unlike Nascha or Trick's bear forms, this one was ghostly. Trick could see all the way through it. It glanced at her, and then gave her the barest of nods. Even that small nod made her feel oddly accomplished, like someone had heaped praise on her for an entire day. She blushed and looked away immediately. When the chant intensified in volume, Trick looked back.

In the circle where the Skinwalker had been there were now two figures. One was a human shape wearing tattered clothing. The clothing was torn, and in some places, of such age that it crumbled into dust. Further, the man looked emaciated. His cheeks were hollow, and his lurid red eyes were sunken. He could have been a stand-in for the skeleton in the science classroom back at her school.

Next to him, radiating viridian light, was the shape of a wolf. The wolf bowed its head to Nascha and the Great Bear. Then it turned to Trick and her friends. It gave them the same bow. Then it trotted off out of the circle. The glowing form of the wolf faded away after a few seconds, and then burst into motes of shimmering aquamarine light.

Nascha's chant trailed off, and all of the light faded. When her voice finally went silent, the light, the ragged man, and the truly enormous ghostly bear faded away leaving the night truly dark. Nascha fell to her knees, and bowed her head. She looked as if she had aged many years. Her face was lined, but her eyes still sparkled with specks of green light. Trick walked closer, with Anabelle floating behind her.

"That was beautiful," she whispered. Nascha smiled.

"The works of the Great Bear often are, child," Nascha said. Slowly, she got to her feet, putting one hand on her knee to help push herself up.

"Well that sure was something'," a voice said from thin air. Shadow Runner, in his same beaded buckskins, came walking out of the shadowed side of the small garden shed on the front lawn. He wolf whistled at the circle of pure white sand where Nascha had done her ritual.

Nascha glared at the man. "You fool," she said before continuing in what Trick assumed was the Navajo language.

Shadow Runner held up his hands defensively. He replied in a few short words. They went back and forth. Everything he said just seemed to make Nascha angrier until she was shouting and shaking her finger under his nose.

[They are talking about the fact that he sent you kids to do something he should have done on himself,] Anabelle said into Trick's head.

Finally, Nascha pointed back towards the shed, and stopped talking all together. Shadow Runner just lifted his hands and turned around. He disappeared into the shadow. Nascha turned back to them and pinched the bridge of her nose. She opened one eye and dropped her hand. She looked them and smiled.

"You poor kids. I can at least get a hot meal into you and let you get cleaned up. I get the feeling you are a long way from the truth you are hunting for. Old Coyote will show up when he is ready. You can wait for him here." Nascha held out her hand towards the door, inviting them to come back inside.

Nascha righted the couch with surprising strength and then returned to the kitchen. She took an apron from the hook by the back door and put it over her head. She tied the strings behind her back, and Trick grinned when she saw that the apron was embroidered with the face of a brown bear. She had given them time to fetch their things. While they were gone, she cleaned up and began getting dinner ready. When they returned, she invited them to use the two bathrooms to clean themselves up.

They all changed into their last set of clothing, and Nascha had taken their dirty clothes to put in the wash. Trick had dried her hair as best she could. She had been the last one out of the shower. She now stood in the middle of the living room, fiddling with the ribbon around the waist of the purple cotton sundress. She had tried three times to tie a bow in the ribbon at the small of her back. Finally, she got it right, and sat down on the edge of one of the reclining chairs.

"I wish I could do more than just feed you. I can't repay what I owe you three. I shudder to think what the creature would have done with the power of my magic," Nascha said.

"How come I could see it but you couldn't?" Trick asked. She dug a brush out of her backpack, and started pulling it through her hair. Anabelle was laying on the back of the chair where Trick sat down. She had alighted there and dropped off to sleep almost immediately.

"The crystal it was wearing had captured the power of another of the children of Bear. It used that magic to shroud itself from me. That was how it controlled me as well. All of us share in the same magic. Can't protect myself from myself." She was rolling out some sort of dough, and the smell of cooking meat filled the house.

"Will Shadow Runner keep his word?" Dylan asked. Nascha just shrugged. Trick looked back and forth between them. Her bright copper colored hair had finally dried enough to braid, and she began doing so.

"Why wouldn't he? We did what he wanted," said Trick. She had used the brush to part her hair in the back, and she used a small purple hair tie with a tiny purple bow attached to it to tie off the second of two tightly-braided pigtails.

"With the children of Coyote, you can never really know, but you kids have done an amazing thing for the Diné. I meant what I said before, and I mean it even more now. I owe you a debt I cannot repay. If he doesn't help you, I will."

Nascha started putting dishes on the bar between the kitchen and dining room. There were padded chairs high enough to sit and eat there. "Get it while it's hot." They all pushed themselves up from where they were sitting. Trick eyed the stools. The backs were solid, and there would be no place to put her tail. For a long moment, she hesitated while Dylan and Eddy climbed up into their chairs.

[Just curl it around your waist as tight as you can like you did before. You should be able to sit in those chairs just fine,] Anabelle said into her head.

She did so, curling her long Cheshire Cat tail around her hips beneath her dress. She climbed up into the chair, and it worked. She was able to slide almost all the way to the back of the seat. Nascha had made tacos completely from scratch. The shredded beef had been in the crock pot in the kitchen, and they hadn't smelled it earlier because the cover had been on tight. They all dug in, and a few minutes later, they were all eating when Nascha looked out at the front door.

"Looks like he is going to keep his word after all," she said. Her eyes sparkled with green motes of light for a moment before it faded away.

"He's here?" Trick asked with her mouth full, putting the taco she had been holding down. Nascha held up a stalling hand.

"Take your time and finish eating. I'll tell the old coot to wait. If he was in a big hurry to talk to you, he should have showed up before we started our meal." Nascha finished the last bite of her own taco. She dusted off her hands and headed out the door. Anabelle had frozen the moment that Nascha looked up.

"There's something really, really big out there," she whispered, fright apparent in her voice. It was like she was terrified of even being overheard. Trick could almost feel something, like a prickling sensation against her skin. She shrugged.

"Nascha said it would be fine." She finished the taco she was eating, and then made another. Anabelle started to fidget nervously. She floated to the end of the counter and then back again. It was uncomfortable for her to actually walk, or she would have been pacing.

"BelleBelle, settle down. Nascha said we should finish eating first," Trick admonished.

"How can you just sit there eating? Can't you feel that?" she trilled uneasily. Trick shrugged. She could feel the power tingling against her skin, but for some reason it didn't bother her like it did Anabelle.

"She can feel it, little one, but she is the control source of your magic, so it doesn't feel quite so overwhelming to her," Nascha said. She closed the door behind her and sighed. "Even a thousand years can't change that old dog. He won't come in here. My home is a place of the Great Bear. It would not react well to old dogface coming inside." Nascha chuckled softly. "How is the food?"

"It's great!" Dylan said around a mouthful.

"Look, I know you three are a little young to understand all of what is happening to you, but I owe you a favor. That is no small thing. The old mutt has told me a little of why you kids are here. So I'll tell you what. If you need a place to stay where Figments can't get to you for a while, you can come back here whenever you need to. If I'm not here any longer, I will leave a way for you to find where I have gone."

"But you're a Figment, aren't you? Why would you help us?" Dylan asked.

"Sure I am, but that doesn't mean I don't care about people. I know what I said earlier and I meant it. You kids have a lot of power, so I felt like you could take care of yourselves. Considering that you saved me, I don't think I was wrong. I'm here to care for Diné. The Great Bear reminded me that all people are one people. Something I should have remembered all on my own. So if you need a place to stay, food to eat, or protection while you are on your journey, return to me."

They had all finished eating, so Nascha started to clean up the dishes. When she was done, she pulled her apron off and hung it back on its hook. After the magic spell that had destroyed the Skinwalker, her clothing had not changed back. The shimmering beaded robes and the belt of living roots had remained just as they were. Nascha had changed into a button up shirt and a pair of jeans. She explained that so much magic had run through the clothing that within a couple of days it would just fade away to nothing.

She waved for them to head outside. "If you want to get some sleep before you move on, you can stay here, but I get the feeling that the old mutt has something to show you that may take a little time, so take your things. You can come back whenever you need to."

All three of them grabbed their packs and put them on. When they made their way out into the yard, they were surprised to find Shadow Runner standing next to the garden shed. Trick turned back to Nascha, who was standing on the front porch.

"It's him. Coyote has godlike power, child. He cannot manifest on this plane without causing problems. He will speak to you through Runner."

Trick turned back to Runner and walked towards him. She fiddled with her dress nervously. She remembered what it felt like when he had talked to her inside of her head. He scared her.

He emerged from the shadow of the gardening shed. He looked the same as he did before, but his eyes had changed. Shadow Runner previously had bright green eyes. Now his eyed glowed a dim amber, and something about the way he walked was utterly different. He walked with such blatant disregard for anything that was happening around him. He was completely confident that nothing could ever happen to him. Then he grinned at her and his face completely changed.

That grin was so warm, so happy, that she felt it all the way down to her toes.

"You got nothing to fear from me at all, child. You have done a great thing for the People."

"How come you say the People, but she says Diné? Doesn't it mean the same thing?" Eddy asked. Coyote looked at him and nodded.

"Shadow Runner was being polite by using English. He does not know that you know what the word Diné means. Nascha is likely not even aware she is using it instead of English. Despite her modern education, she is very old, and some words do not translate directly to English. Diné is one of these words. I cannot convey all that it means by simply saying the People. You understand, little brother?"

"I think so," Eddy said. Coyote nodded slowly.

He walked with them into town, and then he turned down the road towards the end of town, where the cave was located.

"You sound really different." Trick accused.

"Different body, different voice." He grinned. "So, Runner tells me that you have a question for me. How can I reward you for your service, little sister?"

"Figments are chasing us, and we're afraid to go home because they'll hurt people to try and get us." Thinking about her parents made Trick tear up. She sniffed back the tears, and went on. "A Cheshire Cat told us that if we wanted them to leave us alone, we had to find out how we got our Figments." Coyote nodded slowly, and then sighed.

"I'm afraid I know what you must do, little sister. I can start you on your way, but it'll be a bit of a journey to get you where you need to go."

Trick, Dylan, and Eddy all exchanged looks.

"Listen to me now, little sister. I can offer you and your friends a way you can go back home until you are older. I can hide you until you are stronger in your magic." Coyote kept walking, but he didn't miss the hopeful look on Trick's face. "But if I hide you now, when the protection wears away, it'll be much worse than it is now. You won't have any time to do what you need to do."

They crested the top of the hill outside of town. From there, they could see the cave across the open desert. It was a beautiful tableau with the sun setting behind it all.

"And if you don't hide us now?" Dylan asked.

"Oh, no, I'm going to hide you either way. None of you deserve what is happening to you. The question is, what will you do while you are hidden? I would not blame you if you went home and dealt with this later when you are better prepared. But you have another option that may be safer for you when you consider the foreseeable future. You can keep going and find out what you need to know to free yourselves from all this nonsense permanently."

Coyote led them towards the cave. Trick stopped outside the mouth of the cave to watch the sun set. Coyote seemed content to let her watch the sun go down.

"We're just kids." She sniffed, but the tears she had held back started to leak out from the corners of her eyes.

Everyone was telling her that she had to do something impossible, something that even her parents would find impossible. She already did something impossible. Wasn't that enough? She crumpled to her knees and started to cry in earnest. Anabelle landed on her lap and worked her head beneath Trick's hand.

"Why do we have to do this? It's not fair!" Trick shouted at Coyote.

He bore up under it well, giving a small, sad smile. He came back to where she had knelt. He scuffed his snakeskin cowboy boot through the sand. Then he got down on one knee in front of her.

"Because you wanted it more than anyone else. People tried to scare you about wanting to do magic, but right here," Coyote touched her chest right over her heart with a fingertip, "in your heart, you knew that was what you wanted more than anything."

Trick knew he was right, but she hadn't known it would do all of this. She said so.

"I know you didn't know, little sister. That doesn't mean that you did anything wrong. Trick, you will do great things with your magic. Fun and wonderous things." He flashed a very silly grin at her. "You have a real big future in front of you if you can get through this. It isn't fair to ask you to choose right now. You are too young to decide. So I'm going to do the best I can to help you, little sister. Between these two things, you can't be wrong.

If all three of you want to go home, I will help make it so that everyone forgets about you for as long as I can. If you want to finish this so you can go home without being accosted by Figments for this ever again, I will help you do that instead. Understand that I can't promise more than that they will no longer come after you for this reason. If you do other things in the future that provoke them, you will have to handle that on your own."

He sighed when he saw the look on Trick's face. He wiped the tears off her cheeks and held out his hands to help her up. Trick put her tiny hands in his, and he lifted her to her feet. "Do you understand, little sister?"

"If we make trouble besides finding out how we got our Figments, you won't be able to help with that?" Trick asked. He touched her nose gently.

"That's right, kiddo. And all three of you have to decide what is best. You can't decide this for everyone." Coyote turned to look at Eddy and Dylan. Eddy, though, didn't hesitate.

"I'm helping Trick. Whatever she wants is what I want to do," Eddy vowed.

Coyote nodded. "You have yourself a real friend in little brother, here." Coyote's grin had gone silly again.

"I've got nothing to go home for unless you guys are there," Dylan said.

"That's a wise choice, Traveler. While I haven't shared my skin with you, I can see you carry more years than you've lived. These two are the family that you need. Don't forget it." Coyote gestured to Trick and Eddy. Dylan nodded.

"I want to go home," sniffed Trick. "I don't want anyone bothering us, either. I want to be all done."

Coyote snapped his fingers, and they were someplace else. The surrounding desert shimmered, and changed instantaneously into the spot just outside of Nascha's house.

"I will point you on your way then." Coyote said. The time had changed too. The sun was setting but it was still higher in the sky than it had been a moment ago. The scene was from earlier that day, when they had been fighting the skin walker. It was a single frozen crystalline moment, just before Trick had crushed the crystal the Skinwalker was using to control Nascha.

"Look at this thing," Coyote said to all of them.

"This thing was once a great man among the Diné. It was a kind soul who healed many hurts, and saved many lives. It did amazing things for those it cared about, Trick. I'm telling you this because to learn what you want to know, you have to understand." Coyote folded his hands behind his back and leaned over, sneering at the Skinwalker about to be crushed beneath Trick's massive bear form.

"What?" Trick asked.

"That even those who have done great good can also do great and terrible evil. Magic can be a gateway to wonders beyond the imagination of mortal minds. It can also be a door to things so dark that even I would shy away from seeing them. Magic is not good or evil on its own, no matter how much anyone would like to blame it for the ills of the world. It is the mind that wields the magic that is to blame. Do you understand, little sister?" Coyote asked.

Trick shook her head. She wasn't sure what he meant. He sighed disappointedly, but then he grinned and he started to talk again.

"Trick, people call people like you Demons. They think that because you have magic that you'll do bad things with it. But would you?" Coyote asked.

Trick shook her head. "I don't think so."

Anabelle floated quietly over Trick's shoulder. She shook her head.

"But you could?"

"Well sure, I guess,"

"And if you did, would it be because the magic made you do it?"

Then Trick understood. She looked at the image of the Skinwalker with her massive bear-self hovering in the air above it.

"No, it would be my fault. I decide the things I change into, and how to use my magic," Trick affirmed.

"Right. Don't forget. Trick, Dylan, Eddy, the magic is your magic. How you use it is up to you."

He waved his hand and the image began to break up like it was smoke that had been somehow colored in with markers, like one of Trick's coloring books when she was younger. It finally dissipated, and they were standing back at the mouth of the cave.

"You have seen the baddest of the bad. To finish this, you need to see the goodest of the good." Coyote chuckled a little and turned towards the cave. He entered, and the rest of them followed him, not sure what to make of what he had said. "What I can tell you is that you didn't get your Figments by accident. But only the White God has the answer as to the how and why of your pairing to your Figments.

To find him, you must first find a missing little boy. He's like you three, but his power is a little out of control. He doesn't understand how his Aura is supposed to function, and if someone doesn't find him and help him, he is going to damage himself."

He led them around the corner to the fire pit. There was a little fire blazing merrily in the pit, and Coyote gestured for them all to sit down around it. He took the large rock on one side of the fire.

"The boy you are looking for is named Brewster Crews. But he does not like his first name so he goes by Bruce instead. I can't tell you where he is right now, but I can tell you where he will be sometime soon," Coyote explained.

He gestured towards the fire, and the flames intensified from orange to bright blue. The heat shimmer over the fire became much clearer. A moment later, an image began to form in the shimmer. It was a young Caucasian boy with dark brown eyes and mussed curly brown hair that looked like it was in the middle of growing out from having been brush cut. He wore a white t-shirt that had the outline of a bird embroidered on the chest in black thread. He had on a ragged set of blue jeans, but wasn't wearing any shoes. Sitting next to his feet was a large white bird. Trick had never seen a bird like it, but it looked similar to a raven. It was much larger.

"Right now, I have no idea where he is. Sometime over the next few weeks, he will be drawn to a hospital in Edinburgh Scotland. It is called Edinburgh Sick Children's Hospital. If you can find him there and help him learn how to control his Aura, his Figment, Eliani, will be able to tell you how to find The White God."

Coyote snapped his fingers, and the fire died down, leaving shadows dancing everywhere in the cave. He made to get up, and Trick spoke up.

"Didn't you say you would hide us?" Coyote grinned his trickster's grin.

"Already did, little sister. Anyone hunting you will never find you now." He blinked his eyes, and they were Shadow Runner's oddly bright green again.

Trick realized that his eyes were very strange because she hadn't seen anyone in the clinic or the town who had anything other than brown eyes.

"Did he keep his word?" Shadow Runner asked. It seemed like he was very concerned with whether or not Coyote had.

"He did," replied Dylan. Trick seemed to be lost in thought, and Anabelle was looking up at her with some concern.

"I'm sorry for anything he did that was out of line," Shadow Runner said.

"What do you mean?" Eddy asked. Shadow Runner whistled a long slow whistle.

"You kids must really be something. That's the first time I ever remember him letting anyone off scot free without playing some mischief on them."

Shadow Runner turned toward the fire. The fire exploded into a two foot wide column of coruscating flame with a whole

rainbow of colors in it. Everyone jumped back from the fire
except for Trick. Eddy tumbled over the log he had been
sitting on and rolled away from the fire yelping. He ended up
perched uncomfortably in a position with his feet well above
his head. Dylan vanished in a flash of white light and
appeared thirty feet away. Somehow, though, he ended up in
almost the same state as Eddy. He was tumbled in a tangle of
limbs, and Tigs was somehow sitting on top of his butt.

Trick, though, didn't even move, though Anabelle
scrambled up her body and sat on her shoulder with all of her
hair standing on end like an angry housecat. Both of her tails
waved like angry snakes. Shadow Runner changed into his
coyote form and tried to bolt through a shadow, but before he
could, a lawn chair that Eddy had kicked in his tumble
crashed to the ground in front of him. Shadow Runner tripped
over the chair, rolling muzzle-first into one of the walls, unable
to go through the shadow like he had obviously planned. He
laid there, upside-down with his paws hanging over his head.

A wild cackle sounded throughout the cave. Shadow
Runner let out a similar yipping cackle, making no attempt to
right himself. He eventually toppled over to his side, and laid
there panting helplessly, his tail wagging in amusement. Trick
finally stood up with a sigh, displacing Anabelle, who floated
next to her. Then she landed on Trick's head, draping herself
over Trick's skull like a hat.

"Come on, BelleBelle," Trick groaned.

"But it's the most comfortable place to lie down!" Anabelle
complained.

Trick rolled her eyes, but she somehow felt better with
Anabelle's warm presence on top of her head. She turned
around, and blinked at the scene of everyone clambering to
their feet. Shadow Runner had changed back to his human
shape, still laughing a low wheeze.

"What happened to all of you?" Trick asked, perplexed.

"Coyote!" they all answered as one, though Eddy and
Dylan groaned it while Shadow Runner sort of chuckled out
the word.

"I'm gonna get a move on. I stay around these parts much longer and Coyote might decide to insinuate hisself into my business again," Shadow Runner said. "Good Luck to you kids."

"Thanks, Runner," Trick replied.

He slid his cowboy hat onto his head and tipped it to her. He switched to his coyote shape mid-step. Then he padded out through a shadow on the wall.

"So what do you guys want to do? Can we even get there?" Trick asked. Dylan nodded.

"I don't have any place in Scotland, but I do have a spot in Ireland in a place called Ards Forest. It's where we went to see the Faeries. I go back there all the time now. It's a nice place, and Tigs likes to talk with the Faeries," Dylan explained.

"Are they really..." Trick made a fluttery motion with her hands.

"Some of them are. But not all of them are tiny people with glittery wings. Some are a lot like us. Dryads look almost human except for the green rooty-looking hair and the pointy ears," Dylan said. "But we should get some sleep. I'm exhausted, and spending tonight in Nascha's house sounds pretty good right now."

"Do we have time?" Trick asked.

"If we get some sleep I can get us to Ireland in a single jump tomorrow," Dylan said.

Trick sighed, but then nodded. The truth was, after everything they had been through that day, she wanted to be in a house too. They all shouldered their packs, and headed back towards Nascha's house.

Nascha had welcomed them back in, and her house was surprisingly larger than they had originally thought. In it were four bedrooms and a third bathroom hidden away behind a door that opened onto a hallway that lead back towards the front of the house. The bedrooms wouldn't be good for much more than sleeping in as they were not very large, but they were a lot more comfortable than camping out in a sleeping bag, at least for the people who didn't sleep floating in the air.

Eddy rubbed the sleep from his eyes as he came out of the bathroom. The sound of cooking floated from the kitchen, and Eddy migrated that way. He got about halfway there when he fully remembered where he was. When they had finally gotten back from talking with Coyote it had been late, but not so late that they didn't have time to do some things. Dylan had teleported to Ireland to make sure that the place they were going was safe. Trick and Eddy had stayed behind to talk to Nascha, who they had found had a surprising knowledge of Figments. After telling her about what they were trying to do over the next few days, she had suggested that it was a good idea for Trick to have more Figments that she could use.

That had been over a week ago. Trick had practiced three new forms. A Hippogryph, a Selkie, which she could only take the Seal form of, but could be useful because of its ability to stay under water for so long, and a Drake. The Drake was her favorite. It was like a tiny dragon. It could breathe fire and had nearly impenetrable armored scales. She went slow because she didn't want to be stuck out of her human form.

Finally, they had started to talk about what they were going to do when they found Bruce. Nascha had been immediately reminded of a Figment from a story that she had once read called a Null Imp. They were very rare, but they did exist in the world. They fed off of magical energy, and while you were within a couple dozen yards of them, it was almost impossible to do magic.

They were odd-looking little creatures, almost like a cross between a lizard and a small child. They had a long thick tail and were covered in black scales. There were two slightly curving horns sprouting from the back of their skull, and they had a very short blunt muzzle. They had long talons on their hands, but no mouth. The most disconcerting part was that they didn't see the way any normal creature did. The Null Imp's vision was almost entirely based on seeing magic. Real solid things were easy enough to navigate but they were just grey shapes. The only colors that they could see were when they looked at magical things.

Trick had agreed to take the shape of one of the Creatures even though Anabelle had warned her that if they didn't wait, it was possible that they would be stuck out of their human form. Trick had said that she would try to change back in her room so she could get used to it before anyone else had to see her. She wasn't there, though, when Eddy came into the living room. Or at least she wasn't in her human form.

She floated above the kitchen counter as a Cheshire Cat. For the first time, he realized that the pattern of mottled blue stripes in her fur wasn't just random. It had hypnotic whorls and swirls in it, and they all flowed towards a spot on her chest where there was a vague circle of knots in the stripes. It was beautiful, and it made her distinct from the other Cheshire Cat he had met.

"Good morning," he said. Trick spun in the air, and then rolled over upside-down.

"Hi, Eddy~" she said in slow melodic tones.

"Good morning. Bacon, eggs, pancakes, help yourself," Nascha said. She piled the last few pieces of bacon onto a serving tray, and brought it around to the dining room table. Trick floated closer, turning right side up.

"Ahem, no eating with those paws. Change back. Anabelle would like some bacon too," Nascha said.

"But I'm all fuzzy," Trick whined. Nascha rolled her eyes.

"You're all fuzzy now," Nascha said.

"Fine," Trick grumbled.

The flash of azure light came and went. When Trick emerged from the light with Anabelle floating over her shoulder, Eddy gaped. She was wearing her favorite purple dress. It was like a set of overalls, but it had a knee-length purple corduroy skirt instead of pants. But underneath it all, it was clear that her last transformation into the Null Imp had caused a serious reaction.

Trick barely looked human anymore. She was covered completely in the same fur she had as a Cheshire Cat. She didn't have the same creepy grin as her cat form, but her face was distinctly more feline than it had been, with fine fur covering her entire face. Her eyes were almond-shaped and also distinctly feline, with slit pupils. Her hands were somewhere between paws and hands, though thankfully she didn't have claws to contend with. Her tail seemed even longer and puffier with fur than it had been before, sticking out of a hole in the back of her dress. She had a miserable expression on her face, but she pulled out the chair.

"What's with that look?" Nascha probed.

"You don't think I look a little too weird?" Trick groused. Nascha started to laugh, a full body chuckle that brought tears to her eyes. Trick scowled at her, and with her new appearance it was a fearsome expression.

"Oh don't be angry, little sister. But come now, I turn into a bear on a regular basis. Eddy has worn the skin of Coyote, and I strongly suspect he will become as used to having fur and a tail as you will. Dylan must suffer the fate of being a child for the rest of his very long life. Trick, this gift you have been given is a wonder, and from what I understand, you love magic. Maybe you should treat it like the dream come true that it is."

Nascha loaded up a plate with food and held it out to her. Trick took it carefully, as if she wasn't really sure how her hands worked anymore, though they worked just fine. She put the plate down and picked up a fork. She cut a piece of pancake, and paused for a long moment. She ran her tongue over her teeth, which had become rather sharp and pointy in the front. She put the pancake in her mouth with almost comical care, but after a second, she found that while her front teeth were quite a bit more feline, her back teeth were mostly unchanged.

"I know you are worried that people will find out about you and they won't treat you well, but does that really matter, Trick? Not everyone is going to understand, but you have friends who will. Besides, you've got magic powers. You can turn into a Manticore and scare anyone who bothers you spitless." Nascha grinned. Trick rolled her eyes.

"Oh, that's a good one!" Anabelle said.

"What's that?" Trick asked.

"It's a huge Figment that's a combination between a lion, a porcupine, and a scorpion. They're super scary. But they aren't very nice. They eat people," Anabelle recited, trailing off with a little trill of dismay at the end.

"Well, you don't have to eat people, silly, but if you look like a Manticore, I doubt that anyone will make fun of you. But it won't be like that for long, Trick. As you grow, and your magic gets stronger, if you want it to be so, you will be able to hide yourself much better. Looking at your aura, there is going to come a time where no one will remember you have magic unless you want them to," Nascha said.

Trick tilted her head. She was about to ask Nascha what she meant when the back door burst open. Dylan was standing there, panting heavily.

"I found him!" He gasped as if he had run all the way from the cave in the morning heat. He was sweating profusely, and Tigs was peaking over his shoulder from where she was clinging to the rim of his backpack. He hadn't seen Trick since last night, and when his eyes fell on her, his words tumbled to a stop. "Whoa," was all that Dylan could get out.

"Found who?" Trick asked. She ate a piece of bacon, and Nascha waved him inside.

"You're letting out the cold air."

He entered the air-conditioned room, and she closed the door behind him.

"The kid! I found Bruce!" Dylan blurted out. He sat down in one of the chairs around the dining room table.

"How long have you been awake?" Eddy asked, looking askance at Dylan, who looked extremely disheveled.

"About three hours. I couldn't sleep so I figured I would have a look around. Tigs has been learning new things that she could never do before over the last few days." Dylan seemed to notice the horrific state of his clothing.

"Oh this isn't because I'm tired. The spot where I usually teleport into the Dryads grew a new tree. Tree is a lot heavier than I am so I took a tumble," Dylan said.

Trick understood immediately from her earlier experience with being in the same spot as Dylan when he appeared in a place.

"What?" Eddy asked.

"Oh the bigger the difference in weight, the faster I get moved out of the way. That's why I don't want to teleport inside of a mountain. I'd probably end up in outer space before I could slow myself down." Eddy blinked and then shook his head.

"I have no idea what you are talking about," Eddy observed.

"We're burning daylight. I'll explain on the way." Dylan shoveled bacon and pancakes onto his plate. "Thanks Nascha! You're an awesome cook."

Nascha chuckled. "When you live alone for a few hundred years, either you learn how to cook, or you suffer the consequences."

Dylan put bacon and eggs between two pancakes like a sandwich, and scooped pieces into his mouth as quickly as he could.

"Slow down, you're gonna choke!" Eddy admonished.

"Yeah, seriously," Trick said. She noticed she had a bit of a lisp on her S sounds. "Great, now I can't say anything that starts with S anymore." She growled, and the sound rumbled deep in her chest. She scowled at Anabelle.

"Hey, don't look at me. You're the one who broke our magic. I'm the one trying to fix it."

Trick shook her head, and then let out an explosive breath. "Alright. I'm a furball, and I'm gonna end up being a furball a lot. I'm over it," Trick said. Eddy burst out laughing.

"We can do different kinds of furball if you get tired of the cat look?" Anabelle offered helpfully.

"Yeah, fine, smartass," Trick said.

"Well, this is a change. Someone is heckling you for once." Eddy continued laughing.

Trick narrowed her huge almond-shaped eyes. Then she pointed at him, and a flash of blue light filled the room. Suddenly Eddy was replaced with a large black and green cat. Trick was a little startled, but she didn't show it. She hadn't picked what he was going to look like, and he looked completely different from her Cheshire Cat form. He was jet black, but his body was covered in various shades of green splotches from a bright, almost neon green one around his left eye, to a dark hunter green spattering that looked like someone had flung paint all over him. All she had remembered was the time she had first changed into a Cheshire Cat and how hard it had been to figure out how to control her ability to fly.

Eddy had no more luck than she had. He floated just above the back of his chair for a moment. He was waving all four of his paws, but then he began to tumble. He bounced off the back of the chair and fell towards the ground. Then he snapped to a halt about six inches from being able to touch the floor. He scrambled his paws at the floor as if he was trying to swim towards it. It didn't work. He began to cartwheel towards the opposite side of the room.

"Trrriiiicccccckkkk!" he yowled in a dulcet version of his regular voice. His tumbling made the drawn-out wail waver as his body spun towards the opposite wall, but Trick couldn't help him. She was too busy laughing. Dylan was trying to hold in his laughter.

"Okay, I deserved this. Change me back please?" Eddy begged.

"Stop trying to stop yourself. Just float there," Trick said.

Eddy squeezed his huge green eyes closed, and his body froze in the air. He opened one eye, and stared at the wall, then at the ground.

"Cheshire Cats float normally. You only actually move in a direction when you think about moving. You can't actually fall unless you want to fall. Otherwise, you'll just float wherever you are," Trick said.

"That makes no sense at all!" Eddy complained. Trick just shrugged. "Please change me back, Trick?"

"Get down to the ground. As funny as it would be to see you end up in a goofy heap of tangled arms and legs, if I change you where you are, you'll fall down," Trick said with a toothy grin.

Eddy flailed his front paws at the floor, but continued to float where he was without moving at all. She ate a few more bites before Eddy finally slowly floated to the ground. He arranged himself with absurdly slow care into a sitting position. Trick nodded at him, and he disappeared in the flash of magic. He sat on the floor blinking for a minute.

"That was off the weird'o'meter. I couldn't even think the way I normally do. All I could think of doing was something fun. It was like I didn't care about anything important. How do you do that?" Eddy finally got up. He came back to the table and finished eating.

"I don't know. I'm always having fun so it isn't hard to just be normal." Trick shrugged.

"Please don't do that again without warning me?" Eddy asked.

"Sure. I'll pick something else next time." Trick laughed. Eddy cleaned the syrup from his plate with the last of the pancake. Then he pushed back his chair and made to walk away.

"Ahet! In the dishwasher," Nascha scolded.

Eddy snapped his fingers. "Almost made it." He grinned and picked up his dishes from the table and went into the kitchen. Dylan was right behind him, and then he stood by the door practically jittering with excitement.

"You might as well explain it to him. I'm not done, and I'm not going to shovel it in like you creatures."

Trick pointed her fork at Dylan and then Eddy. She speared a piece of bacon and held it up for Anabelle, who snatched it off the fork. She flipped over onto her back and began to munch on the bacon, holding it between her two front paws. Dylan explained what happened when he teleported into a place where something already existed.

"So it moves me. But if something is a lot heavier than me, it can throw me pretty violently. It also depends on how big the thing is. With walls or trees, they aren't so much bigger that it has to move me very far, and even then, I can get moving pretty fast. A couple of times when it was something really big, I had to teleport to a spot over water so that I could slow down without hurting myself. But if there was a few hundred feet of mountain that it had to move me for," Dylan shook his head.

"I have no idea what would happen. Tigs just says it would be very bad. The biggest thing I ever teleported into was a huge redwood tree in California. Tigs and I have developed a reflex for instantly teleporting up high into the sky when it happens. Gives me time to figure out how to slow myself down, and, if I have anyone with me, to get them slowed down too. It's one of the first things we learned."

"Do all Figments learn like that?" Trick asked.

"Not all. Though like I said, I was never part of a Spelled pair. I don't know the answers you are looking for. I'm sorry," Nascha said.

Trick shrugged. "Guess we'll just have to do what Coyote told us," Trick said. She finished her pancakes and got up to take her dishes into the kitchen.

"Got a small present for each of you," Nascha said. She opened a drawer next to the stove. "But I can't make them work without your help." She took out three tiny bags on leather thongs. The little bags were made with leather, and were edged all the way around with red, blue, and green beads. Trick took one, and when she touched it, her fingers tingled.

"Wow." Trick put it back down.

"It'll only tingle like that until you make it yours." Nascha explained.

"Make it ours?" Dylan asked.

"These bags are my gift to you, and you three will be the only people on earth ever gifted with one of these outside of the Diné," Nascha explained. "I have been permitted to gift one of these to only one person in my several thousand years of life. I certainly never thought I would give them to three young warriors not yet old enough to be out of their parent's sight. But the vision that shook me from my sleep last night made it quite clear that you were worthy to carry them."

"What do they do?" Eddy asked.

"These, once we give them each a drop of your blood, will heal the bearer of one mortal wound. Something that would have otherwise killed someone wearing one of these will be healed as if it had never happened," Nascha explained. Eddy and Trick looked frightened, but Dylan looked awed.

"That's freakin' amazing!" he burst out. Nascha nodded.

"I can't make these on my own. You have caught the notice of the Great Bear or I would not have these now. I suspect that the part you took in defeating the creature has drawn the attention of many of our divine ones. You three really are something." Nascha pulled the longest, biggest needle that Trick had ever seen out of the drawer. It was so close to being a spike that she could barely call it a needle.

"There is no freaking way you're stabbing me with that thing!" Dylan shouted.

"No there isn't." Nascha chuckled. "But it always gets a rise out of everyone." She slid it back into the drawer. She went to a basket on a table next to one of the chairs in the living room. She took out a small plastic box filled with sewing pins. They had tiny yellow balls on top. She opened the box and took out three.

"Now, each of you take one of the bags and hold it in your hand. I'll prick a finger on your other hand, and you let a drop of blood fall into the bag. You'll feel light-headed afterwards, but just take a deep breath. It'll go away."

They each picked a bag. Trick held it in her left hand, and
Nascha took her right. Trick hissed when she pricked her
index finger. There was a paw pad there now, and that made
it a little easier to squeeze out a drop of bright red blood.
Nascha went to the other two, and a second later, they were all
rubbing their fingers. She hung the bags over their heads.

"Now don't let these make you stupid. They only work
once, and dying is not something you want to experience,"
Nascha said. "Luck," she added.

"Thanks, Nascha," they all said. Then they vanished in the
light of Dylan's magic.

"So, I found him just outside Edinburgh. He was sleeping in a tree in the form of that huge white bird that Coyote showed us. I didn't wake him up, and if we're lucky, he'll still be there," Dylan said excitedly. "Okay, hold on tight to Tigs. This is gonna be really fast."

It was. Things blurred by so quickly that it was impossible to identify where they were. A few seconds later, they came to a stop, standing in a farm pasture. They were in one corner of the pasture, which was fenced off with a ragged looking barbed wire fence. Directly in the corner of the fence was a massive oak tree. But nowhere in the tree was there a big white bird.

"Crap. He must have woken up. He could be anywhere by now," Dylan groaned. Trick reached out to Anabelle.

"Yeah, he could be anywhere, but I bet his smell is still here," Trick said.

Anabelle landed in her arms, and after a quick flash of blue light, a massive white werewolf stood where Trick had been. Unlike a normal wolf, werewolves have retractile claws, and they were the equal to those of any big cat. Trick jumped into the tree, her claws sinking into the bark. She pulled herself up into the tree, and her nose started sorting through the smells until one spoke to her. **This is the smell of a bird that is not a bird**, it said. She inhaled deeply, and tried to memorize the scent. She jumped down out of the tree a moment later, landing with a heavy thud on all four paws.

[Don't worry. I'll remember it when we change again,] Anabelle said into her head. They changed back.

"I've got his scent, and we know he's going into the city."

"Yeah, but you can't really run around Edinburgh as a werewolf," Eddy pointed out.

"Watch me," Trick said. "Besides, if anyone tries to stop me, I can just switch to a Cheshire Cat and vanish."

"And what about us?" Eddy reminded.

"If I'm going to use the werewolf, I won't stay near you guys. If we get separated, we can meet back here."

"It's like ten miles to Edinburgh from here," Dylan observed.

"A werewolf can run ten miles in about fifteen minutes," Anabelle supplied.

"Alright, let's go," Dylan said.

They all vanished. It was a burst of images flashing by Trick's eyes before they appeared on a wide street surrounded by trees. Dylan pointed with his thumb behind him.

"The hospital Coyote mentioned is over there."

A large building made of red stonework with a large blue and white sign out front stood behind them. There were people all around, but no one had noticed them yet. They backed up against the large stone wall on their side of the road and sat down in the grass.

"You guys should wait here to see if he shows up. You're normal looking, so you won't draw any attention. I'll change and go to see if I can find him before he gets here," Trick said.

"Be careful," Dylan said.

Trick nodded, and then Anabelle landed in her arms. She trotted off down the street. She made sure she was out of sight of Dylan and Eddy before she changed. One step to the next, she slipped into the werewolf. She knew that she couldn't stay hidden. The werewolf shape was enormous, and she would have to keep moving if she wanted to keep from scaring everyone that saw her. Thankfully, her nose was extremely powerful so she could smell everything around her even at a near run. The downside to this was that she could smell everything around her. The scents were extremely confusing.

[Trick, find a place to hide. You are going to overload your brain if you don't stop and give me a minute to help translate all these smells.]

[What?] Trick stumbled to a halt.

[I don't know what all these smells are, so I can't translate them all for you. Slow down.]

Trick slowed to a trot and looked around, sniffing the air. She slowed down to a walk and got closer to the road. She sniffed the road, and then got closer to a parked car. She sniffed at the tailpipe of the car. Then she sneezed.

[That's gasoline, then,] Anabelle said. *[All these human smells are vile, but I think I have them mostly sorted out. Let's go.]* No sooner had Anabelle's thought come through that there was a shout.

"Holy shite, is that a werewolf?" a man on the street screamed.

Trick folded her ears and growled at him reflexively. He ran off down the street, screaming at the top of his lungs.

[Oh good work. That's gonna be fantastic.] Anabelle groaned into her head. *[He's not anywhere nearby. Let's be the cat and go around the other side. We can sniff around there for him.]*

As quickly as that, they had shifted shape to the Cheshire Cat. She concentrated on fading away and appearing across the street. When she was there, she did it again until they were out of sight of the parked car. Then they shifted back to the werewolf shape. She trotted off down the street in the new direction, and Anabelle helped her sort through the scents.

This is a human you don't know, were the words that kept repeating inside of her mind as she followed this scent trail or that. She went around another corner, and paused for a moment to lift her head to look where she was going. That was when she caught the scent. **This is a bird that is not a bird,** it said the same way that it had earlier. She looked around but didn't see a big white bird anywhere.

That was when she spotted the commotion. Across two streets, under some trees, two men were wrestling with the white bird, trying to stuff it into a cage. Trick bolted straight towards them. She leapt completely over the street, clearing two cars, but by the time she made it to the second street, they had crammed the cage into the back of the van. They sped off down the street.

[Anabelle, the cat, now!] Trick shouted inside of her own head.

The change was instantaneous. She could still see the van as it blurred off down the street. She concentrated, and then vanished. She appeared inside the back of the van.

Surprisingly, she floated neatly in the center of the space, moving as quickly as the van was. The cage took up most of the back of the van. Trick floated down to the cage door. Just as she reached for the latch on the cage, the bird looked up at her. Its eyes went very wide, and then there was a loud banging noise. She translocated on reflex. She appeared on the street outside of the van.

[What happened, BelleBelle?]

[They tried to shoot us. Cheshire Cats can't be harmed, but the way they do it is if anything is about to hurt them they translocate away from the danger. It's a reflex.]

[They what?!] Trick choked. Trick spun in the air to look for the van, but it was long gone. *[How are we going to find him now?]* Trick groaned unhappily.

[Same way we did just now. We can sniff him out if we hurry, but I don't think he's going to come back here now. No reason to have Dylan and Eddy wait for him anymore.]

[Okay. Let's get back to them.] Trick concentrated and vanished. *[How come this feels so different from when we teleport with Dylan?]* Trick asked as she faded into view on the other side of the street.

[Because Dylan's ability to teleport goes through a different type of tunnel. The place he has to go through to go such huge differences is farther away. The place Cheshire Cats use is much closer to this world,] Anabelle explained.

It didn't make much sense to Trick, but she figured she would just understand when she was older. When she faded into view, she startled a woman with long red hair wearing a pair of pajamas covered in printed-on kittens. Trick slowly rolled upside down and grinned.

"I love your PJs," she churred. The woman swallowed audibly and then smiled tentatively.

"Thanks?" she said.

Trick let herself fade away, leaving behind her upside-down grin for a few moments before it too vanished. She appeared down the street not far from where Eddy was sitting. Dylan was missing. She floated to the top of the stone wall and landed on her back. She let her head hang off the wall upside-down, looking down at Eddy.

"What happened to Dylan?"

Eddy jumped and looked up so quickly that he bumped his head on the wall. He rubbed the back of his head.

"He'll be back in a minute," Eddy grumbled. "He went to make sure that the kid wasn't in the hospital already."

"He's not. Someone just shoved him into a cage and drove away with him." Trick rolled over onto her stomach and pushed backwards off the wall. She vanished, leaving behind a puff of blue smoke and appeared floating next to Eddy.

"Eeesh, can you not do that?" Eddy said.

"Do what?" Trick asked. She vanished from one side of him and appeared on the other, looking towards the hospital. Eddy pulled out his phone.

"Is that going to work here?" Trick asked. Eddy shook his head.

"Probably not. You can go in looking for him." Trick nodded and then let herself slip out of reality. She appeared in the lobby of the hospital. She thought for a minute about changing back to her normal human shape, but until the magic leaked out of her body, she wasn't going to draw less attention that way.

[Can we change into something that can be human?] Trick asked.

[No. There are some Figments we can't become because their magic is really similar to ours. Shapeshifters especially. Like our werewolf. Werewolves can change between human and their wolf. We can't become a human version of a werewolf. I wish I could explain better.] Anabelle said.

Trick gave a mental shrug, then spun in a circle until she noticed a nurse behind the emergency room triage desk was staring at her, completely unnerved. Trick lifted a front paw and waved at her. She let her body fade away and appeared in the slowly-closing elevator down the hall. Trick looked at the elevator buttons, and then pressed the one labeled with the number two. The elevator went up with her floating weightless at its center.

[We can't search every floor unless you get a lot better at going invisible without translocating,] Anabelle said.

Trick had spent a few hours the first time she had become the cat trying to do it. It was hard because part of translocation was first becoming incorporeal. Anabelle had explained it but Trick didn't understand. She said that becoming invisible was actually using magic to move their body out of phase with the current dimension. Translocating did the same thing, it just moved you a little further into the other dimension, and then you came out in another spot.

[How am I supposed to stop?] Trick asked.

[I don't know. Just try to fade away only a little.]

Trick tried to do what she said. When the doors to the elevator opened, she tried to concentrate on fading away. She felt her body moving. It was like taking a tiny step backwards. She concentrated on not taking any more steps into that other place. The doors started to close, and she lost concentration. She slipped a few steps further into the other place and popped out the other side a few feet into the hallway. There was a desk about ten feet away, and a woman looked up from it at the elevator bell. Trick concentrated furiously on taking just a single step back into that place. This time, it worked. She felt herself fade away, but she didn't appear somewhere else. She looked around, and it was like looking through a sheer white curtain. There was a sort of white film between her and everything else.

[I think I did it.]

[Yep. Good work.]

[Yeah, but now how do we move?]

[The same way. You just don't fade back in at the end. It's how they seem to be able to move around so quickly.]

Trick tried it. To take those tiny steps back into that other place. The white film got thicker, and when she got closer again, she was at the far end of the hall where she had wanted to go. It seemed that the building was sort of a big U shape. She followed it all the way around, disappearing from one spot and appearing at the next without ever actually becoming visible again. She didn't see Dylan anywhere. She discovered when she got to the other end of the U shape that there were another set of elevators here.

She floated closer to the window, still looking through that ghostly transparent current. It was odd how she could see it but if she didn't try to look directly at it, she couldn't see it at all, which was why she hadn't really noticed it before. She was worried that Dylan had gone down another elevator while she was coming up. Sure enough, when she looked out the window, she saw Dylan crossing the street back to where Eddy was sitting.

[Can we just...] She made a mental gesture towards the window.

[Sure. We aren't really in that world right now. You can float through anything. Like a ghost. You can also just translocate down there.]

Trick floated out through the window just to see if she could. She passed through it just like it wasn't even there. When she was floating outside of the second floor window, she took those tiny small steps back out of reality and then appeared on the street next to Dylan and Eddy. When she appeared, Eddy was explaining what Trick had told him. Dylan looked around for her.

"I can search the hospital and find her," Dylan said.

Trick concentrated on getting back out of that place outside of reality. She felt herself fade back into sight next to Dylan and Eddy. This time, Eddy managed not to jump.

"I couldn't catch them." Trick's slow, melodic voice had a severe downturn of unhappiness.

"It's not your fault. But how are we going to find him now?" Dylan asked.

"Anabelle thinks we can still sniff him out. The werewolf's nose is super powerful, but we have to hurry before the trail goes away. So just try to keep up with me." Trick switched forms to her werewolf shape.

[Are you sure we can do this?] Trick asked mentally.

[Yep. Just get back there, and start sniffing. I'll help you.]

Trick bolted down the street. She didn't want to stay close to here. A bunch of people had already seen her both as a werewolf and as a Cheshire Cat. Someone was sure to have called the police by now. Werewolves were known to be very dangerous. Dylan appeared on the side of the street ahead of her. She didn't stop running, she went right by. She darted across the first street, zipping between two cars that slammed on their brakes and blew their horns at her. She ran back to the spot where the men had pushed the cage into the van.

She began to sniff around there. After a moment, the scents started to speak to her. **This is a bird that is not a bird. This is the van that took away the bird that is not a bird.** Trick turned in a circle, following the scent around, and then it trailed away down the street.

[The Van actually has its own scent?] Trick asked skeptically.

[Yes. But if we don't hurry, it will get lost in all the other car scents.]

Trick started to run down the street the way the van had been heading. She kept darting into the street, much to the dismay of the people driving through the city. She was running much faster than any of the cars were going. At her size, she didn't think anyone would want to crash into her, but she was still careful not to get hit by any of the cars. She ran until the scent took a sharp turn to the left. Then she lost it in a wash of other car scents.

She slowed down and trotted to the side of the road. The intersection was large, with 5 streets leading away from it. The van had been going to the left, but it was very busy, so the only way she could try to find the scent again would be to stop traffic so she could sniff around in the middle of the road. She waited until there was a break in the traffic and then stepped out into the street. She was almost as large as the red compact car that screeched to a halt when she sat down in the middle of the road. She snorted at the car when the horn started to sound. Trick stood up, and started to cast around with her nose close to the ground.

[I can't find it,] Trick complained. At that moment Dylan and Eddy appeared in the flash of white light she was getting used to seeing.

"What's the matter?" Dylan asked. Trick just stared at him for a long moment and then rolled her eyes and resumed sniffing the street. "Right, you can't talk, sorry."

The man in the car had stopped leaning on his horn, and was now talking frantically into his phone. Trick let out a huff

of annoyance, and then trotted down the street, casting about
with her nose until she got to the other end of the street. The
intersection there was of three streets, but she had no idea
where to go from there. There were a lot of cars going through
this intersection as well, but this time Trick didn't even
hesitate.

She walked right out into the middle of the road, to the
displeasure of the people driving. She could hear sirens now.
She tried her best to ignore them. Even if the police did find
her, she could just change to the cat to get away. After a long
moment of casting around with her nose, the scent hit her.
This is the bird that is not a bird. It was odd that she caught
that scent and not the scent of the van. They had taken the
street to the right, and she took off in that direction, following
the scent as fast as her paws could carry her.

Old brick facades flew by as the sirens faded away into
the distance behind her. She took a second right as the scent
went around a long curve to the left. She leapt over a green
car that ground to a halt when the driver saw her going over
its hood. She got to the other side of the street where the scent
continued. Trick started to pant as she came down the street.
It was odd because she noticed that the buildings on the left
were old looking brick buildings while the ones on the right
were much more modern glass and concrete structures. Trick
hadn't spent a lot of time in big cities, but she thought for a
moment that she would have to ask Eddy if it was weird.

[How long can we run before we get tired?]

*[A long time. But we're really going pretty slow compared to
how fast we could go if we didn't have to follow the scent.]*

Trick was panting pretty hard, but she didn't feel tired. She
was getting more than enough air to keep going. She tried to
speed up, but when she did, she lost the scent. She stopped
twice, turning circles on the side of the road until she found
the scent again. She ran on at the slower pace. With all the
traffic, she was hoping that maybe the van was caught in it
somewhere, but as they got to the outskirts of Edinburgh, the
street went into four lanes. The traffic started to thin out. She
hadn't noticed in her frantic attempts to keep the scent, but
Dylan and Eddy had kept up with her the entire way. She was

about to stop and change to talk to them when she spotted the
van.

[There it is!] Trick shouted inside of her head.

[You don't have to shout. I'm inside your head.]

[How do we make them stop?]

*[Just get up next to it and jump into the side of it. We weigh
enough to knock it off the road,]* Anabelle suggested.

[We could hurt him,] Trick objected. She felt a mental
headshake from Anabelle.

*[He is merged with his Figment. His Figment has incredible
healing powers. If he gets hurt, he will heal almost instantly.]*

Trick still didn't want him to get hurt, but she didn't see
any other way to get them to stop.

*[They haven't seen us yet. Maybe we can just jump in front of
them?]* Trick suggested. Anabelle gave a mental shrug.

[That could hurt if they don't stop.]

The conversation only took a few seconds, but at the speed
they were running they were coming up on the van very
quickly.

[Alright. Body check it is then, I guess.]

She sped up as fast as she could go, getting alongside of the
van. She dodged around a car in the driving lane, and then
darted back towards the van. She leapt and slammed her
shoulder into the van. The van rocked violently up onto two
wheels for a short moment. By the time it returned to all four
wheels, it was too late for the driver to save it. It spun wildly
off the road, sliding into the driveway of a hotel on the right-
hand side of the road. Its wheels hit the curb sideways, and
the van flipped onto its side.

Trick leapt into the air. She landed with all four paws on
the side of the van, crushing the side of it a few inches from
her sheer weight. The door to the van popped open, and a
man's hand pushed it open the rest of the way. The second
hand that came out of the door was holding a pistol. Trick
lunged forward and bit his hand. It was an extremely gentle
bite, considering how hard she could have bitten him, and she
still tasted blood. The man yelped, and the gun clattered to
the ground. Trick shoved her head in through the door and

growled at the man who had fallen on top of the other. A flash of white light delivered Dylan and Eddy just behind the van.

"We weren't going to hurt him!" the man yelled in terror. He had an odd accent that made him hard to understand. Trick didn't recognize it at all. She narrowed her eyes at the men and lifted her lips away from her fangs.

"Please don't eat us!" the second man begged. Trick rolled her eyes at him and snorted. She pulled her head back out of the door and jumped down from the side of the van.

"I can't get over how huge you are," Dylan said. Trick swapped back to her normal form.

"Those jerks tried to shoot me!"

Anabelle floated above the van, watching the door to make sure they didn't try to get out. "Can you get him out, Dylan?"

"They tried to what?" Eddy shouted.

"They tried to shoot me. That's why I bit that guy in the van," Trick said. Anabelle floated down past the van and grabbed the gun from where it had landed on the driveway. She floated up into the air, and then over the van. There were trees behind where the van had fallen. Anabelle threw the gun into the trees, and it vanished into the foliage. Dylan nodded to her.

"Seemed like a good idea," Anabelle said.

Dylan vanished, and then appeared again a moment later, holding the huge bird cage. Inside was the enormous white bird.

"Bruce, we are here to help you. We'll get you out, and then you can change back," Dylan said.

The bird watched him with odd silver eyes. They looked like tiny round mirrors.

"You can't take him!" The man that Trick had bitten was scrambling out of the van. His hand was bleeding, but he had tied a handkerchief around it to stanch the blood. Trick turned to him.

"If you try to stop us, I'm going to take a bite out of a lot more than your hand!" Trick shouted angrily at the man. When he noticed her distinctly feline features he shrank back away from her.

"What the heck are you, demons? You're not kids," the man said.

"Idiot. We are kids, we just have Figments," Eddy shot back. "Well, they have Figments. I'm just here to help my friends."

"We need him," the man said.

"That doesn't mean you can just take him," Dylan said.

He grabbed the padlock on the cage. The flash of his power came and went. He only moved about two inches, but the padlock had moved with him, coming out of the cage hasp. He tossed it aside and opened the cage. Bruce hopped out of the cage. His body began to change. Unlike Trick's transformation that happened in a flash of blue light, Bruce's transformation took a few seconds.

His bird body expanded like a balloon, and colors began to run over his body. Then, the blob of colors split into two. One was pure white and quickly reshaped itself into the form of the giant white bird. It shook itself and its feathers fluffed up then laid back down flat. A moment later, the much larger of the two blobs reshaped itself into the boy that Coyote had showed them. He looked a little bewildered.

"I need to go," he said. The bird looked up at him. Then it looked at Trick.

"I can't make him understand," the bird squeaked. Trick was startled for a moment.

"You can talk!" Trick exclaimed.

"Why does everyone think we shouldn't be able to talk?" Anabelle blurted out.

Before anyone could answer her, Bruce started to walk away down the street back the way they had come. The bird made an odd motion with its wings that showed it was worried somehow. Trick had no idea how she knew that, but she knew.

"He needs help. I can't make him understand his magic," the bird squawked.

Then it hopped off down the street after Bruce. It beat its huge wings once, and then it was in the air, gliding down the street to catch up with him. Trick looked at Dylan and Eddy

with an expression of confusion. Dylan shook his head – he
didn't get it either. The men started to follow Bruce, but Trick
turned to them. She switched back to her werewolf form. She
growled, and they froze where they were. She looked at Dylan
and Eddy. She shooed them on with a paw, and they
disappeared. She turned back to the men, and peeled her lips
back from her fangs. She growled again, and they backed off
even further. Trick switched to what passed for her human
form.

"What's the matter with you? He's just a kid," Trick
shouted angrily.

"We need him to heal someone that's sick!" the man
shouted.

"Then you ask for his help. You don't steal him. I don't
care what you need him for. If you don't stay away, I'll hurt
you until you do. Come on, Anabelle." Trick stalked away
from the two men. She reached out to Anabelle, and they
changed into the cat.

"She'll die without his help," the man said. Trick ground
her row of sharp teeth. She spun around, and narrowed her
huge eyes at them. "Who will die?"

Dylan hurried along next to Bruce. He had an odd expression on his face, and he wouldn't respond to anything either he or Eddy had said. His Figment glided down and landed on Bruce's shoulder. She flapped her wings gently as she got a careful grip on the boy's shoulder so that her talons wouldn't dig in.

"He can't hear you," the bird said.

"You're Eliani, right?" Eddy asked. The bird gave a very human nod.

"How did you know? How did you know Brewster's name?" The bird squawked the questions so fast that there was no time to respond.

"It's a long story, but someone sent us here to help. Why can't he hear us?" Dylan said.

"Because he can only hear the call. When Bruce imagined me, his mother was sick. He wanted desperately to make her better. Part of our magic is that we can feel sick people so that we can find them and help them, but something about our magic damaged his mind somehow. He doesn't understand how to turn it off, and he won't learn. I've tried to explain. If he doesn't stop soon, we'll die," Eliani explained.

"From using your magic?" Dylan asked.

"No. He won't sleep unless he passes out, won't eat unless he gets too weak to walk or change. I can't get him far enough away from people so that he won't feel them needing him anymore."

"Is that all you need? A place really far away from people?" Dylan asked. Bruce continued walking back along the road. He seemed entirely oblivious to their conversation.

"I don't know. I can't learn new things about our magic with him like this." Eliani's voice got a little frantic. "He's going to make us change again. He knows he can get back to the hospital faster if we are together as a bird."

Tigs jumped off of Dylan's shoulder and into Eddy's arms. He caught her at the last second. Dylan grabbed Bruce by the shoulder. Then they were standing on the side of a mountain. The wind was howling insanely, and it felt as if it was going to blow them all off the mountainside.

"Come on, we have to get inside!" Dylan shouted over the wind. He pointed towards a white wall of snow behind them, at the back of the small plateau that Dylan had brought them to. Bruce was looking around blankly, and Eliani had fluffed up all of her feathers until she looked like a white ball. Dylan put his hands on Bruce's shoulders, guiding him towards the wall.

"Where are we?" Eddy shouted over the wind.

"Near the peak of a mountain in the Himalayas called K2. I don't think anyone knows there's a cave here!"

When they got closer to the wall, Dylan teleported them inside. Eddy blinked and looked around. The inside of the cave was surprisingly clean and neat. There were half a dozen sturdy industrial shelving units to the left hand side of the cave. Stacked on them were neat rows of canned food. Some held camping gear, and one of them held neat stacks of money.

"Dylan, if no one knows this is here, where did all this stuff come from?" Eddy asked. Dylan shook his head.

"Don't ask." He moved to the right hand side of the room and carefully started the camp heater he had set up there.

"How many secret places like this do you have?" Eddy probed.

"Only two. I only have ten spots where I can go without seeing them. You've seen Hawaii and the spot in Arizona. There are three more at home, the spot in San Francisco, this one here, the spot in Ireland, and two more that I will show you when we get back to Trick."

"It's not working," Eliani squeaked dismally. She looked at Tigs, and her gleaming silver eyes focused tightly. Dylan could hear Tigs' side of the conversation, but not what Eliani was saying. Tigs had to do something to help Eliani

[You need to give it time, Eliani. How long has your magic been running without stopping?] asked Tigs.

[Weeks. He spent a lot time flying over the ocean. He used our magic to make it all that way.]

[Then you definitely need to wait before you give up. Your magic will take time to run out of him after all of that.]

[He's so weak. How long will it take?]

Tigs made a little shrugging motion with the plush paws.

[As long as it takes, and if it doesn't our friend can help you both.]

Eliani finally nodded, and seemed to calm down a little. Bruce, for his part, stood where Dylan had left him, staring blankly into space. Dylan guided him to a chair near the heater.

"We'll help you both, Eliani. Tell us more about your magic?" Dylan asked.

"I don't know as much as I should because I can't learn new things without his help, and he isn't trying new things with our magic. We can make people better from sickness and pain. Lots of people all at once. It works better in places where there are more happy people."

"Why does that matter?" Dylan asked.

"How much positive energy there is matters to our magic, but I'm sure if he was able to help me, we could do much better," Eliani chirped.

"Ok, and you said you can sense where there are sick people?"

The bird nodded. "I was hoping if we got far enough away from people that it would make the magic go away, but I can still feel them faintly. Brewster isn't going to stay still very long. He's exhausted. That's why he hasn't moved yet."

"Are you hungry, Eliani?" Dylan asked. The bird nodded vigorously.

"I haven't been able to eat in two days."

"I'm sorry I only have canned stuff here, but you can have anything on the shelves that you like."

Eliani flapped her wings and landed on the back of the blue camp chair sitting in front of the shelves. She peered at the neat rows of canned and prepackaged goods on the shelves. Dylan got up and joined her at the shelves. He reached out and picked up a packet of tuna with dressing in it. He tore the package open and threw the torn off top in a trash bin before removing a fork from a coffee can full of utensils. Eddy joined them a minute later. He took a bag of sour cream and onion chips out of a box filled with small bags.

"That smells good." Eliani pointed her beak at the pouch of tuna that Dylan was eating.

"Can you eat out of one of these, or do you want me to put it in a dish for you?" Dylan asked.

"I can eat out of it if one of you hold it for me. Or give it to Brewster. He'll hold it while I eat. He cares about me, but his mind is so cloudy. I can't make our magic stop."

"But our friend Trick can help you with that."

Dylan tore open another package of Tuna, and took it to where Bruce was sitting. He held it out to the boy. "This is for Eliani, and I have more if you are hungry."

Bruce didn't respond, but he did reach out and take the packet out of Dylan's hand. Eliani let out a sigh and flapped over to the chair where Bruce was sitting. She landed on the arm of the chair and stuck her beak into the pouch of tuna.

"Eddy, I don't want to leave you guys here because there's no way out of this cave without me. That's why I don't think anyone knows it is here," Dylan explained.

"But you can't really take Bruce with us because he'll change shape and leave," Eddy finished for him.

Dylan nodded. He finished eating the tuna, and Eddy balled up the empty bag from his chips. He tossed it into the trash can, and Dylan followed him.

"Eliani? Where are we?" Bruce asked confusedly. Dylan and Eddy spun around. Bruce was blinking at them owlishly. "Who are they?"

"It worked!" Eliani chirped ecstatically. She threw herself off the arm of the chair and against Bruce's chest. Bruce tried to juggle the pouch of tuna and the huge bird. He hugged her to his chest.

"We're friends, Bruce, and now that you're back, we can help you get control of your magic. But to do that, we need to go get our other friend. Would you mind waiting here until we can get her and come back?" Dylan asked. Bruce looked around the cave in a daze.

"What happened to us?" he asked, still clearly confused.

"I'll tell you," Eliani volunteered. "You two go on and find your other friend. We'll stay here."

"Alright. We'll be back soon, I hope," Dylan said. He held out a hand to Eddy and they both vanished.

It took them only a few minutes to find their way back to where they had left Trick. It was an anthill of activity now. Police cars and emergency vehicles were swarming over the hotel parking lot and van. It took Dylan and Eddy a long few minutes of listening from various places around the site of the accident before they were able to piece together that someone at the hotel had heard the crash and seen the van flip over. They had also seen an enormous werewolf attack the two men in the van. None of the talk was good when concerning the werewolf. No one knew that Trick had been trying to get Bruce out of the back of the van at all.

"She'll have to be careful not to be a werewolf around here again or people will remember this mess," Eddy said. Dylan nodded.

[She isn't here, Dylan. If she were nearby, I would be able to talk to Anabelle mind to mind.] Tigs' telepathic voice was concerned.

[She can be Figments that are literally immune to being hurt. Don't worry. I'm sure she and Anabelle are fine.]

"How are we gonna to find her?" Eddy asked.

Dylan teleported them away from the scene. It took them a minute to get over the ten miles, but finally they were back by the tree they had left earlier that morning.

"I don't want to take the chance that anyone saw us there earlier. We're going to find her the hard way. You wait here. She said if we got separated, she would meet us back here. I'm going to teleport around the city and look for her. Even if she is using her normal shape, she'll stand out in a crowd with all that fur," Dylan said.

Eddy nodded and sat down under the tree. "Hey, wait. We should get new phones that work here," Eddy suggested.

"How?" Dylan asked. "My parents got my phone."

"They sell them in convenience stores. They aren't as good as our phones, but we can call each other on them. Throw them away when we are done with them."

"How do you know all this?"

"Don't watch much TV do ya?" Eddy laughed.

"Not really."

Dylan vanished with the signature flash of white light. About twenty minutes later, he came back to find Eddy had pulled a book from his bag and was reading it. Dylan had three small plastic packages in his hands, and Tigs was holding another between her plush paws from her spot on his shoulder.

"Took a couple of minutes to find a store that sold them. I just got ones that looked kinda like my phone."

He put the packages down in Eddy's lap. Eddy took out a little swiss army knife that his dad had given him on their first camping trip that year. He tore open the plastic packages, and started turning on each of the phones. Eddy took his knife and started scratching at the plastic backs of the phones.

"What are you doing?" Dylan asked, a little alarmed.

"They all look exactly the same. I'm scratching a letter into each one so we know which one is which." He fiddled with each one until he finally held out one of them to Dylan. This one had a letter D scratched into the back.

"This should be pretty much like your phone. I put the new numbers into the phones so you can just dial any of us by the names. Texts work too," Eddy explained.

"Alright, I'm gonna see if I can find her. If anyone sees you, text me right away. We aren't supposed to be here, and if anyone hears you talk, they're going to know it," Dylan said. Eddy positioned himself on the side of the tree facing away from the road. There were no houses in sight, so unless someone was really looking for him, they shouldn't see him. He leaned back against the tree and took his book out again.

"You think you'll find her?" Eddy asked. Dylan shrugged.

"I've no idea which way she went. I'm going to try to go the same way the van had been going first," Dylan said before he and Tigs vanished.

The men explained why they had tried to take Bruce. They had been hired by a man whose daughter was very sick. Trick had not wanted to listen to them. After all, they had tried to hurt her. If she hadn't been wearing the Cheshire Cat body, they could have killed her. She kept wearing that form the entire time she was talking to them just to make sure that they couldn't hurt her. She had already decided that she wasn't going to help them, but the little girl they were telling her about, she could help that little girl. If she could just find out where the girl was.

They had gotten away from the hotel and crashed van by walking back into the hotel parking lot. The parking lot had a road on the opposite corner that they followed into another parking lot. This one belonged to a hospital. That was two hospitals in such a small area.

"Tell me where I can find this girl. I'll help her, but not you," Trick said in a metered, melodious voice. The two men exchanged a look.

"We don't get paid if we don't bring back help," one of them said.

"That's not my problem. You should have thought of that before you tried to kill me and steal a little kid," Trick admonished, rolling over onto her back.

"We can't deal with a freaking demon!" The larger bald headed man growled.

She grinned as insanely as she could at the men.

"I don't like either of you very much. So tell me where to find the girl, and I'll help her, or don't. You can tell whoever it was that hired you that you couldn't get what they wanted. Now go away, and stay there." Trick started to fade away, and one of the men shouted.

"Wait! I'll tell you where you can find her, but it's a long way away in Oxford." Trick vanished and appeared by the smaller of the two men. He was the one with brush cut brown hair and green eyes. The one that she hadn't bitten.

"Do tell," Trick purred practically into the man's ear.

He jumped back and flailed his hands at her. He was clearly terrified of her, despite the fact that he looked like he was a pretty strong guy. The larger of the two men cuffed the smaller one on the back of the head. He was about to say something when Trick narrowed her eyes at him.

"You should stop talking now." She turned back to the other man. "Last chance," Trick said.

The shorter man took a notepad from his pocket. It was in an odd leather case. He flipped it open and quickly scribbled something onto one of the sheets. He tore it off, and held it out to Trick. Trick snatched it in her front paws. Trick wondered idly why all animals didn't have paws like the Cheshire Cat's. Thumbs were apparently extremely useful. Trick vanished and moved away from the parking lot.

She went back the way she had come, eventually appearing in the parking lot at the hotel where she had come from. She could see that there were still tons of flashing police car lights on the other side of the hotel. She rolled over right side up and read the paper. It was an address, but it was weird, not quite like her address back home. She would have to get back to Eddy and Dylan so that Dylan could take them somewhere that their phones would work. Then she could look up where this place was and go there to help.

She didn't stay very long in the parking lot. Police were coming around the building to search for the people who had been in the accident. Trick vanished and appeared in the trees on the other side of the parking lot. This took her back towards the city a little ways. She disappeared again and appeared another few hundred feet down the road. Once the sound of the sirens had faded, three translocations later, she paused.

[How are we going to find Dylan and Eddy again? Our phone doesn't work here,] Trick asked Anabelle.

[We should try the tree on the other side of the city. We said we would meet them back there if we all got separated.]

[I have no idea where that even was.]

Trick floated slowly back towards the city.

[The werewolf will remember how to get there.]

[What?]

[Oh, what I mean is, we have access to different senses when we use different forms. If you change back to the werewolf, I can use its senses to remember how to get back to the tree.]

Trick initiated the magic, and they changed back to the werewolf. Anabelle could tell that Trick was getting better at controlling their magic. She could feel Trick's surprise that she had done that transformation instead of Anabelle doing it for them. It wasn't always best to do it that way, but the less Trick had to depend on Anabelle, the better. It was faster that way, and sometimes speed counted.

[Okay. Turn in a circle and keep your nose up in the air.]

[Okay,] responded Trick reluctantly.

She did what Anabelle said, keeping her nose up and slowly spinning clockwise in a circle, taking little steps to the right with her front paws and to the left with her hind paws. Finally, after she turned almost all the way around, Anabelle spoke inside of her head.

[It's this way.]

[How far?]

Trick felt that mental shrug from Anabelle. She didn't know exactly how far it was.

[Just go. It won't take us too long to get there.]

Trick went. She had been running for about five minutes when her stomach began to growl. It was well past noon, and the last time she had eaten anything was that morning at Nascha's.

[Does doing a lot of magic make us hungry?] asked Trick curiously.

[Sure it does. Every time we use our Aura, it uses magic energy, but there's no limit on that. But we use up little bits of our own energy to get the magic to do what we want. Eventually, we get tired and hungry. Just like running around playing all day makes you tired and hungry. We use the same kind of energy get the magic to do what we want.]

Trick tried to run in as straight a line as possible, but the city got in the way. They had to dodge around houses and zip down streets, much to the dismay of the people who saw her. After the first few minutes, she thought she had gotten completely out of the city. Then they came to a collection of buildings that Trick realized was a school of some sort. She ran all the way around the outside of it to avoid running into anyone there, but people still saw her. Some even took out their cell phones and held them up, trying to take pictures of her, she thought. As soon as she saw that, she sped up to her fastest run. She didn't know if it would keep them from taking any pictures of her, but she was sure it wouldn't hurt.

Trick was running so fast that when Dylan popped into existence at the other side of a field she was running across, she almost didn't have enough time to stop. She gave a little hop, and then spun her body violently midair. She dug her claws into the ground, and leaned her whole body forward to slow herself down. She ground to a halt only a few feet away from Dylan. Her paws were bruised and the pads of them were a little cut up by the time she got stopped. She danced from one set of paws to the other, turning in a circle to face Dylan again.

"Oh God, I'm sorry, Trick! I didn't mean to do that," Dylan said, gritting his teeth, trying not to laugh at the sight of an enormous, terrifying, werewolf dancing in a circle like its paws were on fire. She gave him a look, and relayed a message through Anabelle and Tigs that she couldn't change back until the cuts in her paws healed.

"That's Okay," Dylan said.

He came tentatively closer, and Trick laid her ears flat at him in displeasure. He shouldn't be scared of her. It's not like she was going to bite him. She relayed this sentiment to him through Anabelle and Tigs again. Dylan eyed her.

"You're the size of a freaking polar bear, your teeth are longer than my hand, and I'm pretty sure you could eat my freaking head in one bite. It doesn't matter that I know it's you inside of there, Trick. You're freakin' scary, and you're never going to convince my brain otherwise."

Dylan walked around to one side of her and put his hand on her flank. They both vanished. After two teleportations, they appeared next to the tree where Eddy was sitting reading a book.

"Finally found her, eh?" Eddy piped up.

"Oh, it took me a whole hour to find her in a giant city! What an incredible waste of your time!" Dylan snarked. Eddy laughed.

"Alright, fine, I deserved that."

He closed his book and slid it into the small backpack he was carrying. A flash of blue light later, Anabelle and Trick emerged. Surprisingly, Trick looked a lot more like her normal self than she had in days. All of the fur and feline features were gone.

"Hey, you look a lot more normal! I thought you said after the transformation last night, it would be a couple more days?" Eddy said.

"I still have the tail and ears. You just can't see them," Trick said. She pulled her purple boonie hat a little further down to make sure her ears were hidden.

"I said it would be a couple more days for all of the magic to fade away. But it bleeds off slow. Every time we do a new transformation to something we haven't done before, it adds more in, but at the same time, it's always leaking out. Eventually, we'll have done enough new forms that it'll be pretty rare that Trick ends up looking off in her normal shape, unless she wants to," Anabelle said.

"What does that mean, unless she wants to?"

"It means we can figure that out later after we get all this cleared up. What happened to Bruce?"

"Well, Eliani said that we needed to take him somewhere far away from people, so I jumped us to a place I like to go to be alone in the Himalayas."

"Where?" Trick choked. "I thought you said the only time you had gone any place else was when you went to see the Fairies." Dylan scratched the back of his head uneasily.

"I guess I didn't want to tell you everything. I didn't know if you guys were my friends yet," Dylan admitted sheepishly.

"He's got a cave full of stolen stuff!" Eddy said enthusiastically. Dylan's expression went sour.

"I didn't take it all from one place! And I didn't steal almost any of it!" Dylan objected. Eddy eyed him skeptically. "I didn't!" he protested loudly.

"You'd be surprised how much stuff people leave behind accidentally when you can check a few thousand campsites all over the world every day. I got most of the money completely honestly, by returning stolen wallets to people in places where there's a lot of pickpockets. People give me rewards. I can make a couple thousand dollars in a day doing it if I go someplace where there are lots of thieves," Dylan said.

"Where did you learn to do that?" Eddy asked. Dylan just shrugged.

"How I learned everything in the last year since I got Tigs. By going places and watching people," Dylan said.

"Doesn't it bother your parents?" Trick asked. Dylan's face went from good natured annoyance to scowling anger almost instantly.

"My parents don't care where I'm or what I'm doing. I told you before. They couldn't care less about me," he said angrily.

"Whoa." Trick held up her hands defensively. "What did I say?"

Dylan sighed. "Alright, look, I know I'm only like a year older than you guys, but my parents don't care about me. They only care about my sisters, so I do everything for myself. Tigs is the only good thing that ever happened to me. Can we please stop talking about them now?"

Tigs looked at him and then flopped backwards so that she was lying across his shoulder. Trick looked confused.

"See? I told you they wouldn't get it."

"Why would they do that?" Eddy asked.

"How should I know? They just do!" He didn't yell, but it wasn't far from it.

"Okay, I'm sorry, Dylan. I didn't know." Trick made a calming gesture. Dylan took a deep breath, and Tigs sat up on his shoulder. She patted a plush paw against his cheek.

"Well, now you do," Dylan said much more calmly.

"When we get back, we'll help," offered Trick.

"Thanks, Trick. What did you do with those guys?"

"I ate them." She said with a completely straight face.

Eddy looked stunned, and Dylan's mouth fell open and he goggled at her. She burst out laughing.

"I talked to them, which is why I'm back here. They were trying to take Bruce because there's a sick girl who needs his help or she's going to die." Trick took the piece of paper from her pocket. "We need to go here so I can help her." Eddy seemed to accept what she was saying, but Dylan looked on with disbelief.

"They tried to kill you! You should've eaten them." Trick made a gross face.

"Yeah but she didn't, Dylan. This girl is just like us, and she's sick. I can use the Bear's magic to make her better. No one ever has to know we were there."

Eddy took the piece of paper and fiddled with the new phone that Dylan had gotten.

"This place is about three hundred miles away. South." Eddy showed Dylan the map he pulled up, but Tigs showed more interest than Dylan. She put her paw on the screen and traced the line.

"She says we can get there in three or four jumps." Dylan looked at Tigs long and hard. "What do you mean? I don't feel any different." Tigs made a little shrugging motion with her paws.

"She says our magic is getting stronger. She can feel if we're going in the right direction, now. If we tell her where we want to go, we don't need to stop to check where we are anymore," Dylan explained.

"But you didn't do that when we went to Arizona," Eddy said.

"Yeah I did. I brought us in lower so I could see landmarks. You guys didn't see them, but I was looking for certain things, and if I hadn't found them, I would have had to stop. But Tigs tells me we don't have to do that anymore. She'll always be able to tell where we are," Dylan relayed.

"Great, let's go then. The faster we get this done, the faster we can get back to help Bruce," Trick said. Dylan sighed in defeat.

"Alright." Dylan reached up and plucked Tigs off his shoulder, holding her out. She turned her head almost all the way around to glare up at him. It was surprisingly creepy.

[*I can get down myself, you know,*] Tigs grumbled in annoyance. She was sick of being tossed about.

"Alright, fine, you can get down yourself. I'm just trying to help. I know it isn't easy for you to move, you cranky little thing."

She turned her head back around, and folded her little arms.

[*I'm tired of this stupid body, and the stupid name your stupid sister called me, and the stupid fact that I can't talk like everyone else! Even the stupid bird can talk! I could just move myself with our magic,*] Tigs complained.

Dylan rolled his eyes. "I wish I could help you, Tigs, but this is the only way I know how. If you went teleporting yourself everywhere, we would be exhausted in no time."

[*Fine, but let me do it myself sometimes. I'm not a toy.*] Dylan looked a little annoyed now.

"What has gotten into you? I never think of you as a toy," Dylan said.

"You uh…" Trick pointed at Dylan and then Tigs. "You two know that we can only hear half the conversation?" Tigs just held out her little paws plaintively at Trick.

"Well I didn't force you to use my little sister's stuffed tiger for a body!" Dylan shouted.

"What's the matter with you two?" Trick asked.

"She's upset she's stuck in this body, and we've been sort of tossing her around like she's actually a stuffed animal," Dylan explained.

"Oh. Well, I guess I get that." Trick took Tigs. Then instead of putting Tigs up on her shoulder, she held her up, and let her climb across on her own.

"Maybe when we learn more, we can help you," Trick said.

Eddy put his arm around Trick's shoulder. Dylan's magic picked them all up and they vanished. The teleportation went incredibly fast this time. They appeared and vanished a half a dozen times in the space of a few seconds. They then appeared on the side of a street, much to the dismay of the people standing around it. Everyone had frozen, staring at the three children and two Figments that had just appeared in their midst.

"Shoot, too close," Dylan said. Then they vanished again. They appeared a second later, standing in a small back yard surrounded by a fence. There was a swing set tucked into the corner of the small back yard that faced the porch of a small white house. Apparently, no one was home because they stood tentatively for a few minutes and no one came out of the house.

"Where are we?" Trick asked. Dylan looked at Tigs for a minute. Then Anabelle, who had taken up a spot on top of Trick's head squishing her hat down a little, spoke up.

"I don't know, but I smell bacon," Anabelle said.

"And what good does that do us?" Trick asked dubiously.

"I'm hungry?" Anabelle trilled.

"Later, after you find a food other than bacon."

"I don't think I want any food other than bacon," Anabelle retorted. Trick laughed.

"You're gonna get fat if that's all you eat," Trick joked.

"Tigs thinks that we're pretty close to that address." Eddy took out his phone and started to fiddle with it, swiping his fingers across the screen rapidly.

"Well, at least the new phones still work here," Eddy mumbled. "We're only a few blocks away. We can probably just walk there."

"Which way, Eddy?" asked Trick.

Eddy pointed at the house. "Back out that way and to the right."

Dylan teleported them out onto the street. Thankfully, there was no one around right then to see them. They walked down the street, and Eddy noticed Trick's striped tail peaking out from beneath her dress.

"Trick, your tail?" Eddy said.

"I just need to stretch it. Keeping it wrapped around my waist sort of makes it cramped." She curled it around her waist under her dress again. "Besides, it's not like they won't notice Anabelle." Trick pointed up at Anabelle, who was spinning lazy figure eights over her head, having vacated her comfy spot on top of Trick's hat. She seemed to notice that she was conspicuous and floated down between Trick and Eddy.

"Sorry," she said. Trick shrugged.

"I'm pretty sure I'm over it. Dylan's been right all along. We aren't going to keep it a secret forever," Trick said, but the way she said it Eddy wasn't so sure. The way people had reacted to her in Edinburgh made Eddy think that it was bothering her more than she was saying.

They trudged down the street and around the corner. The house they were looking for was on the next street over. They walked down the street, which was lined with big brick and stone houses. Sculpted hedges blocked some of the houses from the view of the street, but they could see the upper floors. The houses all seemed deserted, which probably meant that everyone was out working. Still, it made the street feel empty, and a little scary. After a moment, they found the house they were looking for.

The houses here were the same brick and stone structures. It was a little weird compared to home, where everything was vinyl sided, and most were only single-story. Here, everything seemed to have at least three floors. They walked across the street and started checking each of the houses. It was really hard to find the addresses on most of the houses, but they finally got it. The house was a huge three story one, and it too looked fairly deserted.

"I'll go in first. If someone is sick in there, then there have to be other people taking care of them," Dylan said. Eddy nodded in agreement.

"No, I should do it. You can teleport around, but it's bright and flashy. I can use the Cheshire Cat. It's quieter," Trick said. "Besides, if I can find her I can just do the magic and we can go." Dylan and Eddy exchanged a look, then Eddy shrugged.

"Hey, she's the one that can turn into a freaking bear the size of a boulder and has magic powers. I'm not trying to stop her," Eddy said.

"Just be careful. Those guys shot at you. I don't think anyone in there's gonna be good people," Dylan warned.

Trick nodded. She held up her hand for Tigs. who got up off her shoulder and walked onto her hand. She held her hand out to Eddy's shoulder, and Tigs climbed on. She took on the shape of the Cheshire Cat, and then faded away.

"So, what do we do?" Eddy asked.

"I'm gonna to go check on Bruce. I shouldn't be more than ten or fifteen minutes. I just hope that Trick doesn't come out of there with anyone on her tail," Dylan said, and then vanished. Eddy tried to stop Dylan, but he was already gone. Eddy started to mumble to himself.

"Stupid deaf, fast-teleporting doofus."

He sighed and put his pack down on the street. He leaned up against a light pole and started fiddling with his phone. He tried to watch the house at the same time he was looking down at the screen, so if anyone did see him, he wouldn't look out of place.

Not for the first time, he ran over everything they had been told in his head. He didn't understand why Coyote had sent them after Bruce. The Cheshire Cat that had sent them to the Navajo made some sense at least. It was pretty clear that Coyote had known more than he had told them about how kids got their Figments, but from what Eddy could tell, Bruce and Eliani had no more idea how they had been placed together than Trick and Anabelle did. He had a lot of questions, and not a whole lot of answers. The only thing he could think was that Coyote knew something about Eliani that they didn't. That was the first thing he was going to ask when they got back to the cave.

Trick appeared just inside of the front door of the huge house. She looked around, but didn't see anyone. Trick thought to Anabelle.

[Can we float through stuff without translocating?]

[You did it earlier. It just takes more practice with staying between this place and the other place,] replied Anabelle.

Trick concentrated and she felt the sensation of taking a tiny step backwards as she faded into that other place. She floated down the hallway and through an archway into a huge living room. Everything looked too fancy to sit on in here, and there was a massive flat television nearly covering one wall.

Through a door on the other side of the living room was a gorgeous kitchen filled with stainless steel appliances. Every flat surface was made of marble or stainless steel. The cupboards were flat white with stainless steel handles. There was someone in this room. It was an older woman with brown hair threaded through with grey. She had it pulled back in a neat ponytail. She was dressed in a dark blue dress with long sleeves. It had an ankle length skirt. Over it, she wore a flower print apron. Trick smelled something cooking in a pot on the stove. Her nose in this form wasn't as good as the werewolf, but she knew it was chicken soup. The woman turned around quickly and looked around.

"Is anyone here?" she asked.

Trick floated past her and out of the door back into the hallway. She looked back into the room, and woman was still standing there, looking around. She finally shook her head, turning back to the stove and picking up a ladle. She started to stir whatever was in the pot on the stove. There was a stairway that went somewhere onto a second floor, but there were two other archways on the opposite side of the hallway.

One went into a big room with huge windows that curved up to become the ceiling as well. She came back out of the room and floated towards the remaining archway on this floor. Before she could go inside, the woman from the kitchen came out into the hallway. She was carrying a bowl of what Trick was now certain was chicken soup. Trick almost ignored her, but then she wondered who the soup was for. Trick spun around as the woman was about halfway up the stairs.

[Whenever I'm sick, chicken soup is the best.]

[Sure?] Anabelle said skeptically.

Trick followed the woman up the stairs to the second floor, then up another set to the third floor. Up on the top floor of the house, there was a hallway with four doors off of it. The woman went to the second door on the right. She opened the door, and Trick slipped through as soon as she did. She stopped just inside the door.

The room was twice the size of her bedroom back home. It was decorated in bright pinks and yellows. The bed was a huge four poster that Trick imagined a princess sleeping in. The girl in it didn't look like a princess, though. Trick could only see her face because a pink comforter adorned in yellow flowers covered her up to her neck. She had long, pale blonde hair that was almost white. Her cheeks and eyes were sunken. There was a tall metal stand to one side of the bed with plastic bags hanging from the top with liquid in them. Tubes ran from the bags under the covers. There was also a softly beeping box about halfway up the pole like Trick had seen when her grandma had been in the hospital last year.

Trick thought that the girl was around her age, but she looked much older than that. Trick fretted about what to do for a moment. The girl was asleep now, and that would be best for her to do her magic with the Bear. It looked like the woman was about to wake her up to give her something to eat. Trick didn't want to wait too long because Eddy and Dylan were waiting. But now that she knew where the girl was, she could come straight back to this room. Trick was about to translocate outside when she realized that she was getting an odd feeling. It was something she had been feeling every time she went invisible in the Cheshire Cat body.

[BelleBelle, why do I feel like I'm not supposed to be here?] Trick asked.

[I'm not sure you'll understand the explanation to that.]

[Can you tell me anyway?]

Trick watched as the woman helped the girl sit up in bed by propping her up with a number of extra pillows.

[Because Cheshire Cats step out of our universe and into another one when they disappear or translocate. The magic specifically allows them to stay in that universe for as long as they want, but we aren't part of that universe. So it's constantly trying to push us back to our reality. That's why when you translocate, it feels like you are getting squeezed through a small space. You can only make hole that is exactly big enough to get your body through it.]

[You were right. I don't really understand all of that,] Trick said with a little mental laugh, *[but I sort of get it, I think. Like trying to squeeze through a bunch of hedges.]*

[Yeah, sort of. We should go. This is gonna take a while.]

Trick concentrated on that feeling of stepping backwards, and thought about the street outside where they had started. She felt the squeezing sensation, and then she popped out on the street. Eddy looked up from his phone.

"Hey Trick, did you find her?" Trick floated closer, rolling onto her back, looking at Eddy's phone upside-down. "Why do you do that?" Trick made a little upside-down shrugging motion.

"Nothing looks quite right when I'm right-side-up in this body," Trick said. "I found her, but there's a woman taking care of her. I'm just waiting for her to go away. Where's Dylan?"

"He went to check on Bruce."

"Alright."

They waited a few long, boring minutes with Trick floating in lazy figure eights around the light pole that Eddy was leaning up against before Dylan popped out of a flash of white light near the end of the street. Tigs was riding on his shoulder, swinging her tiny legs. Trick floated down from her figure eights.

She was about to ask Dylan how Bruce was when someone shouted from behind her. Trick immediately took that little step back into that other place. She spun around, and found a police officer coming down the street towards them. He had a hard accent that made him hard to understand.

"Oy, what are you kids doin'?" he said, but it took Trick a long moment to puzzle it out.

[Can Dylan and Eddy hear me while I'm invisible?]

[Yep, but it'll be like a whisper, so you have to get close to them.]

She floated closer to them. "Just pop around the block a few times. I'll wait in the house until the old woman leaves the girl alone."

Dylan nodded. He grabbed Eddy's arm, and they vanished. Trick floated closer to the police officer as he stopped when they disappeared in a flash of light. His mouth dropped open, and then he immediately looked around, completely agog.

"What the bloody hell was that?"

He went to where Eddy and Dylan had been standing. He went down to one knee and touched the concrete sidewalk. Trick floated away from him and back towards the house. She concentrated on the magic, and then she squeezed through to the other side of the door. She floated up the stairway, and then stopped at the end of the hall. She wasn't sure what would happen if the woman walked through where she was floating.

[*Nothing would happen. We aren't part of her world right now. She would walk right through the spot,*] Anabelle advised.

Trick still floated to one side of the hallway. A few minutes later, the woman came out of the little girl's room carrying a nearly full bowl of soup. She was shaking her head, and she looked very worried. Trick floated past her, and then translocated through the closed door. When she appeared on the other side of the door, she was careful to stay in the other place so that no one would see her. It was a good thing she did, because the girl was still propped up in her bed.

She was awake and watching cartoons on a big TV on the wall across the room. Trick sighed in frustration. It would have been much easier to do this with the girl asleep. She couldn't stay invisible and make the girl better. She had to be the Bear to use the healing magic. She flew across the room and spun around so that her face was just above the girl's head. She still didn't make herself visible yet. She wasn't sure what to say to put the girl at ease.

"Hello. Can you hear me?" Trick asked. The girl tensed a little and looked around the room.

"Y-yes?" She asked skeptically.

"Good. My name is Trick, and I'm here to make you better, but you can't scream or tell anyone I was here."

The girl looked up, zeroing in on the direction of Trick's voice. "How come I can't see you?" The girl had a similar accent to the police office outside.

"Because I didn't want to scare you before you knew I was here. Promise you won't scream?" Trick asked.

The little girl nodded. Trick floated down beside the bed, and then concentrated on that feeling of taking a small step

forward. She felt herself fade into view. The girl took a deep
breath, and Trick zipped forward. She put her front paws over
the girl's mouth.

"You promised!" Trick said. The girl looked up at her, and
then nodded. Trick floated away.

"You're a Cheshire Cat!" the girl said. It was louder than a
whisper, but still hushed.

"Not really. I can just be one. Actually, I'm just a kid like
you. A kid with a Figment." Trick took her human shape and
made sure to keep her tail and ears under her clothing. "See,
just like you."

Trick felt the miniscule weight of Anabelle on top of her
head. She had flopped herself over the hat, letting her paws
hang off in the front and back. Trick pointed up at her. "This
is my Figment, Anabelle. She's going to help make you
better." Anabelle lifted one of her paws and waved to the girl.

"Hi!" Anabelle trilled. The girl's eyes went really wide.
She squeezed the top of the covers in her fists, and grinned.

"A real Figment!"

"What's your name?" Trick asked.

"Elemindrada, but everyone just calls me Mindy."

"Okay, Mindy, what's making you sick?" Trick asked.

Mindy's expression melted into a deep frown that made
her face look a little scary.

"I've got Large Cell Non-Hodgkin's Lymphoma," she said,
but her voice changed as though she had heard someone else
say it so many times that she was merely copying their words.

[Can the Bear fix that?] Trick had no idea what that all
meant.

Anabelle's telepathic response was a firm nod. *[The Bear's
healing magic can fix anything as long as the person is still alive, but
it's gonna use a lot of magic. We're gonna be really tired
afterwards.]*

[Will we still be able to change back to the Cat so we can leave?]
Trick asked.

[Sure. We can always do that.]

"We're going to make you better, Mindy," Trick started just
as she caught the sound of footsteps just outside of the door.

Quick as thought, the blue flash of light came, and she took the shape of the Cheshire Cat. Trick darted to the corner of the room behind the door. She held her paw up to her huge mouth in a shushing gesture, and then stepped back into the other place just out of sight. The woman from earlier opened the door to look in on Mindy.

"How are you feeling dear? Did I hear you talking to someone?" the woman asked.

"A little better. No, just the TV. I'll turn it down," she said.

"That's fine dear. So strange. I could have sworn I heard someone."

The woman shrugged and backed out of the room, closing the door. Trick was suspicious, though, and floated to the room door. She squeezed through the other place and appeared in the hallway outside. There, she found the woman with her ear pressed against the door listening to the little girl watch television. Annoyed, Trick pushed through the other place and appeared in the kitchen downstairs. She noticed something she hadn't before, and her Cheshire grin spread from ear to ear.

She looked around for something heavy enough to accomplish her mischief, but light enough that the cat would be strong enough to swing hard. Hanging in a square above the island in the middle of the kitchen were over a dozen pots and pans. All Trick needed was something heavy to bang them with. They would all make such a racket that it would not only scare the woman upstairs trying to eavesdrop half to death, but it would bring her racing downstairs to see what was going on.

Trick found it a moment later, a big stainless-steel spoon holder next to the stove. She snatched it up by the curved handle and zipped up to the pots and pans. She spun in a circle grinning like a maniac and smashed it into a huge copper pot on the end. It let out a deafening sharp metallic bang of sound that echoed through the house. Then the predictable cacophony of noise followed. Trick zoomed back to the countertop and put the spoon holder right back where she had found it. Then, she faded back into the other place until she squeezed through and popped out in Mindy's room upstairs. She could hear the woman banging down the stairs to see what was going on. She appeared next to Mindy's bed and changed back to human form.

"I don't think I have a lot of time. Don't be scared. I have to change into another Figment to make you better. It's big, and I'm going to have to put a really big scary looking paw on top of you to make ya better. I promise you'll feel all better when I'm done," Trick explained quickly. It seemed to flow right by Mindy, but she nodded a little like she had heard.

"What did you do?" the girl asked, wide eyed.

"I shook the pot holder thing hanging in the kitchen so all the pots banged together like a big huge noise maker." Mindy giggled. "You ready?" Mindy nodded her head, and Trick changed to the Bear.

She sat very still, trying to get a grip on how her huge body worked. Mindy drew a deep breath, but she just let it out slowly as her eyes roved over Trick's massive body. Trick finally got things worked out, and she lifted one huge paw. Mindy cringed a little when she saw all the claws, but she pulled on a brave face. She nodded, and Trick put her paw down gently on top of Mindy's blanket above where her chest was.

[How do we do this?] Trick asked.

[I'll help, and next time, you'll remember how to do it,] Anabelle said.

Trick felt an odd cool, calming presence flowing through her mind. She closed her eyes and let Anabelle control things.

[The Bear's magic is a calm thing, so you have to empty out all the thoughts in your head to let it in. Just sort of let the inside of your head drift without thinking about anything.]

Trick did what Anabelle said, and suddenly she felt something warm inside of her chest. It spread through her body. When she opened her eyes, all of the colorful markings in her fur were glowing softly. The three bands of color around the leg on Mindy's chest were the brightest, and then they dimmed as the magic flowed out of her body through that paw. Mindy actually glowed for a long moment in a soft blue. TrIck took her paw away and let out a deep breath.

Mindy looked incredibly better than she had. Her face still had that sunken look, but the dark bags under her eyes had faded away. She lifted her hands and looked at them.

"I feel good!" Mindy said excitedly.

Trick switched back to her human form. "You still look pretty thin," Trick said unhappily.

Mindy shook her head. "But…" Mindy's eyes filled with tears. "I haven't felt good ever since before they told me I was sick."

She threw off her bedcovers. Underneath, she was wearing a long dressing shirt that hung all the way to her ankles. It had multicolored ponies all over it. She swung her legs out of bed, and Trick noticed how bad she really had looked under all of that. Her arms were terribly thin, but she threw them around Trick's neck.

"Thank you, thank you, thank you…" Mindy cried as she hugged Trick with surprising strength for how frail she looked.

[She's so happy,] Anabelle said into Trick's mind.

[She's been sick. I haven't ever been sick for more than a few days, but it was awful. I don't know how anyone could lay in bed sick for longer than that,] Trick replied. She put her arms around Mindy, and hugged her back. Mindy reached up, and petted Anabelle with one of her hands.

"You're welcome. But Mindy, I have to go. I can't stay, or we're both going to be in trouble."

Trick carefully extricated herself from Mindy's hug and then helped the girl back into bed. Mindy tried to wipe the tears off of her face, but they kept trickling out of her eyes.

"Will you come back?" Mindy asked. Trick grinned and then took on the shape of the cat.

"If you want me to, I'll try." The slow melodic tones of her cat voice seemed to soothe Mindy now.

"I'd like that," she said.

Trick concentrated on her magic and faded away into the other place. Then she thought about it a little harder, and translocated to the spot on the street outside.

[That felt really good,] Anabelle said.

[Yeah, but it took so much magic to make one person better. That seems like it's a really little good.]

Eddy and Dylan popped out of his flash of white light. They looked around a little frantically.

"That cop has been walking around here ever since we left, trying to find us. Let's go," Dylan said.

Trick floated over and landed herself on Eddy's shoulder opposite Tigs. They vanished into Dylan's magic.

They appeared in the cave that Eddy had talked about earlier. It was freezing even with Trick's fur, and she immediately migrated towards the warmth of the propane heater that Dylan had left for Bruce.

"He's still having some trouble," Eliani said from her spot crouched on the back of Bruce's chair.

"It hurts not being able to go to them," Bruce said.

"I can help," Trick said, becoming a Null Imp.

[I really don't know how this works,] Trick projected mentally to Anabelle.

[Don't worry. I'll help you. This'll actually help us get back some of what we lost healing Mindy,] Anabelle said, and then Trick felt cold for a moment. Soon, she felt quite warm as energy started to trickle into her body from Dylan and Bruce.

[Can we do it just for Bruce?] Trick asked. Anabelle replied with a telepathic negative.

[Not really. If you stand on the other side of him, though, we can make the circle small enough that Dylan won't be in it.]

Trick turned and took a moment to get her balance. The Null Imp's shape required her to lean pretty far forward to walk comfortably. Her front talons were nearly touching the floor as she walked around to the other side of Bruce. She crouched there, which was much more comfortable than sitting down in this form. Her tail balanced her. The biggest problem with spending a whole bunch of time in this form was that she couldn't talk. The Null Imp literally didn't have a mouth. She would have to relay messages through Anabelle to Tigs to Dylan before they would get anywhere. Still, clearly she was having an effect because Bruce was perking up.

"Hey, it's working!" Eliani exclaimed. Bruce was holding his head.

"The voice is gone. What did you do?"

"Trick is making it so magic doesn't work here right now. While she does, your Figment Eliani is going to try to explain how to control your magic." Eddy replied.

Eliani began talking, but it wasn't long before she went silent. Bruce kept nodding, but it was clear they were communicating telepathically. It seemed like every Figment could do that with the person they belonged with. Dylan looked at his watch, and then moved to the racks. He took down two battery-powered lanterns and turned them on.

"These ones are gonna go dead."

Dylan turned off the two lanterns that were lighting the area around the heater and put down the two new ones. "It's getting late, and I'm getting hungry."

[Trick says she's hungry too,] Tigs relayed.

"I could use some food," Eddy said.

"Bruce, you hungry?"

"Eliani, too."

"Anyone gotta use the bathroom?" Dylan asked. Everyone except Eddy shook their heads.

"Where we goin'?" Eddy asked.

"I figured we'd go back to Nascha's house first. She might not have food for us, but we can use the bathroom there." Eddy nodded in agreement. Before they could run off Trick thought to Anabelle.

[Hold on, can Eliani hear us? Otherwise, we aren't going to be able to talk very much,] Trick asked.

Anabelle sent a message to Tigs to tell Dylan to hold on for a moment. Then she concentrated on trying to make a mental connection with Eliani. The big white bird sat up immediately and looked at Trick.

[She can hear us. She actually says now that he can't hear his magic telling him about all the sick people, it's going well,] Anabelle said.

She relayed a message to Dylan that he and Eddy could get going. They backed up all the way to the other side of the cave so Dylan could use his magic, and then they disappeared in the typical flash of white light.

[It is so super weird not having a mouth,] Trick said.

[Null Imps are solitary, but they do have some telepathic capability if you practice it. Telepathy is super hard to do if you don't practice a lot, though. That's why I do it for you, and not all

Figments can do it, so you wouldn't always have the power to do it,]
Anabelle explained.

[So you're trying to tell me I should just let you do it?]

[Yep!] Anabelle said brightly, and Trick let out a mental
groan of annoyance. *[Eliani says that soon Bruce is going to have
to go someplace with people to test out what she is trying to teach
him.]*

*[Does that mean we can change out of this creepy no-mouthed
body?]*

*[Not yet. She says she needs a little more time, and this Figment
can be really useful. Not only does it eat magic, but it can use its
magic to destroy things completely without a trace. It's a very
powerful Figment.]*

Trick shivered a little.

[I don't want to destroy anything.]

[No, I mean,] Anabelle paused as she thought about how to
explain. *[Look at the guy with the gun earlier. You had to bite him
to get him to drop it. In this body, we could have just made the gun
not exist. We wouldn't have had to hurt him or worry about
throwing the gun away.]*

*[I get it. Well sort of. We would have to be awful careful with
something like that though, or someone could get hurt.]*

*[Sure, but that doesn't mean we should just never use this
Figment again.]*

*[But it's so gross and scary. Look at the claws, and it doesn't
even have a mouth. Big creepy silver bug eyes and this goofy tail
that I could actually sit on. And my skin feels like I'm wearing
cardboard boxes. It looks so weird.]*

Anabelle gave her a mental eye roll.

*[Actually, most Null Imps do learn to coil them and sit on them.
Your skin feels so weird because the Imp doesn't really have skin. It
has an armored hide. You never complained about having armored
hide when we were the drake.]*

[You're not helping.]

[Besides, Bruce doesn't look like he's scared of us.]

That was when Trick looked up and found that both Eliani
and Bruce were watching her. She held her long clawed talons
up in a little shrugging motion as if to say 'What?'

"Well, I just wanted say thanks. That voice in my head, the one that tells me there are sick people that need my help. It wouldn't ever go away. Not even when I was trying to sleep. I couldn't hear anything else until you and your friends came to help. So even when you do look like a scary alien monster, you're still the coolest person we've ever met."

[See told you so.] Anabelle said.

[Quiet, you.]

"Can you come a little closer? This is the first time I've seen a… " He paused. "well, whatever you are."

Trick moved a little closer, stepping fully into the light. She hadn't wanted to scare him, so she had stayed mostly behind one of the chairs that Dylan had set up. She peeked around it now, putting her talons around it so that she had a better sense of it since it was hard to see for her. She couldn't really see the light. The gray shapes of tables, chairs, and other non-magical things loomed out of a hazy background in her sight. The two battery-powered lanterns had two tiny pin pricks of white where the light would normally come from.

Bruce and Eliani, though, were two shapes made of coruscating colors, green and blue at the center followed by a wide band of white around it, and then a hazier, more nebulous blue that filled out to the edge of their silhouettes. He shivered when he got a better look at her, and she almost drew back as she did not want to scare him.

"No, it's ok."

She noticed he had an accent too, though it wasn't like Mindy's. Trick had an aunt and uncle from Tennessee that talked like Bruce did.

"You've just got really big claws. Like an eagle. I saw an eagle at a fair once with big ol' claws like that."

Eliani lifted one of her talons and looked at it. Then she clutched it at Bruce.

"Yeah, they're like yours. Anyway, thanks. You can turn the magic back on now if you like. I think I've got a handle on how to," Bruce looked at Eliani

"Disable your magical senses," Eliani squawked.

"That."

Trick was about to switch back when she realized something about the Null Imp. It didn't have a nose or a mouth.

[How are we breathing?] Trick asked Anabelle.

[We're not.]

Trick became alarmed.

[You mean we've been not breathing all this time? How are we alive?]

Trick became a little frantic.

[Relax. Null Imps don't need to breath. The magic they take in fuels their bodies. The environment around them has enough magic in it to keep them alive if they can't take in big sources of magic, but that's why you usually only find them near places where there are lots of other Figments. So they don't go hungry. They're just as alive as you and me. They just live a little different way,] Anabelle explained. A moment later, Trick changed back to her human form.

"I know you didn't really see me earlier, but this is what I really look like. My real name is Teresa, but my friends call me Trick."

"Well, I'm Bruce, and this is Eliani, but you already know that. How do you know that?"

"Well, that's a long story. Someone told us that you needed help, and that we could help."

Dylan and Eddy popped back into the cave.

"Alright, so Nascha said that if we wanted to eat, we should bring Bruce and go back to her house. How is he?" Dylan asked.

"We are much better," Eliani croaked.

"That's good," Dylan said.

"Bruce, this is Dylan and Eddy. They're my two best friends, and they were the ones that brought you here."

"Where are we anyway?"

"Do you know where you were this morning?" Dylan asked.

"Not exactly. I know I wasn't in the United States anymore. We flew across the ocean and landed somewhere. I could only really hear the voice telling me that there were a lot of sick people that needed help where we were going."

"But why here? I mean where are you from in the United States?" Eddy asked.

"Texas. I live in a city called Tyler." Bruce said.

"So if it's sick people, you must have gone past dozens of hospitals full of sick people to get here. There are places with tons more sick people than here. Why here?" Eddy asked again.

Bruce just shrugged. Even Eliani didn't seem to have an answer for that, and she should know a lot more about how their power worked than Bruce did. Eddy groaned.

"Alright, so Eliani, what do you know about how kids get Figments?"

"Oh, everything!" Eliani hooted. "I was one of the Spelled in the last age!"

"Well, at least Coyote was right about that," Eddy groaned. Eliani shrank back.

"You talked to Coyote?" she croaked unhappily.

"Yessss?" Trick drew out the word uncertainty.

"What did he say?" Eliani asked. Trick, Dylan, and Eddy all exchanged looks.

"What do you think he said?" asked Eddy slyly. Eliani narrowed her silvery eyes.

"I may look like a bird, but I'm not an idiot."

"Okay, I'm sorry. He just said that you and Bruce needed our help, and that you'd be able to tell us how people get Figments." They all stood there expectantly for a long minute.

"I'll tell you how it happens, but I'm starving and you said there is someplace we can get food?"

"Sure, we made a friend in Arizona. We helped her stop a…" Dylan paused not sure if he should say what it was. "…monster," he finished lamely. Eliani stared at him.

"It'll be a good place for Bruce to test his powers, too. Not a lot of people there," Trick said.

Bruce shook his head.

"No, we can't go yet. We flew all the way here for that hospital, and we have to fix the sick people there," Bruce said. "Can you take us back there first?" Dylan shrugged.

"Sure I can, but let's go, already. My stomach is gonna eat the rest of me pretty soon."

Tigs rolled her embroidered eyes exaggeratedly on his shoulder. "Sorry, this is Tigs. She's my Figment. She's a drama queen." Tigs waved and gave her plush grin. He held up his hand to Tigs, who got up off of his shoulder and walked onto his hand. He held her out to Eddy. She climbed across onto Eddy's shoulder. Trick took Eddy's hand.

"So how does your magic work?" Bruce asked. He got up from his chair and held out his arm. Eliani climbed carefully onto his arm to make sure her talons didn't bite into it.

"Everyone has to be touching, but it's best to get a good grip and hold on tight. Just grab my hand, and don't let go for anything," Dylan said. "If you fall down or throw up when we stop, don't worry. Not everyone does well with teleporting the first time."

They appeared first in a forest, then, in a half a dozen quick flashes of images, they were standing on the street across from the hospital. Bruce stood for a long moment, taking deep breaths.

"You Okay?" Trick asked.

"Yes, just feel like I left my stomach back in that cave."

"How does your magic work?" Trick asked.

"Um, well, it's kinda..." Bruce trailed off. "I usually do it as a bird. It's easier. I have to scent all the sick people I'm going to heal. Their smell is a little tiny piece of them. Then my magic pulls all the sickness out of their body and into my body. Once it's inside of me, the magic makes it go away."

"Ok that sounds kinda..." Trick made a face like she was gonna be sick. Bruce gave a grim little smile. He nodded.

"It doesn't feel great, either. Thankfully, it passes in a few seconds. Our magic is really good at getting rid of nasty things."

"How many people can you do all at once like that?" Eddy asked. Bruce shrugged.

"A lot. The first time we used our magic, it made everyone better at the hospital in Tyler. Broken bones, cancer, even people who were dying of old age got better. At least, that was what my parents told me. It was about a week later that the magic voice in my head started," Bruce said.

They went across the street and waited at the edge of the driveway while cars left and came in.

"How do you get into all those hospital rooms? Don't people try to catch you when they see a big bird in the rooms?" Trick asked. Bruce shrugged.

"Only if they see us," Eliani squeaked. "They don't see us for the most part. That's why we just smell instead of doing it other ways. We don't have to go into the rooms to do that." She tilted her head and looked up at the building.

"Lots of open windows here," Bruce said, and Eliani gave him a very human nod.

"Other ways?" Trick asked.

"Sure. To make someone better, we need a little bit of the person inside of us. So we could lick everyone, or taste a tiny bit of their blood, but smells are easiest to get," Eliani squawked.

"Oh, gross!" Trick said, but then she remembered biting that man with the gun. When she was wearing the werewolf shape, it didn't taste all that gross. Bruce gave a little shrug.

"Not so bad when we're both in Eliani's body," he said, echoing her thoughts about the werewolf. "Still, she's right, smells are easiest."

"How are you? Is it still hurting?" Trick asked. Bruce smiled and shook his head.

"No, it doesn't even hurt when I turn the magic on now. I don't have to fight with it. That's why it hurt before, because I was trying to fight it off," Bruce explained. "Come on Eliani lets go."

Bruce's skin began to give off a slight white glow, and then he began to shrink. Eliani and he seemed to melt together, and then they both resolved into a much larger form of Eliani's body.

"I'll help. If anyone sees you, I'll distract them. This'll be fun!" Trick said.

"You're not leaving me and Eddy out of this!" Dylan exclaimed enthusiastically. Tigs gave a little thumbs-up from her perch on Eddy's shoulder. Trick took the shape of the Cheshire Cat, which was quickly becoming her favorite.

"Dylan, why don't you and Eddy just make a big flashy racket on every floor? I'll stay with Bruce so if anyone tries to grab him, I can help him," Trick suggested.

"We should do what she says. She's pretty good at getting away with making a mess," Eddy laughed.

"Alright, lets go. We'll make a racket all right," Dylan chuckled.

Bruce flapped his way up to the window, and Trick followed him by translocating into the room he was headed for. She didn't come fully back into the real world, though. She stayed in the other place, just watching what happened. Bruce didn't stay long. He actually decided to fly to all the open windows first. It didn't matter very much, because a few seconds later there was an enormous crashing sound from somewhere in the hospital. It was horrendous, and Trick could not imagine what Dylan and Eddy were up to. Whatever it was, it certainly got the attention of the hospital staff, because at least half of the nurses and doctors went scrambling down the hallways towards the stairwells at the front of the building.

Trick stayed with Bruce, though, translocating from room to room as he flew about the hospital. It only took him about fifteen minutes to get to all the rooms with open windows. He didn't stay at any of them for very long. That was good, because Trick noticed there were security guards swarming the halls now. "What had they done?" Trick wondered to herself. But when Bruce zipped in through one of the windows and didn't come back out, Trick immediately squeezed through the other place and came out in the room.

Bruce and Eliani were perched on top of one of the tall poles next to a hospital bed. He was waiting for her. Trick faded into view just long enough for him to spot her. He gave a little nod, and then swooped down and out of the door into the hospital proper. Trick followed him, but it looked like he really wasn't going to get spotted. Trick was waiting outside of a room with sliding glass doors when she saw a flash of white light down the hallway.

Dylan appeared there, sans Eddy. He looked around then vanished again. He came racing back a moment later with half a dozen security guards chasing him. He ran screaming at the top of his lungs towards the stairwell door. When he got to it, one of the security guards lunged for him, but caught only empty air as he vanished in a flash of light. The men all slammed into the door and wound up in a pile except the last one, who managed to stop in time to save himself. He stared at the pile of his fellow guards, and then grabbed at his radio.

"There are bloody demons in the hospital!" he said.

Trick could barely understand a single word of it through the man's thick accent. He started to help the other guards up. Trick started to laugh, but then watched as Bruce worked the sliding glass door open. He was in the room and back out in a second. He looked directly at where Trick would have been if she popped out into the real world.

[Eliani says that they're done here. Next floor.]

Things went on like that for almost half an hour. Every time the guards started to get themselves organized, Dylan or Eddy would come screeching through the halls, smash through them like a pile of bowling pins, and then vanish in a convenient burst of light. Trick still had no idea what the huge crashing noise was that had started the whole cacophony, but clearly it had stirred up the whole hospital like a hornets nest. Trick followed Bruce down a hallway on the main floor.

[Eliani says there's one more left. Their magic is telling them it's down this way.] Trick followed Bruce.

[I don't like this. There are no windows and stuff down here. No place to get away or hide. Can Tigs hear you?] Trick asked.

[Sure. I'll tell her where we are so that Dylan and Eddy can meet us down here.]

Trick followed Bruce down the hallway as he zoomed towards a set of double doors at the end. He back-winged and landed just outside the doors. He stuck his large beak in between the doors and shoved one of them open. Trick translocated to the other side of the door. Inside, there was a waiting room. A little boy was sleeping on a bed on wheels.

Unfortunately, there was also nurse in there with him. She looked up from fiddling with some tubing that was going into the little boy's arm. She spotted Bruce instantly, and then stared for a moment.

"That's the biggest damn bird I have ever seen!"

The woman had a thick accent that made her almost unintelligible, just like the security guard. She came around the bed and made like she was going to try and kick at Bruce. Trick faded into view.

"You should be nice to the pretty birdy. He's about to make your job a lot easier."

Trick grinned her Cheshire grin, and the woman yelped and jumped back. Bruce took the opportunity to hop up onto the railing of the bed. He nosed over the kid in the bed, and then looked up at the woman.

"Don't worry. When he wakes up, he's going to feel a lot better," he squeaked.

The woman looked back and forth between Trick and Bruce. Then, Dylan, Eddy, and Tigs appeared just inside the door in his signature flash of white light. "Oh my god, you're demons!" That was apparently more than the woman could tolerate. Her eyes rolled up into her head and she passed out. She collapsed to the floor, and Trick let out a little chuckle that she didn't mean to.

"Can we go now? I'm pretty sure we are going to be in a lot of trouble if anyone actually catches us," Eddy said.

"Chicken," Trick purred.

"Creeper," Eddy laughed. "Still, we made a pretty huge mess in one of the store rooms. I hope we aren't on any cameras anywhere."

Dylan shrugged. "We're from the other side of the planet, and no one knows we're here. Let's go."

Trick landed on Dylan's shoulder. Eddy closed his eyes and then held out his arm for Bruce and Eliani. They very carefully wrapped their talons around his arm. Everyone appeared on the street outside.

"Okay. I'm gonna do it. This is so much better than before. I can do it when I want to now," Bruce squawked.

His body began to glow like he was going to change shapes. Then the glow got a lot brighter. It wasn't white, either, but rather a soft yellow, like sunlight. It brightened until it was blinding, like it was going to fill the whole world with light. When it faded away, Bruce and Eliani's feathers had changed from white to shimmering gold. They were all staring when Bruce finally opened his eyes.

"Oh, yeah. Uh, we look like this for a while after we use our magic. I can't change back for a bit yet, either, or I'll puke all over the place. It takes time for the magic to get rid of all the problems," Bruce squeaked, sounding almost sheepish.

"How do we know it worked?" Trick asked.

"Because I wouldn't look like this if it didn't. I would still be white. Eliani says our feathers change color because of the magic we radiate when we get rid of all the sickness."

"Then, all those sick kids in there?" Eddy asked.

"Good as new," Bruce said.

"That's a lot of good as new," Eddy whispered in wonder. Then they noticed security guards spilling out of the doors of the building and into the driveway.

"Uh, we should probably go," Trick warned.

In a flash of light, they were gone.

They first appeared in the cave, but after a few quick teleportations, they were standing in Nascha's living room. They found the house quiet and empty. Clearly, Nascha had been called away for some reason, or maybe she had just gone into work. It was nearly eight o'clock where they had just been in Scotland, but here in Arizona, it was only two.

"When we were here earlier, Nascha was just getting ready to go to the clinic. She said there were leftovers in the refrigerator if we're hungry. She said we were responsible for the dishes too," Dylan said. He went directly to the fridge and pulled open the door, pulling out containers and setting them on the counter.

"So, what are we eating?" Trick asked.

Dylan shook his head. "I have no idea. She just said leftovers. She didn't say what they were. We really didn't give her time. We sort of just flew in here, used the bathroom, asked her for food, and then vanished before she had a chance to tell us anything more than leftovers." Dylan laughed. He had half a dozen containers out on the counter before he started popping them open.

"It looks like she made us sloppy joes and vegetables. I'll start heating things up. You want to tell us what we asked about earlier?" Dylan looked at Bruce and Eliani. Their feathers were still gold, though at the tips they were starting to bleed back to white.

"I'd like to hear the story too," Bruce's voice, heavily toned with birdlike squawk, came out first. Then Eliani's more female voice came from the bird's beak.

"It was a long time ago, and some of this is going to be hard for you kids to understand. I'll try to make it simple for you," Eliani said.

"Ok," Trick said, sitting down on the couch. Eddy stayed in the kitchen to help Dylan with the food.

"If you hadn't guessed yet, this isn't the first time that people have gotten magic powers. But last time, all the magic got used up, and we had to go back to the place between until more built up. I don't know exactly how that part of it works, but about fifteen hundred years ago, all of the magic from the last Emergence finally ran out.

It was used up by the last of the great wizards from the last Emergence. Once that happened, magic started building up in the real world again. It took all that time for it to build up to reach a new Emergence. That was how Figments got out into the world. Back then, they called us Familiars, Totem Spirits... there were a lot of different names. People weren't able to communicate as quickly as they can now, so in those days there were many different names," Eliani explained as Dylan and Eddy started putting out plates at the dining room table.

"Food's up. How long until you can change back?" Dylan asked.

Eliani lifted her wing and looked at the feathers. She stuck her beak into them, and twitched her head a little, putting some of the feathers back into place.

"It's probably going to be a couple of hours before we can change back. We can't change back until all of our feathers are white again."

"Okay, well, we'll make another plate for him when you two can separate."

"No bun for my meat, please. Just one less thing I have to peck apart before I can eat," Eliani said.

"How do you and Bruce switch out like that?" Trick asked. She was sort of curious. When she and Anabelle transformed, Anabelle was always sort of a passenger in the back of her mind. It would be a lot easier if she could just let Anabelle talk sometimes. Eliani just made a little shrugging motion with her wings.

"Can you let her control your body when you two are transformed?" Eliani asked as Dylan put a plate down for her.

"Sure."

"You just let her have full control. She'll be able to talk while you ride along," Eliani said.

"So, the other Emergence?" Dylan prompted. Eliani pecked at the veggies on her plate.

"Right. I'm getting to what you wanted to know. The first part was kind of important. So, the last Emergence ended, and with it, all of the magic went out of the world. I, like almost all of the magical folk, had to return to the place between. Because one of the humans did something. I don't know what that was, but I do know this much. As a familiar, I was placed with my partner by being one of the Spelled. A magic that is cast by The White God to link together a human with one of people of magic. In the last age, the powers given to us were chosen by the White God."

"And who is the White God?" Dylan asked. He bit into his sandwich and found it to be delicious.

"The White God is the living spirit of your world. They are responsible for being the gatekeeper for the place between and the real world. You can think of them as the most powerful Figment in reality. They choose each pairing of magical being with human partner."

They had all stopped eating.

"What would they want with us?" Trick asked. Eliani finished eating the small pile of green beans on her plate.

"I have no idea, but I know where you can go to find out." Eliani started in picking up the pile of spiced meat on the plate. "Oh, this is very good, much better than eating out of a McDonalds dumpster."

Dylan snorted and then began to cough violently as soda trickled out of his nose. Trick and Eddy were both laughing uncontrollably. Even Dylan's temporary pain couldn't stop him from laughing. Eliani looked around the table tilting her head curiously. "What did I say?" She squeaked. Trick finally wound down.

"Nothing, Eliani. We're just sorry you had to eat out of a dumpster." Trick wiped tears out of her eyes.

"So, where do we go to find this White God?" Eddy finally asked.

"Where the Cheshire Cats are. In London," Eliani said.

"What? Why them?" Trick asked apprehensively. Everyone knew that the Cheshire Cats had taken over London at the start of the Emergence.

"Because they're the ones who protect the dwelling of the White God. There's so much to tell all of you that I don't know what to give you and what would be better left for you to find out from them," Eliani added. She scooped up a last mouthful of the seasoned meat in her beak and swallowed it.

"They're not what everyone thinks they are. They're not even allowed to harm anyone. People don't actually know why they left London. It wasn't because of the cats. It was because that was where the White God manifested. Normal humans can't stay too close to where the White God dwells for very long. The massive amounts of magical energy are harmful to them. Their instincts tell them to move away even if they don't know why. The cats were just a convenient excuse."

All of them just sat there eating for a while digesting that information.

"So, all the stories about the cats driving people mad and chasing them out of the city?" Eddy asked.

"Just stories. You see, the White God needs no protectors. They protect what the White God keeps with him. Kept in that place is all the knowledge of magic on your world. You can learn everything there is to know about your magic there. Everything there is to know about all magic, it is all there, but no one is allowed to use it yet. That's all I really know. The cats can take you to the White God."

They had long since finished eating and had all just stayed around the table while Eliani had talked to them.

"So, was the whole point of this just to get us to go to London?" Eddy asked no one in particular.

"I don't think so," Trick said. "I think we were supposed to learn something from all of this. Remember what the Cheshire Cat told us when we started all of this?"

"That we had to follow our own path to get to the White God," Eddy recited.

"I guess all we can do is go to London, and hope we have learned what all these Figments were hoping for?" Dylan asked.

"Oh, hey, your feathers are all back to normal." Trick pointed at Eliani and Bruce.

"Oh, good," Eliani said. She hopped down from the chair, and a moment later, Bruce was standing there. Eliani, now much smaller than she had been, hopped up onto the back of a chair. She flapped her wings once to make it to the countertop and sat there.

"Okay, so, I don't get how eating works for you guys?" Eddy said, changing the topic completely to something that had been annoying him.

Anabelle floated down from where she had been watching the entire conversation. She had been napping upside-down with her paws touching the ceiling. She was still upside-down, but she took over the explanation without turning back over.

"We don't have to eat, but we do feel hungry, especially when you're hungry, because we're tied to you through our magic bond. But our bodies don't process food the same way. The food is broken down magically and converted directly into energy. When we eat, it replenishes our combined magic more quickly." Anabelle turned slightly towards Eliani. "You've done this before. Will we stop learning new things at some point?"

Eliani nodded. "Yes. There is a limit to how much you can magically draw on the knowledge. Eventually, you'll either need to go to the White God to learn more, or pick it up on your own. Especially now that we have so many different magic powers," Eliani squawked.

Bruce had made it into the kitchen and was fixing himself a plate to put in the microwave oven. "So, should we go with you? You might need our help."

Trick shook her head.

"Nah, I think we should get you home, Bruce. You've been gone for a long time."

Bruce sat down with his plate and started to eat. He exchanged a look with Eliani. "Are you sure?"

"Yeah, Coyote didn't say anything about you. I think we are supposed to be the ones to go. I don't want you to get into trouble if we are supposed to be the only ones going to London," Trick said. Bruce looked down at his half-finished plate.

"You guys fixed my Aura."

"Nah, you fixed your magic. We just got you someplace quiet to do it," Anabelle said.

"They're right, Bruce. We've been gone for three months. Mom and Dad have probably lost their minds by now," Eliani squeaked.

"Okay, but if you guys get hurt or sick, you can always come back to me."

"I can make people better too," Trick explained.

"Oh," Bruce said. He took a bite of his sandwich.

"Not like you, Bruce. I can do one at a time. What you did at the hospital was way more amazing than anything I can do," Trick reassured.

"You can help way more people if you go home. You can tell your parents how your Aura works. Maybe they will be able to help you use it. But if they won't help you..." Dylan opened his backpack and took out a little pad of paper. He scribbled his e-mail address onto a piece of paper. "Send me an e-mail, and we'll help you." Bruce took the paper.

"Thanks, you guys. I would really like to see my parents again," Bruce said. Eliani nodded enthusiastically.

"Finish eating and I'll take you home. You'll have to tell me where you live. You said Tyler, Texas, right?" Dylan asked.

"Yep," Bruce said. Eddy held out his phone, showing the map on the screen.

"Here, type in your address and I'll help Dylan figure out how to get you home."

They had left Bruce at the end of his street, but they had stayed close by until he made it to his house. None of them wanted to see his reunion with his parents, not until they had gotten home to see their parents. Dylan hadn't wanted to see it for other reasons. They all had opted instead to go back to Nascha's house. They cleaned up the mess they had made with their late lunch and got all the dishes into the dishwasher for Nascha. She had shown them all how to run it earlier that week. Once that was done, they all looked at each other expectantly.

"Well, I don't know what the heck we're going to do. I mean, we can't just walk into London," Trick said.

"Other people have," Dylan said.

"Yeah, and they never came back out," Trick shot back.

"Yeah, but after what Eliani told us, maybe they didn't want to come back out," Eddy suggested.

"What do you mean?"

"Well, if you could learn everything there is to know about your magic, would you want to leave?" Eddy asked. He looked from Dylan to Trick and back again.

"Huh. Good point," Trick replied. She looked at Dylan and Tigs. "Speaking of learning new things, before we go to London, Anabelle and I have something for you."

Trick pointed to Tigs atop Dylan's shoulder. Dylan held up his hand to help Tigs down onto the table, and she tottered across it to sit down in front of Trick. She tilted her head as if to ask what Trick wanted. Trick smiled at her and then reached out her hand, placing it atop Tigs' head. The plush tiger was swallowed in a familiar flash of blue light.

When the light faded, Tigs was still there, but she had changed. She was a little larger than she had been, and her plush appearance was still there. But it was more, somehow. Her paws had individual digits besides the thumb, and looked far more useful than they had been. Her hind paws had similarly changed, gaining tiny plush toes with little plastic claws. The fabric her body had been made out of was now a short fur like a real cat rather than the pattern of a plush.

Most of the changes were in her head and face. It had a much more realistic big cat shape with a real mouth. Her teeth were still plush, but they were much more detailed than they had been. Her eyes were no longer embroidered, but had become some sort of glassy substance. They had black pupils and bright blue irises. Tigs looked down at her little paws, and then she touched her chest. She looked up at Trick and tilted her head.

"Oh, not me. Her." Trick pointed up to Anabelle spinning lazy figure eights over her head. "She's been working on this ever since she met you, and didn't spring it on me until just now." Tigs pointed at her chest. Anabelle relayed a message from Tigs.

"She wants to know how it's different from how she was before," Anabelle said aloud for everyone's benefit.

"Well, I don't know. Anabelle said it would let you move around easier, and let you talk." Trick grinned when Tigs put her new little paws on her muzzle.

"It might take you a little while to learn how to talk, but you can now, and your body isn't just stuffing inside anymore. I can't give you a real flesh and blood body like mine right now. I'm not sure we ever can. Making a life is extremely powerful magic. But this transformation gave you a few little adjustments. If you break a claw or get a cut, it'll heal up. Your more alive I guess?" Anabelle tried to explain.

Tigs got up and started to walk around a little on the table. Clearly, she could move a lot more easily and smoothly than she could before. She even jumped a little, which had been totally impossible for her before. She got down on all fours and ran around the table for a moment. She finally slid to a halt near Dylan and plopped down on her rump. She looked up at Trick and Anabelle and smiled. She stood up on her new hind paws and folded her little front paws in front of her. She opened her new little mouth uncertainly. After a long, hesitant moment, she finally spoke in a squeaky, very toylike female voice.

"Thank you," she said.

"That's the cutest thing I have ever seen in my life," Trick said. "Did you make her sound like that?" she asked Anabelle.

"Not on purpose. Our control on our magic isn't good enough for things like that. It's her magic that's doing that," Anabelle said.

"So, what are we going to do about London?" Trick asked.

"I think we should just go. You heard what Eliani said. The cats are only there to make sure people don't learn things they shouldn't. Besides, you two can be Cheshire Cats," Dylan said.

"Not me. It was weird being that cat," Eddy said.

"The magic doesn't make your brain a Cheshire Cat brain, Eddy. It can help you think like they do so you can blend in, but you still control everything you do," Anabelle explained. Eddy shivered a little, but nodded.

"Alright, I can do it if it'll help."

"Thanks, Eddy. I didn't want to go in there alone."

They both looked at Dylan and Tigs, who had climbed up onto his shoulder on her own. She kept staring at her new paws and flexing the little digits.

"Alright, let's get going," Trick said. She got up from the table and shouldered her backpack.

"I don't have a direct teleport to London. The closest I can get is Ireland, so it's going to be a few jumps to get there. Hold on tight."

Dylan moved closer and Tigs got up off of his shoulder. She jumped from his shoulder onto Eddy's, landing there on all four paws. She turned herself around, and sat down on Eddy's shoulder. Trick took Eddy's hand, and Anabelle landed on her shoulder. Eddy shouldered his pack with his free hand. Dylan picked up his pack, as well.

"Alright, here we go," Dylan said.

They vanished.

When they reappeared and it wasn't just an image flashing by, they were standing on a deserted street outside of a huge deserted city. The buildings here bordered on dilapidated. There were no cars driving on the streets. There were no people walking anywhere. The skies were overcast, and it looked like in no time at all, they were gonna get soaked if they didn't get inside. But none of that was what drew their attention.

Across the skyline was something that no one outside of London had ever seen. If they had, there was no question someone would have heard about this. The whole world would know about this. Standing in the center of the city was a tree that dwarfed skyscrapers. The canopy of the tree spread for miles across the city, engulfing the tops of abandoned skyscrapers. The underside of the canopy was covered with huge, bell-shaped flowers of every color imaginable. Each flower glowed almost too brightly to look at them directly. There were many more white flowers than other colors, and they lit the city below almost as bright as daylight. The tree trunk itself appeared from that distance to be thousands of enormous trees twisted into a single tree trunk.

"My god, it has to be two miles wide," Eddy said in wonder.

"Guys, we've got a long walk. I can't teleport us any closer than this."

"End of Line," Tigs piped unhappily.

Trick quickly switched to her Cheshire Cat form. She squeezed through to the other place and appeared about two dozen feet down the street closer to the massive tree. She came back a moment later, popping out of the other place right beside Eddy.

"I can still use my magic to get closer, but maybe it's time to try something you guys suggested earlier. I'm going to change into the Hippogryph that I practiced while you were looking for Bruce. First take us to the top of this building." Trick pointed to a four story building with a flat roof next to the road.

They appeared up there a moment later. "It'll be easier to take off from up here with you guys on my back. Eddy, get a piece of rope out of your pack. I know you have some. Put it in my beak, and you can use it to hold on. I practiced enough to know I can keep you both on my back as long as we don't have to do anything too crazy. Just don't yank on the rope too hard or I won't be able to steer very well." Trick switched shapes to the Hippogryph.

Dylan stared at her in awe. "You look just like one from the movies!" he exclaimed.

Trick nodded. She carefully laid down with her paws and hooves tucked under her to make it easier for Dylan and Eddy to get on. Eddy put his pack down on the roof and started to fiddle through it.

"Flying is probably the best idea. Who knows what monsters are in the city. The Cheshire Cats can't be keeping out all the Figments, and they tend to show up where there are no people," Eddy said.

A minute later, he came out with a length of rope. He held one end of it out to Dylan, and then brought it up next Trick's head to measure how long it needed to be. He then doubled it and cut it, tying some loops in the end. He tested the loops by putting his hands through them to make sure they were big enough to fit. Trick ducked her head, and Eddy swung the rope over her head. She took it in her beak. Eddy and Dylan climbed up on her back. Dylan was bigger, so he sat in the front. He put his hands through the loops of the rope and pulled it gently until it went taut in Trick's beak. She closed her beak on the rope with it closer to the back, away from the sharp edges of her beak.

[*Tell them to hang on tight. It's gonna be a little bumpy getting into the air with them on my back,*] Trick projected to Anabelle. She spread her huge wings, and flapped them a couple of times, testing to make sure everything felt the same as it had when she had flown at Nascha's in Arizona.

"Ready back here," Dylan said.

Trick felt the rope tighten in her beak a little, and she tried not to shake her head too much. She started to trot around the roof, picking up speed as fast as she could. She finally came completely around with her head pointed towards the tree. Eddy started to scream.

"Holy crap, we're gonna die!" Eddy screeched.

Dylan, though, shouted enthusiastically, right over the top of Eddy.

"Go for it, Trick!"

Trick leapt over the edge of the building and beat her wings down. It flung her surprisingly higher than she thought it would with all the extra weight on her back. They soared into the air, and Trick steered slightly to the left to line them up with the street. She figured if she stayed over streets, it would be easier to get to the ground without anyone getting hurt if they got into trouble. She tilted her body slightly back, and flapped her wings, lifting them higher into the air. The underside of the canopy was still a few hundred feet above them. Trick thought about getting closer to get a better look at the glowing flowers.

[Ask Tigs if the boys are ok with going higher. I want to see the flowers better.] Trick asked mentally.

A moment later, Anabelle responded. *[They're fine, just take it easy]*

[I'll go up in a nice slow spiral.]

She tilted her body just slightly and flapped her wings, putting her into a big circular spiral that took them up much higher than they had been. When they finally got nearly close enough to touch the underside of the canopy, they realized that the leaves, and especially the flowers, were enormous. Each bell-shaped flower was big enough that even Trick's Hippogryph form would fit inside without a problem. The leaves of the tree were nearly five times the size of the biggest leaf that Dylan had ever seen. Trick tilted left and right between the glowing bells of the massive flowers, flying through beams of multi-colored light.

"I think I'm okay with this being the rest of my life even if I don't get my own Figment!" Eddy shouted over the wind rushing by.

Trick banked gently towards the tree trunk again. She glided lower as they covered the ten miles from where they had come into the city to the trunk of the tree. But when they got about a mile away, the air began to swirl violently. Trick tilted brutally when it hit her wings, and she tried to stay upright so as not to jostle Dylan and Eddy.

It quickly became impossible. She had to turn sharply away from the tree to gentler air. She tried again, but the wind seemed to be even worse the second time. Dylan pulled hard on the rope in her beak trying to stay on her back. She banked away again. She leveled out, but Dylan was still gripping the rope pretty hard.

[Please tell Dylan to let off the rope so I can turn my head. I need to see where we're going so I can get to the ground.] Trick asked Anabelle.

A moment later, the rope slackened, and she turned her whole body into a gentle spiral towards the ground. She finally got lined up with one of the roads. She tilted her body down, gliding towards the ground as gently as she could.

[Tell him to pull the rope tight and hold on. The landing could be kind of bumpy if I have to back wing to slow us down.]

She put her head down and kept her neck stiff. She felt the rope tighten in her beak, and she bit down harder to keep it from sawing at the back of her mouth. She took a deep breath through her nose and angled her body further down towards the ground. Landing had been the part she had had the hardest time figuring out. If it was just her, she could back wing to put herself in a kind of hover to touch down fairly lightly. With Dylan and Eddy on her back, if she back winged, it was likely to tilt her body so violently it would throw them off.

[You can do it!] Anabelle encouraged her.

[Maybe you should do it?]

[Maybe I should, but I'm not going to. Go ahead, Trick. You practiced a lot. It's on you.]

Anabelle retreated into Trick's mind. Trick took another deep breath, and then she tilted herself down into a glide just above the street. She let her legs down from the crouched position she was instinctively holding them in. She let her rear legs down first, and her hooves skidded on the pavement a little. She tilted her wings back, which took her back into the air a little, but also slowed her down. She managed to get her feet going when they touched the ground the second time. Her front feet hit the ground and she galloped down the street. She was able to slow herself down quickly, trotting to a stop, breathing hard. She tugged forward on the very tight rope, and Dylan let slack into it.

"Sorry, Trick. That was really intense. Didn't know I was still holding it so tight," Dylan apologized.

Trick folded her legs, and laid down to let them both off. They swung off of her back. Eddy set her pack down for her and Trick dropped the rope out of her beak. She changed back a second later.

"That was awesome!" Trick said.

"That was terrifying. I'm never riding on your back again without a freaking saddle or something!" Eddy shouted. Trick began to laugh.

"Not even the Spelled can approach the tree without speaking to us first," a voice floated from the side of the road. They all jumped and spun around.

There, lounging in a beam of red light, was an enormous Cheshire Cat. He was floating about a foot off the ground. His body was sideways, and his grin looked like a crescent moon made of sharp triangles. Trick walked toward him, and Anabelle floated at her side.

"Well, well, you have finally made it. Clever of you to fly over the city. You avoided quite the cornucopia of troublesome Figments who make their homes on the outskirts."

"You sound a lot different than the last Cheshire Cat we spoke to," Trick said. The cat chuckled.

"Yes, I'm sure that I do. Do not mistake my body for the mind inside, child. Many of those among us who are searching the world for those of the Spelled might actually make the choice take their job of being vague very seriously."

"Come, come. Let us get you some refreshment, and perhaps a conversation about why you have come." The Cheshire Cat began to float away down the street.

They all shouldered their bags quickly and followed him. He spun around backwards and floated in the direction he had been going.

"Oh, my, no, that won't do. You have come a long way. Allow us."

The cat pointed a finger at them, and their bags floated up off of their backs. Then they began to float along behind them.

"Uh, that is not something Cheshire Cats can do," Trick said.

The cat chuckled. "Look again, child."

Trick looked over her shoulder and then she saw it. Each bag was being carried by another Cheshire Cat. They grinned at her, and one of them even gave them a friendly little wave of her paw.

"Do you have a name?" Trick asked.

"Of course we have names. Don't be silly. I'm Indola. That cats carrying your bags are Skol, Tria, and Hessa. Do not worry, you are perfectly safe. Even the Figments on the outskirts of the city would not hurt one of the Spelled. They would just be mischievous." Indola led them down the street for a few blocks, and then he turned right down a street.

"I'm afraid that the White God is currently indisposed. I'm sure that he will soon manifest a body here to speak with you. He is quite interested in your progress. Until he returns, I'm sure that you have many questions that we can answer for you." Indola floated across an empty street and into an enormous building that looked like it was a castle. It had a huge clock tower in the middle. The clock face was not moving, though.

"Where are we?" Eddy asked.

"This building is where most of us live, and it is also where we study this new age of magic. We have done some very heavy architectural modifications to the castle to support our activities. Your pairing is one of our most interesting subjects, Trick. The ability to use all of the forms and abilities of almost any Figment. Do you realize this makes you one of the most powerful of the Spelled in all of history?" the cat wondered.

"No?" Trick drew out the word into a single long syllable with a clear question mark at the end.

"No, of course you wouldn't. Silly me, you are still so young. I wonder how he expects one such as you to make the choice," the cat mumbled to himself.

"What choice? The other cat wouldn't tell me."

"Of course he wouldn't. You hadn't gone down the correct path yet, but I cannot tell you. That is for the White God to decide. But what of your magic? You must have questions about your magic!"

He led them through hallways, and then stopped in front of an elevator. He pushed the button, and it dinged. "Marvelous, the technology of this age. Not much use to we cats, but for those who cannot translocate about so useful."

"How do you still have power here?" Eddy asked.

"You mean electricity? Magic, dear boy. Very easy to convert magic to electricity. Very similar energy signatures." The elevator doors opened, and everyone climbed inside. "We have food upstairs, and there are some of the Spelled here as well. Those who did not do well in the outside world came here."

That triggered something in Trick's memory. Something her mother had said when she had first found out that Trick had a Figment.

"Is there a woman here from Germany? She would have been one of the first kids to get a Figment of her own," Trick asked as they rode the elevator up to the fourth floor.

"You must mean Nedra. How would you know her?"

"My mother knew her, and when I got my Figment, she mentioned her."

"If you want to meet her, she would be up on the roof this time of the day with her Figment Feuer. He's a phoenix. Nedra and Feuer can control flames, and Feuer can carry loads many times heavier than he should be able to. He can easily fly carrying Nedra herself. Skol, you have her bag, will you take her up to the roof to see Nedra?"

"Of course, Indola. Come on, Trick, let's go see Nedra. She's very nice." Skol's voice was much higher pitched than even Trick's when she wore a Cheshire Cat body. It was a really cute voice, and it made Trick smile.

"Will you guys be alright?" Trick asked Eddy and Dylan.

"They'll be fine. Eddy, if I'm correct, is interested in how he might get a Figment of his own, and Dylan, I think you and Tigs would like to know how to use your powers to go places directly without having to make a bunch of little teleports in between. We have those here who can answer those questions. The White God will sense your presence soon and manifest a body here to speak with you I'm sure. The choice must be made soon," Indola assured Trick.

"Maybe we should stay together. I can't teleport here," Dylan said.

"Oh, no, your magic will have been released here, Dylan. You can go anywhere you want. We have to take precautions about anyone approaching the Source without first knowing who they are. The Spelled are perfectly safe near to the Source, but normal humans would quickly perish near it. That is why we have spells in place to prevent people without Auras from getting too close. Unfortunately, some of those spells by necessity must block traveling magic that could bring those without Auras too close to the Source for safety. Now that you have been identified to the protective magics, you can return, and use your magic here as you always have."

The doors popped open on the fourth floor. Dylan teleported a few feet into the hallway.

"Awesome," Dylan said. He appeared back next to the door.

"I see that your Figment's body has been altered. Can you tell me who cast this magic?" Indola asked.

Dylan pointed at Trick.

"Truly?" Indola spun gently in the air and looked up at Trick. His eyes were a little wide. "That is quite amazing. Did you draw this knowledge from the Ether?" He was clearly talking to Anabelle, who floated just over Trick's shoulder. She shook her head.

"I couldn't. I tried, but it wouldn't release the information, so I used what I already knew about projecting our power onto another to construct the spell that made her new body. Trick helped too," Anabelle said.

"I only held all the energy while you told me what to do," Trick said.

The elevator doors dinged, but one of the other cats, Tria, put one of their backpacks into the elevator doors to stop them. Indola came back.

"You did this unaided?" Indola asked. Anabelle nodded. He narrowed his huge amber eyes at them. Then he blinked, and his mouth fell open.

"Well, that is unexpected," Indola said. "It is an amazing magic. I could not have done better myself, short of giving her a truly living body."

"Can the White God do that?" Tigs' squeaky voice asked. Indola turned back to her.

"There are few things the White God cannot do, but I think that this is likely the best form you will gain in this age. I know you have not been one of the Spelled before, but there are some limits once you have been chosen to be one of the Spelled. Come, let's go. Answers waiting for the two of you. Go on, Skol, take Trick to see Nedra." Tria lifted Dylan's bag, and the elevator slid closed.

"You managed to startle Indola," Skol said as the elevator started moving up again. "You must have done something awfully special to get a look like that from him," Skol purred.

The elevator stopped again and the doors popped open. What was outside of the doors did not look like the roof of the castle they had walked into. It looked like a lavish jungle. There was a path through green leaves. Sprays of tropical flowers in blue, pink, and yellow decorated either side of the path.

"I can take my bag," Trick said.

"Oh, no, it's fine. Trust me. It is much lighter for me than it is for you," Skol responded. She let go of it for a moment, and the bag hovered there in the air. It started to fall slowly, and she grabbed it with her front paws again. She grinned at Trick.

"Wow. You'll have to teach me how to do that," Trick said.

"We can extend our anti-gravity field a little ways, especially to objects we are touching. If what Indola said is true, you can do it too if you can be one of us,"

Trick touched Anabelle, and they switched in a flash of blue light. Skol was colored much differently than Trick. Her fur was a yellow-orange color like the inside of a peach, and she had lilac purple stripes that twined around various parts of her body.

"Oh, I love your patterns. You're so pretty. Look at those swirls." There was a roar of sound from somewhere off through the plants. Trick changed back, a little startled.

"Oh, it's nothing. Nedra is practicing her magic. It's perfectly safe," Skol said. Trick nodded, and Skol floated down the garden path.

"I like your colors a lot better than mine. You're so cute, and I'm that nasty blue grey," Trick said.

They came around a corner in the path, and the pathway opened up into a large open area. There was short green grass covering the large space, and all the larger foliage was pulled back to the edges of the roof. Sitting on the grass in the middle of the roof was a small woman. She had her eyes closed. She had light, cream colored skin just like Trick's mom. She was wearing a simple orange sun dress. She had silver hair that hung down to her waist in a thick braid. Sitting next to her was an enormous red and orange bird. Hovering over its head was a halo of bright orange fire. Above her in the air was a basketball sized sphere of what looked like roiling blue fire.

"Now focus on the central compression point. Compound the energetic focus into the central mass, and this time, contain the energetic reaction." The bird spoke in a whistling musical voice. The sphere of blue fire compacted itself down to something about the size of a grapefruit. The blue fire became a seething mass of blinding white light. The bird seemed to notice Trick and Skol.

"I would look away if I were you," the bird whistled. Trick and Skol turned away quickly.

"Very good, Nedra. You are doing perfectly. The strain is acceptable. We could sustain this for a few hours every day." The bird almost sang the words. They had a beautiful cadence to them. "But we now have visitors, so I think you can release this."

There was an amazing roar of sound. Trick stumbled forward from its volume. She almost fell down. She spun around, and found the woman now standing with her hands behind her back, smiling brightly.

"Hello, Skol. I see you have brought a little friend. I take it she didn't do well outside?" Nedra said.

"Oh, no, it's not like that at all, Nedra. This is Trick. She is here for the choice, but she thinks that her mother knew you when you were younger," Skol purred.

"No. Hannah? Hannah Muller? You look just like her! Well, except for that red hair." The woman's German accent was very faint. Trick switched to German.

"Mama said that people were not very nice to you when you first got your Figment. I'm Teresa, but everyone calls me Trick."

"Hannah taught you German! No one here besides my Figment speaks it, and you speak it so well!" Nedra seemed genuinely delighted. Skol put her bag down near the edge of the green grass.

"I'll let you two talk. Trick, Nedra can show you the way to the libraries when you two are done," Skol said. She faded away before Trick could say anything.

"We don't have to speak German, but I would love to just talk about what happened to your mother after Fire and I left home." Nedra smiled.

"I can speak either, but I'm not sure Anabelle can."

"I speak it just fine, but frankly, I think I could use a nap. Wake me when you're done," Annabelle said. She floated to a spot in the sun about ten feet above the foliage. Nedra sat down in the grass, and motioned Trick to sit down next to her.

Dylan and Eddy followed Indola down the hallway. Something was bothering Eddy as he walked along the floor.

"Indola? You said you did a lot of work on this building?"

"Quite a bit. As I understand it, this building was used as a place where the government of this country made decisions. The building was quite open without any real floors to work with. However, it is the ideal location so we decided to use the building. We employed several Figments who are adept at working in stone and wood to do the construction. It was done in such a way that we can very easily change it back to exactly the way it was before we started using the building. It is quite possible that this city will once again be home to many humans when this is over," Indola explained.

"But it looks like this was all done at the same time. I'm just a kid, but the stone all looks like the same stuff," Eddy said.

"It's an astute observation, young man. Yes, we have bent the rules a little here, and used magic to mine and place the stone in such a way as to preserve the building's construction time-wise. In the event that the humans find our modifications to the building useful, we hope that they will not feel we have defaced the building's history. If they do, we can release the magics holding our modifications in place and return the building to its original state."

"Amazing," Eddy said.

"Magic, properly utilized, is often quite amazing, young man. But I'm sure that on your path that is a lesson you have learned."

Indola lead them all the way to the end of the hall, and then went through two large wooden doors. Inside, there was an enormous room. It had a large, wide open space with long tables surrounded by chairs. There were Cheshire Cats everywhere. Multiple colors of fur and stripes were on display as the cats zipped this way and that. There were dozens of shelves, and the whole room looked like an enormous library. But there were no books. Instead, softly glowing spheres of glass, each about the size of a grapefruit, floated about above desks and in small clouds near to cats that were moving about the room.

"It looks like a library," Dylan said. Eddy nodded in agreement.

"It is, but books are somewhat inefficient when it comes to storing knowledge. They are an excellent stopgap, but with magic, you can do much better. These are magical matrices used to store information in such a way that it can be accessed telepathically, so you can learn things just by touching the spheres. However, they are not safe for humans yet. Not even perfect for the Spelled. We are still adjusting their magics, and we could use your help specifically, Eddy. You, as of yet, do not have a Figment or magic of your own, which means your biology is still entirely human. This means you can help us to safely adjust the magic so that it interreacts properly with humans."

Indola lifted a cream colored paw and waved over another of the cats with the same color fur. They also had the same crosshatched teal colored markings as Indola. "This is my offspring, Ikona. Dylan, she can be very helpful in teaching you and Tigs about how to better utilize your teleportation spells."

"Hello." Ikona waved a paw. "I have never met one of the Spelled. It is a pleasure." Indola shooed them away.

"Go on. You're in good paws with her. She knows a great deal about intradimensional tunneling," Indola said. Ikona floated away towards the other end of the library. Dylan followed her.

"So, you know about the last age?" Dylan asked.

"Oh sure, we were there then as well. I have been alive for the last two ages. I haven't always looked like this." She held up her paws and then grinned at him. But it wasn't scary on her even when it spread all the way from ear to ear.

"Do you like it?" Dylan asked.

"Well I could have done with some more interesting stripes. The crosshatching is kind of boring." She rolled upside down as she floated. "But the central gravitational disruption is a great deal of fun and makes sleep ever so comfortable." Ikona rolled back right side up. She turned down one of the aisles of shelving, leading him all the way down to the end.

"So are we really safe here?" Dylan asked. Tigs had been silent the entire time. She finally spoke.

"This is safe place," Tigs assured him. Her ability to speak was getting a little better. He trusted Tigs not to lie to him.

"Oh, I take it that you have recently been given the ability to speak?" Ikona asked. She spun in the air and floated backwards. Amazingly, she dipped between and below other Cheshire Cats without hitting anyone, despite her inability to see them.

"Yes. Hard to make new sounds," Tigs squeaked.

"I can help with that. Just go to the end of the row and take a seat at the table there." She pointed back over her shoulder and then faded from view.

Dylan and Tigs exchanged a look then Tigs made the shrugging gesture with her paws. They walked down the aisle, and then Dylan sat down at the table. He was there for less than ten seconds when Ikona popped out into the air. She was surrounded by two hovering spheres. She pointed at one of them, and it floated down to the table.

"This one is for you, Tigs. This sphere contains the complete knowledge of the human language of English, which it appears all of your friends speak. This includes knowledge of all of its vocalizations. If you touch this sphere, it will teach you how to speak properly. But be warned. These spheres can be a little dangerous to use if you don't keep your concentration. The spells are very new, and we have just started to research how to place safeguards on them. So just put your paws on the sphere and concentrate on what you want it to teach you." Tigs nodded and Ikona turned to Dylan.

"Dylan, this is for you. As I understand it, you had a rather strong initial release on your magic that halted the aging process. I'm a little hesitant to give you this, but my progenitor thinks that because of your inability to age, it could be useful to you." It floated down to the table in front of Dylan. It hovered there for a moment, and then it changed color from soft white light to soft yellow light.

"What is it?" Dylan asked.

"It is the comprehensive knowledge of your entire school curriculum all the way until your graduation from high school. My sire thinks that you would benefit from the knowledge." Dylan stared at the sphere incredulously.

"No way. You mean..."

"If I can walk you through the procedure for using this sphere, you would not need to go back to school," Ikona said.

Dylan reached out his hand hesitantly. "Wait. Not yet. Tigs will have a much easier time of this than you will. Also, if you use this sphere it will be a long time before you can use any others. This is many years worth of knowledge, and it will be months at least before your brain is able to adapt to all of this new knowledge."

"So you weren't planning on using one of these to teach me about my magic?" Dylan asked, drawing his hand back from the sphere. Ikona gave him a soft, comforting smile that made him feel better, even with the smile being so huge.

"I was, but my sire has explained to me that it must be your choice. I can teach you some things about your magic the normal way. Indola thinks that it might be more important to give you the option to be more independent," Ikona explained to him.

"But I can't just…" Dylan trailed off. Ikona gave a put upon sigh.

"Dylan, my sire is a very intelligent individual. Further, he knows about your situation with your parents. There are things you can do with this knowledge," Ikona patted the sphere. "You would be able to make a place for yourself in the world without anyone's help."

"My friends, though, what about them?" Dylan asked. Tigs, who had been staring into the sphere Ikona had given her for the entirety of their conversation, finally lifted her head. The light from the sphere faded back to a soft glow from its intensity, and Tigs looked up.

"That is disconcerting," Tigs said. Her voice was still the slightly squeaky toy-like voice, but she spoke very clearly now. She took her paws off the sphere, and it floated up from the table, returning to Ikona.

"Much better than spending months forgetting words though, I'm betting." Ikona's slow melodic tones put them both at ease. She turned back to Dylan.

"Your friends have families, Dylan, and this wouldn't keep them from being your friends," Ikona said.

"I lost all my friends when I got Tigs, and I've never had much of a family. I don't think this is a good idea," Dylan said. Ikona nodded.

"It will be here if you decide that you need it. For the record, I think it's a good choice. Sometimes, it is better to learn things on your own. One second." Ikona faded away again. A moment later, Eddy sat down at the table across from him. He had a sphere in his hands, and Indola was floating nearby. Ikona faded back into view.

"Told you so, sire," Ikona said.

"We had to offer. Eddy has given me the interface parameters for normal humans that we have been missing. As soon as he arrives, everything should be ready for him," Indola said. Ikona floated another sphere to the table in front of Dylan.

"This sphere contains an incomplete knowledge of your particular teleportation magic Dylan. I have not completely worked out how it functions, but there are some things this sphere can teach you that you and Tigs would not easily learn on your own," Ikona explained.

Dylan reached for the sphere.

"Remember, you have to mentally command the sphere to give you only knowledge of things you do not already know. Otherwise, it will just try to shove everything it contains into your mind all at once, which could damage you."

"Okay," Dylan said. He touched the sphere, and his eyes went out of focus.

Trick faded into view wearing her Cheshire Cat body. She spoke a stream of a language that Dylan and Eddy couldn't understand.

"Trick, you're speaking German," Eddy said.

"Oh, Sorry. Nedra said that I should come back down because the White God should be coming soon."

"So I will." The new voice was deep and sounded very grandfatherly.

They all turned to see a man emerging from the shelves. All of the cats bowed their heads and slowly withdrew, leaving Trick, Eddy, and Dylan alone with the man, though

Indola, Ikona, and Skol remained. They had bowed their heads, and didn't look directly at the man. He looked elderly, but spry. He had a well-kept mane of silvery hair that was a little past shoulder length, tied back into a pony tail. He was wearing a white button-up t-shirt beneath a white and silver vest along with a neatly pressed pair of slacks, and no shoes at all. He had tan feet with perfectly pedicured toenails that were painted with silver polish.

"You are…" Trick said slowly. She was still wearing her Cheshire Cat body.

"The White God. Yes, that is what they call me. Indola, how are your efforts in memory suffusion going?"

"Well, my Lord, your latest charges have been most helpful in advancing our efforts. We are actually waiting for Dylan to emerge from our latest test sphere. He should be coming out any moment."

"Very good, Indola."

A moment later, Dylan gasped. "Wow! That was so intense." Dylan handed the sphere back to Ikona. It floated next to her.

"Did you learn anything?" Ikona asked. Dylan nodded.

"You and Ikona may go. Skol, please stay. I have a question for you," the man said.

"We can talk more later. Thank you, my Lord," Ikona said.

"Thank you, my Lord," Indola added. He and Ikona faded away.

"You three have proven to be more amazing than even I could have predicted. Eddy, I had hoped that you would make it here with your friends. It was not always a sure thing. There was a chance they would be too worried about your lack of powers to bring you with them. I'm glad friendship won out."

The man came to the table. He looked at it for a moment. "Oh, this won't do at all." He waved his hand, and it was like the whole world changed around them. Suddenly, they were in a cozy living room with a roaring fireplace off to one side. Four comfortable chairs were arranged in a circle. On a small table next to each chair was a comfortable looking cushion.

Trick changed back to her human form, and Anabelle landed on the cushion next to Trick's chair. Trick climbed into the chair. The White God took the chair across from Trick. Eddy sat down, and Skol landed on the cushion next to him. Dylan and Tigs took the last chair and cushion. Just as he sat down, there was a huge roar from outside. It sounded like hundreds of people chanting something. Trick's head snapped around to the window.

"No need to worry about them. Indola and our friends among the cats will shoo away the monsters who have come in from the outskirts. They are just excited because they know you are here," the elderly man said.

"What do we call you? The White God is a bit of a mouthful," Eddy said.

"And if that was the only name I had to give to you, young man?" he asked with a smile.

"Then I would use it, sir."

"Truly, I do not have any given name, and had never had to have the idea," he said musingly. "Let us be simple, then. Call me Spirit."

Chapter Twenty-Two
"Spirit"

"I suppose now that I have lured you to my lair, I should explain what you are doing here," Spirit said. They all began to feel a little apprehensive. A moment later, Spirit let out a huge belly laugh. "No need to worry. No one is going to harm you here. No, we rather need one of you three for something very important, though I'm still not sure which one it is. So, I'm going to tell you the whole story as best I can. You are still very young, and so it is unreasonable to think that you will understand everything I'm about to reveal to you. I think you will understand enough, though." Spirit folded his hands in his lap and looked out the window at the massive trunk of the impossible tree.

"This is not the first time that we magical folk have visited your world. Every world that develops intelligent life also eventually develops a parallel magical realm because one universal constant of all intelligent life is belief. It may not always be belief in a god, but belief always develops. Belief is an energetic force, and when it develops, it builds up like a lake that has a dam but continues to take on water. Eventually, if there is nothing to drain the excess, the dam overflows. So, too, does belief.

When it does, a doorway is torn between your physical realm and our magical one. The tear creates a great imbalance in energies. Then the beings of the magical realm are thrust upon this physical one. But that does not completely repair the imbalance." Spirit drew in a deep breath.

After a pregnant pause, Eddy spoke up. "What does?"

"Well, you do, of course," Spirit said. He continued to stare out the window at the tree.

"Me?" Eddy yelped.

Spirit chuckled. "No, dear boy, you as in humans. The intelligent species that fosters the vast majority of the belief must choose what to do with all of this built-up energy," Spirit explained. The fire cracked and popped loudly, making everyone except Spirit jump a little.

"So, you want one of us to pick what to do?" Dylan asked apprehensively. Spirit nodded his head slowly.

"Yes, but let me finish the story because you have to understand what is going to happen when you choose. You see, the amount of energy that is sufficient to form a bridge between our two worlds is also sufficient to destroy both worlds if not directed by this choice. The choice is between two possible things. This is the part that you all need to understand, and I can't imagine how to help you." Spirit fiddled with something small he was holding in his hand. "Some God I am, eh?" Spirit chuckled again.

"Can't you just like..." Eddy twiddled his fingers in a magical gesture.

"I could, but your minds are fragile little things. If I tried to force everything you need to know into your brains, it could damage you. I guess I will just be blunt. Our little world is not the only world in the universe with intelligent life. Not all of these worlds are friendly places. Some are quite hostile and would not be kind to us if they discovered our little blue world.

There are two ways to protect our world. The first choice is to use all of the energy that triggered the Emergence to build a magical shield around our world to keep it hidden. The second choice is to distribute that magic to the world. Everyone who is young enough for their body to adapt to the magic and has the desire to use it will get their own Figment. But if you use the energy to build the magical shield, all the Figments and magic will eventually fade away out of the world in a few hundred years. The cycle will start over again.

One of these two ways is not truly better than the other. One of these two ways is more secure than the other. If you build the shield using all of this magic, it would take the full effort of another world using all of their magical talent to breach our world. There are almost no worlds that are willing to trade all of their magic simply to invade our world. Our world would be mostly safe. If you choose to give knowledge of magic to your world, there is no going back to that safety. In time, though, you would learn how to defend our world just as well as if we had continued to remain hidden. Unlike the shield, though, we will have to defend it. It will be up to all of us to keep our world safe. One of you can make this choice." Spirit finished. He sat back in his chair.

"Which one?" Eddy asked.

"Well first, it has to be one of the Spelled. So, there is a small piece of business to deal with first." He smiled at Eddy. "In the last age, magic was done differently than it is now. Each of the Spelled had a Familiar that allowed them to use their magic in a variety of ways. Beliefs and rules have changed, though, so I cannot give you magic just like that. However, I know that you have a fascination with our feline friends."

Spirit gestured to Skol. "Skol, you have been a loyal Protector of Knowledge through four Emergences. Many times, you have asked to be part of a Spelled pair. Would you like to be Edmund's Figment?"

"You mean it, my Lord?" Skol asked excitedly.

"If you think that you can enjoy that body for the foreseeable future, and if Edmund can remember what sort of magic he is most interested in doing."

"Oh, I think that this body will do just fine. I just hope that he has an interesting magic for us."

"Well, Eddy?" Spirit asked. Eddy seemed to become slightly shy, which was completely not like him.

"He used to write these little magic words all over everything. He had his own little language," Trick said.

"No." Skol spun back towards Spirit. He grinned at her. "You sneak! How long have you known?" Skol grinned a wide grin at the spry old man. He chuckled.

"Only a few years. I have not, in fact, known since the last age. I only picked up on Edmund when I first noticed Trick here," he said holding up his hands in a mollifying gesture.

"I always loved writing magic spells. I'm such a nerd." Eddy seemed horrified that Trick had revealed that little bit about him.

"Edmund, what you do not know is that the written word was invented during an earlier Emergence. Skol was born during this Emergence, and she helped to pioneer the idea of the magical spell book. I believe you would find her absolutely delighted to help you to develop a completely new form of written magic." Skol nodded her head with incredible enthusiasm.

"How do we..." Eddy trailed off.

"It's has already begun. As soon as you sleep again, the bond will fully form," Spirit said.

"Can I ask one more question sir?" Eddy blurted it out as if he wasn't certain he would get the chance if he didn't.

"Of course, dear boy." Spirit replied.

"Why don't they remember?" Eddy gestured at Anabelle, and then Tigs.

"The answer to that is a complicated one Eddy. I will try to simplify it for you. Spelled pairs are created in one of two ways. One is the way I'm making your bond. An already living magical creature has a power that aligns well with the desires of the human of the Spelled pairing. In this case how much the magical being remembers of their past depends heavily on how much belief their kind received in the previous age.

Sometimes, like in the case of the Protectors like Skol, the energy is sufficient for them to retain all of the memories through their passing into this world. In other cases like Tigs they were not well known, and so the energy they retained upon leaving this world was only sufficient to sustain their existence. So they do not remember their past. They are born anew with the Emergence."

"And the other way?" Trick asked.

"The other way is how your pairing happened Trick. Sometimes a person's belief is so strong that it births an entirely new and unique magical being. In these cases the magical creature has no past, and have only basic instincts about how their powers function. That is why Anabelle only knows some things, and not others. Since magic is so complex I tend to help newly born creatures along by giving them a little extra magic to help them learn faster." Spirit paused, and when they all nodded he continued. "I suppose there is one other question each of you would like to know."

"Why us?" Eddie asked.

"Why you," Spirit said. "The answer is different for each of you, and it may not be what you expect." They each nodded.

"There are several reasons I choose someone to be one of the Spelled. For Dylan, it was his great need that called my attention to him. I chose you because I knew that you needed Tigs in your life. Tigs is a Veysper, a spirit of air and travel. She is a rarity among us, and her energy is very particular, so we couldn't make her fit in with the beliefs of this time. She needed a physical body, and a new way to express her particular sort of magic. She fit in with you perfectly, so that is how you got paired together. Tigs was Dylan's imaginary friend when he was younger before he gave her to his sister, which is why Tigs ended up in the stuffed animal body. I knew you would do good things with your combined power," Spirit explained.

"My parents," Dylan said just loud enough that everyone could hear. Spirit's frown was a little frightening, and when he spoke, his voice was similarly transformed into a slightly dark scary tone.

"Yes, your parents. Unfortunately, many kids in your situation do not have the strength of character to manage magical talents like yours. That is why I chose you Dylan."

"But Trick and I don't have any reasons like that," Eddy said. Spirit chuckled at him.

"I chose you, Eddy, because there is no one anywhere on this whole world that wanted magic more than you do. But unlike so many of the kids who wish for their own Figment, you are one of the very few who think almost exclusively of helping others with your magic. You will be an irreplaceable blessing to the world for the foreseeable future," Spirit finished. He looked to Trick and smiled at her so fondly.

"Trick, I Spelled you for the simplest reason of all. You're good. You're always going to do what you feel is right, even if it might not necessarily be of greatest benefit to you. Someone like you can do anything, magic or otherwise. So now we are left with which one of you will be able to choose."

"I can't," Dylan said immediately.

"Do you know why you cannot, Traveler?" Spirit asked. Dylan just shook his head.

"It is because you are too unbalanced. You are strong, Dylan, and some day that strength will pull you up to greatness. But right now, you know that magic is your only saving grace. It isn't true, but that is the way you feel. So, you would choose magic regardless of how it will affect the world. Which means you are not choosing, you have already chosen. Do not worry, Dylan, this does not make you a bad person. It simply means that you will grow a great deal in the years to come." Dylan nodded his head. "Nothing to be ashamed of, my boy."

"Not me, either," Eddy said. He looked up at Skol. "I think it is worth having magic no matter what," Eddy said.

"You're very right," Spirit said.

"Me? You think I can choose something like that?" Trick's voice cracked. She had been quiet the entire time trying to absorb the information that Spirit had given them.

"You are the only one among your friends who has the potential to do it, Trick. You and Anabelle are the only ones who can, but no one can force you. Even if you cannot do it, we will continue to look for another who can. I'm only asking you to consider it. Eventually, it will be too late if we are unable to find someone who can choose, but that does not mean it has to be you. There are other candidates."

Trick nodded, but she had to ask. "What's going to happen if no one picks in time?"

Spirit sighed. "You know the answer to that question. I don't want to stack that on your tiny shoulders. Can I just say that it would be bad?"

"Yeah, that's good enough," Trick said. Anabelle landed in her arms and Trick hugged her. "Can we just do it here?" Trick asked. Spirit shook his head.

"Not here. We must go to the Source. I will take you if you agree?"

"Can my friends come with me?"

"Of course. They have come all this way. It wouldn't be right to not let them finish this with you."

"I'll try," Trick said.

"Very good."

Spirit lifted his hand. The world seemed to shift around them again. Suddenly, they were all standing on a deserted street just underneath the trunk of the incredible tree. The tree's trunk was miles wide and seemed to stretch to the horizon from where they were standing. From where they were, they could not see the base of tree, just the beginnings of the roots as they dove into the heart of the city.

In front of them was an enormous staircase of stone at least a hundred feet wide. The steps were carved at human scale, but the width of the staircase made one think it might be used by a giant, at least for the first few stairs. Clearly, something had happened, though, because the hill had swallowed huge swaths of the staircase. This left only an S-shaped path up the steep hill towards the base of the tree. There were no railings, but with all the plants surrounding it, it didn't seem unsafe. The land around appeared to have exploded with flora of all imaginable species, and even some that Eddy was sure were not native to earth. The hill itself seemed to naturally contour itself to holding up the stair way.

"This is it. These stairs lead up to the Source. This is where my energy first manifested once the humans had cleared the city. Unfortunately, many of the buildings here in London were destroyed when the tree grew. I did my best to minimize the damage to the city since I hope to return this settlement to prosperity as soon as is possible. Also, you three were looking a little rough around the edges, so I have taken the liberty of replacing your clothing and restoring your vitality," Spirit said.

They all looked down at the clothing that they were wearing. It had changed drastically from what they had set out with.

"Those were my favorite coveralls!" Trick complained. She was wearing a blue knee-length dress. It was two-tone blue, the bodice a deep navy blue. It had pleated shoulders. On the front of the bodice was a knot that was somehow tied into two panels of a light blue skirt. The other panels were sewn to those two, hanging down just past her knees. It was a beautiful dress, but she had been wearing her favorite Cheshire Cat overalls.

"I'm… sorry?" Spirit apologized.

"It's a pretty dress," Trick frowned.

"But you'd rather have your coveralls back." Spirit grinned.

He held out a folded set of clothing in purples and pinks. They looked brand new. The boys' clothing had been restored to brand new as well, though Dylan's clothing hadn't changed. He was still wearing the leather bomber jacket and jeans. They looked brand new, though. Eddie's clothing had changed from his t-shirt and jeans to an odd set of black robes edged with silver thread. Trick took her coveralls back. Then she looked up at Spirit with a question forming.

"But what about the cats?" Trick said.

"Oh, they will be fine. If the humans do not wish to be reasonable about sharing their city with our furry feline protectors, we have made arrangements to take some spaces that are currently uninhabited by humans," Spirit said.

"Alright," Trick said. She started up the stairs, and she was about a dozen steps up when someone finally spoke again. But it wasn't Spirit, or anyone else that she expected to hear.

"Trick!" It was her Father's voice, and she whipped around, startled by the voice. When she saw them standing there next to Spirit, she bolted down the stairs.

"Mom! Dad!" she screamed and ran to them. Her father scooped her up and hugged her.

"I have taken the liberty of explaining to your parents exactly what you have been doing all this time," Spirit said. Spirit put his arm around Dylan and knelt down next to him. He whispered something in his ear, and Dylan nodded. Eddy's parents were there too, and his mother was clutching him like she wasn't ever going to let him go again.

"I'm sorry. I didn't know what to do. I'm sorry," Trick said. She felt her mother's arms around her, squeezing her almost too tightly for her to breath.

"It's okay. It's alright, we understand. We know, Trick. He explained it," her father soothed until she calmed down. She turned herself in her father's arms until she could see her mother.

"I saw your friend, Mom. She is okay."

"My friend?" Her mother seemed confused.

"Nedra. She is here, and she is doing well."

"You found Nedra?" her mother asked, confused.

"Yeah, she's been living here ever since she left home," Trick said.

"That's amazing. I'm sorry I didn't want you to keep Anabelle." Her mother petted Anabelle.

"It's alright. You were scared, and you were right. It was dangerous," Trick said. It sounded like Eddy was having a similar discussion with his parents.

"I apologize for the interruption, but as I explained, it is not safe for you to stay here yet. I will take you to your homes, and soon I will return your children, as well. You have my word," Spirit said.

Trick's mother finally stepped away, and her father put her down. Her mother walked over to Dylan, and she knelt down in front of him. She put her hands on his shoulders.

"Dylan, we didn't know what your parents had been doing to you. When you get back, you're welcome in our house whenever you like, and there are people that can help with your parents."

Dylan nodded and ran his hand over his brush cut hair. It had gotten a bit longer in the last couple of weeks.

"Thanks, Mrs. Strand. I'm sorry we made you all worry."

"Yeah, well Trick is gonna be grounded for a while when you all get home, so you'll have to visit her at our house, but you did good, Dylan. You all did good," Trick's mother said.

"I apologize again, but I must insist. Your bodies will soon begin to degrade in this environment," Spirit pressed.

"What about Edmund?" Eddy's mother asked.

"Edmund is protected by his previous encounters with Trick's magic, and now by his new bond with his Figment Skol."

"Figment?" his father asked skeptically. Spirit gestured to Skol, who had been floating a polite distance away during Eddy's reunion with his parents.

"Oh god, I totally forgot," Eddy said and pealed himself out of his mother's grip. He turned to Skol. "I'm so sorry."

"It's okay, Eddy. I'm sure it'll take some time for me to get used to the arrangement as well," Skol squeaked. She waved her paw at Eddy's parents and smiled. The smile did not seem to reassure Eddy's parents. "Hi, I'm Skol. It's nice to meet you."

"Edmund?" his mother said.

"I promise I don't bite," Skol added. His parents seemed at a loss for words as they looked between Skol and Eddy. Skol sank down and landed on Eddy's shoulder. "Um, did I break them?" she whispered to Eddy uncertainly.

"No, they're fine. They'll catch up," Eddy chuckled. Spirit moved closer to Dylan.

"Is everyone ready to go?" Spirit asked. All the parents gave the kids one last hug.

"We'll talk when you get back," Eddy's mother said and petted Skol gently. Eddy nodded. Skol seemed a little taken aback at the petting, but not in a bad way. Spirit waved his hand, and they vanished without ceremony. Trick sniffed back tears, and she felt Anabelle wrapping herself around her neck. She put her hand on Anabelle's head.

"I'm okay, BelleBelle. I just want to go home," Trick said.

"So you shall. No matter your decision, I will see to it that you are returned home safely," Spirit said. Trick took a deep breath, and she started up the stairs again. This time, though, Eddy and Dylan walked up with her. When they turned to see if Spirit was following, he was gone. They all shrugged and turned back up the stairs.

"He was planning this all along," Eddy said to Skol.

"Yeah, he was. He always knows what a child's imaginary friend is. That's why you haven't gotten a Figment yet. He had already chosen one for you," Skol explained.

"But aren't people's Figments usually their imaginary friends?" Eddy asked.

"Well, sure, but did you have an imaginary friend?" Skol grinned knowingly.

"Yeah, but it was a he and looked like the Cheshire Cat from the Alice in Wonderland movie," Eddy said.

"Oh, the animated one, or the one voiced by Steven Fry?" Skol asked. They all stared at Skol.

"What?! We watch movies, and our bond hasn't formed yet, so I don't know which one he means yet!" Skol said defensively. Trick laughed, and so did Dylan.

"I guess we were just surprised that you would have any interest in movies," Trick said.

"Oh, human entertainment is the best! What you all have been able to do with special effects without any magic is amazing!" Skol did a full barrel roll excitedly and then came down to rest on Eddy's shoulder again. They were about halfway up the stairwell when Eddy paused.

"All this is so huge. How did you grow stuff this big so quickly?" Eddy asked, pointing to a huge bank of enormous flowers growing along the wall.

"Well, the standard answer is magic," Skol said, and Eddy scoffed.

"Okay, fine. The manifestation of the Source causes an initial increase in the growth of flora around the site, but the energetic imbalance is what causes everything to get so out of control like this. Time itself is accelerated around the site for the first few months until the energy output from the Source becomes constant. These flora are a result of vastly augmented evolution," Skol finished, then rolled her huge eyes.

"Show off," Eddy said.

"You asked for it." Skol laughed like tinkling bells.

"Well anyway, the newer movie," Eddy finally replied.

"Well, we sourced our forms from the original descriptions from Lewis Carroll's version, though I suspect that some of the imaginations of kids around the world had a small influence on our forms. We are kinda shaped like the one from the newer movie, huh?"

Skol levitated off of his shoulder and spun around so she was floating through the air in front of them. She did indeed look a little like a smaller version of the live action movie Cheshire Cat. Her fur was vastly different in coloring and markings, but the rest was very similar, right down to her triangular-toothed grin.

"But if you are truly unsatisfied with my form, you will have the opportunity to change it tonight when you sleep, though I rather do like the peach and lilac color scheme."

"Well, you're never going to scare anyone looking like that," Eddy said jokingly.

"Oh no?" Skol said. She faded from view and then whispered into his ear. "You would be surprised what one can do when..." the sound changed from one side of him to the other in an instant. "...one does not have to obey the normal laws of reality." Her huge lavender eyes popped open in front of him.

Eddy jumped back with a little shout and almost fell down the stairs. He felt small paws against his back steadying him. Skol stuck her head over his shoulder.

"Just because I look like a pretty flower doesn't mean I can't be scary."

Eddy began to laugh. "Alright, you've convinced me. The peach and lilac can stay."

They reached the top of the stairs a minute later, finding a large clearing surrounded by much smaller evergreen trees of a sort none of them had ever seen. Up ahead was what looked like a cave made of wood. A large void in the roots of the tree was filled with soft light in cool blues and warm yellows.

"I suppose that's it?" Trick said.

"That is the Source," Skol said.

They made it to the cave over the course of a quiet minute. None of them spoke, and when they stopped inside of the mouth of the cave, they were surprised to find that the light did not seem to interfere with their vision despite how bright it seemed from the outside. Inside the cave was a surprisingly smallish space covered with more bright green grass. It might have been fifty feet from wall to wall with a ceiling no more than thirty feet overhead. You could have comfortably tucked a small house into the cave, still it was tiny compared to the tree above.

Hanging from the ceiling of the cave was a huge crystal that glowed very brightly. It was almost too bright to look at, but they could make out the shape through the warm yellow light it was giving off. Near the back of the cave below the crystal was a large pool of sapphire blue water. It was too blue to be real water, but it moved like real water.

"Why does it look like that?" Eddy said.

"Because the stones below are sapphires. It makes the water that unusual dark crystal blue color," Skol explained.

"But what are we supposed to do here?" Trick asked. She walked in, and Anabelle floated in figure eights above her head.

"Well, this is the Source, Trick. This is the manifestation of all of the magic. To make the choice all you need to do is walk up to the edge of the water and speak your choice."

Trick turned back to the four of them.

"What do you guys think I should do?"

Skol held up her paws in a shrugging gesture. "You already know what we all think, Trick. You heard what Spirit said. You have to pick."

Eddy and Dylan both nodded to her. Even Tigs just waved her on. She turned and walked towards the edge of the pool while they all waited at the entrance to the grotto. Trick stopped at the edge of the pool, and Anabelle glided out over the water. She came back a moment later.

"It's so beautiful." Anabelle landed in Trick's outstretched arms.

"I don't think I can do this," Trick said. Anabelle looked up at her.

"Sure you can. It's just a few words, Trick," Anabelle said.

"Yeah, but no matter what ones I say, a lot of people are gonna get really hurt."

Trick remembered the look on the face of the Skinwalker when it saw her watching it through the window. All those people it must have killed to stay alive. It couldn't have done any of that without the magic. Then she remembered all the kids that Bruce had made better at the hospital. She remembered how happy Mindy looked when Trick had used her magic to make the girl better. She stared into the water and realized that it really didn't matter. No matter what she did, there were going to be good and bad things in the world. Even without magic, people were able to do unspeakable things.

She sat down on the ground and stared into the water. In the end, the only thing that mattered was that she had to protect everyone. When she spoke the words, the whole world seemed to shake around her. She hugged Anabelle to her chest. A voice that seemed to fill the entire world with sound spoke in reply. The words rang out like someone had struck the largest bell in all of existence. Light began to flood up from the water as waves of magic exploded away from the sapphire crystals.

"The choice is made."

~ The End ~

9 781963 266085